EL HERMANO

EL HERMANO

a novel by Carmen Baca

&

WESTERN EDGE PRESS • SANTA FE

ISBN: 1-889921-54-8
ISBN 13   978-1-889921-54-9
Library of Congress Control Number: 2017935763

Design by Jim Mafchir
Edited by Cinny Green

Frontispiece: La Morada, photo courtesy of Sally Kruse
Photo of La Muerte courtesy of Ruben E. "El Jefe" Archuleta

Sherman Asher Publishing
P.O. Box 31725
Santa Fe, NM 87594-1725
www.shermanasher.com   westernedge@santa-fe.net

Dedication

I dedicate this book to my father, José Ismael Moises Valdez, and my mother, María del Carmen Valdez. My father willingly and humbly devoted his life to Christ as an Hermano. He raised me to cherish his grandfather's land and to thank the Lord daily for our blessings. My mother piously devoted her life as a Veronica and a Catholic Daughter. She taught me the value of heritage and culture, from her delicate embroideries and her delicious Spanish recipes to the many antiques and documents she collected for me to discover my roots. Thank you both for blessing my endeavor to write your story; I hope I made you proud.

Table of Contents

FOREWORD   *ix*
ACKNOWLEDGEMENTS   *xi*

El Hermano   3

Conciencia   13

Recuerdos   23

Imaginación   36

Tentación   43

La Vida Jóven   50

La Muerte   57

El Hermano Difunto   63

Revelaciones   76

Confesión   86

Domingo de Ramos   93

La Semana Santa   97

Hermanitos   101

Resoluciones   116

La Última Cena   132

Novicios   137

Brujas   140

Sangre de Cristo   148

Las Tinieblas   159

Resurreción   168

Amor   180

Esperanza   188

Aceptación   208

AFTERWORD   *211*

Foreword

Before you read my story, I want to offer a bit of explanation, justification, if you will, for writing about los Penitentes, their ceremonies, and their reasons for doing what they did (do). I only mean to provide my own perspective of what it was like to grow up among them, to interact with them in everyday tasks, and to pray with them.

Other books on this subject provide historical descriptions or observations, mostly from a third person perspective. Some seem to relish the shock value of what los Penitentes did in the past while others seem to condemn such acts of religious fervor. Through the eyes of José, however, I provide a glimpse of what it was like to actually become an Hermano and offer a first person viewpoint of what it was like to live and worship with them: the elders of my past who commanded such respect from their community.

The descriptions of los Hermanos themselves, their processions and ceremonies, come from my own memories; and the words to their *alabados* and their prayers come from the few prayer books I have which belonged to my ancestors. The description of the initiation ceremony comes from my imagination since my father never disclosed what they did behind the closed doors of the *morada* in the late hours of the night. The few rules I included which governed their *cofradía* are genuine and all were submitted for approval by Bishop Juan Leoniro in Santa Fe, New Mexico, on April 11, 1850, according to their documents.

Acknowledgements

Because "with God all things are possible" (Matthew 19:26), I owe this story first to Him for giving life to everyone who made this book a reality. Thank you, Lord, for my best friend and husband, Mike, and my sons Michael, David, and Andrew. Thank you all for always pushing me to do this, for encouraging me through rejections, for allowing me my alone time to get my father's story finished, and for providing positive, but biased, feedback on my ideas.

Then, of course, there are so many friends, relatives, colleagues, and former students who never wavered in your support of my endeavor. I beg forgiveness for not mentioning you all by name.

However, there are a few I must acknowledge: my closest confidants who never allowed me to give up my dream, Margie Seay, Christine Rodriguez, Linda Montoya, and Margaret Johnson. And two new friends who reached out to me, Irene Perea and Jon Aranda, who give me hope that los Hermanos will live on. *Los agradezco mucho.*

I'd like to give special recognition to the following individuals. Thank you for your services in assuring my Spanish was colloquially correct: Betsy Gomez, the late Pita Jaramillo, Yolanda Garduño, and Dr. Belinda Laumbach, Spanish experts and women mentors all! Thank you, Barbara Villaseñor, owner of Charles Publishing Co., for reading my manuscript in 1995 because your words of encouragement and praise of my writing style and my story kept me striving to succeed. Thank you, Rudolfo Anaya, for actually writing back to me when I asked for publishing advice; the fact that you wrote handwritten letters served as inspiration for me never to give up. Thank you, Angelo Archuleta, for advising me when I had specific questions about what I could and shouldn't write because I didn't want to offend los Hermanos. Thank you, Jeanette Yara, for helping me find the words to describe our unique New Mexican cuisine; and thank you, Dr. Sevllyn Gurulé, my wonderful former student, for your input regarding my questions about illness and health. Thank you, *primos* Fred, Jeffrey, and Benji Espinoza for caring for the morada and for allowing me to visit it again. Thank you, Sally Kruse, my fellow aspiring author, for your wise advice and photography skills. Thank you, Renee Moody, for caring enough about me to write a newspaper article about my achievement. And thank you, Vera Jo Bustos, another talented former student and now aspiring author, for hiring me as your editor—your confidence in me is humbling.

Lastly, but most particularly, thank you, Jim Mafchir, publisher and granter of dreams, for appreciating my father's story enough to publish it as a living legacy for people to understand what it really meant to become an Hermano. You gave me a platform to impart many customs, traditions, and superstitions we New Mexico Hispanics want to keep alive for future generations. Thank you for assembling your team of talented individuals, award-winning author and editor Cinny Green, world-renowned folk artist Diana Breyer, and award-winning author James Santiago Baca, who helped make my dream a reality. You four valued my father's story enough to do your best in your areas of expertise to assure that *El Hermano* exists as a record of *la gente del Cañoncito de las Manuelitas*.

EL HERMANO

El Hermano

The young man trudged home shortly after midnight. His lonely journey went unseen except perhaps by the eyes of God to whom he whispered prayers of heartfelt gratitude for his fellow Hermanos and for the *cofradía* which he had just professed to embrace. He cast himself from the protective warmth of the sacred morada, insisting that as part of his *penitencia* he wanted to walk home alone amidst protests from los Hermanos who offered their assistance. He was a *novicio*, a novice, who only hours before had taken the vows of the Penitentes and need not have chastised himself. But he had stubbornly maintained to his Brothers that he was compelled, had begged his *Hermano Mayor* to let him do what he felt he had to do. With his heart weighing heavily in his chest, the elder had agreed, and the novicio departed alone into the night.

Hours earlier, he had prepared himself for the ritual of his initiation, dressed in what the Hermanos provided: cream-colored, loose-fitting trousers sewn by one of the penitente's wives for the ceremony. The young man stood out amongst the Hermanos, not only because he alone wore the traditional ceremonial garb, but because he was by far the youngest. In the dark room lit only by kerosene lamps and numerous candles, the others watched as the novicio knelt upon the wooden floor, inhaling deeply as tiny pebbles embedded themselves in his flesh, to prove, more to himself than to his Savior, that he could endure the penance he had set for himself. As the secret ceremony unfolded, the novicio was overwhelmed by an almost giddy lightness of heart that came when he took the vows of his forefathers.

Home was a dark speck only a short distance away. Now, however, he fought fatigue and shivered against the February cold, blinking away the tears forming in his eyes, noting with disappointment that he couldn't stop them.

They ran down his face as he succumbed to his emotions and let himself fall to the ground. Yet even as he rolled onto his back and felt the chill of the frozen ground permeate his body, the novicio knew the reason for his tears. They stemmed not from the pain or emotional fatigue, but rather from his earnest entreaty for God's forgiveness for having been a coward. For four years, he had declined his father's invitation to become one of them, fearful that he couldn't live up to the Brothers' expectations. Finally, having decided to join them because of his uncertain future in the military, he embraced their support.

The shrill cry of a lone coyote barely echoed through the valley before it was joined by the chorus of its pack. As the novicio berated himself for giving in to his inner turmoil and began to struggle to his feet, he became aware of two shadows bending on either side of his body, lifting him to his feet carefully and raising his arms over their shoulders, speaking to him softly, their voices a welcome caress to his spirit. Los Hermanos had come, he realized, as grateful sobs took over him. His efforts to thank them as they half-carried him home were unnecessary. He realized that too as they quickly and efficiently took care of his wounds and put him into his bed before they left. And as he fell into exhausted slumber, the novicio was comforted by yet another realization: He was part of the Brotherhood now, and his Brothers would never desert him. He would never have to fear that he was alone in his struggle to live a humble existence emulating the life of Christ.

—

The novicio could've been any one of the many male ancestors who came before me: *mi bisabuelo, mi abuelo, o mi papá*. But he was my older brother, Miguel, and the year was 1928, a time that marked a great change in all our lives. So it's no wonder that I often reminisce upon the events which began that year and which still affect me deeply in the autumn of my life.

I woke with a start before dawn that morning, wondering for a moment why I felt such a feeling of foreboding. Then I remembered. The first day of Lent, Ash Wednesday, was yesterday; we'd spent the evening praying las *Estaciones* with los Hermanos, also marking my brother Miguel's induction into the cofradía as a novicio. I wondered what he'd had to do in los Hermanos' secret ritual. I also wondered if he was hurt like my *tío* had been the year before. I cursed myself for having fallen asleep, and then I smiled at my mother's craftiness. Remembering that although I had struggled against sleep when we'd returned without *Papá* from the *capilla*, *Mamá* suspected I would defy her and sneak out into the darkness to my aunt's house where Miguel was staying. She saw to it that I succumbed to slumber before she did.

Miguel had come home Monday after enlisting in the military and completing his physical examination in Albuquerque. He seemed different than when he'd left and yet somehow the same since he'd made the decision to become a Marine. The fun-loving youth returned with a playfulness that had always been there, yet at times he became pensive and closed-mouthed to my inquiries, masking whatever he'd discovered about his irrevocable decision. His acceptance at last to join the Brotherhood surprised me because in the past he'd always rejected my father's invitation to petition for admission, saying he wasn't ready. And although I wondered what had finally changed his mind, I didn't know. At the time, I think I didn't want to know, afraid that if I prodded him too much he would tell me things I'd rather not hear.

I snuggled beneath my quilt a bit longer, letting my thoughts turn to the Brotherhood instead. I knew that in becoming an Hermano, I, like my brother, would have to take a vow to help the others just as they would me. Since childhood, I knew I wanted to become an Hermano myself, yet I had gotten tired of waiting year after year to petition only to be put off because I was "not yet old enough, mature enough to know what I wanted," the very words spoken by my father and uncle who had listened time after time to my pleas with a sigh and a shake of their heads, words spoken only because of their sympathetic insight that I needed a reason, although it was an inadequate one.

At least I had thought I needed one—until the year before when I turned fifteen, the year I stopped asking and started wondering what being an Hermano was all about. That was the year my cousin Filiberto discovered his father had either been hurt or had hurt himself in some procedure performed at the morada while we so innocently slept. Because of what Berto told me, I began to have second thoughts, fears even, of what being an Hermano was all about. And because they never spoke a word about what went on during their closed meetings, I wasn't about to ask my father, *Hermano Mayor de la Cofradía de los Hermanos del Sagrado Corazón*, or Elder Brother of the Confraternity of the Brothers of the Sacred Heart.

Remembering that my only brother had undergone whatever ritual had been required of him in becoming a novicio the night before, I cursed my weakness for falling asleep before I could sneak out of the house to see for myself that he was fine. The crowing of the rooster in the hen house told me I'd have no time to check on Miguel before school if I didn't hurry, so I flung back my blankets and jolted out of bed to dress before my mother came in.

By habit, we were all early risers, but having only one bedroom, we got up in intervals, providing a semblance of privacy for one another. When he lived with us, Miguel had been first, until he acquired a job in Las Vegas and returned after only two months to find our great-aunt had moved to Colorado with her daughter and left him her house.

Now it was I who slept in the kitchen on an army cot given to Miguel by my uncle, and I would get up first, taking over Miguel's job of preparing the fire in the wood stove for my mother. She would rise next to put on a pot of coffee and start breakfast as my father dressed.

My former doubts and fears assailed me anew. I offered my morning prayers for my brother as I slipped out of the house, sure that I'd be damned if I didn't say them during Lent, of all seasons, sure also that somehow, some way, they would help Miguel.

I looked back over my shoulder as I ran up the hill behind our house rather than risk being seen running down the road to my brother's house. When I got to the path to Miguel's house, however, I had second thoughts about entering. After all, if he'd gotten home late as I suspected, he would probably still be asleep. Maybe, I thought, I would just peer in through one of the windows and see. As I rounded the house to the south, I could see there was a lamp burning in the bedroom window, and my dog, a mix of collie and who knew what else, was lying on the ground near the door to the kitchen. Spotting me instantly and letting out a cheerful yelp, Red came to me with a wagging tail that set his entire rear swaying. I pressed my back against the wall, shushing him with a quick pat to his nose. So, intent upon seeing Miguel for myself, I hadn't even noticed Red's absence at our house. I knew there was only one reason he would be here at all: my father was inside.

I peered into the window, crouching beneath the ledge, when my suspicions were confirmed. Mumbled voices told me my brother was awake, and though I knew I would catch grief if my father saw me, I squatted again, stayed low, just enough to see inside. My grandmother was there too, bent over my brother and rubbing what I knew was a salve into the wounds I also knew had come from whatever he endured the night before. As the sun came over the mountains to the east, a few words drifted through the window: "*Está bien*," my grandmother said. "*Bueno*," my father said, "*voy*." He headed for the door. I ran.

As my father trudged home, I started feeding the horses and cows. Holding the pitchfork high with hay, I tossed it to make yet another pile from which the animals would feed until there were only seeds and few scraps left for the crows and magpies. I knew he'd seen me though he hadn't called out, and I took my time until I knew the chickens would have left at least a few eggs that I could take up to my uncle's house.

When I entered our two-room adobe, my father was sitting at the table having coffee and my mother was bustling around our small *cocina*. I said good morning to them both, hoping neither would know where I'd been. I realized I had fooled no one when I saw the look they exchanged as I took the steaming kettle from the wood stove, poured water into the washbasin, and proceeded to make myself presentable. Neither spoke, other than to say good morning, and I knew from the silence that I'd interrupted something.

We would have eaten breakfast in silence too, but my concern for Miguel wouldn't let me. I blurted my question into the thick quiet. "*¿Está bien Miguel?*"

My father chased down a bite of egg and tortilla with a swallow of coffee before he looked me in the eye and asked a question of his own. "Why did you get up so early today?"

Debating inwardly about lying, I opted for a half-truth. Looking back into his eyes, I explained. "I didn't sleep well because I was worried about my brother."

"Your brother is fine, just tired from having stayed at the morada late."

I bit my tongue from asking why my grandmother had stayed with him if he was just tired, realizing that I'd be giving my earlier whereabouts away. Instead I said, "I think I'll go over to see him."

My father nodded but added, "José, go over later, after school perhaps."

So I finished the rest of my eggs in silence and said my goodbyes, explaining I was meeting my friends before school.

I gathered up our leftovers for Red who was waiting for breakfast and for the exercise he'd get following or, more often than not, leading me wherever I went in whatever direction I'd take. Knowing I shouldn't defy my father and run to my brother's, I still felt compelled to see if in fact he was alright. Shivering a little in the cool morning, I waited for Red to finish his food before I made my way up the hill behind our house again, jogging to the east end until my plan was thwarted by a blood-curdling yell that could only come from tiny Tino's throat. "Last one to the caves sucks eggs!"

I couldn't resist. It was early, after all, and as Tino and I raced one another up the hill behind my house to the caves where we usually met after our chores were done, especially on Saturdays, I forgot the cold. In my peripheral vision, I caught a glimpse of two more boys who'd also taken up the challenge, running and jumping over rocks in their path. Through scattered oak and dense pine, we raced, slipping on pine needles and half-melting snow all the way. Careening down one arroyo and up yet another hill, we ran, panting along with our dogs.

"I won." Tino breathed hard as though the rest of us were unaware of the fact. The smallest of our lot, he was also the quickest, and nine times out of ten he won. It was a given. What rattled the rest of us was that he always announced it.

Catching our collective breaths, four of the five of us fell against the boulders we called the caves. Truly, they were just big flat rocks with ledges and niches we could crawl into, and right between the two biggest rocks was a space about two feet wide where a refreshing waterfall fell after a rainstorm which we used for summertime dunking matches.

Glancing to my left, I took a moment to look at my motley group of *primos* and *amigos*. Four of the five of us were here, all cousins of sorts, each related to the other by mother or father, and we had been the best of friends since birth, since we were all about the same age. I don't ever remember a time when we didn't all play together as children. When we were each about ten, we established ourselves as the Cañoñcito gang, swearing a solemn oath to our band. Since it had been Berto's idea, it was also decided that he should be our leader. At fifteen, he was not the eldest of our gang, but ever since I could remember, Filiberto possessed an inherent magnetic quality that drew the rest of us to his side. And no matter how many times we'd gotten into trouble for following his lead, none of us sought to replace him, though in suffering one punishment or another when we'd been caught, each of us felt the compulsion to throttle him until he begged for mercy. But we didn't because chopping so much wood and racing after his father's sheep at sun up and sun down gave him a stocky, muscular frame, Filiberto also had a temper when he was riled and wasn't one the rest of us would challenge. Even Pedro, who was the biggest and the oldest, had never challenged him.

As we waited for Horacio, the chubbiest and therefore always the last to clamber up the hill, Tino started making snowballs, quickly readying a dozen or so to pelt the unsuspecting and most innocent of our group when he came into view. Chuckling, Berto joined in, and just as Horacio's red head appeared over the ridge, they loosed a few icy balls. Because of his perpetual tardiness, Horacio knew what was coming and kept between trees, lobbing some missiles of his own.

After receiving an especially hard snowball hit to my chin, I finally called a halt to the fight which left us all with red hands and a few smarting spots on ears and cheeks. We waited impatiently for Horacio to join us. He lumbered forth in his signature slow gait, whining that we'd been unfair again. When we were all lounging against the rock ledges, it was Pedro who finally asked what we would do with the afternoon hours between school and evening chores.

Berto pounced, having waited for the moment when we were all together to hatch yet another of his plans. Without preamble, he blurted, "I have a plan for tomorrow night."

"Night?" Horacio squealed. It was a known fact among all of us that anything pertaining to the dark hours after sunset would meet with his disapproval. Like me, Horacio hated the dark, feared it even. But whereas Horacio had let his fears be known (the poor guy became the easy target of night time practical jokes), I had kept mine relatively concealed from the gang. I followed Berto's lead no matter what time, regardless of my qualms about meeting with anything in the dark like the wailing *Llorona* my cousins from town told us about or the *serpiente* of our mountains one of the elderly men of our valley swore he'd once seen.

"Well?" Tino prompted, after having teased Horacio until he squirmed. "What's your plan, Berto?"

We heard Berto out with no interruption. But once he finished, we looked at one another in silence, our misgivings racing through our heads a mile a minute as we sifted over the probable consequences if we were caught. This time, unlike his former ideas that were met with approval from the rest of us— primarily because fun was the basis of his plans—there was a serious quality to Berto's proposal, one which appealed to all of us because of what we would discover about our own futures. Yet there was the very real probability that we'd be caught, and none of us was willing to face the music if that happened. To be discovered doing what he planned could very well mean ostracism from the society to which we all aspired before we even had a chance to join.

But Berto, our fearless leader, looked at us, his gang, his gray eyes gleaming with pent up enthusiasm. As though he experienced not one of the fears the rest of us worried over, Berto's sun-bronzed face beamed. He looked expectantly at the rest of us with a myriad of expressions as he always did when he was unsure of our thoughts or of our approval. He tossed his head to rid the unruly lock of brown hair that always fell over his brow and began to glare at our silence. He crinkled his nose and raised his upper lip in a snarl as though he were a dog. Yet still he waited, his eyes focusing expectantly first on Pedro.

Also fifteen, Pedro had developed into a tall, husky young man, the hint of what he would look like as an adult already apparent in his stature and demeanor. At five foot, seven, he towered over us, and when he'd look down into our faces with the darkest eyes I've ever seen, Pedro's stare was intimidating indeed. With his boyish good looks, females of all ages were drawn to him like bears to honey. Once captured by his eyes, they seemed hypnotized by his gaze and by his gallantry. He already knew what he wanted out of life: employment and marriage, in that order. And the rest of us, except for Horacio, envied his self-assurance because we weren't ready to meet our futures head on.

Berto's glance next flickered to Celestino, a name too long for such a short guy, so we'd shortened it to Tino, practically from his birth. At four foot, ten, he was both tiny and quick. Tino's greatest pleasure was in sneaking up on one of us when we least expected it, emitting a blood-curdling yell into an ear that sent his victim jumping into the air, chagrined in the realization that it was just Tino—again. His cherubic face was deceptive; adults thought the smile that always etched his countenance was pure innocence, but we knew otherwise. That smile was a warning that someone was about to find himself the victim of another one of his pranks. Only Tino wasn't smiling now, his forehead was creased in concentration. I knew he, like I, was thinking of the ramifications that would come if we decided to carry out Berto's plan.

Filiberto's eyes flickered to Horacio, the bookworm of our group. School was alright for me, but to Horacio, it was his future. At fourteen, like Tino, he'd already decided to follow in Maestro's footsteps and become our little valley's future teacher. Never without a book, Horacio even carried one with him when he did his chores, plopping down next to the pig pens or chicken coop to take in a few pages before he was caught. Horacio hated his daily chores, but like the rest of us, hated being whipped with the ever-ready willow *chicote* even more. He looked away from Berto's steady stare, shuffling closer to a tree as if he could burrow behind its trunk and make himself invisible from Berto's questioning eyes. Always a follower, Horacio never spoke first, always waiting for the rest of us to decide and following our lead for fear of being left out.

I found myself almost cringing under Berto's gaze as he looked from Horacio to me, and I wondered what he saw. I was a little older, but something about him usually made me agree to whatever he planned should be our next quest. And though my conscience shouted for me to stand up to him on a multitude of occasions, many were the times I let myself be carried on the wave of his exuberance. And many also were the times I had suffered one punishment or another because one of his schemes went awry. Perhaps I was too much like Horacio, more of a follower than a leader. Scrawny as an unstuffed scarecrow, I was five feet of pure muscle. I had to be to keep up with my father and my uncle and keep our small farm running. I had my uncle's hazel eyes, but I also wore the curse of our ancestors on my lean face: the Valdez nose stood out prominently, evidence that I had come from Indian roots.

"¿*Pues*?" Berto looked at us expectantly after he'd blurted out his new scheme. "¿*Qué piensan*?"

"What do we think? ¡*Que estás loco*—that you're crazy!" Pedro mumbled with a shake of his head as he absently scratched his Labrador behind the ears.

Horacio nodded, and Tino chewed on his lower lip. I only stared, wondering what had made Berto even think of such a plan in the first place. Then realization dawned and I knew the reason for his unbridled curiosity—because only that morning I had begun to share the same obsessive quest for answers myself. I bit my tongue, a habit I felt would only increase as time went on.

"That's alright," Berto scoffed, spitting on the ground before adding, "if you're all *gallinas*, cowardly hens, I'll go alone. But don't expect me to tell you what I see."

I should have known then and there that he was bluffing and that he wouldn't dare go alone because there was no way Filiberto was capable of keeping a secret from any of us. Oh, he would hint and tease us with his intimate knowledge for a while, but the novelty would wear off and he'd be bursting at the seams to share his story, no matter how embellished with fictional details, and the rest of us would be able to discern the truth. Yet even as I wondered about the same thing Berto did, especially with my brother lying in bed after whatever had happened at the morada during his induction into the Brotherhood, I had another matter to worry about. I gave it more than a few moments of thought.

"I don't know about the rest of you," I spoke up finally, "but I don't think I have that much longer to wait. Either this year or next I'll be a novicio. There's no way I'm gonna ruin my chances just because you want to satisfy your curiosity about …." I left the rest unsaid for it was a sore spot to mention it in Berto's presence.

All our fathers were Hermanos, but Berto had been rudely awakened to the evidence of what being a Penitente meant the night he'd seen his father return home injured by one of their rituals. The incident was taboo; the rest of us learned quickly not to bring it into the conversation. But evidently it had been festering within him all this time, the curiosity to see for himself what los Hermanos put themselves through in their rites of penitence. I knew only too well today what fears he needed to put to rest before he himself would join. Didn't I have the same doubts?

"He's right, Berto. What if we get caught?" Tino asked hesitantly.

The look Filiberto threw at the youngest of our gang made me glad it wasn't directed at me. As for Tino, his face resembled that of a puppy that'd been told to go home when all he wanted was attention. "If we get caught we say we were just trying to cure Horacio from being afraid of the dark, eh?" Berto proposed. "It won't really be a lie either 'cause we've been trying to do that anyway."

Pedro nodded. "And we were just passing by ..."

"Right!" Berto grinned, his eyes sparkling with eagerness.

"In this weather?" Horacio stammered, blushing.

"So?" Berto parried.

It did seem a sure-proof plan, however, a way to catch a glimpse of what would be expected of each of us when our time came to join the Cofradía of Penitentes of which my father was the leader. And though my conscience screamed at me to remain in ignorance until my time came, I too shared the curiosity, for my father never spoke of their rituals in my presence. And now there was Miguel.

"It might just work," Pedro agreed finally, but when he looked directly at me I knew he shared my fears. Being the same age, we knew our time was near. To jeopardize our chances was to have to wait yet another year to prove we were worthy.

"José, how's Miguel?" Berto asked me. Did I detect a mild taunt in his voice?

"That's right," Tino blurted, "he became a novicio last night, huh?"

The moment he spoke up, my eyes sent daggers into his and Tino tried to swallow his words a moment too late.

"He's fine," I answered, not wanting anyone to know my brother would lie in his bed for most of the day.

Horacio had been a silent listener. He rose and said, "Shouldn't we think about this?"

"Fine," Berto scoffed, also rising and tossing a last taunt over his shoulder as he walked away. "Take till tomorrow to decide. I'm going with or without you."

Daring us to go along with him, Filiberto had gotten us all into trouble so many times we couldn't count them if we tried, and we cursed ourselves afterward for being stupid enough to let his taunts get to us. It was this thought that kept me preoccupied the rest of the day. None of us dared voice our doubts aloud in Berto's presence. Instead we each weighed the pros and cons in silence. As the rest of the gang went their separate ways, I went to my brother's house.

Conciencia

My grandmother would keep my secret, I knew. So my conscience was clear as I lifted my hand to knock on the kitchen door. Abruptly, it opened and my gramma's weathered face peered out at me for a moment before she stepped back for me to enter. I did, kissing her cheek and bidding her a respectful good morning.

"*Yo sabía que ibas a venir*," she said, knowing instinctively that I would come. "*Venites esta mañana*," she confirmed, and I nodded, knowing she'd seen or sensed me here earlier in the morning.

Wondering how my brother fared, I asked, "*¿Como sigue?*"

"*Bien*." She nodded. "He needs rest right now, that's all."

She motioned with her chin for me to take a look for myself, which I did, tiptoeing to the bedroom and seeing that Miguel, though a bit pale, slept peacefully.

"Come back later," my grandmother whispered. "You know your papá will not like that you did what he told you not to do."

I nodded, wondering not for the first time why my grandmother always seemed to know more than she ought. But Miguel was alright in my gramma's care, and I knew I would catch more than the chicote if my father learned I'd been here. Knowing my gramita wouldn't tell on me (she never had), I left feeling comforted that Miguel was indeed better than I thought he would be.

I raced to school, a mere seventy yards or so up the road, a daily ritual Miguel had started, one he enjoyed more than I did, but a habit I continued in his absence, one I couldn't seem to break. By unspoken challenge we would look at each other for a split second as we reached the road at the edge of our yard and take off, huffing and clutching our books until he reached the rock wall of the one room schoolhouse a few seconds ahead of me. Never had I won, and never would he let me forget it. For even after he had finished school, he interrupted his chores to race me there each morning, ribbing me good-naturedly as always. "*¿Cuando, chivito?* When will you ever win?" I never minded, knowing I was three years younger and would probably never beat him. I would smile, humoring his superiority for being the oldest. And I continued to race, the memory of my childhood with Miguel urging me on.

Arriving at the schoolhouse a few minutes before my friends, I leaned huffing against the rock wall to wait for them, and I wondered where they'd all gone. School was something I always enjoyed, not only for the fun I had with primos and *compañeros* during recess and lunch, but for the sheer pleasure of learning. Maestro Rubel made our lives rough if we deserved it, but he had a knack of making whatever we were studying at the time extraordinarily interesting. An avid reader with an insatiable interest in world history and cultures, he told countless stories of each country he introduced, coloring each by mimicking the accents as he spoke words or phrases in foreign languages, opening the pages of his texts to show us pictures as he roamed the long room so we could all see.

We visited vast Chinese empires and the cold regions of the Poles with him, traveling in our imaginations to each corner of the world. And although he taught all grades (first through eighth) and we ranged in age from six to sixteen (older if retained), when he introduced us to the world, he left all of us inspired, mesmerizing us by his colorful tales and awakening in us a hunger for more.

In his early sixties, he had taught our elders before us, having been maestro of the Cañoncito valley for over almost thirty years, coming down from the village of Rociada a few miles to the north in his horse-drawn buggy until 1915, when he shocked humans and sent animals scurrying in a frenzy as he drove proudly through our valley in a real car, the first most of our community had ever seen. It was a Ford Model T, for which he had saved pretty much his entire life, knowing—he told us—that mankind was bound to achieve something he'd want to purchase eventually. In his case, this vehicle became that achievement, bought for an incredible eight hundred and fifty dollars! Of course, to us that was a fortune and we all fancied him our own resident millionaire.

Of the many anecdotes I begged my Tío Daniel to retell countless times and even now sends me into spasms of laughter, the first time Maestro Rubel came clattering down the dirt road through our serene valley has always been one of my favorites. The people who had been outdoors that early morning crossed themselves in anxiety, thinking the rumbling and unexpected noise was a tremor in the earth. Tío said that my gramma later confessed to having grabbed up poor Saint Medard (patron saint for protection from bad storms) from her little altar and, standing in the center of the kitchen, raised him in the act of genuflection while turning to the four directions, always a surefire way to ward off a bad storm. (My wife and later my daughter did this all the way into the twenty-first century. Some people tossed salt in each direction hoping to ward off evil while others even genuflected with a knife. The process called "*cortando las nubes*" means cutting the clouds.)

Anyway, Tío Daniel was chopping kindling, he said, when the noise became noticeable. He yelled at the top of his lungs for his wife and mother (still clutching the santo) to get out of the house and take to the hills, which they did in short order, stumbling over rocks in their night gowns and *chopos* (slippers), their long braids whipping their backs in their haste. About to run for cover himself, he glanced down the road to see the horses in Primo Juan's pasture galloping toward the barn just before the glossy, black machine rounded the curve between the capilla and the schoolhouse, sending the smaller children gathered there running home in tears. When Maestro Rubel pulled up beside the school and cut the engine, the backfire sent more farm animals racing in panic and magpies and crows screeching in outrage.

The shock also caused quite a few accidents that morning as Maestro Rubel innocently and proudly arrived in his new acquisition. Berto's older sister, a thin, lanky girl, stumbled over her brother, Manuel, as she ran from the school in her haste to reach home. He did a complete somersault in the air, coming down badly on his arm and dislocating his shoulder. As he yowled in pain, his mother raced to the rescue, only to be thrown accidentally backward by two small screaming boys who didn't see her and rammed solidly into her stomach, knocking the wind out of her even before she landed.

Primo Victoriano's cows in the corral across the road from the schoolhouse broke through the latillas that were supposed to hold them, stampeded up the road, and scattered a few more children into the trees of the *monte*. The pigs in Don León's pen broke loose, and when most of the neighboring children had calmed down enough, they were recruited to round up the squealing creatures, all eight of them. Needless to say, school was canceled for the day as Maestro Rubel, overwhelmed with guilt, shamefacedly assisted in all that he could to quiet the valley once more.

Of course, no one blamed him. After everyone and everything was taken care of, we all congregated around the vehicle to check it out up close. As long as it stood silently, no one feared it. In fact, those who had over-reacted stood laughing at themselves and cutting jokes about the shock on the faces of others. Everybody who had never seen an automobile was rather impressed, which is how Maestro Rubel had wanted them all to react in the first place.

Yet the uproar caused everyone's chickens and geese up the two miles from the main road to stop laying eggs for an entire week until the shock wore off. It took about as long for the horses to stop running away and the cows and pigs to remain docile as Primo Victoriano with half the children and Don León with the other half surrounded the corral and pigpen the minute the approach of Maestro Rubel and his new conveyance could be heard. School was delayed an hour that whole week, and after-school chores were delayed just as long for Maestro Rubel to crank up the vehicle and leave our otherwise quiet valley with a final backfire to signal his departure each afternoon.

"Yaaaa!" The scream in my ear nearly sent me two feet in the air, bringing me out of my daydream with a shock as Tino crept up beside me. I should have known. It was a prank he just couldn't resist whenever he could get away with it, running away almost before the scream faded from his victim's eardrums and before the person could catch his breath enough to take after him.

"San-a-ma-gón!" I breathed hard. "You did it again!"

"Wet your pants?" he asked with a wide grin, as he always did.

Before I could retort, Berto strode up, spitting a wad with importance and wiping his lips on his sleeve before greeting us.

"*Órale*," he said with a lift of his chin, looking at Tino but avoiding my eyes as he spoke.

I knew he knew it would be Pedro's and my decision that would sway Tino and Horacio to carry out Berto's plan for the next evening, and I debated whether to respond or just to walk away. I knew he was still angry about my reluctance to support his scheme. Even when he was wrong, Filiberto was well known for holding grudges, yet fearing exclusion, he'd always enter the realm of buddies again.

Before I said anything, the rest of our motley gang arrived. I took stock of the boys, wondering what, if anything, Berto had told them in my absence. Horacio stood by, the round pinkness of his face sporting a wide smile and the chipped tooth he received in the last water fight at the river. Though he was large and big-boned, he was soft, pudgy—the scaredy cat of our group. Sniveling when thwarted and running home if we teased, which we did unmercifully at times, Horacio was easy prey for Berto. Often after joining in the teasing, I would make myself kneel before my mother's altar in penance afterward. My mother's altar, like most Hispanic mothers' altars at the time, was very special although it really was just a cabinet upon which was a linen cover she'd cro-cheted herself and upon which stood her numerous saints and candles. In my prayers, I wished I was strong enough to prevent the others from starting up on Horacio, hoped to find the courage one day to fall away from the rest and to rise above their pettiness. But needing their approval to remain one of them, at fifteen I, too, succumbed to the playfulness in teasing my cousin.

Once, when we were out behind the *ladera* on the mesa behind my house playing baseball, Berto tumbled accidentally into Horacio's paunch as he slid into third. Horacio yelled for the ball. Unfortunately, he was standing directly on the flat rock we used for the base. Sending Horacio unexpectedly into a per-fect backflip, Berto twisted his body to the left as he fell and Horacio landed on his stomach with a muffled "ooof!" When he came to, Tino was kneeling astride his chest, slapping his head from side to side to bring him around. We all wondered afterwards if Horacio would have come to on his own without the howl that rumbled up out of his throat at awakening to find Tino smiling with each slap. Horacio rose up, pushing Tino to the ground in one move as he screamed, catching Tino unaware before Horacio ran all the way home. Tino clearly enjoyed the satisfaction of slapping Horacio's cheeks, since his cousin was three times his size and unconscious.

And because he was the tiniest, Tino's enjoyment came primarily from ril-ing Horacio or Pedro, the two biggest of our lot. He'd creep up behind either, catching each unaware so many times we couldn't count. One or the other would jump a mile at whatever Tino was up to, sputtering, "You'll be sorry, Tino, if I die of a heart attack!" Once, he'd even caught Pedro trying to kiss Luciana in her father's barn. He probably would've gotten his kiss if Tino hadn't peeked, thrown the door wide open, and hidden from view, yelling in a gruff voice imitating that of her father, "¡*Bésala y te mato*!" (Kiss her and I'll kill you!)

Needless to say, we laughed so hard at Tino's rendition of how Pedro jumped a foot in the air and threw Luciana backward into the hay so hard she was buried. Then he stumbled over the hens in his way, getting unmercifully pecked in the groin by her father's rooster, before he made his escape. Pedro was the lover, thinking all the girls in our valley had crushes on him, but Tino was by far the most fun-loving.

"Órale," Tino spoke up, "just scared the pants offa José again."

"So what else is new?" Horacio scoffed. "I swear, Tino, one of these days …" which was a common threat he used on Tino at least fifty times a day, only making Tino's eyes twinkle at the thought of how to scare Horacio in a new way next time he got the opportunity.

Berto broke in quietly, "Well?" Looking at me for the first time, he added, "Are you going or are you gallinas gonna vote?" Waiting for a response which didn't come quickly enough, he looked at each one of us, stretching out the silence for emphasis before he persisted. "Are you with me or not?"

Pedro broke the silence first, trying for a bit of levity, "I'd rather peek into Luciana's bedroom window any night."

Tino snorted, "You always think with the wrong head, Pedro."

After the laughter died down, Horacio asked soberly, "You never did find out about your father, didja, Berto?"

I looked at Horacio with trepidation. Even knowing what a sore spot the topic was for Filiberto, Horacio must've summoned up every bit of courage he could find to ask what the rest of us wanted to ask but were too intimidated by Berto's temper to attempt.

But Berto only raised a brow in surprise and shook his head. "No," he replied shortly, glancing toward the morada rather than at any one of us directly. To place the embarrassment on other shoulders, he looked at me then and added, "Miguel's been in bed all day, huh? I thought you'd wanna know why. But if you're too chicken …"

Tino started in on me then, teasing, flapping his arms and scratching at the ground with the tips of his boots. "Bak, baa-aak, bak," he clucked.

I squared my shoulders and looked at the group. "It ain't that. It's just that I want to be an Hermano bad, you know that. And I don't wanna do anything that will stop it from happening if we get caught. Besides, I thought we had till tomorrow to decide."

Berto scoffed at the pensive quietude of the others, "Bah, it's not that big of a deal. If I'd known you were all going to be chicken I would've never brought it up. I'll do it alone. Who says I need you, any of you?"

Pedro slammed a palm on Berto's chest as he made a move to stalk away. "I didn't say I didn't want to," he said with quiet firmness.

"Wait!" said Horacio. "Say we go up there and someone goes outside to piss or something and we do get caught, what'll we do?"

"I thought we already went over that," Berto spat. "We just gotta get our story straight before we go, just in case. After all, what's confession for?"

"Ya," Tino nodded, "but …"

"But nothing," Berto crossed his arms across his chest. "I'm going; you vote if you want to." He threw the words over his shoulder dismissively before he walked away.

The rest of us looked at one another, thinking deeply of the consequences, shuffling at the dirt with our toes, looking away, waiting to decide as a group as we always did whenever one of Berto's schemes was bound to get us in trouble.

The rumble of Maestro Rubel's automobile announced his imminent arrival, so we began to line up at the door of the schoolhouse.

"Today at recess," Tino proposed, "we better decide."

The morning passed slowly for all of us. Unable to concentrate on one thing for long at any time, Tino's daydreaming during arithmetic caused Maestro to stand him in the corner balancing an extremely large textbook on his head when we were let out for the usual fifteen-minute recess, thus postponing our vote until lunch. Then right before lunch, Pedro's note-passing to Luciana caused Maestro once again to mete out punishment, after he read Pedro's note to the class. " '*Chulita*,' " he read and mumbled to himself, "yes, she is a pretty child," before continuing, " 'meet me by Primo Victoriano's barn for a sweet lunch, okay?' " The numerous snickers and giggles that passed around the room in a soft wave caused Maestro to cut them short with the slap of his willow stick on Pedro's knuckles. We all knew any one of us could be next if we were stupid enough to laugh again. Thus, our vote was again postponed, for Pedro had to spend lunchtime doing all manner of tasks Maestro Rubel demanded and go without food while Maestro himself enjoyed his burrito loudly with gusto. The rest of us were dismissed to our homes for our own lunches.

Maestro was a strict disciplinarian, but he could also be fair-minded. As I sat at our kitchen table for my lunch of the usual buttered tortilla, a boiled egg, a bowl of *frijolitos pintos*, or a slice of whatever meat we had on hand, I reminisced about a particular time I was on the punishing end of Maestro's discipline. In the not too distant past, Teresita, one of the Luceros, was running late to school, having had a delayed start on dishwashing before getting her younger siblings and herself ready in the morning. It so happened that when she arrived, we older students were in the process of silent reading while Maestro was at the front with his back to the door as he worked with the younger kids. Since it was springtime and the front door was wide open, we all heard a noise outside. It sounded like a shuffling of feet, quickly followed by a thud. Looking up from my reader, I was just in time to see a pair of arms windmilling wildly and the rest of Teresita's body following in such a forward slant she was almost horizontal. Her body flew past the door so quickly, I wasn't even sure I'd seen what I'd seen, but when I heard a gasp followed by a thump, I knew she'd hit the dirt—literally. I know I should've rushed out to assist, because that's what Pedro did. Instead, I found myself in the throes of uncontrollable laughter. Oh, how

I struggled to make no noise, even hiding my face under my crossed arms. But no matter how I tried to hold it in, an occasional guffaw escaped. And my upper body shook so much from the effort of holding in the giggles, it felt like I was having convulsions. When I finally lifted my head, it was just in time to see Pedro leading Teresita in by the elbow; one look at her dirty face sent me into spasms once more. Hiding my own face again, I tried in vain to think of something serious. However, when I closed my eyes, Teresita's smudged nose and cheek, her pink frock covered in brown dust, and the look of confusion on her countenance set me off again.

When I finally thought I could control myself, I looked up—right into Maestro's face. Leaning over me with his most serious and frightening teacher expression, he asked, "*¿Acabates?* Are you done?"

Talk about instant sobriety! Oh, yes indeed, was I finished. With a gulp and a straightening of my shoulders, I responded, "*Sí, señor. Dispénsame, maestro; no pude controlarme.*" Lame, I know, but at least I was honest when I said yes, sir, excuse me, I couldn't control myself.

"*No vas a comer hoy. Vas a trabajar por toda la hora de la comida.*"

I only nodded. Of course, I'd skip lunch and work for the full hour for him. To this day I can't explain why poor Teresita's mishap caused such a hysterical reaction from me, nor could I explain the many other times I'd been stricken by such uncontrollable mirth. It even occurred once at a rosario, a rosary for a dead relative. It so happened that when a heavy woman was trying to make her way across several people already seated in the pew she also wanted to occupy, she let out a little fart—a little "wheeew" that escaped her behind—right in front of my face as I was kneeling at the time. Because we were at a church function, for Pete's sake, I mumbled to my mother seated beside me that I needed some air and made my way quickly outside. Once there I ran to the outhouse across the road and muffled my laughter until I could gain control of my senses and rejoin the prayer session.

When I reached the door of the capilla opposite the altar, however, I looked inside and saw my mother holding her handkerchief to her nose and the flatulent woman half kneeling in the pew in front of her, fanning her face with her own kerchief—and I ran right back across the road before anyone could catch me in a renewed bout of the giggles. Let me tell you, it took almost to the end of the rosario for me to finally control myself and return.

This time Pedro suffered the consequences of his indiscretion. By the time the afternoon wore slowly on and school was over for the day, I was on pins and needles. Berto had refused to discuss the matter for lunch, sensing he already had Pedro's vote. Knowing, too, how Horacio and I felt about it, Berto also realized it would be Tino who would cast the deciding vote. Under no circumstances would Berto let us do any talking that would convince Tino to vote our way. After school, we all ran straight for the center of an *arbolera* where there was an apple tree with gnarled branches upon which we all could perch comfortably above the ground, swinging and horsing around. It was this spot, which was sacred to our gang, the spot where all our decisions as a group were made, just as the caves were our designated spot for hatching plans.

As we stood or fell to the ground catching our breaths, Berto spoke, knowing we had but a few moments to come to a decision since we always had to return straight home after school to do our chores before we were allowed time to ourselves.

"Vote," he demanded. "I say sí."

"No," I said quickly.

"No," Horacio echoed.

"Sí," Pedro said defiantly.

All eyes turned on Tino, Horacio's and mine imploringly, Pedro and Berto's probingly as Tino weighed the alternatives a final time. He looked at each one of us somberly, catching the almost imperceptible shake of my head and the noticeable tightening of Berto's fists before he nodded and mumbled, "Yes."

The decision made, Berto raced away with a whoop and Pedro crossed the fence in the opposite direction, leaving Tino, Horacio and me alone.

"We'll catch hell for it if we're caught," Horacio moaned as he made his way to the ladder-like bridge over the river to cross the three properties between his home and mine.

"Sí," I sighed, speaking mostly to myself while Tino remained silent, alone with his conscience as we walked up toward the road. I offered no words of reprimand, nor did I lash out at him in anger, knowing that if he hadn't voted as he had, the others would have branded him gallina for the rest of his life. As much as I cared for Tino, I knew I couldn't act as his guardian angel every moment of the day, and so I had only myself to blame. If I had consented to go along with Berto from the first, the entire matter never would have involved the gang. I knew Berto, knew he would have been satisfied if only I was involved. Instead, now I had not only my own soul to worry about, but three others.

Friday dragged on until there were only a couple of hours left before the *Estaciones* would begin, and I awaited the setting of the sun with trepidation about what the evening would bring. I had avoided my father as best I could the entire day to keep from being alone with him for fear he might sense what the boys and I had planned for the night. And when I did happen to catch his eyes upon me, which was quite often, I imagined it was my own guilty conscience that made me see suspicion where there probably was none.

As usual my mother, with her maternal insight, discerned something was amiss. Her watchful eyes seemed to widen in unspoken question whenever I caught her glance. As if she knew that Berto was at the root of my problem, once she even advised, "Don't let Filiberto make you do anything you don't want to. Listen to your *conciencia*, *hijo mío*." So much for keeping a secret from a mother's intuition.

Recuerdos

——————

I sat beneath the towering pines atop the ladera behind our house to pass the time. I whittled at a small piece of wood that I struggled to shape into a pistol to give my little primo on his upcoming birthday, picturing in my mind the revolver my Tío Daniel used to scare off coyotes. The February winds were blowing lazily as they always did during this holy month, and I looked down upon the pastures with spots of snow and patches of grass sprouting here and there, the memories of past pious days of Lent bittersweet, mingling with my anxiety of what this night would bring. I eagerly awaited my first glimpse of los Penitentes making their way from the morada, where at times an Hermano emerged assisted by his Brothers to his home because whatever he had undergone there had made him too weak to make his way on his own. I thought of my brother and all I could do was conjure up images of frightening, painful tortures like the ones my Tío Daniel had relived in his nightmares when he came home from the war. All that I had ever been allowed to participate in was the praying of las Estaciones. Since I still hadn't talked to Miguel, whom I sensed would keep the details of his own initiation to himself, how was I to know whether to be frightened or eager to prove myself worthy?

How could I have known that this year would be different? After all, I had turned fifteen just that October and yet nothing had changed. Little did I suspect in that middle year of trust and naïveté between child and adult that I was to be led into the awareness of adulthood by my cousin Filiberto who wanted as much as I to see into the secret world of los Hermanos, hoping for a glimpse of what our futures would hold when our time came to join the sacred Cofradía of los Penitentes. What we discovered during that most sacred season of Lent when we were unknowingly called has stayed with me all my life.

When I heard the first mournful rising of the notes of the *alabado* sung by the Penitentes, I glanced up across the road, the meadows, the river, and a chill coursed up my spine with the crescendo of their voices. It was not exactly a shiver of fright of the Penitentes themselves. I did not fear these men, all of whom were either related—uncle and cousins—or known as *compadres* to me. We were raised to think of our elders with trust and respect. However, there was a fear of what they did, of what they forced of themselves and of one another. And yet the coldness creeping up my body did not dampen the twinge of expectation or diminish the reverence in my heart. I recognized it for what it was: a longing deep within me to conquer my fear of the unknown, to become one of them.

They had begun to walk slowly down to the capilla from the morada up on the little knoll across from Don Juan's house. I could see them now—a procession of the hard-working, respected men of our small community called Cañoncito, meaning little canyon. There was my Tío Daniel—*el Celador*, the warden of the society, in the lead, carrying the *bandera*, the crimson-colored flag bordered in gold tassels and bearing a hand-embroidered Sacred Heart. Worn, calloused, but God-fearing men were *los Penitentes de la Capilla del Santo Niño*. Behind Tío Daniel was my father—el Hermano Mayor, the eldest brother, not in age necessarily, but the leader, carrying his black leather-bound book of alabados, prayers sung as hymns. Following in twos were the rest of los Hermanos: Don Donacio, Don León, Don Juan, Primo Gabriel, Don Procopio, Primo Esteban, Primo Melaquías, and Primo Eufemio, all living around us in our section of Cañoncito or a bit north up the mountain at Las Cañadas, the Big Canyons, except for Primo Melaquías, who lived to the south, in Las Vegas, "the city," population almost 4,000. And last in the procession came my brother, the newest member of their elite society. Though I couldn't tell from this distance whether he was in pain, I thought I detected the hint of a limp.

Each Hermano held his own small, worn, ink-smudged copy of hand-written alabados, most which had been penned by the hands of their fathers. As each harmonized as best he could with his Brothers, all tones and pitches of voice, cracked and rusty, combined in a doleful, funereal hymn that sent chills of awe and a kind of anticipatory terror down my head to my toes as if a shroud of death like the ones placed over the saints during Holy Week were being draped over my body, emanating electric-like prickles as it went.

Crossing myself quickly and putting my pocketknife and piece of wood in my pocket, I ran down the hill to our house. Finding the two rooms empty, I realized my mother had already left to go to the church, though I hadn't seen her. I locked the screen door by turning a four-inch piece of wood that swiveled on a nail on the door frame, meant more for locking out cats and dogs than humans. I walked slowly down the dirt road to the capilla. I knew it would take los Hermanos some minutes to reach the church and so I took my time, listening to the rise and fall of their wailing voices echo down the valley. I glanced at the pine trees waving their clustered needles at me from atop the mountain which rose to my left, ending in a flat mesa where my cousins and I played ball on those cool summer evenings when we weren't herding cattle or sheep in the sierras of Las Cañadas and reached by hiking up the ladera a few hundred yards behind our house.

My eyes turned down toward the fields, where neither the brown earth nor the snowy patches gave a clue as to what would sprout with the early days of summer after spring plowing. Looking beyond Primo Juan's square of land to the rutted track of a road between his property and another where Miguel now lived, I caught a glimpse of the red and yellow banner held high as my Tío Daniel led the Penitentes. He wore his usual army green attire, the only remnant of the military career of his youth besides the few medals earned honorably in World War I. The flag swayed with the gentle wind around his five-foot-five lean frame as he took step after slow step, providing the tempo for his Brothers who followed behind.

Although he was too far away to see clearly, I could visualize his face—the sharp, light brown eyes, so like my own, that would be beady with tears of religious fervor as his voice rang out in a tremulous tenor. I could see his short cut salt-and-pepper hair ruffled by the afternoon breeze, and his long, aquiline nose pointed upward, his head lifted proudly in this prestigious parade of wise men. His high glossy cheekbones would be aglow with pink, partly from sun and wind burn from his long days of tending to the land and the livestock and partly from the pride that came from holding the lead position in this procession of faith. His face, like all of us Valdezes, Montoyas, and countless primos, compadres, and tíos of this cañon, mirrored the Indian ancestry that had permeated our Hispanic culture in centuries past.

So did the nose.

It came in variations. In the primos from Colorado, those self-acclaimed relatives from the north, some of whom were big city *pachucos* who had left our community in the years before I was born, the nose was prominent with a Roman quality to it, that Roman step that slides sharply downward to end in a long semi-sharp point. When Ricardo or Larry, two of the seventeen cousins of Rocky Ford, looked at you, the nose pointed at you accusatorially as if it had a personality of its own. It said, "*Hmmpf, ¿qué miras, jodido?*"

Then there are the noses of the Apodacas who live in Las Vegas, numbering in the teens, too. These nineteen twenties, poor years without electricity, were hard ones. The long winter nights afforded little in the way of entertainment, and it is a common practice of later generations to teasingly attribute the large families of our era to this fact. With such an Indian-begotten, long bulbous sniffer, people could tell how we were all related. This protruding piece of the Apodacas' countenance was long, as long as ours, and thin, like ours. But where ours ended almost as sharply as those of the Colorado primos, theirs ended in what can only be compared to a lightbulb or plant bulb. Ours, the prominent honker, is a combination of these two. My gramma had it, my Tío Daniel had it, my father, all of us had it. We were all cursed to find peace with it.

I ceased my contemplation of our curse, stifling my urge to laugh at the portraits in my mind and renewing my appraisal of the Hermanos who were still making their way slowly down toward the capilla, a sight that sobered me immediately. I focused on my father, wearing the customary work pants, a plain, long-sleeved shirt, and the tough leather work shoes that had to last for years and did. He stood a few inches shorter and was even thinner than his brother. He had begun to grow bald at a young age so the roundness of his head was quite evident. So was the prodigious nose, with classic high cheek bones, red-brown from years of long, hard work in the sun. His voice, a low bass, blended in with his brother's, so hauntingly harmonic that their chords renewed the chill down my spine as if the wind had picked up the ribbon of notes on their staff and brought them to me, wafting over the *pasturas* and would-be *jardines* of the neighbors.

The Penitentes approached the bridge of vigas that stood through all types of weather conditions, except the *crecientes*, the spring run-offs or floods from the sierras of Rociada and Gascón. The waters usually took the bridge of logs with them as they rushed downstream and had to be dragged by horse and manpower back to its original place or rebuilt altogether by these same Penitentes.

I could see, crossing the bridge behind my father, Primos Gabriel and Esteban, brothers themselves and cousins of my uncle and father. These two looked as different from each other as my father and uncle looked alike. Primo Gabriel reminded me of a huge, hairy, but gentle bear, one with a soft and low trembly voice because lately advancing Parkinson's disease began to afflict him. His face, light-complected and quite wrinkled, exuded kindness. And his small, twinkly eyes and plum-shaped, rosy cheeks were always accompanied by a toothless, but cheerful, smile. Primo Esteban, on the other hand, was short, stout, and sly-looking, like a crafty fox that always had ulterior motives up his sleeve. Though I was sure my impression of him was groundless since to be a Penitente was to hold life holy.

Following them were Primo Juan and Primo Eufemio, two of our neighbors on either side of us. Primo Juan could have been my father's twin. They looked so much alike, both short and thin. Even their bald heads and bony faces could have been carved from the same mold. Primo Eufemio, whose rimless glasses perched on his nose, hid his small, piercing, dark brown eyes which took in the words of the alabados at a glance before they looked toward the heavens as he stepped in unison with his Brothers, blending his gruff voice in with theirs.

Next came Primo Donacio and Don Procopio, both of Las Cañadas, a few miles behind our house deep within the forests of pine and blue spruce. The road to their homes was deeply rutted and could only be traveled by foot or by horse, but they never failed to attend to their duties as Penitentes, no matter the weather. Don Donacio, visible always and everywhere because of his white hair, reminded me of a white freckled giant. No one in our valley was tall, so we children revered his height of six feet. We felt small as mice when we were younger and we'd gather around his heels to hear tales of how things were in the "old days." Grampo Procopio, who was my father's father-in-law, was light-complected and lean, closely resembling my Tío Daniel—with the omission of the horrid honker. He was a cheerful man with twinkling eyes that hinted of mischief. He was notorious for his practical jokes and was always the life of the party at communal or family gatherings.

Primo León, short and very stout, made up the last pair with his brother. He was one of three primos who came from Las Vegas to uphold this holy tradition of our simple, religious valley. He reminded me of a jolly *Santo Clos*, just as round and red-faced as a human could be. And since his brother, Melaquías, frequented Maloof's Mercantile, he always had a pocketful of Christmas *dulces* for us. Those ribbon-like, hard and rainbow-colored candies were a treat that was prized and long-awaited by us children who so rarely ate a candy at all. A pocketful was more candy than we had ever even seen, and we all longed for the honor of our elder brothers or sisters who got to accompany our fathers to Maloof's on rare occasions like the Fourth of July fiestas. Manuel, one of Primo León's five sons, would boast that at Maloof's a large wooden wine barrel was filled to the brim with a colorful assortment of Christmas candy all year long. I dreamed of this mythical barrel of candy often. Just to see it would be enough since I knew my father had no money to buy any for us.

Last, of course, I could see my brother, looking more like my uncle than my father, only taller, and I winced with each painful step he took as his limp was indeed noticeable now that he was close. My pride in him swelled as I realized that he'd made this last procession a self-penance before he had to leave us again. I imagined myself walking at his side, wishing that I could offer him a shoulder to lean upon.

As the church came into view around the bend in the road, I could see the Penitentes arriving at the front double doors. Entering the capilla, they filed down the dimly lit aisle to kneel before the altar. Following in subdued silence were those of us who came late, called by the tolling of the church bell or by the wailing sound of the Penitentes' alabados, both of which could be heard throughout the cañon.

The capilla was decorated and kept clean by the women and children of the valley. My mother had been here early that very morning with Prima Juanita and her husband, Primo Victoriano, replacing candles in the hand-carved wooden sconces high up on the two walls that ran parallel to the altar and connected in a wide vee-shape behind the altar. The interior walls were painted a pale salmon color with *caliche*, a creamy hand-mixed tint that rubbed off on your back if you leaned against it. The old wooden floor creaked here and there as if weary of sustaining so many generations of us who passed through here on our journey of life. The altar itself lay in semi-darkness, glowing ethereally in the light of dozens of candles on and around it. A knee-high white with blue trim picket fence divided the sacred altar from the rest of the church, enclosing it and the two side tables holding numerous santos, wooden crucifixes, and candles, some in ornate glass holders and others in black wooden holders. The altar was nothing more than a large wooden table with a raised shelf at the rear, all of which lay covered with white linen cloths, *manteles*, which had been trimmed with lacy, delicate patterns crocheted by the women: wives and mothers, sisters, and daughters of the Penitentes, and all known as *Carmelitas, Veronicas, Auxiliarias*, or *Paduanas*, depending on the individual societies of Hermanos.

The santos, donated by the people of the valley, were a motley lot. Some were hand-carved of wood, created and painted by the ancestors of the present day Hermanos. Others like the Santo Niño for which the capilla was named were brought from Mexico and sold at stores like Maloof's. Made of *jaspe*, a ceramic-like substance, they all exhibited signs of age in the form of faded paint, chips, and/or missing appendages; toes, hands, tips of noses just fell off with the continued cleaning of the women.

The numerous hand-carved wooden crosses, painted black and uniquely fashioned by each Penitente as symbols of the trials each must undergo in his lifelong term as an Hermano of the morada, were carried in by all and placed one by one atop the altar and side tables. Above the altar in line with the fence were white curtains, gathered at each corner and tied with string and cloth flowers.

The Penitentes, kneeling before the altar, awaited Primo Juan, who, turning the matracas, circled the exterior of the capilla three times before the Estaciones began. The wooden *matracas*, about ten inches in length, whirred with an ominous clatter to symbolize the impending doom created by the death of Christ as it turned on the peg which was its handle. And the church bells were rung by Primo Donacio one last time, announcing to any and all late-comers that the Estaciones were about to begin.

Primo Juan joined Primo Donacio at the double doors, and they both walked importantly down the aisle on either side of the narrow rectangular wood stove situated in the center at the back of the church and passed all of us seated in the tall-backed wooden pews, handmade, too, by the fathers and grandfathers of our present day Penitentes. Joining the other Hermanos already kneeling before the altar, Primos Juan and Donacio knelt, signaling that we should do the same.

"*En el nombre del Padre, del Hijo, y del Espíritu Santo, Amén,*" the Hermanos chorused and we all joined in: the older men, too old now to be active in the procession; the younger men, now only two who had chosen to follow in the footsteps of their forefathers as farmers and ranchers rather than leave our little valley for the big cities and who had yet to become Hermanos; and the women of all ages, who, no matter how strongly they may have wanted, could never hope to join the Penitentes' society. Unlike the Penitente practices in Spain where children are inducted as infants and women are welcome as members, very few northern New Mexico fraternities ever allowed women to be Penitentes that I know of. Last were the children, though our gang disdained being called children like the younger members of our community who had no active part in any of los Hermanos' ceremonies except for assisting in the preparations for Lent and joining them in prayer.

My father led the prayers that were concluded by the rest of los Hermanos and us in unison. I never heard my father's voice so tremulous, so proud, as I did when he prayed. Even as a child I sensed that he was filled with a tremendous pride, an honor to have been elected by his fellow Hermanos as their leader. Listening to the words of each prayer, I searched the front of the church, trying to see my father, but I was too short to see above those in the pew in front of us when we knelt on the wooden kneeler.

I imagined I knelt next to him, a book of alabados in my hands as it would be when my turn to join the cofradía came. Each Lent, I knew, brought me closer to the year when I would be taken into their society. But my father had yet to reveal when that would be. All he would say to my question of "when" was "*tú vas a saber,*" a disappointing "you'll know." I thought I had known ever since I could remember participating in the Estaciones. So how would I really know?

I was brought back to the present by my omniscient mother, who always sensed when I became lost in thought and who pinched me none too gently to bring me out of my daydreams just in time to hear "*Gloria del Padre, del Hijo, del Espíritu Santo …*" I rose quickly from my knees and crossed myself, humbled, as the Penitentes moved down the aisle facing the picture of the first Station of the Cross.

The year before on the way home after the Estaciones, Mamá had asked me why I daydreamed when I should have been praying. When I confessed as to the content of my visions, she had looked at me deeply. As if seeing my sincerity, she blinked away tears rising in her keen eyes and said no more. When her pinches came more softly thereafter during the hours of prayers, we both knew they came not of chastisement, but as a reminder to make me aware that others might think me insolent or disrespectful.

"*Primera Estacíon,*" my father read, his voice filled with passion. "*Aquí es endonde fue sentenciado a muerte nuestro Redentor.*" Here is where our Redeemer was sentenced to death.

I looked as if for the first time at the *cuadro* on the far-left wall closest to the altar, Christ kneeling before Pontius Pilate, accepting his sentence wordlessly, the soldiers around him, in their hands the scourges they would use upon Him mercilessly as He would be forced to carry the heavy cross to His place of death.

In a mournful tone, my father described the countless, horrible agonies endured by Jesus Christ on His way to Mount Calvary. The Penitentes joined in the prayer that followed, and then, joined only by my uncle, my father began the verse of the alabado, the part of the Estaciones that never failed to affect me.

"*Oh oooh, Suavísimo Jesús, que quisite padecer como vil esclavo delante del sacrilegio pueblo. Esperando la sentencia de muerte que contra tí daba el tirano juez. Suplícote, Señor mío…mortifique yo mi sabiduría, para que sufriendo con humildad las afrentas de esta vida te goce en la eternidad.*"

In tones, which can only be described as sorrowful, el Hermano Mayor and his brother sang to their sweet Jesus, who like a despicable slave before the sacrilegious city, awaited His sentence of death, placed upon Him by a tyrannous judge. The rest joined in, voices rising and falling dolefully in imploring Jesus in their own mortification and in their passion, so that by suffering with humility for the dishonor done to Him in His life, they, too, would rise to share in His eternal bliss.

Their voices rose in the anguish and desperate hopelessness that accompanies death wherever it strikes. But because this tribute was sung to our Savior in His moment of impending death, the effect was far more moving than any alabado used for the *rosarios* and *velorios* for loved ones of our community who succumbed to death. The alabados sung at las Estaciones inspired such a sense of doom in my body. I can feel it still, whenever the hauntingly religious memories of Lent arise. The inharmonious rising and falling of the woeful notes sung by these humble men touched our very souls, leaving us desolate as we all were taken back through time to the painful experience of the crucifixion of Christ. Not one of us, even the children, left the capilla on those evenings unaffected by our Catholic faith.

Abruptly, the chorus of the alabado ended and the low tones of the prayer resumed. One by one, my father grievously lamented the fourteen Stations, representing the tribulations experienced by Christ, each followed by the consecutive prayers and alabados of his Hermanos on either side and behind him. Their somber, tremulous voices filled with such emotion as if they had indeed borne witness to the countless agonies of the actual crucifixion of Christ. In my mind, never having seen what actually went on behind the closed doors of the morada where they met for hours both preceding and after each recital of the Estaciones, I wondered if perhaps they had.

The portraits of each Estacíon hung around the side walls of the capilla, interspersed only by the candles with their inconstant wavering light and by four windows, two on either wall. As each Estacíon was described and lamented over, the Penitentes knelt in front of each portrait as they moved down the aisle for the first half and moved back up for the second. We, in turn, knelt with first one knee and then the other in our attempt to face the Estacíon as well. At the sixth Station, which was directly across from us, los Hermanos stood with their backs to us and I finally caught sight of my brother. I saw that he lowered himself to his knees slowly like the others, but I sensed it was from discomfort rather than from the stiffness of age. After all, he was only eighteen. And since I couldn't see his face, I wondered whether he fought with himself not to grimace with pain. We, on the other hand, knelt sideways on the narrow kneeling board, holding on with one hand to the edge of the pew to our left and with the other hand clutching at the back of the pew to our right. It was truly an effort to attain one's balance before pitching forward face first onto the seat of the pew to one side of us, and it became a penance indeed to maintain this unnatural position while focusing one's eyes and mind on the prayer at hand.

This maneuvering was difficult, and with each consecutive Estacíon, it became increasingly clear that our slow but sure revolution around the walls of the church became harder before it became easier. We turned counter-clockwise in this fashion until, at the conclusion of the fourteen Estaciones, we again faced the sacred altar of venerable saints, their countenances appearing even more somber with the fluctuating, pale candlelight. The sun had set, leaving only the utter blackness of the moonless night outside the windows. I shuddered, feeling as if the ghosts of my ancestors were seated here beside me, to share this ageless experience of communal prayer with the honored Penitentes.

"*Padre Nuestro, que estas en los cielos,*" my father and uncle began The Lord's Prayer, and I prayed, consciously aware of the throbbing pain in my kneecaps that was already beginning to numb them. But then I glanced at Primo Gabriel, already in his sixties, Primo Victoriano, at age seventy in the pew ahead of us, these men who had lived out long, fulfilled lives here in this very cañon. Were they giving up now—to sit back, to relax in the pews when they could no longer kneel in penance to the Lord? They never did; never did any of the Penitentes or the former Hermanos who were now too feeble to stand and kneel without a pew or a bordón to lean upon. Never did they sit back during any part of the services. Only Primo Victoriano, with the help of his crooked *bordón*, handmade from a latilla and smooth with wear and age, occasionally rose stiffly throughout the service to feed the fire in the wood stove or to tap out a candle too small to do more than flicker and spew bits of wax on the walls, pews, or unsuspecting heads of his *vecinas* or *comadres*. It was he, too, who came to light the candles and start the fire each Friday evening a half hour or so before the arrival of the others. I drew my strength from these men, examples of humble piety that I hoped I could live up to when I grew up.

"*Santa María, Madre de Dios,*" the Hail Mary began, recited or whispered with bowed heads by all except the very young who were merely present to share this wondrous experience with no real concept of its importance in the molding of one's soul. But they remained respectfully silent throughout as though, even in their naïveté, they could sense the awe of the rest of us participating in the Estaciones.

I let my eyes drift upward slowly without lifting my head, always watching the Penitentes who gave me such a proud feeling of partaking in something unique, something awe-inspiring when I came to pray the Estaciones with them. There they were: the ten elders who comprised such a secretive order, and my brother, the novice. And my own father led them, a group of ordinary men—ordinary to me because I took them for granted. They were there as they had always been. I had the impression that since all los Hermanos, relatives or not, were such good men, all men were of this nature. These ordinary men of Cañoncito were farmers, though compared to the rich farmers and ranchers of the Midwest that we had heard about from our Primo Melaquías (who owned a radio), the farmers of our proud, little section of New Mexico were not considered even that. The few hundred or so acres owned by each were merely enough for each household to cultivate a *jardín* and afford small sections for grazing a few animals and growing alfalfa or oats. Most of the acreage was mountainous, covered with pine, blue spruce, and small oak trees, the ridges of land rising and falling as far as the eye could see, yet affording grazing space and plenty of wood for building or burning.

My musings were interrupted by the creaking of the old wooden floor. This signaled the rising of the Penitentes who were crossing themselves and coming to their feet laboriously from kneeling on the uneven planks. Low mumbling among them made me wonder what they had planned now. I knew from past experiences that they would soon retire to the morada in singing procession once more, each carrying his own crucifix in one hand and prayer book in the other. This time, however, since the night was so dark, a few of the men interspersed among his brothers held a kerosene lantern and here and there a flashlight to guide them to their prayer house.

It was an otherworldly scene, indeed. I couldn't then have imagined one more haunting, awe inspiring, yet tinging my thoughts with something akin to fear because of the unknown. Like everyone, I had heard stories of the secret rites los Penitentes performed within the silent walls of the morada. Like everyone, I, too, had seen the Hermanos who appeared the day after, struggling to conceal their pain from whatever had occurred in the midnight hours as we slept. And because of my brother, I both feared and longed to see for myself what I would undergo when my turn came.

The men were seating themselves in the front pews, the rest of us rising as if in slow motion, supporting ourselves as we leaned upon one another or grasped the backs of pews for support. Primo Juan, on the left side of the capilla near the walls which mirrored the pale butter yellow color of the candlelight, rose and crossed the aisle stopping to face the altar, kneel, and genuflect before moving on. With outstretched hand, he approached my father, congratulating him for a service performed well. They all rose then, shaking hands all around, giving us the signal that we too could rise and converse quietly, at leisure with our relatives and friends.

While my mother spoke with her Comadre Marta and Prima Raquel in the pew ahead of ours, I took the opportunity—as casually as I could before my mother could catch sight of me and make me stay seated next to her—to stroll over to where my father now stood with his Hermanos near the altar. People blew out the candles on the walls. The Penitentes began snuffing out the ones on the altar and side tables, an honor I usually enjoyed, pretending that I was one of them as I blew out a few and touched the santos with reverence, offering prayers from my heart that I would someday be one of the Brothers. The Penitentes held lanterns that cast the only remaining light into the velvety shadows of the capilla. Women like my mother carried tin candleholders to light their way home alone with their children. This time, however, I fought the urge to help them with the candles and opted instead to do something I thought would show my father I was no longer a child.

Just as I thought I had hidden safely behind my father I heard, "*¿Quien viene aquí?*" Who comes here, my Tío Daniel teased, clasping me in his customary bear hug. Not really wanting to hide from my uncle, I returned his hug, remembering when I was small that he would toss me high enough to bump the long age-smoothed ceiling vigas softly with my back. No matter where we were and no matter how big I thought I had grown, my uncle greeted me in this manner everywhere until I got too heavy. He made me feel special.

Now, as he let me go, he turned purposefully toward me, his eyes twinkling in the soft glow of his flashlight. Avoiding his knowing eyes, I knew he knew the question in my mind. Quickly I looked back at my father, who had turned toward me, placing a solid hand on my shoulder, knowing what I was about to say, and resisting the urge to smile. I had made myself a nuisance, I supposed, begging my father to let me accompany him to the morada, wondering each year if he would finally say yes. But my father, looking at me with a tolerable patience, slowly shook his head from side to side each time.

"*No es posible, hijo,*" he'd smiled gently. "*Ya tú sabes eso.*" It's not possible, son. You already know that.

Yes, I thought, I knew the answer before I had even asked. Remembering the year before, disappointed yet again, I had nodded in subdued acquiescence as my father gently turned me back toward the doors, my uncle giving my shoulder a gentle pat as he chuckled softly at my retreating back.

This year, I vowed to bite my tongue as the question out of habit came to my lips. I would not be disappointed yet another time. Instead, I extended my hand like the other men had done and congratulated my father for a good service. The look of surprise on his face slowly erasing into one of approval as he nodded was worth my silence; the look of thunderstruck shock on my uncle's was worth it, too. Longing to speak to my brother, I only gave him a nod. Clamping my mouth shut to keep silent, I sensed their eyes on my back as I walked out the door.

Looking for my mother among the dark shapes surrounding the doors inside and out in the lantern light, I felt a sense of pride that I had not succumbed to the actions of childhood.

"José." My mother's voice came from the darkness to my right.

Searching the faces floating in the orange-yellow glow, I made my way between people and dogs waiting for their masters on the threshold of the capilla. I caught Berto's knowing gaze. When he shrugged, I knew my primo thought I had failed again to convince my father to include me in whatever ceremony awaited them. I didn't bother to explain; that my father had not offered an invitation told me enough. It was not yet my time. We stood there together next to the big yellow cross at the center of the large slabs of *laja*, watching as the Penitentes took their places facing the road that would lead them back to their original starting point, the morada. The vast blackness of the night hid it from our view, giving no hint at what would soon occur within its walls.

"Oh oooh," my father began the rising notes of the alabado as they moved away, step after slow step on the rutted dirt road. The Penitentes added each of their individual voices to the chorus, trudging purposefully down the dark path as one body to yet another of their secret sessions at which I so longed to be present and from which I was still excluded.

Imaginación

About fifteen of us stood in silence outside the capilla, each affected by this age-old ritual. The Penitentes' secret vows inspired our palable awe and humility. We stood as if mesmerized by the alabados heard through the black night. No one moved as we watched their lights slowly move away, the glowing, golden orbs getting smaller as the men neared the bridge of vigas a few feet above the cold, slow-moving water of the river.

"*Bueno, pues, que pasen buenas noches,*" vecinos and compadres wished each other a good night and shook hands all around. Berto and I bid proper farewells to the adults before everyone turned to walk in small groups up or down the road toward home. We each treated adults with the respect due them without the embarrassing reminder of the cuff on the side of the head or pinch on the arm accompanied by the disapproving looks of our elders. Berto's mother joined mine and Prima Marta relinquished her lantern to Berto. As we lagged behind, we could no longer see the three women only a few yards away. They spoke in low tones since the Penitentes' singing could still be heard across the river. The darkness had already swallowed all eight of the Luceros, too, as they also walked ahead of us to their home up the road a quarter mile or so from ours.

For once Filiberto was silent, only holding the lantern in front of us to light our path. I was left alone with my thoughts. Looking over my shoulder toward the sound of the somber singing, I glimpsed the only visible evidence that the woeful music was of this earth: the faint up-down movement of the lights of the procession. The Penitentes were enveloped in the blanket of the night on their solitary path to meet their destinies, as the rest of us walked on our paths to the warmth of our abodes.

I shivered, wondering what each Penitente was thinking as he and his Brothers, mournfully singing of Christ's last days of life on earth, trudged forward to make their own penances secreted in the morada. Christ, too, on His holy way to Mount Calvary, must have had much on His mind of the actions of His Brothers and of His own strength and resolve. The Penitentes, Brothers of the Church, had similar thoughts, I was sure. Only God knew what ceremony they would now perform, whether in penance or pre-arranged rituals passed from generation to generation. And I wondered, as I always did when they made their way to the morada one last time in the darkness, what role my father would play in their secret rites. I had heard from numerous primos or *parientes* who swore that rituals of blood and tears occurred while we innocently slept.

Yet many were the sleepless nights I spent in fearful contemplation of the kinds of ceremonies that my overactive imagination supplied. Filiberto had told me that he had seen his very own father come in after one of the Penitentes' private sessions the year before. His labored movements made Berto stare in shock at his father, who normally was strong and healthy, and never complained of any ailments.

Berto sighed heavily, breaking into my quiet reflection with his whisper, "Well, d'you think we'll be able to get away?"

"Probably," I answered disconsolately under my breath, "only after tonight I wonder if los Hermanos will ever let us join."

"Don't say that." Berto groaned as he, too, glanced over his shoulder toward the silent morada. "Don't you wanna find out what they do when they're alone?"

"Of course, especially since you told me about what happened to your father," I added cautiously, knowing it was a sore spot for Berto. Since Berto slept in the combination parlor, kitchen, and at night, make-shift bedroom, I knew that when his father came in after Berto was in bed, he would have surely seen him. I knew Berto wouldn't lie about something so serious, especially since the next day I, too, had seen our Primo León limping painfully as he did his daily chores. So I believed Berto when he told me that he had seen his father move in anguish into the cocina, setting the lantern on the table to ready the basin with hot water from the kettle on the warm stove, and then grab a towel hanging from a peg on the wall and sit heavily on one of the wooden benches at the table to laboriously remove his work boots. Then he slowly hitched his pant legs up one at a time and exposed his knees. What Filiberto had seen next was what had made him stare wide-eyed under the cover of darkness. His father's knee caps were an angry red, the flesh indented with dozens of whitish pock marks. Berto had said that to keep from crying out, he'd bitten his pillow so that his father would not catch him looking. Grimacing with the pain and inhaling a hissed breath, his father dabbed at each knee with the warm cloth for a long while before shuffling off to bed. What could have happened? Who could have done that to him? Did all the Penitentes come home like this at one time or another? And what had happened to Miguel?

"I still don't actually know what happened that night," Berto whispered. "All I know is what I saw when he came home; I sure won't ever ask him. He doesn't even know I saw him. How he got that way I guess I'll never know, unless ..."

I had no memory of my own father coming home in a similar condition, but then I was always sound asleep when he arrived. Mamá once mentioned that he returned at midnight at the earliest. With this in mind as we rounded the bend in the road, I peered through the darkness once more in the direction of the barely audible singing. The moonless night made it impossible to see anything other than the fluttering of the Penitentes' lights bobbing like fireballs across the river. My thoughts raced ahead as I planned how I could stay awake long enough to see my father return later. Shivers crept slowly like prickling needles up my spine in anticipation, and a tinge of fear overcame me as my imagination supplied horrors similar to the one seen by my cousin Berto.

As we came to the uneven, rocky path which led to our doorway, my mother said, "*Éntren, primas,*" inviting the elderly Prima Marta and Berto's mother, my Prima Cleofes, in for coffee and fresh bizcochitos to aid in the passage of the long hours of the night until their husbands' return.

Entering the house first as Berto held the door open for the women, I grabbed a handful of *ocote*, small strips of kindling to light the fire, from the woodbox and made my way to the stove. Tossing the thin strips in, I revived the smoldering embers to fire up the tepid warmth of our adobe home. Its walls were nearly two feet thick, keeping it warm during winter and cool in the summer). My mother lit the kerosene lamp in the center of the table, telling her guests to be seated as she did so.

Once I got the fire going, my mother began preparing coffee and laying out the table for the women. Prima Marta, meanwhile, sat chatting away, leaving little room for Prima Cleofes' interjections before my mother could actually sit down and pay proper attention. Reminding me of a plump mother hen-like character from one of my few storybooks, Prima Marta was one of those people who never seemed to have a bad day. Whenever I saw her, whether it was hard at work weeding her jardín or doing something even more laborious, she wore a smile that crinkled her eyes into slits and made me wonder how she could see at all. The wife of Primo Eufemio, she was one of our most highly respected neighbors. As the mayordomos of la Capilla del Santo Niño, they both took care of the needs of our little church. Her job was to organize all the other women in charitable functions like cleaning the capilla and morada as well as aiding vecinos in times of need.

Prima Cleofes, on the other hand, was a thin, quiet woman, forever scowling at Prima Marta's constant attempts to make her laugh, yet succumbing to a smile or two at the other woman's *chistes* and *cuentos.*

While the coffee heated and the women chatted amiably, Prima Marta reached into her large apron pocket and withdrew a small drawstring cloth sack filled with punche, tobacco. Prima Marta tapped out a small amount of tobacco onto the square of cigarette paper and then pulled the string with her teeth until the bag closed. She distributed the punche evenly lengthwise along the paper before her fingers deftly rolled it all up into cigarette form and, with one lick of her tongue, closed it. This procedure of rolling one's own cigarette never failed to interest me. It always looked so easy to do, so gratifying when, with a flick of a match, satisfaction came over the smoker's face with the first puff. It seemed everyone who smoked home-rolled cigarettes did it so comfortably that they made it an appetizing vice for those of us who didn't.

I caught the almost imperceptible nod of Berto's head toward the door, so taking a few bizcochitos, we asked if we might be allowed to join the gang for a while. The twinkle in my mother's eye, her mirth evident in the light of the lamp, disappeared. She knew I didn't like going farther than where the light from the window illuminated the yard. My overly vivid imagination, coupled with stories told by my father and his primos, had made me fearful of the dark in my youth, a sore spot in my character for which I suffered the indignity of constant ribbing and practical jokes at the hands of my Tío Daniel and had yet to overcome.

As my mother hesitated to grant her permission, I could tell Berto was trying to come up with a reason why we wanted to go outside into the dark again with the gang. I, on the other hand, was trying to plead with my eyes, trying to make my mother understand that since I had to conquer my fear of the dark some time, it may as well be tonight. Yet to be honest, I silently hoped she'd say no and thereby thwart Berto's plan.

To my mixed relief, it was Berto's mother who said no, perhaps some other night. I know I will never forget the look of amazed surprise on his face. He'd planned every detail of this night, leaving out the one factor that could prevent him from carrying out his scheme: his mother. I looked at him out of the corner of my eye, though I longed to give him a taste of his own medicine and smirk at his discomfiture. Instead, I bit on a cookie and concentrated on chewing so I wouldn't laugh outright at his befuddled expression. There was nothing he could do, and he knew it. It was unthinkable that he protest, for his mother would tell his father and Berto knew what the consequences of such ill-mannered behavior would be. Ever the actor, he shrugged his shoulders as if the matter was of no importance and asked if we couldn't just sit outside instead, to which both women only nodded.

Grabbing and lighting the lantern, I followed Berto outside. "¡*Que friega*!" he hissed once out the door, muttering a few more expletives until I reminded him it was Lent. We knew we couldn't risk being seen making our way down the road, so instead we went up the hill, over a shallow arroyo, and around a couple of young pine trees and numerous large rocks barring our path.

Since my fear of the dark was not common knowledge among my friends—my uncle's teasing was never intended with malice and he promised to keep it our secret until he could "break" me of it—I led Berto with false bravado. He was behind me, so all I could hear were mumbled oaths and something about telling the guys we wouldn't be going tonight after all.

Glancing atop and beyond the ladera as we trudged upward, I searched the many pines at its edge, black silhouettes that supplied images of coyotes or bears crouching in wait behind or beneath them. Inwardly chastising myself for my vivid imaginings, I reached the biggest outcropping boulder and scrambled up with Berto right beside me over its high edge. We had made it to the high ladera without mishap. Both a little out of breath with the effort, we stood for a moment in silence. The black sky, dotted with innumerable stars of differing degrees of brightness and twinkling as if to divergent melodies, supplied a stillness to the night that was peaceful yet mysterious.

Perched on the ledge facing the back of my house, we both looked across the road beneath the pine-covered hills toward the morada, but there was no evidence of the inner activity behind those sanctified adobe walls. In fact, we couldn't even see the morada itself in the dark. It was merely through knowing where the building was that our eyes instinctively peered in its direction. Lost in our wonderings of what might be occurring there and nervously munching the cookies we'd pocketed earlier, neither of us spoke, fearful of what visions our own private thoughts would create when put into words.

"Hey!"

When Berto's sudden exclamation broke into my thoughts, I jumped, almost losing my balance on the rock ledge. "¿Qué?" I asked, choking on my last bite of cookie. "Por Dios, don't scare me that way! You almost made me fall!"

"Sorry," Berto smiled sheepishly, "I just saw a light moving to the capilla, probably Tino and Horacio. *Vamos.*"

"We're not still going, are we?" I blurted, shocked that he would stoop to disobey his mother.

"Don't be *estupido,*" he scoffed. "I just gotta tell 'em we aren't going, that's all."

I swallowed my relief and followed him down the hill in the direction of the church. I lost myself in my thoughts in the silence broken only by our panting breaths and the rocks and pebbles scattering from beneath our feet. Knowing that no one was allowed to see the secret rites that were performed when only the Hermanos were present, not even a hint of what went on there came from the men. Each, as far as I knew, was as closed-mouthed as a mute about the whole thing like my father and Berto's, and I felt grateful about this short reprieve from going ahead with Filiberto's plan.

But I knew one Friday of this Lenten season would bring the revelation I secretly wanted though I had always had a problem with dishonesty, and my conscience shouted out even now that this was something forbidden to me until I was of an age to learn for myself. Could I live with myself in later years when I became an Hermano, knowing I had seen something I should not and harboring in my heart the secret of a boy's adventure while keeping up the pretense that I had no idea what awaited me as a member of such a prestigious society?

Berto, on the other hand, had no problem with a case of a guilty conscience as far as I knew. When we were younger, he was the one Maestro Rubel caught pulling Constancia's *trenzas* and putting the garter snake in Luciana's desk. Last year he was also the one who wrote the answers to Maestro's spelling test on the bottom of his shoe for our last exam. His only penitence, at first, had been despair because most of the words had scuffed off on the way to school, and he couldn't make them out sufficiently to pass the test anyway. But when Maestro saw what he was up to, Berto knew his cheating days had come to an end. Between what Maestro did to him at school and what Berto's father did to him at home for the next week, the punishment made him realize the error of his ways.

My constant reminders that if we were to become Hermanos in our future we must set examples of good conduct only served to anger Berto and alienate him from me for days until he cooled down sufficiently enough to come around as usual as if nothing had ever happened between us. Berto hissed at me, bringing my thoughts back to the present and I followed him steadily, keeping away from the shadows of the pines as I kept him in sight. My former fear of the dark dissipated, in intensity at least, to be replaced by a new fear: the temptation of the forbidden fruit of knowledge which had been thrown into my hands by the demon called deceit.

Tentación

After walking Prima Marta home around about ten o'clock, I returned to find my mother had already retired. Relieved by this, since with her sixth sense she could tell if I even thought of doing anything deceitful, I went to bed myself after turning the lamp wick low enough to shed a soft flow in the kitchen for my father. As quietly as I could, I lay in the cot my mother had readied for me, listening to her steady breathing in the next room as she slept in the larger of our two beds because she swore that my father turned and tossed the night away, preventing her from sleeping. And this I believed to be true, at least until Miguel, who was three years my senior, informed me that it was my mother's sense of modesty that made her sleep alone.

Miguel had told me that I was old enough to know what goes on between men and women at night. They slept together until I was five; now, of course, they couldn't because we boys were old enough to understand. But I wasn't, I had protested. What should I know? Miguel had only laughed mockingly, as though he were so much older and wiser than I, and he had called me chivito, chuckling that I was still too young to realize, or maybe our mother kept me tied to her apron strings so long that I was still ignorant about such things. Leaving me and my curiosity piqued but unsatisfied, Miguel winked and walked away.

I sighed softly in the darkness, wondering if I were now "old enough" to know about the many facets of life which thus far had been kept from me. I fought back a chuckle that rose in my throat when I thought back to an hour before when we had found Tino and Pedro waiting on the church stoop, Berto inquired casually about Horacio before admitting that the plan was off, for this

43

night anyway. The boys said they stopped by only to be run off by Horacio's mother who informed them he seemed to have caught another cold and would-n't be going anywhere. Berto laughed then, scoffing that Horacio probably faked illness rather than go out in the night. But when Pedro asked if the rest of us were still going, Berto threw a stern look at me when he told them that he had second thoughts about the evening's plan because his mother had told him los Hermanos were disbanding earlier than usual this night. Before either Pedro or Tino could respond, we raced off again to my house where we found Berto's mother yelling for him and Prima Marta ready for me to walk her home, even though it was only maybe a hundred feet up the road from ours.

And though Berto hadn't either the time or inclination to qualify the lie he'd told the others, as surely as if it had been truth, los Hermanos came home unexpectedly early that evening. It was ten-thirty when the screen door squeaked open and my father entered the cocina quietly so as not to disturb my mother, whispering that he wasn't tired enough to sleep yet so he'd stay up and read awhile. I sat up as well, trying to concentrate on a geography lesson in the flickering light of the kerosene lamps. Our community was too poor to meet the cost necessary to equip our small valley with electricity until 1931. It seemed only minutes had passed before the silent peace of our home was dis-turbed by a furtive knocking on the door, startling us all—even my mother.

It was my Tío Daniel who refused to enter, instead he called my father out-side where they spoke in hushed tones for some time. Though my conscience spoke up to prevent me from listening, my deep sense of curiosity prevailed when a few disassociated words wafted in on the evening breeze.

"Primo Esteban," my uncle said.

What could it mean? I wondered, especially when my father came into the house and donned his jacket, shifting his eyes at me pointedly before looking into the bedroom where my mother whispered, "*¿Qué pasó?*" Whatever he replied to her question of "what happened" was too low for me to hear. All he told me was he wouldn't be gone long.

Pedro hadn't mentioned his father being ill. Could something have hap-pened at the morada? A chill permeated my bones with the images this thought inspired. My fears mounted when my father joined my uncle and they made their way quickly down the road, but somehow I felt that my intuition was wrong. Whatever had happened, it had nothing to do with los Hermanos' cer-emony. My mother made the excuse of needing to speak to my Tía Clara as she donned her shawl and prepared to slip into the night, leaving me to my own thoughts as she ran to confirm her own.

But as she opened the door, she wondered aloud, "*¿Qué pasaría?*" What could've happened?

Deciding to go back to bed since there was nothing I could do, I mumbled cryptically, "*Lo que no debería de haber pasado.*"

She only looked at me in bewildered silence, nodding as my words sank in: What should never have happened.

That weekend we bade farewell to my brother whose life in the military had only just begun. We had spoken little during his short interlude with us. Though I waited as patiently as I could for him to reveal what being a novicio was like, he never spoke of it. I even imagined he was avoiding me. While he spent most of his spare time helping my father, when he did have time to himself he'd closed himself in his home alone.

My father, uncle, and Maestro Rubel drove Miguel to Las Vegas where he would catch the train. I stood with my grandmother, mother, and aunt along the road, waving until the car rounded the bend and we lost sight of it. I wondered whether his having become a novicio would affect him so far away from home. It wasn't until after he'd left that my grandmother, in her ageless wisdom, took me aside and explained, "Miguel was plagued with doubts about his decision to leave home." She added that his situation was more difficult because he hadn't been able to see Carolina, the object of his desire, before his departure. She'd been away helping a relative in Taos with her new baby. "He needed the time alone," she whispered, "to make himself strong to take on what lies ahead of him."

I realized I wasn't the only one he'd seemed to shun: it was all of us. "Then how did you know, Gramita?"

And as was her custom, she only smiled, leaving me to wonder for the hundredth time why she knew about things none of us even remotely suspected.

That weekend, there was much to do to keep me occupied, but as I cleaned out the chicken coop and the barn along with my other chores, my thoughts never strayed from Miguel and the Brotherhood.

The only time I saw the gang was at church Sunday morning, and even then, it was only briefly. I glanced sideways at Berto when we walked up the aisle to receive Communion; the smirk on his face made me wonder whether he'd confessed the lie he'd told the guys Friday night. Horacio went up as well, head bowed, eyes screwed tightly shut, and I wondered if he'd lied about being ill. Then too, there was Pedro with his parents, acting as though we were invisible and ignoring us completely. And though by no means did I consider myself

my friends' keeper, my confusion about them kept running through my mind
throughout the day.

Monday, we encountered quite a subdued Pedro at school; he refused to
meet our eyes again and refused to join in any games throughout the day. At
lunch, Luciana walked up to where Pedro sulked on the hill by the spring across
from the schoolhouse, yet even she had been unable to cheer him or distract
him, flinging her long red hair back and shrugging her shoulders as she left him
alone with his problems.

Tino had been at him all afternoon, teasing in a sing song voice, "Didn't
Luciana wanna kiss ya, huh? Didn't she?"

Pedro simmered until, like a pot boiling over, after school something broke
deep inside him and he furiously rose to the bait. Unable to stand Tino's barbs
any longer, Pedro turned on the smaller boy smashing his knuckles into Tino's
mouth before any of us could stop him. As Tino fell, Pedro straddled his stomach, fist raised once more as he growled, "¡Jodido! Mind your own business!"

Both Berto and I grabbed Pedro's fists, pulling him back off Tino before
the little kids could yell there was a fight and get us all in trouble. By the time
the lower grades were dismissed, we had crawled under the fence and hidden
ourselves behind the chicken coop by our barn so Tino could dip his face into
the clear, cold water of the acequia and so Pedro could calm down before going
home.

As a rule, whenever something bothered one of us, something big, none
of us spoke, affording the troubled party time to collect his thoughts and his
emotions. If he wanted to share his problem with the rest of us afterward, fine;
if not, that was fine, too. Sitting there under the quiet coolness of the shady
cottonwoods, listening to the water rippling over the time-smoothed rocks and
licking at the yellow weeds along its edge, I remembered the time Tino's mother
had given birth to a still-born infant.

Tino, who had so wanted a baby brother, was crushed. Striking out at all
of us in rage at first, Tino pummeled our chests while we stood still for him,
wincing quietly as a few connecting punches or kicks caught us squarely. When
he spent his anger at God's cruel justice, he fell to his knees at our feet, asking
why, why an innocent little boy had to die before he could even begin to
breathe. He bewailed never being able to take him fishing and horseback riding;
he mourned not having the chance to be a supportive shoulder to lean upon
when the kid scraped his knee or got hit by a baseball.

For a while, none of us could find words of *consuelo* that he so desperately
needed, until finally, moved by his tears, we all seemed to speak at once, offering

our naïve yet heartfelt advice to relieve him of his burden.

"My gramma says when a baby is taken before its time, it's because something was wrong with it from the beginning," I said quietly.

"Ya," Pedro agreed. "It woulda probly been crippled or something and woulda been in pain."

"Just think, Tino," Horacio added, "you got your own guardian angel to watch over you now."

Even Berto softened, a rare occurrence, offering consolation the only way he knew how—to point out the negative. "Think about it, Tino, ya won't hafta clean up *vomito* or change *pañales llenos de cagada*, phew." He pretended to choke down vomit while changing a soiled diaper.

We all laughed tentatively. Tino joined us after a time, until we all romped and wrestled on the grass, beginning our healing of Tino by making him forget, moments at a time, that he had lost the only brother he would ever have before he had even seen him.

Now, we waited quietly, offering silence like a healing balm to Pedro, whose heavy panting returned to normal, but who looked intently at the ground as if to look at us would cause him to lose control again.

The rest of us avoided looking at him, giving him privacy until he was ready. A deep shuddering sigh coursed through his body before he spoke. "My father," he began his confession, his voice barely above a whisper. "Papá was hurt the other night."

Having been to the Estaciones, we all suspected that what he referred to had occurred when los Hermanos went back to perform their secret ritual. Our imaginations provided all kinds of ghastly visions. Hadn't I even had my doubts?

"¿Qué?" Berto gasped, feeling a certain kinship with Pedro now that both their fathers had undergone a great penance for something they had done. He looked at me quickly, and I knew he thought also of Miguel.

Horacio cleared his throat self-consciously while Tino whistled softly and I remained silent, keeping my thoughts to myself.

"His body's covered with bruises," Pedro continued, "I only noticed last night; he went up to the monte with the cows before I got up yesterday. I shoulda known something was wrong. He always wakes me up before he goes."

"So how d'ya know he got hurt at the morada and didn't fall up in the monte or som…?"

Pedro's glare stopped Horacio, "It didn't happen at the morada. They don't beat each other up; I'm not as *pendejo* as you think."

"I only thought maybe …" Horacio muttered, "I didn't say …"

"Take it from me," Pedro interrupted, "I know what happened. After José's papá left, my mamá and papá had such a terrible fight I had to cover my head with my pillow—even with the door closed."

"¿Qué pasó?" Tino breathed, wide-eyed as he voiced what we all wanted to ask: what happened?

"Papá didn't do nothin' wrong," he explained. "But my Tío Pablo did. My papá went into Las Vegas with yours, José, when they took Miguel to the depot, to try to talk to my tío, but it was too late. He had taken stolen property from a *camarada* in town, had known it was stolen when he took it. Some camarada, the guy split when one of the other Hermanos from town saw them and found out what he was doing. And he told papá that he had done it for his *familia*, the only way he could get them things they needed, but that didn't help 'cause Papá had smelled liquor on his breath."

Pedro finished, "One thing led to another, and before he knew it, my papá was fighting, really fighting with my tío. He got pretty banged up." Shrugging, he added, "Then when he got home, he went up to the *valle* with the cows, and on the way back he fainted. If it hadn't been for Chato, running to the house barking his head off, we'd a never known."

"He'll be alright, Pedro," Tino said quietly, "you'll see."

"I know," Pedro sighed. "It just makes me mad, that's all."

We nodded, knowing how we would feel if one of our fathers got beaten up like Pedro's.

Horacio broke the silence with a thought all of us harbored, "I'm glad he didn't get hurt at the morada though."

"Yeah!" Berto sputtered, leaping to his feet. He slammed a fist into his palm, "But we still got us a damn good reason to go see for ourselves what los Hermanos do, what our fathers do."

"How d'you figure?" Pedro asked.

"If your father weren't an Hermano, he woulda just minded his own business maybe. But Hermanos always look out for their own, even members of their familias that aren't Penitentes. Look at what that got your father, Pedro."

"What're you saying?" I blurted before I could stop myself, my anger rising like heat through my body. "D'you think it's some kind of brain washing? Is that what you think being an Hermano is all about?"

"How would you know?" Berto snickered.

"I don't," I spat, "but it's my father who's Hermano Mayor. Are you saying he controls the others like … like some monster?"

"Maybe he does," Berto barked, looking at me accusingly. "I bet it's the Hermano Mayor that gives an order, and the rest do things, like the beatings when they do get hurt at the morada."

"Don't be estupido," I argued, my anger overriding my fear and rising at his accusation of the role my father played as Hermano Mayor. "My father would have never hurt Miguel, and besides, look at what Primo Esteban did all day. Walked by himself, punishing himself even more by climbing the monte with the *vacas*. It was even more penitencia he did to himself. Nobody made him."

"Berto-o-o-o," Manuel, Filiberto's brother, called. "*Ven ayudame, huevón.*" He could be heard on horseback, clip-clopping down the road, yelling, "Come help me, lazybones" again before muttering, "Lazy sanamagón, when I catch him …"

"Oh, yeah?" Berto asked, rising and moving away. "None of us really knows, do we?" As he disappeared behind the barn, he threw his final words over his shoulder, "But we'll all know, one way or the other, this Friday night."

"Don't pay attention to him, José." Horacio sniffed once Berto'd gone. "*No sabe nada.*" He knows nothing.

"None of us does," Tino added, nudging me in the ribs with his elbow, "but he sure as heck made us want to find out for ourselves, didn't he?"

We laughed then, all of us realizing that Berto's taunts would only make me want to prove him wrong, and what other way to do that than go through with his plan for Friday night?

The others quickly scattered like leaves in the wind, each going more light of heart in the general direction of home, and I turned quickly to my own chores. It wasn't until I went to bed that night only to remain awake again, trying to dispel the fear that had pervaded my heart on Ash Wednesday, the beginning of Lent. I kept trying to dismiss as imagination the premonition of what was to come into our lives. It played itself over and over in my mind and would reside in my memory for the rest of my life.

La Vida Jóven

The rest of the week crawled sluggishly by like a slow-moving snake, thoughts of the night's adventure writhing in and out of my awareness, leaving twinges of fear like pieces of shed snakeskin that clung to my mind in a time-slowed dream. No matter how I tried to avoid thinking of what would happen in the late hours of Friday night, the images came unbidden, slithering into my consciousness.

I sensed it was the same with the others. Tuesday morning Tino fidgeted in his seat so much, Maestro Rubel came up from behind and whacked his fingers with a willow rod so suddenly that Tino jumped a foot. Needless to say, he sat so still thereafter I was afraid he'd collapse from the effort. We were all so preoccupied none of us even thought to give him a bit of his own medicine with our taunts when we were let out for recess.

That Friday we attacked our lessons as best we could, all except Berto, who hated school and only attended because the promise of only one more year kept him going. Out of the corner of my eye, I watched as he wriggled nervously in his seat. When he looked up and caught my gaze, he winked sardonically before lowering his eyes to the tablet before him. I struggled to concentrate on my lessons, certain that Berto kept himself out of trouble that day mainly due to his reluctance to spend time after school in the corner. That would only serve to postpone his scheme for yet another week.

For a fleeting moment, I was tempted to cause some mischief of my own to keep me after school, forcing my mother to make me stay home after the Estaciones and thereby keep me out of trouble. But when I glanced up again and found Berto watching me, his eyes narrowed in suspicion and he moved his head slowly from side to side as if to warn, "*Ni lo pienses*—don't even think about it." I knew if I did anything, it wouldn't protect me from Berto's wrath. The weekend could bring many surprises, not to mention accidents.

Even though I was older, we all had established Berto as our fearless leader. We knew that to do so was, at times, folly, but the plain truth was that we feared him. Berto had a way of turning the tables on us by fingering one of us as the guilty party when we got caught at something we knew better not to do, coming out free and clear in the process, hidden from our elders' accusing eyes and pointed fingers. Camouflaged like the changeling chameleon that he was, he escaped countless interminable lectures and strappings with a horsehair cattle whip always ready for one of our backsides.

I guess I was about ten years old when poor Primo Pablo came to visit us from Las Vegas. Because he was blind, he needed to be led everywhere lest he trip and break a bone. He was reed thin and feeble with age. Berto and I were playing outside when my mother called for me to take our primo to the outhouse. I guided him by the elbow on one side while he used his bordón to tap the ground as he walked. Well, our outhouse was located about seventy feet from our house on the other side of the road where you had to walk across large rocks placed in the water of the acequia. It was only maybe two to three feet across with hardly a bank on either side. As we made our way ever so slowly— I hoped his need to relieve himself wasn't great, for at this pace we'd take at least ten minutes—Berto motioned for me not to let on that he was there. I don't know why I agreed, but I kept up a steady conversation with my primo as we walked, ignoring Berto as he followed.

At the outhouse, I helped Primo Pablo safely inside, and I walked a little way off to give him privacy. Berto whispered, "Let me lead him back; let's see if he can tell it's not you."

I shrugged, thinking surely this would just be an innocent experiment. What could go wrong? So when Primo Pablo emerged, Berto sprang to his side and resumed the position I had held before. But instead of leading the elderly man back to the house, Filiberto turned him in the direction of the acequia and promptly guided the old man straight into the water before I could even react.

"Ahhh!" Primo Pablo yelled. "*¡Qué estás haciendo conmigo, cabrón, desgraciado, malcriado!*"

Yes! I thought to myself, what're you doing with him, Berto?

I leaped forward intending to help him out of the water as I fought powerful giggles. It was a good thing the water was only about six inches deep where Berto had guided him, but it was more than enough to soak Primo's poor worn out boots and socks. Next, everything seemed to happen at once. As Primo Pablo fought to keep his balance while trying to get out of the ditch, he raised his bordón high and then simultaneously struck Berto and me on top of our heads. I clutched my head and fell to one side while watching Berto's eyes roll back as he plopped down into the middle of the acequia on his backside.

"¡*Perdóname*, primo!" I apologized, trying to come up with an explanation and trying also to help him while avoiding more blows from his cane. I glanced over my shoulder at Filiberto, who was shaking his head like a dog. But before I could come up with anything that wasn't a lie, I looked up—right into the face of my mother, who'd heard her primo's shout and came running to his rescue.

Needless to say, I was the one who had trouble sitting for what seemed like weeks but was probably only days. If the spanking wasn't enough, I did double the chores for the next month and the padre's sermons covered every topic concerning wayward children for four consecutive Sunday masses. Oh, and Filiberto? My mother didn't even see him sitting in the middle of the water beneath the leafy branches of the apple trees. And since Primo Pablo'd never even been aware of his presence, he got off with no punishment at all. After all, I knew better than to rat him out.

Berto wasn't mean to the point of intentionally hurting someone, but his past reactions to our inability to back him up or to follow his lead had caused consequences we'd have avoided if we'd only gone along in the first place. The rest of us had learned at an early age to bite our tongues instead of whimpering, "Berto, it was Berto," or "Berto made us," which only made our fathers lash the whip across our *nalgas* more solidly or more times, because we acted as *ratas* and *chavalitos*. We weren't rats because we cried out for equal justice (in vain, no less), we were teen-agers, no longer chavalitos. We were chavalos, becoming vatos! We felt we were too grown up for the whip, but our fathers always accompanied their strappings with a similar version of the dicho, "*Si quieres vivir sano, haste viejo temprano.*" Or rather, if you want a healthy life, get older (and wiser) quickly, which we knew meant we'd never have the upper hand over our elders, who would always be older and wiser than we.

And Berto, ever the respectful young man before our elders, basked in feigned innocence, receiving praise from those who saw only the mask he put on for their benefit, never seeing the real face he wore for us, his peers, his partners out of fear more than choice.

This endless Friday, I looked away from Berto and spotted Pedro, his head nodding as he struggled against sleep. For Pedro had been rudely awakened by the chicote striking his fleshy fingers on a number of occasions. And I stifled a smile as he fought to keep his eyes open, unfocused on the page swimming before him. Perhaps if someone else got into trouble—no, that wouldn't work either, unless the other four were at least implicated. There was no way out of Berto's plan.

I sighed, knowing I had to concentrate on the lesson at hand, but still unable to keep my thoughts from straying. I looked up and saw that Maestro Rubel was busy with the second and third graders who were reading their catechism aloud near the back of the room. On Easter Sunday they would make their Communion with Christ as we had done several years before.

I let my eyes wander to the window to my left where the fields and the montes beyond were visible. While I took in the view, my mind drifted once again to more pleasant thoughts. My father's words, which he spoke often enough to be branded in my brain, entered my awareness: "*Lo que ves es para ti y tu hermano.*" What you see is for you and your brother.

The fields, soon in the early growth of spring, would be covered in the summer with long green grama grass and alfalfa, the ground beneath barely visible. It was crucial that the cows be kept away from the alfalfa when it was maturing, for it became a deadly hazard if they got into the meadow and ate their fill. The plant would cause them to bloat soon after, their stomachs expanding as though they'd burst. My thoughts were softened by the view of the ridges beyond the river. The men usually planted *aveno*, or oats, by hand, and after harvest, the fields made excellent grazing for the livestock. The tree line began halfway up the mountainside. The forest was thick with a species of oak, *encino*, its trunk just as densely structured as its eastern brothers but no thicker than my calf. It made the choicest firewood, burning longer than any other wood in our area. Livestock ate the oak leaves and the wildlife fed on the nuts. If there was plenty of grass, they'd ignore the encino but if there was a drought, it became their only choice besides pine needles. And these could also be dangerous, causing miscarriages or deformed calves. Behind the encino was the dense forest of tall blue spruce and enormous pines that sported clusters of out-spread needles and rust red bark, with moss, wild mushrooms, and lime green ferns thriving beneath their shade. Since forests took up hundreds of acres of our property and our neighbors' as well, there was little left for planting. Each family felt grateful each year to have *becerros* or *maranos* to butcher, *verduras* from gardens to eat, and enough hay to sustain our herds of cattle and other farm animals through the long winters.

And though I truly loved this land that had been my grandfather's and was now my father's, knowing that someday it would belong to my brother and me, my thoughts became bittersweet. With my father's legacy came the responsibility of his sons to keep his vision alive, dispersing our own dreams like ashes in the wind.

I knew Miguel harbored his own tie to the land, but he would be gone for many years. And when he joined the Marines, he hinted to me that if it suited him, he would make the military a career. I conspired with my brother to keep his hope a secret. In following his own dream, Miguel would leave my father's unfulfilled. That left only me.

I had always loved school and had hoped somehow to further my education. And only a few weeks before, my own aspirations had flown on the wings of hope, but only for a moment. Maestro Rubel, pleased with my scholastic ability, had approached my father with the idea of sending me to medical school. My father had looked at me with a mixture of pride and something else I couldn't quite discern. He left the decision to me, let me ponder the question in silence. For just a moment, I allowed my own subdued dream to surface, only to be repressed almost immediately by the knowledge that money hindered my desire. Could I crush my father's dream, ask him to sell some of his beloved land, to realize my own?

In the weary lines that etched my father's face, in the haggard stoop of his shoulders, I realized that he was getting old, and if I were to keep his dream and his memory alive, it was to be through my own commitment to the land. I thanked Maestro with both gratitude and a tinge of regret. The bittersweet decision marked the end of my education but it also marked a beginning: I would be taking an equal portion of the responsibility with my father and uncle in sustaining the farm for generations to come. In the spark of hope that shimmered in my father's eyes that day, I found the strength to make his dream my own. The land was my future. Within the year, mine would be the hands that would man the reins of the horses as I tilled the fields alongside my father and uncle. And for many years to come, ours would be the boots that trod the earth of the mountains herding the cattle. Ours would be the hearts that would keep the farm going. It was to be my last year of school.

In a few weeks, Pedro and I would be like fledgling swallows leaving our nests, officially to enter the world of young men in the fall. In the following year, Berto would be moving to Mora, a small community to the north where he would work at a cousin's butcher shop. Pedro would leave for Las Vegas where he would learn the trade of welding as an apprentice to his uncle—the prospect of being able to provide for Luciana and marry her before the end of the year spurred his decision. Only Horacio would remain in school for another two years as a "graduate" under Maestro's tutelage to obtain a teaching license. Tino, after one more year of school, and I would be farmers.

Maestro Rubel, clearing his throat behind me, brought me quickly to the present. I looked down at my lesson before I could be caught daydreaming. Though trouble with him would be somewhat welcome, I reminded myself that I would suffer more pain at Berto's hands than at my teacher's.

After school, I would go with the rest, to fish for Friday's supper at the *représ*, the small dam, and we would devise some means to get out that night and reach the morada, where the answers to our future awaited. But, unknown to us, the novicios of the future and the specters of the past would keep them hidden from our view.

La Muerte

Perhaps it was our silence that enabled us to catch so many fish that afternoon. We sat quietly immersed in our respective thoughts, experiencing anticipatory twinges of trepidation, or in Horacio's and my case, full-fledged tremors and chills about what the night would bring. Or perhaps it was God, offering us the bounty of His river in exchange for our change of heart about the night's adventure. The last thought gave me a pang of guilt that weighed so heavily in my heart I gasped and feared I'd drawn my dying breath, punished with a heart attack for even thinking of attempting to thwart my fate by learning that which I should not yet know.

Little did I suspect my nervous belly boiled with gas and I suffered from a heartburn I had never before experienced, brought on by my lunch of *chile colorado con torta de huevo*, delicious red chile with egg torts. By the time the wave of intense heat abated, I was ready to crawl home, tail between my legs, shamed into being called gallina forever, sure that it was God's *castigo*, or punishment, for agreeing to go along with Berto's scheme. But the cramp passed and I was once more brought out of my thoughts by the anxious whispers of my friends.

"*Ya vienen*," Horacio whispered, raising his head over the reeds.

"Sí," Pedro agreed somberly, "there they come."

Looking toward the road, I could barely see over the high *popotónes* and willows that rose a bit higher than my head, but here and there I caught a glimpse of the men walking in no great haste down the rutted road to the morada. We fished off a small dam only a few hundred yards down the road from the prayer house, hidden from their view. We crouched among the tall reeds along the water's edge, watching their progress as tips of their heads covered with hats of different sorts bobbed up and down, getting slowly and steadily nearer.

It was time. As usual, they carried only their paper sacks with food, eating together in communal seclusion either before or after the Estaciones, I didn't know exactly when. Sometimes after a hard day's work, my father would eat before departing, so I thought they would eat after the Estaciones, yet at other times, he didn't eat at home and I wondered if he made himself suffer the penance of fasting in addition to whatever else he was compelled or forced to undergo.

With their approach, their voices floated on the breeze over our heads.

"Duck! Pronto!" Berto hissed.

We dropped to the ground, flattening the reeds as we propped our long willow sticks with string and a store-bought hook on some rocks. We crawled away from the noise of the water as it flowed over the ledge of the dam and lay in the weeds, peering through thin reeds and straining our ears to glean some insight.

"*¿Como sigue Esteban?*" Primo León asked how Esteban fared.

"Bien," answered Primo Esteban's older brother, Primo Gabriel. "*Viene más tarde.*"

My eyes shifted to Pedro, whose face flushed furiously at the mention of his father's condition. Although our primo's words confirmed that Esteban was fine and would join them later, I was afraid Pedro blamed the others, mostly my father, for his father's predicament. Silently, we waited, hoping for some revelation of what would occur within the walls of the morada. The men continued to speak, but it was of inconsequential matters, and we were left once again in the dark.

Each lost in his own thoughts, we cleaned the two buckets full of trout quickly, dividing them equally among ourselves to take home to our mothers.

It was Horacio who broke the silence on our way down the now deserted road just before he turned toward his house directly across from the morada, "See you after las Estaciones."

"Yeah," Berto agreed, looking over his shoulder toward the dark building which looked quiet and innocent in the late afternoon light. "Tonight we'll find out for ourselves, one way or the other, what goes on in there."

We made our way to home, wondering what exactly we would discover in the midnight hours of the night to come.

When I arrived home, my mother surprised me. She had baked apple pies and held one out for me to take back to the morada. "Hurry before los Hermanos finish their meal," she warned. Grateful for the excuse to go to the morada before the Estaciones began, I took the pie and hurried as quickly as I could through the fields rather than taking the road for fear Filiberto would see me and invite himself along. Trying not to jostle the pastry too much, I half-ran, hoping I wouldn't drop it and have to return, shamefaced for having destroyed los Hermanos' dessert.

Arriving at the kitchen door of the long, low structure, I knocked, wishing that someone would invite me in rather than take the pie from my hands and send me home. My gramma had told me that in the past when my grandfather was Hermano Mayor, no one was allowed near the morada before the Estaciones, that there was even a guard posted outside the door to prevent anyone from approaching. Back then, the cofradía was so much more secretive that an Hermano who had had to do a penitencia wore a black hood over his head from the morada to the capilla for the Estaciones and back again, only the eye-holes in the hood that permitted him to see at times gave evidence as to who was hidden beneath if he were a novicio. If he were an already established member, well, it must have been only a matter of recognizing the rest of the brothers and noting who was not visible to know the identity of the one wearing the hood. It had only been after the death of my grandfather and most of the elder members that they shed their hoods and proudly began to assert their membership in the religious order, for which I, for one, was grateful.

It was bad enough that *La Muerte* with her frightening countenance inhabited the morada. Did any of their rites have to do with encounters with her? And there was still the question of what we suspected had happened to Berto's father. This in itself was more than enough to make my curiosity about my own future membership more than a little colored with anxiety. And yet the longing I felt to become a novicio one day was still there. But would it have been such a great a desire had I seen an Hermano beneath the black hood, doubtless inspiring more fear of the unknown? I didn't know.

Tío Daniel answered the door with a broad smile and then opened it wider to let me in. The Hermanos were all seated at the long trestle table, conversing quietly as they finished their meal. Setting the pie down, I greeted each with a handshake before I made my way back to the door. My questions of just a moment before dissipated. I felt a sort of peace in the mere presence of the revered men who sat at the table before me in the sacred morada. Visions of the Apostles as they must have sat at meals with Christ ran through my mind. These wizened, God-fearing men, primos and compadres all, whiskers and lines of age and wisdom lining their faces, inspired the image of the Last Supper. I felt blessed, not afraid, to be among them, even if only for a moment.

Reluctant to leave, loath to let go of the feeling of humility that permeated my being, I leaned toward Tío Daniel, seated once more at the table and asked quietly if I would be allowed to say a prayer in the prayer room. He looked at me deeply before he nodded soberly. I knew that he saw how affected I was by being in their midst here more than at any other place. From the kitchen, I walked to a steep, short set of three steps into a small storage room that, in turn, led to the door of the prayer room. I paused at the doorway, my eyes riveted to the altar, already aglow with candles and kerosene lamps. I entered quietly and knelt before the figurine of the Blessed Mother. In Her arms, She held the dead Son for whom She mourned. I offered Her as fervent a prayer as I could, appealing for Her intercession to become a novicio one day soon so that I might worship Her and Her Son with my father as a fellow Hermano.

The sun began to set and flickering flames cast the rest of the large room in shadows. I crossed myself and rose, blinking in the darkening room. Then I saw the skeleton of La Muerte, Death, perched on a wooden stand to the right of the altar. I shuddered, looking behind and around me, but the room was empty except for the large wooden cross in the corner, the heavy crucifix that one Penitente would carry on his back during Holy Week. I shook off my rising anxiety and took a deep breath before looking askance at La Muerte. She never failed to seize me with dread.

Also known as *Doña Sebastiana*, La Muerte is death personified and is the Hispanic equivalent of the Grim Reaper. She was a hand-carved wooden effigy, clothed in a dress and shawl of black. Her bony arms were bent at the elbows, her hands closed around an equally black bow and arrow, which she held poised, aimed at anyone who stood directly before her—a feat that I had yet not dared to do. Her skeletal countenance displayed a lipless mouth revealing bared teeth in a perpetual grimace of terror. But it was the hollowed holes that were her glossy black eyes, which always filled me with fear, for they seemed to follow me always. Never having looked at her throughout the entire time I had been at prayer, concentrating on appealing to the Blessed Mother, I looked at La Muerte from one side, too scared of her to risk standing directly before her.

I gasped when Tío Daniel placed a hand on my shoulder, scaring me out of my wits. I had not heard him come up from behind. Chuckling quietly, he apologized, then whispered, "*¿Le tienes miedo, hijo?*"

I nodded as I stood up, yes, I was afraid of her. I wondered when, if ever, I would get over my fears, fear of the dark, fear of Berto's schemes and the trouble they would bring, fear of Death itself!

My tío moved to stand before me, wrapping his hands around my arms and looking me in the eyes. "When you're an Hermano, you'll learn that Death is not to be feared." He turned me by the shoulders so that I was facing La Muerte once more and said, "It is life that is to be feared, hijo mío, not death. For in death, you will rise with Christ."

"But why then is La Muerte so ugly?" I whispered, afraid she would hear and be offended, and feeling somewhat silly because I sensed she could hear one's every thought. What were mere words to hide from her knowing gaze? "I mean," I added, nervously looking at the bony visage out of the corner of my eye, "not ugly, exactly, but ..."

My uncle struggled to hold in his laughter; the prayer room was not meant for mirth. Waving his hand at me, he tried to look grim. "Perhaps it is meant to scare us, to show us that to be afraid is unimportant."

I knew that he referred to my fear of the dark, and I began to smile, but his next words saw into my soul. I wondered if all of Los Hermanos had some kind of sixth sense that enabled them to know what was on our minds.

"Then again," he spoke over his shoulder as he left, "perhaps La Muerte is ugly to remind us of the kind of death we will have with el Diablo if we do not follow Christ in our life on Earth."

I gulped. Did he somehow know about our plan for this night, and had he taken it upon himself to talk me out of going? I looked at La Muerte again. Her eyes followed me darkly, and I made myself slowly, fearfully, stand before her for the first time in my life. Her skeletal grin was indeed ominous, chilling me to the bone. In my overworked imagination, I thought I saw her bow quiver, as if she barely restrained herself from letting the knife-sharp arrow find its home in my heart. As my knees quivered in response, I quickly apologized in my mind for calling her ugly. Feeling my legs buckling in fear, I fell to my knees before her; her arrow now pointed directly between my eyes, and her grin mocked me. I shut my eyes tightly, offering her the most heartfelt prayer of gratitude for giving me the inspiration to live a virtuous life, telling her that I would remember always what she represented. Tentatively, I opened my eyes, looking into the shiny black orbs that were hers, hoping that I would find in her gaze some indication that she was pleased I had paid her homage, but her visage remained unchanged. I rose to my feet, unable to take my eyes from her face as I backed slowly away, still fearful that she would teach me a lesson and pierce me mortally for seeing my intent to return later that night. And though my uncle had told me death itself was not to be feared, I could not picture anything more horrifying than La Muerte coming for me in my moment of death.

I wavered between deciding to come back or not. The power of the faith instilled in my soul by my presence in the sacred morada beckoned me back, yet my fear of what La Muerte represented urged me not to return.

My father called from the doorway of the storage room. "Time for you to leave, José." Tearing my eyes away from La Muerte, I walked as calmly as I could outside. Once the door shut behind me, I ran, racing the darkness, imagining Death behind me all the way, her arrow poised at my retreating back. I even heard her wavering voice over the thudding of my heart and the pounding of my feet on the hard earth. "Do not return tonight. For if you dare, you will see my work!"

El Hermano Difunto

It would have been a sure proof plan, and our escapade would have remained our secret that night had it not been for the ghost. But then again, I'm certain that 1928 would have been like any other year had it not been for our encounter with the ghost that preceded a season of change in all our lives.

That evening I arrived at the capilla the same moment as the Penitentes, and my father beckoned me to his side, taking from his jacket pocket a small black book that he held out to me. My mouth fell open and my eyes rose to meet his. "*Para ti*," he said simply. For you.

I took the book of sacred alabados from his hand reverently, knowing that it had been his father's, a noble man I had never known, and I swallowed the lump in my throat, honored that he trusted me enough to let me use it to follow along, knowing I was being allowed to join my voice with his in the haunting hymns of sorrow.

"Now go, eh?" he smiled softly, knowing without my having spoken that I was touched beyond words by his gift.

I nodded, leaving him outside with the others who would enter as one body directly to the front of the church. Reaching the pew where Berto sat, I slid in beside him and knelt, still somewhat shaken at what I considered to have been a true encounter with La Muerte only an hour before. But fortified by the gift from my father, I touched the ragged cover of the book, carefully opening the yellowed pages held by worn strings losing the grip that bound them. The script of my grandfather's hand was firm and elegant, in some places dark where he had just dipped the pen into the ink, in others faded and almost illegible from candle wax. I felt a tingling in my fingers, a prickling of the hairs on my neck, and I sensed a communion with the *abuelito* who had died when my father was a boy, one of our valley's original Penitentes, a wise and educated man, a highly-respected teacher who was elected councilman of our community.

About the only story of him I could recall was when he became an unwitting witness to thievery. He'd been on his way back home to Cañoncito on horseback when he saw a wagon approaching in the distance. Since he couldn't tell if it was friend or foe, he took to the bushes to await its passage. Suddenly, from behind he heard the racket of many galloping horses and personally witnessed Vicente Silva and his band of thieves accost the man in the wagon. It turned out that the man was bringing a shipment of *mula*—moonshine—to his friend in Las Vegas who had a saloon. Well, it was well known that Vicente Silva had his own saloon on the plaza in the very same town, and without even a shot fired, he confiscated the man's supply of liquor and left him in the middle of the road to walk home. After the thieves disappeared, my abuelo befriended the victim and offered him a ride. He swore, according to my father, that had he had more than a pistol full of bullets, he would've taken action against the infamous villain. But because he was outnumbered against a group of about fifteen, he chose to do nothing and lived to tell the tale. I smiled at the memory as the last toll of the church bell echoed from above.

As the Estaciones commenced, I imagined it was his voice that beckoned to me from the hand-penned words of the alabados: "*Ampáranos, Madre, para poder verte, ampáranos ahora y en la hora de muerte.*" Protect us, Mother, so that we may see You, protect us now and at our moment of death.

Yes, I thought, protect me, Mother. Please, don't let me encounter La Muerte or her work tonight as she said I would. I prayed fervently that what I had planned to do later with my friends would not be held against me.

Finally, I backed into the pew where Berto's questioning gaze made me want to tell him of the warning I had received; however, I only lifted the book in my hand, offering, "*De mi abuelo,*" in explanation as though I had deliberately misunderstood his wordless inquiry.

The services that night were of hundredfold importance to me. This time as I prayed, I had my grandfather's legacy to guide me through each Estacíon, filling me with strength and humility.

Speaking to all who were gathered together in our humble capilla, my father finished the prayer of the first Station of the Cross, "*Considera, Alma perdida, que en aqueste paso fuerte dieron sentencia de muerte al Redentor de la Vida,*" forcing us all to consider, in our own souls, that in this picture the Savior of Life was given the sentence of death.

As each Estación was described in vivid detail, from the number of scourges Christ received, to the placing of the crown of thorns, down to the number of steps He took to get from one to the other, my heart overflowed with pity for the burden our Savior took upon His shoulders to become our Redeemer. I was filled with remorse for each sin I had ever committed or even contemplated.

"The fourth Estación," my father announced, standing before the portrayal of the Blessed Mother reaching out in agony to Her Son, who stood bent under the weight of His cross, the soldiers' whips raised to hasten Him on to His destination. "*Costa de sesenta pasos, aquí es donde encuetra Jesús a Su afligida Madre.*" My father's tone of voice, so poignantly sorrowful, created the image of Christ, stumbling under the weight of the cross as He walked about sixty paces to where He encountered His grieving Mother.

We knelt, our right knees on the pew, our left legs bent at the knee, supporting our weight as we knelt sideways to face the picture depicting the meeting of Mother and Son.

My father continued, his voice breaking in sorrow at what he had to remind us of the suffering of both Christ and His beloved Mother, "*Considera cual sería en tan reciprocó amor la pena del Salvador y el Morticio de María.*" He forced us to consider seriously what it must have been like for our Savior whose love for His Mother was truly returned and what it must have been like for the Blessed Mother who was indeed mortified by the plight of Her Son.

On the dying echo of the last of my father's words, the alabado began, rising in intensity as each Hermano added his voice to the hymn of sorrow, "*Oh, Señora, la más alfigida de las mujeres, por el cruel dolor que traspasó tu corazón mirando a Jesús, tu Hijo….*" My voice, softly at first, gained strength in unison with those of los Hermanos, and I, too, sang the mournful dirge in tribute to the Holy Mother, the most afflicted of all women, who had to suffer the cruel pain of seeing Her own Son in agony.

The thirteenth Station of the Cross was by far the most painful for our souls to bear, for it was this painting that showed the Blessed Mother with Her dead Son in Her arms. And as the *oración* or alabado began, I feared I would burst with sorrow, for the voices of los Hermanos quavered emotionally, as though they fought back tears in contemplation of what had passed centuries before to the Savior they tried so hard to follow in their own lives.

"*Oh, Madre de mi misericordia, por aquellas penas que padeciste, cuando pusieron a Tu muy amado Hijo en Tus brazos, y fue ungrido por Ti, Te suplico me alcances un grande dolor de haberle ofendido, y compasíon de Tus muchas penas.*"

The pain of our souls rose with our voices, as we appealed to our Blessed

Mother, the Mother of our mercies, for the hardship She suffered when they placed Her beloved Son in Her arms, He who was anointed by the Lord for Her. We beseeched Her to listen to us, wailing our sorrow for having offended Him and imploring Her to believe in our compassion for Her many pains.

When the Stations of the Cross ended that evening and we made our way out the double doors of the capilla, I felt my conscience struggling in its renewed battle against my temptation to join the gang in our scheme. When los Hermanos gathered together, Pedro took me aside, "*Mira*," he pointed with his chin. I looked. There, among the Penitentes were two others, Horacio's primo Jorge, and Primo Gabriel's *ahijado*, or godson, Pablito, the only younger men who were left in our valley. Both barely nineteen, neither had ever accompanied los Hermanos to the morada after the Estaciones, so I was fairly certain they were novicios, novices who wished to enter the Brotherhood. They stood somewhat self-consciously, shuffling their feet and taking sidelong glances at those of us gathered outside to await the departure of the Penitentes. There had been no ceremony, not so much as a hint from any Hermano that any new members were to be taken into the cofradía this night. As if they had walked with los Hermanos always, the two initiates took up the rear as the procession started down the road back to the morada.

"How d'you like that?" Tino breathed, coming up beside us as we watched the procession depart, somewhat awed by the way the two novicios had been taken in with no preamble.

Berto motioned us over with his head to the side of the church where he stood pleading with my mother to let me go for a short walk. She glanced at me only once, and I, unable to meet her gaze, stood in silence, wondering whether her intuition made her hesitate. A part of me longed for her to say no; my conciencia whispered into my mind that I had had enough for one day. Yet another part of me, that part which I called *tentación*, temptation, feared she would say no, putting a halt to what I was already looking forward to: a last walk back to the morada and a revelation of what I half-consciously hoped I would see. The initiation of the two novicios would leave no doubt of what I would undergo when it became my turn.

I wondered whether my mother would have said no if Horacio hadn't joined us just then, announcing that he could stay out for a while, too. Looking from Filiberto to Horacio to me, she nodded briskly, latching onto Prima Marta's arm for the short walk home. "*No muy tarde,*" she said softly, reminding me not to stay out too late. "*Y cuidado,*" she tossed over her shoulder, warning me to be careful.

Left on the front stoop of the capilla with only one small, wavering flame from the lantern Horacio had brought and the new moon that cast a little light upon the meadows, we sat on the cold laja in silence, listening to the wavering notes of alabados as los Hermanos went back to the morada for the last time that evening. We watched the fading light of their lanterns until, after what seemed an eternity, they reached the long, low structure and entered, closing out the black night.

"*Bueno*," Pedro rose, "*vamos si vamos.*"

Yes, I thought, let's go if we're going. We stood huddled together for a moment, then as if we all sensed someone watching, we glanced around, assuring ourselves that we had indeed been left alone. But when we started off, we moved slowly into Primo León's pasture, toward the arbolera as if it were our destination, still sensing a presence that we couldn't quite see.

Horacio whispered, voicing all our thoughts aloud. "I feel like someone's watching."

I almost told the boys of my encounter with La Muerte that afternoon. I still struggled with the fact that it could have been, must have been, my imagination, and I feared being branded scaredy-cat for the rest of my life, I remained quiet, huddling so close to Pedro that I suffered a cuff to the head when I trod on his heels one time too many.

From time to time as we made our way to the river, one of us would look over his shoulder, and none of us knew if our fears were from the dark or from some unknown entity that knew our intent. When we reached the river, Horacio reluctantly lowered the lantern wick to hide the flame and we backtracked to the bridge of vigas in silence, stumbling in the darkness, crossing over to the dam, running to the edge of the forest, and going behind the morada to hide in the trees while we caught our breaths.

"I never noticed before," Berto whispered to no one in particular, "but from behind, the morada looks like a *cajón*."

"Whadda ya mean, a cajón?" Horacio whispered, clutching my arm so hard I winced.

"A cajón," Berto repeated, "*un cajón para un difunto.*"

"A coffin?" Tino gasped.

We all looked at the long, low structure intently. Sure enough, the back part was straight, but where the altar stood, it was vee-shaped like the part of a coffin where the difunto's head rested.

I felt Horacio shuddering next to me, but whether the shaking came from his body or mine I didn't know. My own knees shook so much I feared the rest of the boys could hear my bones striking one another.

"Maybe we shouldn't," Horacio began, but he was cut short by Pedro.

"Go home then," he whispered, then his voice shook. "I-I'm not."

Tino stuttered, too. "B-bu-besides, we're already here."

After some time, we gathered our courage and, grabbing the sleeve of the one closest, made our way stealthily to the rear of the morada. We hugged the wall with our backs as we slipped toward the prayer room. Sidling along in single file until we reached the front of the building, we stood in silence, straining our ears for some evidence of activity within. But the adobe walls were two feet thick, so our efforts were in vain. We heard nothing save the distant chorus of crickets that combined with the occasional lowing of a cow or the squawk of Primo León's chickens, as if to drown out intentionally the sounds we ached to hear.

In the lead was Berto, who kept snaking forward around the corner inch by inch until he reached the window. He crouched below it. Tino joined him, and the rest of us stood pretty much squished together beside him, trying to see inside without being seen. Locating ourselves by the window was risky, to say the least, for it was next to the front door I had exited hours before. However, since we could see if anyone approached the door, we figured we could run quickly around to the back before being seen. So we stayed where we were, hoping for a glimpse of the initiation.

There was shuffling inside, and for a moment we nearly bolted, afraid one of the men was about to come outside to relieve himself. But Berto raised his hand and we stayed where we were, exhaling the breaths that we unconsciously held. Peering inside, I saw that the two novices garbed only in white pants stood in front of the altar before my father. The rest of the men formed a semi-circle around them. My father read from a gray-covered ledger. Bits and pieces of his words came through the window, and I realized he was reading the rules by which they would be judged to ascertain whether they were worthy enough to become members of the cofradía.

"*Segunda regla,*" my father's voice wafted out into the night, "*después de una examinación … información de la conducta moralidad.*" What I could catch was that each novice would have to undergo an examination whereby the rest of the members would present information of his moral conduct. Then I heard, "*faltas graves … no se permitirá que forma parte de la Hermanidad.*" If the novice was found to have grave faults, the Hermano Mayor and other officials would observe his conduct, and if they found the novice unworthy, they would not allow him to become a part of the Brotherhood.

I saw my father raise his head, knowing that his keen eyes were boring into those of the two young men, sensing if either was hesitant to continue in the process of initiation.

"*Tercer regla*," my father continued, "*si alguno de los Hermanos quebrantará el cigilio será severamente corregido al dispocición del Hermano Mayor y Celador … pudiera ser excluido de la Hermanidad.*"

At these words, I caught my breath sharply, shivers of fear slithering up my spine as their meaning sank in. It seemed the third rule applied not only to the initiates, but to all the Hermanos. If any one broke any of the rules he would be severely punished according to the disposition of the Hermano Mayor. Worse yet, he could be excluded from the Brotherhood.

So my father *did* have a power beyond my imaginings as Hermano Mayor! To know that he had been appointed by his Brothers to set the example of moral conduct for them to follow was one thing, an honor to be proud of indeed. But to think he ordered whatever discipline he deemed necessary to correct the immoral behavior of another was a power I could not imagine. I knew he carried much in his mind when he sat pensive and quiet from time to time, but never had I suspected that he was somber because he held all the souls of his Brothers in his charge, that he made them see the error of their ways. And to think of the weight on his shoulders when he had to expel one who had sinned and could not be encouraged to change.

Suddenly the back door to the morada opened, light spilling out in an elongated square on the ground a few yards before us. Like rabbits we leapt, stumbling over one another in our haste to reach the back of the structure. We hugged the wall, listening as best we could over our heavy breathing and the pounding of our hearts. I heard one of los Hermanos hefting wood into his arms and another set of footsteps made its way toward the front of the morada where we had crouched.

"Run!" Pedro whispered urgently, taking off into the trees behind the building. We followed, tree limbs slashing at our cheeks, rocks and fallen branches tripping us in the darkness as we ran deeper into the forest over the hills behind Horacio's house. Reaching the barbed wire fence at the edge of his property, we stopped, stooped over, or dropped to the ground to catch our breaths.

"Th … that was close!" I huffed between breaths.

"Damn!" Berto cursed. "We didn't get t'see nothin'."

"What did you expect?" Tino answered. "Jorge and Pablo are new; they weren't gonna be punished just because they only joined."

Horaco quietly asserted, "Miguel was," before looking away.

For a moment no one spoke, waiting, I supposed, for me to respond.

"At least now we know the truth about who does the punishing," Berto added. I could feel his eyes on me even though it was too dark to see his face. "José, your father, gives the orders, just like I thought."

"That's not true!" I countered. "He sets the example, and he says who has to be punished, but everyone else has a part in it too. You heard what I did; you can't say you didn't. If someone does something wrong, he has to pay the price, and all the Hermanos decide together."

"Besides," Horacio added, "we didn't hear all of it; you don't know who actually does what. Maybe he just says who has to be punished, and the rest do it or the one who sinned does it to himself out of penance."

"I don't care," Berto argued stubbornly. "The Hermano Mayor is the one to blame."

"You're just mad 'cause your dad got caught doing something he wasn't supposed to," I replied, anger that he refused to face facts coloring my words. "*Malíciala*, Berto, the only one to blame was your father. Mine only wanted to make him realize that he broke a rule they all promised to follow." No one said that the same probably applied to Miguel.

"¡*Cabrón*!" Berto spat, leaping toward me and smashing his fist into my jaw before I could react.

His weight threw us both to the ground where he struck at my chest and ribs blindly. I didn't want to hit back, knowing he struck me only because he was angry at my father, angrier still at his own father for having done something he knew he shouldn't have.

The others pulled him away from me, leaving me to writhe on the cold earth with my throbbing belly as he stumbled away and fell to his knees, sobbing with inner pain that his own father had caused. For awhile no one spoke, letting Berto have this moment to himself as he fought for control of his emotions, struggling to come to terms with what he knew was the truth.

But after a while, it was Berto, of all people, who finally broke the silence with unexpected words of wisdom. "It's true," he admitted quietly, tossing his unruly lock of hair from his brow. "Last year my father did something he shouldn't have. It's none of my business, but I know he didn't do it again, and he never will. Whatever went on in the morada that night taught him a lesson that he never forgot, and the way he treats your father, José, well, you can tell he doesn't hold it against him. I guess the same goes for your brother."

We all pondered this for a moment, stunned. All our eyes focused on Filiberto, the one who led us astray, the one who lied, the one who cheated, the one most likely to go to hell. He had learned a valuable lesson from our eavesdropping, and we all learned something that night, too, of the boy who had spoken like a wise Hermano.

Pedro rose and held out his hand to Berto, who after a moment of hesitation, took it, and followed him to where the rest of us sat. Berto mumbled what, for him, was as close to an apology as I ever got from him. "I guess I shouldn't a hit 'cha."

Relief bathed us all with its healing balm and we reinforced our ties the only way we knew how, by rumbling on the ground, punching one another playfully, and rolling in the weeds. Finally, exhausted with giggling, we lay quietly looking up at the stars.

"Let's go home." Tino yawned.

"I'll walk you guys halfway," Horacio offered, though his house was just yards below us.

Following the cow path single file until we got to the fields below, we laughed, knowing halfway to Horacio meant halfway to the river, which wasn't even halfway for us to get home. After hearing legends of la Llorona from our cousins who lived in town, Horacio avoided going anywhere near the river at night, fearful he would see her in her nightly walks through eternity searching for the lost children she herself had drowned. Sometimes the screams of the frogs were enough to set him off, swearing it was the cry of la Llorona we heard. And we had had many a laugh at his expense when we would all shriek that it was and run helter skelter, watching him from the reeds by the river as he stumbled and fell only to jump to his feet, running like a madman all the way home. I knew it must have taxed his sense of bravery plenty to have even joined us this night.

"Ooooooh," Tino teased, his voice rising eerily in the darkness. Never one to pass up giving Horacio a good scare, in a ghostly whisper he added, "There she goes, Horacio, la Llorona."

"Stop it," Horacio demanded. "Leave me alone, Tino."

"I'll bet she dresses in black, she cries like a ..."

"Look!" Pedro stopped in his tracks, the rest of us bumping into his back as we looked where he pointed. Directly ahead of us, barely visible, was a figure in black, making its way across the meadow in the direction of my home.

For a moment we stood and watched, sure that it must be la Llorona ready to take a couple of us to replace her children or La Muerte coming for one of us since we had crouched under the window closest to where she sat in the morada and surely she had known we had been there.

We were all about to run for home, but Pedro spoke again, "Es Don Epifanio. ¿Qué no?" Then repeating in English for confirmation, "It is him, right?"

"Yeah," Tino breathed, the relief in his voice calming us all. "That's who it is. Let's catch up to him. We'll walk him home."

Don Epifanio Tafoya, who was already in his seventies, lived a little up the hill from the Lucero homestead. He was notorious for his midnight jaunts through the meadows and fields. Paying late night visits to all his neighbors from time to time and staying a bit too late most often, he would be seen walking briskly home at all hours of the night. Thinking it was he going home from some vecino's house, we thought we'd catch up to him and perhaps keep him company on his way. Never mind that we were all jumpy after what we had just been through and the thoughts of the ladies of the evening whom we had no desire to encounter alone. We needed Don Epifanio's company more than he needed ours.

"Don Epifanio!" Berto called. "¡*Espéranos*! Wait up!"

But at Berto's voice, it seemed Don Epifanio picked up his pace, walking even faster through the field. We ran to catch up; however, when we closed in, he reached the barbed wire fence separating Don Juan's property from the next. Sure that he would stop there and wait, we slowed down. But what happened next I wouldn't have believed if I hadn't seen it with my own eyes. The figure didn't stop. Instead, it kept on walking, right through the barbed wire fence! It didn't hunch to cross through the wires, it didn't step over as if the wires were sagging, it walked straight through as though they weren't even there!

We stopped in our tracks, clutching at one another's arms, frozen as though we had been turned into statues. We looked at one another with wide and disbelieving eyes as we each tried to make sense of what we had seen.

Tino spoke first, not exactly talking, but wheezing; "¡Un muerto, un difunto!"

And what happened next seemed to occur in the space of seconds. It was so fast.

"¡La Llorona!" Horacio shrieked at the top of his lungs.

We still hadn't moved. I guess we were trying to wrap our minds around the fact that we could be seeing an actual apparition. I know I was, blinking my eyes and telling myself I had imagined the whole thing. Horacio's terror-filled screech snapped my concentration and I turned to shut him up. But Berto was already trying. He wrapped an arm around Horacio's neck and clamped a hand over his mouth just as Horacio was about to let loose another blood-curdling yell. But though Berto was tougher, Horacio was larger. And because his fear made him stronger, Horacio shoved him backward and ran, stumbling back up the hill for home.

Maybe we could have gotten away with our midnight escapade if he'd simply run, but Horacio screamed at the top of his lungs *all* the way home, alerting just about everyone in the valley to the fact that we were up to something—again—something that had scared Horacio half to death so that he ran blindly into the darkness and fell, spraining his wrist in the process. His screams echoed through the hills, and we winced that everyone for at least a mile around knew that something was very amiss. And even that wouldn't have been so bad, except for the fact that los Hermanos were still in the morada just yards from Horacio's front door. Their secret ritual was interrupted by the ruckus. As the rest of us fell to the ground to watch, we cringed when the door to the sacred house opened and in the rectangle of light behind them, we saw the silhouettes of several men emerge to see what was the matter.

After the door slammed behind him, Horacio's screams of terror and pain were muffled, and the men only grunted. We caught words that wafted to us from the darkness. "Era Horacio …" and muffled chuckling "la Llorona otra vez." They knew Horacio's fear of the dark made him see the fabled lady of darkness whenever he ventured out at night. And one by one they shook their heads and retreated into the sacred abode once again, much to our relief. Little did we know, Horacio's cousin would be sent to fetch my grandmother within the next few minutes to see to his wrist, and our discovery was imminent.

We turned as one back to the shadowy figure that had slowed but was still steadily making its way across the meadow toward my father's land.

"Who … what could it be?" Pedro whispered.

"I du-don't know," I stammered, afraid that indeed La Muerte had truly spoken to me, that she had kept her promise that I would see her work, afraid that it had been a difunto, a ghost!

"There's only one way to find out." Berto broke away from my clutching hands. "¡Vamonos!" he challenged. "¡*Siguenlo*!"

It was a good thing that when Horacio panicked, he'd dropped the lantern or we'd have been running blind. So catching up the handle of our only source of light, Berto ran to the fence and ducked between the taut wires. Pedro gave chase.

"Follow him?" Tino yelled, "¿*Estás loco*?"

Tino looked at me; I looked at him. We glanced behind us and ran. Catching up to Berto and Pedro, we all ran as fast as we could in the darkness toward the figure. As if sensing our pursuit, it again picked up its pace. When it approached the fence marking our property, as before without hesitation—it didn't pause to duck beneath or between the wires—it walked right through! And though it was enveloped in a black blanket of night, the sliver of the new moon shed enough light for us to see that the stranger paused to turn slowly in our direction.

When Berto, who had been pumping his legs with all his might in chase, saw the figure turn as if looking at him, he hit the brakes with his heels, stopping so quickly on the sloping incline that he fell back on his rump with an "oof!" Pedro, hot on Berto's heels, had no warning, no time to stop. Running directly into his primo on the ground, the point of his right boot connected with Berto's butt; and the forward motion of his left foot flipped him over Berto's head like a sack of grain. "Yaaaaa!" Pedro yelled, landing spread eagle on his back. The fall knocked the wind out of him, and his yell cut off abruptly. He gasped and lifted his head like an overturned turtle too surprised to struggle. Only a couple of feet behind, Tino and I swerved to either side of the two in our path, stopping in our tracks so fast we were both propelled head over heels. Putting out his hands at the last minute, Tino was able to land on all fours. I, on the other hand, wasn't so lucky or so quick. I landed face first sprawled in the dirt, my chin connecting with the ground so hard my head bounced back.

All this occurred in the space of seconds, yet our eyes remained glued to the figure at the fence. Through stars dancing in my eyes, I saw its head turn toward us, but the thin slice of moonlight didn't reveal any detail, just a dark countenance facing our way before the head tilted back as if silently laughing at our antics—as though we were clowns performing for its pleasure rather than the scared-out-of-our-minds boys that we were. Then it resumed its brisk walk. None of us made any move to take up our chase again. The figure reached the willows at the river's edge and just disappeared.

Scared as we were, we wondered afterward why we didn't run, scream, do anything but watch. It seemed as if in a daze, we merely moved (or hobbled, more accurately), Berto rubbing his backside, Pedro hugging his stomach, Tino massaging his wrists, and I clutching my chin, to the riverbank on our side of the fence. Still gasping for breath, each of us looked to the others for a plausible explanation for what we had seen. None of us spoke. And though after a moment, like zombies, we began to walk silently home, none of us wanted to put into words the fear that what we'd seen was unequivocally something unknown.

By silent agreement Berto and I walked Pedro and Tino to their homes since they lived a bit farther away. Each of us knew whatever courage we felt in our pursuit of the dark figure was gone and none of us was brave enough to get home on his own.

"Un difunto." Tino's voice began to repeat itself in my mind.

Had it really been a ghost? I wondered silently. Had it been the specter of a Penitente from the past come to warn us? Or to chastise us for spying on something which was not meant for us to see?

Pedro whispered my thoughts aloud when we reached his yard, "Tino was right. Era un difunto, un Penitente muerto."

Tino nodded, his voice cracking with emotion. "Ya, the ghost of a Penitente who saw what we were up to and wants us to leave los Hermanos alone."

I shuddered, wondering at the coincidence of our thoughts, trying to convince myself that it was only natural we all thought the same thing after sneaking around the morada.

"La Muerte warned me," I mumbled.

Through the light emerging from Pedro's kitchen window, I saw their eyes turn to me in surprise.

Tino gasped. "Whadda mean, La Muerte warned you?"

Knowing we were all about to have unwelcome nightmares as it was, I bit my tongue. I looked at each of them, wondering whether they would believe me and, if they did, would I bear the brunt of their anger that I hadn't spoken up when we all sensed a presence watching us earlier? I hesitated. But the need to share my innermost fears overrode my caution and I blurted out my experience at the morada that afternoon, sure to tell them I thought it had been my over-active imagination, at least until now.

When I finished, they remained silent, and I waited for evidence of wrath or disbelief in their eyes. But there was neither; only grim acceptance was written on their faces.

Pedro nodded somberly. "*Te creo.*"

And when both Berto and Tino's nods followed, those words meant much coming from three of my closest friends and cousins: they believed.

"We better keep quiet about this," Berto cautioned, "if we don't want to catch trouble for what we were doing."

We agreed with Berto, though I knew we had our doubts about Horacio, who was probably already sobbing his story to his mother and catching hell for our scheme.

But all the way home, Tino's words echoed in our minds and in our hearts "un difunto." We knew it to be the truth: a ghost. To this day, I still believe that we encountered a warning, a gentle, silent, yet frightening warning sent indeed by La Muerte so that we should await our futures with no interference.

Revelaciones

We changed. Our encounter with the unknown left us all a bit different, a mite wiser as to what our lives should embody. Horacio had spilled the beans but not, as we had feared, about our nocturnal visit to the morada as the Horacio of the past would have done. He admitted just to having seen a difunto. And only because he had returned so frightened that he had no time to glue himself together before being set upon by his mother. He would never lie to her. Surprisingly, no one punished us.

The day after our adventure, Tino rushed over after his morning chores, making his presence known with a quiet hello instead of trying to scare the pants off me. Smiling sheepishly, he shrugged. "Don't seem right scaring you no more. We were scared out of our *calzones* last night more than …" He lost his battle to find the right words so I nodded in quiet understanding. He was sincere though the thought of him without his scare tactics made me sad. He never snuck up on any of us after that night, and he was never quite the same fun-loving character.

Even Berto changed. He came over to lean against the fence around the chicken coop when I was raking. With his hands clenched around the wires, he looked like a convict behind bars. I was about to crack a joke about it when I saw the gravity in his eyes. I leaned the rake against the door frame and stepped out of the enclosure. "What's the matter?"

"Horacio spilled his guts last night."

"You mean about the morada?"

"Nah," he spat, "about the difunto. I got ahold of him a while ago, told him what was in store for him if he told about that. He'll keep quiet."

I only stared, shocked. Had the night's adventure really shown Filiberto nothing then? Were his words of wisdom of the night before a farce and was he really going to resume his uncaring ways?

He must've seen the expression on my face because he scoffed. "Don't look at me that way. Whadda ya think I did, threaten to break his legs? I only told him all of us would be in for it if he told, that's all. I was gonna remind him of how we all want to join the cofradía someday, but he told me not to worry, that he had already thought of that."

I would not have believed it if I hadn't seen the sincerity in Berto's eyes, about Horacio and about himself.

Later Pedro came to the fence bordering my father's property and Primo Eufemio's where he had been cleaning out the pig pens. Though we spoke for only a moment, it was evident that Pedro's sullenness had evolved into something akin to pensive thoughtfulness. He chose his words carefully as though to avoid alienating me, something unknown in the former Pedro.

As for the change in myself, I wasn't totally aware of any, except that as the weeks wore on, each Friday's nightly vigil with the Penitentes held a deeper feeling than it had before. I went home content to wait until my father decided it was time for me to accompany him.

As March blew itself out, April meekly arrived with the first green shoots of *lirios*, or lavender and white irises, rising in the meadows out of spurts of dark alfalfa and gramma grass. When the apple, plum, and chokecherry trees of the arbolera began to blossom, we all prayed fervently for warmer weather, knowing that a frost would kill any hope for the fruit we would harvest to feed us in the year ahead.

Miguel wrote, once to my mother and twice to me. In his first letter he apologized for not having spent more time with me, and his explanation was almost the exactly the same as my grandmother's. His letters were colored with anecdotes and descriptions of friends he'd made, but each one ended with a page he bade me give to Carolina, fearing her father wouldn't allow her to receive a letter directly from him. And each time I sent my reply, I accompanied it with her response, written on lilac-scented paper. I wondered what his friends thought of the perfumed letters he received that were supposed to be from his brother. I was sure his explanations, if he offered any, were met with much ribbing.

The Saturday of the first week in April was a day that we boys looked forward to each year: the annual cattle drive up into the high country. At the break of day, we accompanied all our fathers, Tío Daniel, and Primo Esteban to the mountains behind our house, some of us on horseback, some on foot or in

Primo Esteban's wagon. The large horse-drawn wagon, filled almost to capacity with our sleeping gear, cooking utensils, food, and fence-mending materials, went the long way on a rutted road a few miles east. We stayed overnight to ensure that the cattle had enough water for at least a week and that the fences were up. Everyone's cattle combined into one large herd that would graze in the montes for the summer, leaving the meadows of our valley to grow lush in their absence. Every Saturday thereafter, two or more of us would take turns checking up on the cows and the fences. We dug up more water from the arroyo which was fed from an underground spring. It was the only source, other than rain collection in large shallow bowl-shaped rocks here and there.

From time to time, since the sierra was roughly eight miles away, a new-born calf or two faltered or fell behind, and one of us would heft it up onto someone's saddle where it lay facedown until it rested enough to follow its mother once more. I remember picking up my first calf at the age of twelve, trying as hard as I could to hold the squirming baby until a rider came by. It bawled the entire time I struggled with it. I guess the mother thought it was in pain and ran toward me, mooing with each step. I knew better than to run—the cow would have chased me down—and the calf weighed so much there was no chance I could if I had wanted to. When the mother reached us, she head-butted my back so hard it was all I could do not to drop her baby. Of course, everyone laughed, catcalling or trying to give advice. Thankfully it wasn't long before my father pulled his horse alongside and my cousin Jorge lifted the calf from my arms and over the saddle, despite my protests that it wasn't that heavy. To be honest, I was relieved and left calf-toting to bigger fellows for the next few years.

About an hour before reaching our destination, we passed through the property of Don Serapio, who lived with his wife Doña Flora, about as far back into the mountains of Las Cañadas as anyone could get. Don Serapio was wait-ing with his cattle to join up with us, and Doña Flora was waiting for conver-sation, as she always was when we came by on our annual drive. We all understood her need for company, so we paid Doña Flora a short visit before continuing on our way, no matter how much we wanted to reach our campsite. She made us sit for a cup of coffee and freshly baked sweets like prune pie, chat-tering away while we ate. During the winter, we rarely saw her because some-times they were snowbound for weeks at a time. Only Don Serapio came down on horseback or on foot for provisions. We also brought gifts from our mothers, hand-embroidered dishtowels, jars of jams and jellies, sometimes supplies such as thread, material, or cooking utensils. Before we left, the diminutive elderly woman gifted us with a round loaf of bread baked in her horno. Tino promptly grabbed it. As he started walking toward the wagon to deposit the bread, Berto gave him a playful push from behind. Tino fell face first in a mud puddle while the loaf went rolling under the wagon. Of course we all burst into laughter and Berto dove under the wagon for the bread before it could roll into the arroyo. He hid it from Doña Flora's sight and brushed the mud off with his shirt tail, hoping she hadn't seen it fly from Tino's hands. We bade her farewell, some of us still trying to regain our composure as the mental vision of Tino's mishap still raised the occasional chuckle or snort as we tried to say thank you and good bye with straight faces.

Reaching the lush green meadow at last, we set up camp next to the nearly always dry arroyo, some of us taking rolls of barbed wire and loading carpenter belts with *grampos,* the U-shaped hooks used to fasten the wire to fence posts, others hacking down saplings for posts, and still others going to the other side of the meadow where the hidden spring fed the arroyo. Pedro, Jorge, and I went to the spring, taking shovels with which to dig a large hole in the soft sand. It filled almost immediately with water as we dug. I had developed a habit of plunging the shovel into the sand before stepping in it because the first time I had come on the cattle drive, I had jumped from the bank from about six feet above the sand only to find myself sinking to my knees and quickly getting sucked down. My father came to my rescue, yanking me out so abruptly he almost dislocated my shoulder and warned me about the dry quicksand here and there in the arroyo. No one knew how deep we'd sink, and no one wanted to find out. So we stepped through the sand carefully.

Being midday, the sun burned on our backs, and before long, Pedro and I removed our shirts, laughing as Jorge teased us about how we would bulge with muscles by the end of the day. Neither Pedro nor I thought anything of it when Jorge, wiping the sweat from his brow, looked at us somewhat morosely before taking his shirt off as well. In fact, we returned his jokes by making fun of his muscles, calling him Hercules and running just out of range when he threw clumps of wet sand at us. We had a minor water fight amongst the cows who stumbled out of our way as they attempted to drink despite our interference. When we went back to work, neither Pedro nor I noticed that Jorge kept us in front of him for close to an hour until he called for a break. He moved away to sit under the shade of a nearby pine, but when he leaned back against the trunk, Jorge winced loudly.

"What's the matter?" I asked.

"Nada," he grumbled. "I musta leaned on a bee."

"Lemme see," I moved toward him. "If the stinger's stuck in your back, I'll pull it out."

"No!" He practically yelled. "Just get me my shirt."

Pedro ran to get his shirt in the grass by the arroyo and tossed it to him before falling supine on the cool grass beneath a tree. We rested for about fifteen minutes before Jorge started rising stiffly to his feet, suggesting that we had better go back and chop wood for the camp. He began to don his shirt but staggered and fell to his side.

"Jorge," I gasped, running to kneel beside him. I saw numerous cuts on his back, some of which had torn open with his shoveling. His watery blood dripped sideways into the grass. I shook my head understanding why he had kept his body hidden from our view. I knew where the cuts had come from, knowing they were fresh from the night before. A few weeks had passed since his initiation into the Brotherhood, and I wondered anew what the wounds meant and why my father had deemed them necessary.

"D'you think he's dead?" Pedro asked, his eyes wide with fear. "I've heard sometimes the heat does that, heat stroke is what they call it."

Putting my hand under Jorge's nose, I shook my head, "He's breathing." I pointed at Jorge's back, "Look."

"Aaay!"

We looked at one another over Jorge's head, both of us fearing he had done something really wrong, something for which he had been made to do a penance at the morada, and at my father's bidding, no less. Pedro sighed deeply, running a hand through his hair, "Whatever Jorge did made los Hermanos put him through this. He musta deserved it."

I nodded soberly, wet Jorge's shirt in the spring, and returned to wring it down above his face and back, rinsing the blood away.

"Ugh." Jorge stirred and mumbled. "¿Qué pasó?"

"You fainted." Pedro took the shirt from me and dipped it into the water again. Then he gently swabbed at the cuts on Jorge's back.

"No!" Jorge sat up groggily, grabbing his shirt from Pedro and clutching at his head.

"Look," I said softly, taking his shirt from his hands and returning it to Pedro, who continued ministering to Jorge's wounds, "we've seen your back. Let us help you."

He looked at us both, shook his head, and leaned on his elbow, lying on his side once more. He allowed Pedro to run the cool water over his back again. "*Que no se diga nada de esto.*"

"No," I assured him, "we won't tell."

Only the lowing of the cattle and an occasional shout of one of the men from beyond our vision broke the silence of the forest.

"I did wrong," Jorge whispered.

Neither Pedro nor I spoke, wanting to hear what had happened if he were of a mind to talk. Yet each of us knew we should tell Jorge not to say any more.

"You don't need to know the details, but I did something I shouldn't have and last night at the morada, I confessed to los Hermanos. What you see on my back I did to myself as penance for my sin. See, I felt like I was facing God when I knelt in front of the altar at La Morada, and I wanted to make Him know I was truly sorry for having sinned against Him, and I did what I had to do to myself to prove it. Remember, primitos," he sighed tiredly, "remember to always be good so that you will never have to prove to your Maker that you are worthy."

We were silent, taking into our consciences Jorge's confession, knowing we would remember his warning for the rest of our lives, knowing also we would tell no one.

Back at camp that evening, Pedro and I were quiet. Having formed a closer bond with our older primo, we took him his supper where he reclined against his bedroll so that he wouldn't have to get up. Our concern didn't go unnoticed. Pedro's father made a joke about it, but we laughed, telling him how old cousin Jorge had worked so hard his ancient bones were weary and we were afraid he would fall over from exhaustion.

After we had all helped with the dishes, the boys and I asked if we could go sleep in the caves which were about a quarter of a mile away. When it looked as though Berto's father would protest, Jorge volunteered to go with us, rising stiffly to his feet. My Tío Daniel looked at Jorge closely, asking if he felt up to it. When Jorge only shrugged and nodded, my tío rose also, saying he would accompany us just to be sure no mountain lions or bears had decided to take up residence since the time we had last been there. Picking up a lantern, Berto took the lead, and the rest of us followed with our bedrolls. My Tío Daniel never left Jorge's side, even assisting him over boulders in our path. I wondered if my uncle felt a twinge of conscience over what Jorge had made himself do to remain a novicio.

Reaching the larger of the two caves, which was about the size of our cocina back home, my uncle took the lead, pointing his flashlight into the darkness to assure that it was vacant while the rest of us gathered firewood to make a small fire on the ledge. Once the flames took hold, we all gathered around. Tino begged my uncle for a cuento before he returned to the main campsite.

"*Pues*," he began as we settled into our sleeping bags or onto our bedrolls, "did you ever hear of the time the Diablo appeared in town?"

"The Devil?" Horacio squawked. "I'm not sure I want to hear this."

Berto poked him. "Go to sleep then."

"C'mon, Horacio," Tino added, "don't be a scaredy cat."

We were all sure if it had been just us boys Horacio would have protested further. Since my uncle and Jorge were there, he shrugged, resigned to at least try for a semblance of bravery.

"Well," my uncle began again, "it was during Lent. And you boys know that during Lent there are no dances, right?"

"Right," Tino piped up, "during Lent we remember that Christ died for us and out of respect we have to be serious."

"That's right. But you also know that some people in town don't share our view, so they decided to go ahead and throw a *baile*, a dance."

I caught Horacio's eye as he shook his head and rolled his eyes. "Some people have no respect."

"Shhh," Pedro admonished. "I wanna hear this."

"This story is what happens when people show their disrespect," Tío Daniel continued. "A camarada of mine was there and this is what he told me happened. The people were dancing away, drinking, you know how bailes are, when a little before midnight, a man all dressed in black appeared. Now, no one had seen this stranger before, and of course, since he was young and very handsome, the ladies were taken in by his mysterious black eyes. He danced with all of them, even the married ones. As you can imagine, the married men whose wives had danced with him were looking at him very closely. What with the liquor they had already drunk, their tempers were getting short and they were getting ready to throw him out."

"Good," Tino interrupted, smacking his fist against his palm. "I wouldn't want my wife dancing with someone else."

"What wife?" Berto snickered. "You don't even have a girlfriend."

"Shhh," Pedro admonished again, but he added softly, "Let tío finish."

My uncle's voice became hushed, enhancing the suspense and making us all wonder what was to come. "When it was almost midnight and he was dancing away with a young and pretty girl, it so happened that the people saw a change come over this dark stranger. But it happened so slowly that for a while they thought it was their imaginations playing tricks with their eyes. His feet had turned to hooves!"

"*¡Madre mía!*" Horacio gasped. "¡El Diablo!"

"Sí," my uncle confirmed. "But the crowd didn't know that yet. My friend, mi carnal, told me they were all rubbing their eyes, blaming the cerveza and the mula, until before their very eyes, a tail slowly appeared from the bottom of the stranger's coat."

We gasped as one, even Jorge.

"But the worst was yet to come. Still the crowd didn't believe what they saw. They stood motionless and stared as if hypnotized. When the girl felt claws come out of his fingertips, she screamed, breaking the hold the stranger had on them. The crowd raced to her rescue, but the stranger just threw back his head and laughed. My carnal told me the laugh was so horrible that all the women covered their ears, the men who had jumped toward the stranger fell back in fear. And when they looked at his face—the face of a goat—they knew who the stranger was. With a great puff of smoke, he disappeared, leaving only his laugh echoing off the walls of the dance hall and the smell of sulfur to tell them he had really been el Diablo who had come straight from hell to teach them a lesson. And that is why, mis hijos, we do not dance during Lent." He paused, looking straight at Jorge as he finished, "That is why we show our respect to the Lord in all that we do."

"Phew." Horacio sighed noisily. "*¡Que barbaridad!*"

"You can say that again." Pedro gulped. "That was some story, tío."

Tío Daniel shrugged, "Believe it or not, but I do."

"So do I," Jorge agreed softly, "so do I."

A long silence followed my uncle's story, and I knew by looking at Berto, Horacio, Tino, and Pedro's eyes what they were all thinking: our own encounter with the supernatural had left many questions unanswered.

As Tío Daniel pulled his bag of punche from his shirt pocket and began the ritual of making a cigarette, he glanced from one of us to the other, waiting patiently for one of us to speak. Filiberto finally cleared his throat and asked whether my uncle believed in ghosts.

"Ah," he nodded, licking the cigarette paper and twisting it closed. "Sí," he continued, "I do believe in ghosts, for I saw one at the *campo santo* myself not so many years ago." He took up the unburned end of a branch and lit his cigarette before he added, "I was walking home and decided to take a short cut through the monte. I was passing right in front of the campo santo when I happened to look to my right and saw a figure in a long black *manto* and holding a candle as it stood over one of the graves. The shape made me think it was

Mamá, you know, small, in a long black shawl. But then I thought, no, what would Mamá be doing in the dark so late at night at the cemetery? I yelled anyway, thinking whoever it was might want me to walk her home."

He paused and took a long puff of his cigarette. The suspense made us all lean forward, and the conviction of his words added to our own confirmation of what we had seen one dark night not so very long ago. He shook his head. "The woman turned to look at me, and what I saw I will never forget, not as long as I live."

"What?" Pedro breathed, "What did you see, tío?"

"The face of death, mis hijitos, it was the face of La Muerte."

Horacio's groan turned to a grunt when Tino slapped his knee. He whispered, "What did you do, tío?"

"Do?" Tío Daniel shook himself. "I crossed myself and prayed all the way home, that's what I did."

He threw his cigarette butt into the fire and laid back on a bedroll, "I heard you boys had an *encuentro* with a difunto the other night, eh? Now it's your turn to tell a story, tell me about it."

"Sí," Pedro confirmed, filling my uncle in with the details and carefully omitting any mention of where we had been moments before our encounter.

We hadn't had the heart to tell Horacio about our pursuit of the figure in black after he had run home, and he looked at each of us in turn with something akin to awe that we had braved the unknown to see the face of the midnight traveler.

"But that's not all," Tino blurted. "Tell him, José."

My uncle's hazel eyes rested on my face, and he only waited to hear what I would add to our story. I looked from Horacio to Berto. Their eyes widened with Tino's unwary addition. And when I looked to Tino once more, his face was red, more from chagrin than from the flames of the campfire. My primos knew word for word what La Muerte's warning had been that evening: "Do not return tonight; for if you dare, you will see evidence of my work."

I hesitated, feeling my uncle's eyes still on me, waiting for me to speak. Could I tell the rest of our story without revealing what the gang and I had done that night? And was omitting part of La Muerte's warning the same as lying? I would have much to confess to the padre during my next confession if it was.

"Well," I began hesitantly, "you remember how we talked about La Muerte, tío, at the morada that afternoon I took the pie?"

At his nod I took a deep breath and let my words tumble from my mouth,

"When I left it was getting dark. I ran through the *vegas* feeling like there was someone behind me all the way."

I looked at my uncle for understanding, "You know I'm afraid of La Muerte and I thought it was my fear of her that made me feel that way, but after what we all saw that night, now I'm not so sure. I heard her tell me that she would show me her work."

At Horacio's gasp, I saw Pedro gently nudge him in the ribs, a gentle reminder not to reveal what we had done.

Hoping to save face for his earlier blunder, Tino piped up, "And that was what we saw, wasn't it, tío, evidence of her work—a difunto?"

Tío Daniel nodded, looking at me solemnly. Was it my imagination or was it disappointment I also saw in his eyes? Unable to meet his scrutiny, I looked away, busying myself with stacking another *leño* on the fire.

"What do you suppose it means?" asked Jorge innocently.

My uncle sighed heavily, "Perhaps it was a warning after all." He looked deeply at us all, including Jorge in his gaze. His next words hit us all like a ton of adobes, and not one of us was left unscathed by his insight. "I looked upon my own encounter as La Muerte being a messenger from God Himself. Perhaps she meant to warn you not to do something for which you may be sorry someday."

Horacio shook so badly we feared he was about to suffer an attack of conscience so great he would confess what we had done. The rest of us squirmed uncomfortably where we sat, willing him with our eyes to keep quiet. Each of us, including Jorge, felt the truth of my uncle's wisdom.

"Bueno," my uncle said, rising, "mis hijitos. Horacio won't get to sleep tonight, and we still have work to do tomorrow."

We laughed shakily, looking at Horacio who stood, trying hard to stop his shivering by holding his hands over the fire. We bade my uncle goodnight and watched as he was swallowed by the dark of the forest. None of us spoke much as we spread out our bedrolls. I sensed that had one of us proposed going back to the camp with the men, none would have objected. But as we tumbled into our blankets, each of us was alone with our thoughts and fears. I was sure we'd be prey to long hours of nightmares as we lay pretending to sleep, fighting our individual battles with both Tentación and Conciencia, which would eat at us tooth and nail until the break of dawn.

Confesión

——————

After our return from Las Cañadas, the remaining weeks of April passed quickly. There was much to do. As my father and Tío Daniel began to plow the earth for planting, the rest of the chores were left to me. Rising early, it was my task to carry water to both our houses from the well (located about a hundred fifty feet away in the middle of the pasture in front of our house). Then I had to feed the animals and gather the eggs from the henhouse. After school I cleaned the barn or chopped wood, taking armload after armload from the woodpile across the road by the outhouse up to both my uncle's and our house. Afterward, I walked up to the vegas where Papá and Tío Daniel were plowing. I hauled a pail filled with cool water and a couple of fresh buttery tortillas wrapped in a dishtowel for their afternoon snack.

The Friday before la *Semana Santa*, or Holy Week, I went alone to the meadow across the river where my father sat beneath the encinos watching my uncle take his turn with the plow. As I made my way to the ladderlike bridge only a foot above the water, I could hear my uncle whistling away as he trod over the clumps of earth being turned by the *arado* before him, his hands deftly holding the horses' reins. I always marveled at the way that both he and my father could stumble over the clods of dirt beneath their feet and yet follow through with row upon row of overturned earth in such straight lines going round and round the vega in an ever-smaller square until they were through. Even when they cut the aveno and alfalfa, they did it in such straight rows that from the monte the swaths of cut grasses looked like an ever-receding square. Whenever I tried, I tripped and stumbled so much that the horses carved a squiggly path like a huge snake such as the one Don Epifanio swore he had seen come down from the monte to slither its way through our meadow.

Don Epifanio had recently helped my father and spent an evening with us. While I watched my uncle plow, I remember the old man telling us at dinner about his encounter with the serpiente. A much younger man then, before I was even born, Don Epifanio had only an acre to his name and not much to do on it. He was known as "the visitor," and a welcome one at that. He spent most of his days calling upon compadres and compañeros, at times all the way to Mora twenty miles to the north or Las Vegas twenty miles to the south. His arrival heralded delight because he was an ever-ready helpmate and hard worker. He plunged into anything from wood chopping for elderly widows to making adobes for whatever building was under construction, it didn't matter. And the only recompense he ever required was to be fed by the woman of the house.

Anyway, the day he saw the serpiente, he had been riding up from Las Tusas toward home when he noticed that the forest became unnaturally still, the usual cawing of crows silenced by something. He wondered if a bear or mountain lion was prowling in the area. Even his horse became skittish and he proceeded with caution, glancing around the woods and in the branches above for any sign of a predator. Since his eyes were primarily focused upward, he didn't notice a log a few feet ahead directly in his path in the dense under-growth. But his horse rose on its hind legs and screamed with fear. Don Epifanio barely managed to keep himself in the saddle, cursed the horse for its stupidity, when all of a sudden, the log moved!

He told us it had been almost impossible to keep the frightened steed in check. Its eyes rolled, it whinnied urgently and it reared. The horse resisted his efforts to control it so he could get a better view of the log. But Don Epifanio stayed in the saddle, straining his vision to figure out what lay before him in the silent and seemingly uninhabited forest.

It happened in a matter of seconds (Don Epifanio snapped his fingers): the horse would not be restrained, and the now animated log curved toward him. The upper sides of a pointed snout revealed two beady yellow eyes with long black pupils like those of a cat and a huge open mouth revealing razor sharp teeth and a forked tongue. A hissing sound like that of a hundred rattlers emerged when it began to slither heavily toward him and the horse. Had he not clung to the saddle when the horse bolted, Don Epifanio was sure that he would have been supper to the largest *culebra* he had ever seen.

Although he was now too old to do much to assist his fellow man, he was welcome at everyone's table at any hour of the day or night. His compadres and compañeros remember every charitable act he contributed in the days of his youth and loved his stories. And though he seemed to have no fear of the dark as he wandered at night from vecino to vecino through the meadows, whenever he made his way over the monte, he kept a shotgun at his side in the saddle or a pistol at his waist. Neither he, nor anyone else for that matter, ever saw the fabled serpiente of Cañon again, yet everyone believed his tale.

I also chuckled, remembering that there were some people he shied away from. He had been quite a handsome man in his youth, he said (and my mother nodded in agreement), lean and broad-shouldered, but he was a confirmed bachelor. Nonetheless widows and single women in need of his hard-working nature had set their traps for him. Don Epifanio sat back and laughed about how many of those women had tried to worm their way into his affections by filling his stomach with all sorts of delicacies from the tastiest *menudos y tripas* to *panochas* and *sopas*. He patted his stomach and joked that he was so well fed that if he had not done so much back-breaking labor he would have grown to the size of a grizzly. He always concluded with a twinkle in his eye, proud that no woman's culinary masterpieces, however tasty, had ever snared him in what he called la *trampa del matrimonio*, the marriage trap.

A clod of dirt smacked my thigh and invaded my recollections. I glanced up to find my uncle on my left in the process of throwing yet another clump, missing my ear by inches when I ducked laughing. If my hands had been free, I would have returned his greeting with a well-placed clod or cow patty of my own, for my uncle was still young enough to play whenever the mood suited him.

"*¿Que piensas, hijo?*" he teased, halting the horses and wiping the sweat from his brow as I filled the scoop with water for him to drink.

"Del serpiente, tío," I answered as he took deep gulps of the fresh water.

Dribbling the remaining water over his head and handing the long-handled scoop back to me, he laughed. "Still waiting to see it yourself someday, eh?" He tousled my hair and, as he went back to the horses and picked up the reins again, called over his shoulder, "Cuidado, remember that sometimes we see things we really don't want to see."

Knowing that he referred to my escapades with the difunto and La Muerte, I shuddered inwardly. I definitely did not want to see the serpent. I'd had enough of supernatural encounters, thank you. Reaching the encinos, I plopped down next to my father, offering the water and tortillas. We sat in companionable silence as he ate, watching my uncle as he completed one row and continued down the mountainside.

"Why didn't you tell me about La Muerte and el difunto, José?" my father finally asked with gentle resolve.

I swallowed, again afraid that I would reveal what the gang and I had been up to that night, knowing that I could not lie to my father. I chose my words carefully, not wanting to hurt his feelings either for not having confided in him and also for knowing that between us there was always an unspoken understanding that made words unnecessary to know what was on each other's minds. "I … I was afraid."

"But wouldn't that have been more reason to tell me?" he asked. "Or were you and the boys up to something you should not have been?"

The time had come: confession. There was no way I couldn't tell him some of what happened; this was my father, el Hermano Mayor. I had to tell him everything. I rushed through my explanation, hoping for understanding. Beginning with my conversation with my uncle in the prayer room and revealing our gang's plan to return later that night to the morada, I told him how La Muerte's voice had come to me in the darkness, warning me not to return. But I told him to consider how much we all want to become Hermanos someday soon, which is why I had tried to convince myself that her voice had been but a figment of my imagination. I told him of the uncanny feeling we all had about being watched, yet how we had watched them from the window by the altar and were frightened away until we encountered the difunto.

He didn't get angry, nor did he chastise me as I thought he would. He simply took out his sack of punche and proceeded to roll a cigarette, his silence punishing me more than words.

It was terrible feeling I had hurt him, had deceived him, had spied on him when he was acting as the most revered of Hermanos. Yet admitting my sins to him made the heaviness I had felt all along in my heart and soul rise from my body. I clung to the feeling of being cleansed as I awaited his punishment. The words I expected didn't come. Instead came revelations which permeated the core of my being.

Lighting his cigarette, he said solemnly, "You are on your way to becoming a novicio, José. You will pray more fervently to La Muerte when you are an Hermano so that you will live a long life of humility and virtue."

Though I was unaware, my mouth must have opened in shock and a passing fly stumbled into my tooth. I spat it out, waiting for my father to continue.

"You probably did receive a message from La Muerte," he said in a low voice. "No, in fact, I am sure that it was her voice you heard, and you should have heeded her warning. *Pero ya tú sabes eso ¿qué no?*"

"Sí, I know that now."

"As for seeing the servicio for the novicios, now you know what will be required of you when you become one. You also know what Jorge revealed, so maybe you better follow the teachings of the church more seriously, eh?"

"Sí, Papá."

"You have questions, I am sure, and you have also received some answers which only serve to bring up more questions, but your time will come. Until that time you will not talk of what you have learned with anyone, nor will you question anyone, *claro?*"

"Sí," I whispered, but then I wondered, since I had already confessed to my father, the man to whom I would have to answer as a novicio if he were still Hermano Mayor then, would I also have to confess to the padre the next day? So I asked.

"Sí," he said. "Only the padre can absolve you from your sins. I can only help you to see the error of your ways."

I had never asked for punishment, but then I had never done anything much that would deserve a dire strapping—until now. I knew I would receive a harsh penance from the priest. I envisioned having to pray countless rosaries for the rest of my youth. But would that be enough? I waited, sitting quietly beside my father for what I thought was an eternity. When it seemed no harsh words of recrimination were forthcoming, I asked with reluctance, yet mixed with determination as well, "*¿Papá, que castigo me va a dar?*"

"*¿Yo?*" he asked with surprise. "I am not going to punish you, José. It seems to me that your own conciencia has done enough to you. You will remember what you have done, what you have discovered this Lent for the rest of your life. *Que no se diga más.*"

He was right. We never spoke of it again.

That Saturday afternoon as my mother and I entered the church to await the arrival of the priest who came up from Las Vegas for confession and mass, I was dismayed at first to see the capilla nearly filled. I visualized taking an interminable amount of time with my confession and probably an equal amount in my prayers for penance, and I shuddered at the thought of what the people would think. My mother, if she waited for me, would be mortified. But as I glanced around, relief overcame my anxiety when I noticed that there were more children than adults, and I remembered that the little ones would be making their Communion on Easter Sunday. I relaxed in the memory of my first confession, noting how Maestro Rubel had sat the children in the front pews, where he would send them one by one alphabetically to their brief confessions before the rest of us would be allowed to follow. By the time my turn came (for

I planned to be one of the last), the church would be nearly empty.

I noticed that Berto was already there, and the rest of the gang was forth-coming, I was sure. Kneeling with bent head, the more I contemplated how my own confession would go, the more I wondered just how much each of the rest of the gang would tell. Since I was aware of the change that had come over my primos since that fateful night of our scheme, I had a feeling we would all bare our souls to the kindly padre of our parish.

After a short period of prayer, I sat back in the pew and tried to look around. I could see the gang from where I sat without moving my head. There was Tino, squirming so much so in his seat, his mother administered a pinch that made his eyes water. Then there was Horacio, head bowed, kneeled despite his mother's prodding for him to sit back lest everyone else think he carried such an overwhelming weight of sin on his shoulders that he would never be absolved. Only Filiberto and Pedro were as still as I, eyes glued to the altar, faces somber. Being that confession is a private matter was, in itself, consolation; I could tell the padre everything and know that no one would know. I knew the gang felt it, too.

Before long, the little man who was our priest hustled into the church, tripping on his voluminous black robe. It looked two sizes too big and fluttered around him much like a storm cloud. Amid the titters and giggles of the very young, who were quickly silenced by a mother's pinch or a nudge, he arrived somewhat out of breath as always, as though he was forever late and hurrying to and fro at the last minute. He was also famous for his absent-mindedness, as if his thoughts always raced ahead of his actions. He had to pause repeatedly in whatever he was doing to collect them and continue with whatever he was saying at the time.

"*Tarde*," he mumbled by way of an apology, "*siempre tarde.*" After a short prayer to bless us all, he took his place in a tiny alcove behind the altar and awaited his congregants. The little ones went first, rapidly reciting their prayers and innocuous indiscretions before they could forget, hurrying back to their places for only a moment of penance before they were hustled out by their mothers. When they were through, everyone pretty much got up and went when each was ready. Occasionally a cumbersome body stepped to the rear of the altar to unburden himself of whatever made his footsteps so heavy. After his confession, with weight released from his heart, he seemed to float back to his pew to fulfill the prayer portion of his penance. The echoes of his steps were replaced by yet another who would also return uplifted.

I had plenty of time as I waited, and I couldn't help but notice that though the girls took very little time with the padre, the gang took about the same amount of time as the little old ladies in no rush to complete their confessions, though what they could be confessing I couldn't imagine, not compared to what the boys and I had weighing on our minds. When Pedro's turn took even longer than Prima Faustina's (the record holder; we had counted once), I got nervous. What would everyone think? After individual penance, most adults had hurried home for chores, so not that many were left. Nevertheless, I was sure those who had remained in the church noticed as well that when Berto returned to his place, Horacio, Tino, and Pedro were still kneeling, their heads bowed in interminable prayers, leaving no doubt in anyone's mind that they had done something that required much contemplation.

Finally, it was my turn. Taking a deep breath, I followed the steps of my cousins and friends, kneeled before the padre, and recited the words I already knew by heart. "Bless me, father, for I have sinned."

Domingo de Ramos

Palm Sunday was upon us, and we rose with the sun. While the men hurried about their morning chores, we younger ones followed the women and the girls of Cañoncito to the capilla to clean it from top to bottom before Sunday Mass. The boys and I usually took charge of the sconces, climbing on pews to take them down and outdoors, using our pocket knives to scrape the wax and replace only those candles that were too small. We also washed the saints on the altar and scrubbed down the pews with the girls. The women swept the vigas on the ceiling, the walls, and window sills, which always seemed to house an endless supply of flies and spider webs. They swept the wooden floor until they had us all sneezing. Finally, they replaced the altar linens and the curtains, leaving the mopping for last. Then we went home to dress for church.

The padre was always late. While most priests would conclude mass in less than an hour, our little padre easily took an hour and a half by the time he found and donned his vestments, taking extra time to chastise himself for his lack of memory. Then he searched for the Communion bread and the wine that he had left behind in his vehicle. While someone ran and fetched the holy articles and artifacts, he talked nonstop to no one in particular, yet to all of us, about the weather or some other inconsequential matter. By the time he began the search for his spectacles, one of the men would holler impatiently, "¡*Ya los tiene puestos, Padre!*" because he had them perched right on the end of his nose. By the time he found the right pages of his prayer book, we already had ours open and sat as patiently as we could, watching with silent mirth. My grandmother used to say that all of Padre's congregations were surely heaven-bound for our perseverance in following such an absent-minded messenger of God as he.

The afternoon of Palm Sunday was always a personal favorite of mine. While we changed into our work clothes, the women packed food and cleaning supplies into a wagon; then we went to the morada to give it a thorough cleaning. The Hermanos, who had gone up directly after Mass, already had a fire burning and hot water ready for the women when we arrived. They chopped firewood or moved the benches outside and the heavier furniture to the middle of the rooms for sweeping and scrubbing the wooden floors. The women tackled the kitchen first, and after swabbing the floors of the other rooms and leaving them to dry, we would eat lunch with los Hermanos.

Some of the girls did the dishes while the boys and I trooped to the prayer room to remove burnt-down candles and take the candle holders outside to scrape out built-up wax with our trusty knives. The glass ones were fairly easy, except for the places which had ornately curved designs. The wooden ones took more time to clean because they were made by each of los Hermanos and we took care not to scrape off the black paint. Having finished the dishes, the girls wanted the washtub emptied outside and the dirty water replaced. Of course, Pedro offered his muscles (with Berto's assistance) to haul the tub. Luciana teased that if he couldn't manage a measly washtub, he wouldn't get her over the threshold when they married. The grimace on his face turned to a blushing grin. "You'd better weigh less than a tub full of soapy water." Luciana gave him a playful slap with her hand. "Yikes … ouch!" he yelped when he backed into the tub and hot water splashed on his pant legs. Our laughter at Pedro's expense came and went throughout the day.

On this day, the adults tolerated our humor. We knew that any sort of play or mirth was not allowed from Holy Tuesday through *Sabado de Gloria*, the Saturday before Easter. And though there was playful chatter between us as the girls washed and dried the santos and candleholders, we all took our responsibilities seriously lest we break anything and be disgraced. We carefully placing them all on a bench beside the door. But in the prayer room, the women did their work in absolute silence. In that room, no one laughed.

Mid-afternoon, we gathered in the cocina and my father offered our prayers before lunch. There were pots of beans, chiles colorado y verde, *quelites* (spinach), boiled eggs, and tortillas by the dozen. The women served plate after plate while the girls carried food to the table for los Hermanos, who were always served first. When the weather was too cold, we sat on benches placed against the wall of the long kitchen, but today was warm so we carried over-filled plates beneath the trees. The women and girls ate when the men finished, and for a short while los Hermanos joined us to enjoy their after-meal cigarettes or last cups of coffee while they rested. They made us feel like men, even for such a short time, as they engaged in conversation that included us. We cringed when our mothers beckoned us to help the girls to do the dishes.

We shuffled morosely over to the tubs where the girls were busily piling dishes for scrubbing and drying, but instead Berto's mother told us to begin moving the furniture back into place. Proudly squaring his shoulders, Pedro flexed his muscles before Luciana, tossing her a morsel of thought to chew upon, "They know where to find muscles."

Luciana's hand clutched her throat as if she were choking. Unperturbed, Berto lifted his nose in the air amid the girls' giggles following his own muscle-man walk into the morada. The rest of us, mimicking his steps in our own variations, stepped into line and sauntered single file past the girls as manly as we could be. I felt my ears turn red and hoped we didn't look like apes. I knew we all wanted them to see the men that existed beneath the surface of our adolescent bodies.

When we were finished, the girls assisted the women replacing clean curtains and altar cloths for the dingy, yellowed ones. We carried in the candleholders and saints, placing them reverently on the altar, a task we relished because when we left, we knew the Hermanos would pray before the altar that we ourselves had adorned. La Muerte was still perched on her stand in the corner by the altar, and I took the time to bow to her each time I entered or left the room. She was right beside the door, and the others squeezed by as far from her as they could get. Curiously, I no longer feared her because my uncle and my father had convinced me that she was another symbol of my faith, not a menacing entity.

Catching Berto's glance one of the times I bowed to her, I shrugged, said simply, "I owe her one," and left it at that.

Prima Marta carried a bucket of sudsy water and cloths over to the woman in black. I asked if I could have the honor. She looked at me curiously, knowing that in the past I had shied away from La Muerte like the rest of the children, but she nodded silently, handed me the bucket and linen, and left me to the task.

My friends turned with a sort of incredulous look of shock.

"I wouldn't be caught dead …" Gregoria began, closing her mouth with an audible snap when she realized to whom she was referring and that La Muerte would, no doubt, be offended.

Even Tino didn't taunt me with words, just shook his head as if to echo Gregoria. Shuddering when he realized La Muerte could probably hear his thoughts as well, he took to his heels out the door. Alone again, I continued washing her, wondering if that was a tingling I felt when my fingertips gently touched the cloth to her forehead and rubbed her bony face with soft strokes? As I worked, I felt compelled to confess to the Lady of Darkness, the one to whom I truly felt obligated, that I was sincerely sorry I had offended her by not obeying her wishes. I couldn't be sure, but I felt a sense of gentleness as I slowly and reverently cleaned her face, as though she were thanking me somehow for my gentle ministrations.

A gasp and whispers brought me out of my daze, and I turned to find Tío Daniel and my mother watching, the rest of the gang and the girls in the background. I smiled sheepishly and I shook my head. "*Ya no la tengo miedo. Porque me ha cuidado.*" Explaining to my uncle that I no longer feared her because she watched over me. I think I gained a new respect from my elders and my peers that day. One can never be sure.

La Semana Santa

Our wait for Holy Week passed quickly, and *Martes Santo*, Holy Tuesday, arrived. *La Cuaresma*, the period of Lent, was the most important to los Hermanos. Those of us who followed their order practiced our faith more actively than any other time of the year. Since these next few days were the most sorrowful in the lives of Christ and His Mother, we showed our respect for Their suffering during Christ's last days on earth. And even though there were still the daily chores during la Semana Santa, plowing, fixing fences, making adobes—everything—stopped. Even school was suspended from Wednesday on, for we would be at prayer with los Hermanos each afternoon until Easter Sunday.

The atmosphere in the schoolroom was muted. Maestro drilled us on our catechism as he did each year on this day. He tried to instill in us the solemnity of the next few days by making us remember why this period of our Catholic faith was so important. School finally ended. We were relieved to have gotten through Maestro's review, but we were frustrated that we were not allowed to play, much less laugh. Instead, from the age of three, when our meager chores were finished we had to sit quietly in contemplation of the season, sometimes for hours at a time. Our mothers made sure we would not forget ourselves and resort to horseplay.

On this Holy Tuesday, I returned home to do only those chores that were absolutely necessary before having a light supper and praying a rosario with my mother. That night, before going to bed, my mother prayed before her altar where she burned at least one candle day and night for our health, and especially now for my brother's safety.

My father had been at the morada since after noon. As usual when he was away during these nights of la Cuaresma, my thoughts turned to images of the rituals performed within the quiet walls of the morada in utter secrecy. But tonight, now that I knew of the inestimable power my father held over the heads of his Brothers, my discomfort was worse. I tossed and turned restlessly. "Perhaps you'd like to sleep in the barn, José." My mother protested. "That squeaking bed will keep me awake the all night if you don't stop tossing around."

I stilled immediately, my body like a board, and without moving around, I willed myself to visualize the interior of the morada which I knew by heart.

In my mind's eye, I wandered through the familiar rooms of the morada, looking at all the objects like tables, cupboards, coatracks. Against a wall in the middle room, there was a heavy trunk with a wooden box beside it, roughly three feet long by one foot wide. The trunk held the numerous linen manteles that covered the altar and curtains for the windows and altars of both the morada and the capilla. The glass candleholders and *chiflones* of the lamps nestled within the folds of the linens. The wooden box, however, held my eyes as it always did when I was allowed in the sacred building.

Ever since reading about Pandora's Box in school years before, the box not only piqued my curiosity, but also turned reverent awe into terrifying temptation. The part of me so influenced by the devil, Tentación, wished desperately to know what holy relics lay within. At the same time, my angel, Conciencia, warned that it was not yet time for me to know. Instinctively, I knew that my childhood innocence would disappear when the contents of that ancient box were revealed.

I moved on in the dream that was not a dream, the slow-moving picture of my mind taking me further through the morada, into the doorway of the room reserved for religious services. About as large and as long as the cocina, the prayer room loomed before me as clouds of fog rose from the wooden planks of the floor beneath. For the first time, I wondered at the detail in my imaginings. Up to then my dream was, I was sure, only that: the innocent dream of a boy who wanted to become a novicio. Had it not been for the fog I could have sworn I was really there, and I wondered what it meant. Surely the billowing fog had some significance. Didn't it?

Glancing slowly to my right, I glimpsed the large wooden crucifix. Its four-inch thick planks—the vertical one roughly eight feet long, the horizontal one wide enough for a grown man's hands to reach to its tips when crucified—glistened with the glossiest, blackest paint I had ever seen. I did not know what wood it was made of, but although it took two men just to move it from one location to another, it was carried on the shoulders of only one Penitente before the Estaciones on *Viernes Santo*, Holy Friday.

From year to year it was never the same Hermano, though the selection process for the Penitente who bore the cross in tribute to our Savior was another mystery. Emulating the steps taken by Christ to His place on Monte Calvario was an honored position. I had my doubts, though, because the cross was so heavy that it seemed a penance, a punishment to carry it from the morada to the capilla. Although it was no great distance from one to the other, by the time the cross-bearer reached the capilla, went through the hour-long service kneeling and rising throughout, and trudged back to the morada for another four to five hours of whatever occurred there, a lesser man would be exhausted and ready for bed. Yet the very next day the honored one was always doing his chores without complaint.

Looking away from the crucifix, I saw La Muerte. I shuddered inwardly. Even in a dream her skeletal countenance, teeth exposed, was ominous, and her shiny black eyes followed my movements. I tore my eyes from hers, for she could see me when no one else was aware of my presence.

I looked at the morada altar, covered with crocheted manteles and constructed like the one in the capilla. It was filled with retablos and santos placed there by the boys and me only days before. The black crucifixes of the Hermanos stood between and among the santos. Aglow from the numerous candles, light emanated from the altar and flickered eerily over the heads of the Hermanos who, in my dream vision, kneeled as one before it. Each wore a candlelight halo much like the tongues of fire given by the Holy Spirit to Jesus' Apostles.

The prickly sensation of awe-inspired reverence pervaded my being just as it did each time I was privileged to see the Hermanos at prayer. Again, the billowing fog permeated the room and enveloped los Hermanos to their thighs. Though I was not actually there, I was a silent and uninvited witness to their ritual.

In shock, I blinked, vividly aware that I was still awake. The scene before my eyes did not disappear. The chill that electrified my body should have warned me than that I should try to let the vision go, that I should pray for it to leave me. But I did not, could not let it go.

As the fog dissipated for a moment, I saw one Hermano clothed only in white pants kneeling before the altar. Since their backs were to me, I didn't know who it was, and I prayed fervently that he was not my father. My dream eyes would not close; instead, they moved down the man's back, where scarlet color seeped into the cloth. With a will of their own, my gaze moved downward to the man's knees where blood also soaked the white garments. I felt chilled to the bone.

A realization suddenly staggered my awareness: my eyes possessed an unnatural power to see even the minutest of details, but they also picked up fragments of earlier things that I had chosen to disregard. I remembered, with a start, the evidence in the kitchen that los Hermanos had eaten, that their coats and hats hung from the pegs, and that they were here. I remembered the absent lock from the wooden box, wondering suddenly how I could have overlooked it before.

In my reverie, I blinked, rubbing my fists in my eyes, unable to shake the images before me. I was forced to look at what I had wrought. My eyes focused, against my will, on the Hermano kneeling before the altar. I saw gravel beneath the knees of the white-clad Penitente, some surely embedded in his skin through the thin cloth.

I looked at my father. He stood and walked through the cloud of mist to the door. In the mute silence of my vision (for I was now sure that this was no ordinary dream), I opened my mouth to protest, to release me from this binding of my consciousness, but he didn't hear me. His eyes were on the door, his mouth speaking words I was unable to hear. His occasional pause indicated that he spoke to someone outside When he reached the door, he admitted yet another Hermano in white, and I noticed in his other hand a horsehair scourge.

When this Hermano knelt beside the other, whose back now glistened with crimson, his face turned slightly, revealing his identity for a moment before he bared his back for my father, who raised his hand a bit higher as if to signal something. The fog rose again from the flooring and covered the unnerving sight of the blood. I backed away, clapping my hands to my mouth to stifle my screams, my eyes wide open in horror. My father turned ever so slowly, his eyes boring into my own.

Merging his thoughts with my own, he said without moving his lips, "¿*Ves*? See what penitence lies ahead for you now because of what you have witnessed this night?"

I struggled to run away, to flee from the disappointment in his keen and knowing eyes. I could not. My efforts were in vain. The fear in my heart froze me where I stood, and as the white fog rose around me, it turned into the blackness of unconsciousness, and I could see no more.

Hermanitos

"Ahhh!" A cry broke from my throat that didn't sound like mine. I jumped as though shot, sitting straight up in my cot. After a moment, I realized the cry had come from me in the depths of reliving the *pesadilla* of the night before. Where was my mother? She was nowhere in sight. When I stood, I caught my image in the mirror over the wash basin. If my mother hadn't risen before me today, she would have been frightened for the pale youth that gazed back, heavy-eyed with the dreams of a troubled conscience. I said a prayer of thanks to God for small miracles.

The sun was well into the sky. I couldn't remember having slept so late before, but then again, I had never had such a dream-filled night. I willed myself to calm my pounding heart, hoping I had time to compose myself. I was halfway through a half-hearted attempt at breakfast when my mother returned, asking if I had finally slept well.

"You were thrashing around half the night, *hito*. It wasn't until early this morning that you finally quieted down." Her next words made the few spoon-fuls of atole I had fought down my throat bubble in my stomach. "Good thing your papá slept at the morada last night, or he would have never gotten any sleep."

I bent over my bowl, hiding my hollow-eyed countenance. I thought I knew why Papá hadn't come home: First, the *Coadjutor* would care for the wounds of the Hermano who had done his penance, then my father would stay at the morada to *velar*, or to watch over him. I forced myself to gulp down another warm, mushy spoonful of atole. I finished quickly, excusing myself to the outhouse across the road. I barely made it before my stomach rebelled.

The pesadilla of the night before weighed heavily in my heart, and the small woman dressed in black who waited for me under the shade of apple trees by the acequia watching my approach thought the same. I saw it in her eyes when I bent to kiss my abuela's cheek.

"*Yo se,*" she said quietly, clasping my arms and lowering me to the bench at the edge of the water. "*Yo se que ha pasado.*"

She knows what has happened? A fist of confused questions clenched my heart at her words, and a silent inquiry emerged. What? What did she know? How did she know?

Her eyes bore into mine in search of the burden in my soul that she would take upon her shoulders, giving comfort to my own. I looked at the tiny woman with her long, silver braid knotted at the nape of her neck. Her aquiline nose and high cheekbones, pink-hued like two summer apples, gave her face a tender expression. Hers was the face that I swam to out of the countless fevers of my youth; hers was the face that calmed me when I was in pain for myself or for my loved ones. She was more than my grandmother. As the *médica* of our small valley, she was the only "doctor" I knew. I trusted her.

Gramma never wore a dress or skirt and blouse combination that wasn't navy blue, dark brown, gray, or black. Though my grandfather had died when my father was a boy, she never remarried, and I always wondered with a pang of sadness if she was in perpetual mourning. Her dresses almost touched the ground. And her apron, its edges intricately embroidered by her own hand, lay ready in her lap for whatever she scooped up within its folds to carry home, eggs from the henhouse or herbs she gathered for seasoning foods or making *remedios*.

This diminutive woman, my grandmother, inspired the respect of the people of our valley, whether they were those thankful many who were grateful for her sagacious knowledge of herbal remedies and medicinal practices, or those thankless few, new to our valley, who feared her and thought her a witch.

Nodding briefly, she relaxed visibly as if her eyes were satisfied with their exploration of my soul. She told me she knew what I had seen, for her own troubled sleep had been marked by a series of images overlapping one another in such rapid succession that she had awakened confused. My cry, however, put an end to her confusion in an instant, and the fragments of the dream she had pieced together revealed their meaning.

My eyes widened visibly, I'm sure, at her explanation, for I was baffled by what she had revealed. How could she have shared my dream? I quaked at the thought that followed on the heels of my first: was my grandmother a witch? The details of her dreams matched my own, with the exception that I didn't sense her presence there at all. And now a new question entered my perception: why?

My knees began to shake, my spine, to quiver, but she continued. "It was an *aviso*," she said, a premonition. "It really is nothing to fear, hijo."

The look in my eyes must have told her I needed more reassurance than that. And her impish smile warned me that she was up to her explanations her way, by always answering questions with questions.

"You have always followed your religion, eh?"

I nodded. "Sí."

"You have not stolen?" She tried to look grave, failed miserably.

I shook my head, "No."

"You haven't murdered?" She fought back another smile, a bit of it escaping. "No."

"You have not coveted?" I shook my head.

"Taken the Lord's name in vain? Committed adultery? None of the others, no?" "No."

She smiled, "Then you have nothing to fear. And when you become a novicio, you will know what is expected of you."

"But that's just it," I blurted, "to have seen what my father did ..."

Her hand rose, halting my words.

She spoke quietly, "Your father does only what is asked of him. You have seen only a piece of the puzzle you must complete. Does that make you so knowledgeable that you can presume to question?"

I blushed visibly under her accusing eyes.

"Do not speak of this to anyone, eh?" she admonished. Before she got my promise, she added, "Think upon what I have told you." Her finger pointing in my face as she rose, she urged, "Think upon what is before you, and think, above all, of what you must do."

About noon that day, Holy Wednesday (*Miercoles Santo*), the boys and I were allowed to visit one another unguarded, having gained the trust of our mothers in the last year—finally. Besides, it was also common knowledge that with the way loud voices and raucous laughter echo throughout the valley, our mothers, who have the inherent ability to discern their own child's voice from that of his peers, would be awaiting our arrival. And none of us wanted to confront the disapproval etched on their faces if we were late; none of us wanted to dispel their trust.

While we waited for the Estaciones to begin at two o'clock, the gang and I sat beneath the towering cottonwoods outside of Horacio's house, directly across from the morada where los Hermanos were ensconced. It was no accident that for the next few days we would abandon our usual meeting place, the arbolera down from my house, for Horacio's. By unspoken but mutual agreement, it had become a practice we had established with the trust of our elders. We congregated here because we wanted to be close enough to hear the faint strains of the alabados, instilling in us a sense of peace and serenity (which I so desperately craved by now). We also wanted to follow their procession to the church in their footsteps, a practice that made us feel that we, too, were a part of them. In truth, since we wholeheartedly shared the desire to become members of the cofradía, los Hermanos had made it clear that they tolerated our presence with pride because we were the next generation of Penitentes.

Los Hermanos had been secluded in the morada since early that morning. We talked quietly and turned pieces of pine in our hands, thinking of what we would whittle as we waited. At any other time, our waiting would not have been so patient, but we were of an age to realize the solemnity of this Holy Week. Horacio's mother was only a few yards away (the door of her cocina open to her watchful eyes and acute hearing to remind us of those times in our youth when we disgraced ourselves by forgetting our respect to our Savior), so we were not about to succumb to the temptation of child play. We heard her chastising her two youngest children, Julio, a boisterous five-year-old, and Patricia, a little girl of seven. Her voice, wafting on the spring breeze, brought vivid recollections. From what we gathered, the two had been caught playing with Patricia's paper dolls—pictures of people and clothes that had been cut from a Sears catalog. Their voices raised in a duet of wails, but quieted shortly, and we knew without seeing that she gave them a glass of milk, probably a bit of tortilla (since we all, young and old alike, fasted for these last four days of Lent) while they were made to sit and listen to their mother tell them quietly but firmly why they could not play. Then they would spend at least an hour sitting in opposite corners, left alone to contemplate their sins until they dozed off. Oh yes, stifling our chuckles and shaking our heads at the frivolity of the very young, the activity in the house provided us with respite from our burdened thoughts. We each remembered having gone through the same punishment in this last week of Lent; perplexity, rather than understanding, governed our actions when we were too young to realize its importance and solemnity.

It was Pedro who began whittling first, and we watched with interest, wondering what he had thought of to carve.

"*¿Qué vas a hacer?*" Tino asked, wiggling his brow. "*¿Animal o mujer?*"

The gang chuckled quietly, for Pedro, talented at carving creatures of the forest, had already created an assortment from deer to squirrels, and he boasted that one day he would take his creations to town to be sold at Maloof's in Las Vegas. Having also a knack for figures, however, he had even carved a woman in the past which became his little sister's birthday surprise, a doll of her own.

When we quieted, he replied soberly, "*Un santo,*" though he would not reveal exactly which one.

Little did any of us know that with that first saint he began to carve on Holy Wednesday, he established his niche in the world, for he would become known far and wide as one of the most talented santeros New Mexico ever produced.

Horacio, too, started carving awkwardly, holding his piece of wood as best he could because of his injured wrist. "*Un crucifijo,*" he announced before we could ask, "my own crucifix for when I become an Hermano."

We contemplated this in silence for a while, wondering if perhaps our time to become novicios was nearer than we hoped, so all of us except Pedro proceeded to make our own crucifixes. We worked in silence for not more than a few minutes before Berto broke our concentration.

"I have an idea," he whispered. "Why didn't any of us think of it before?"

"Qué?" Tino asked. "What is it?"

Simultaneously, Horacio groaned, cradling his arm, "If it's anything like your last idea, I don't want any part of it. Count me out."

"I don't think it's anything that'll get us in trouble," Berto said dryly, frowning at Horacio's lack of faith. "I just thought, since we know a little of the rules the novicios have to follow, we can follow them ourselves until we're really allowed to join. It'll be like a secret trial period to see if we can handle it."

We greeted his proposal with silence, whether of protest or serious thought, I wasn't sure. "My gramma told me they were really secret back in my grampo's day," I blurted, for lack of knowing what to say. I revealed what my grandmother had confided to me about the black hoods, looking at the others nervously for fear that they could somehow sense that I harbored more of my grandmother's wise words in my heart.

"So will we have someone act as hermano mayor and the other officers, *secretario del mandatorio, rezador, cantador,* and the rest?" Horacio, always the worrier of our lot, added, "Which, I have to remind you, we know nothing about."

"They're elected," Tino piped up, "I heard my father tell my mother once that they vote for everything."

"Well, then," Horacio interrupted, "first, let's vote on whether we do this

or not. Think of everything else los Hermanos do. Will we elect an Hermano
Mayor to be responsible for ordering our punishment if we ever need it?"

"He's right," I agreed, the images of my dream returning. "I'm not sure I
want to be whipped or told to whip myself if I do something wrong." The implication was apparent to the others. I trusted none of us with that kind of responsibility. If we did this, I knew we would be sincere in trying to act as real
Hermanos. And the fact remained that they did, from time to time for whatever
reason, suffer dire penances under their own hands. I added, with much reluctance, "At least not until we're real novicios under the authority of the real
Hermano Mayor."

We contemplated this worrisome thought, resuming our whittling and
wondering with trepidation how any of us could possibly act as leader. We had
changed, of that I was certain, but would the power and the responsibililty of
the one chosen as leader make him merciful or merciless? An image of a whip,
raised to strike, returned from my dream to make me shudder inwardly.

Pedro leaned forward, his elbows on his knees. "I don't know about you
guys, but with all that has happened to us this Cuaresma, I don't think I, for
one, will ever do anything really bad again."

Our mutual nods confirmed that the rest of us felt the same.

"But what if ..." Horacio began again.

"Then we'll come to that when or if it happens," Berto interrupted. "If
any of us does anything that he really should be punished for we can decide together what it will be."

"What we really need is a set of rules to follow," Tino proposed, leaving
for the moment the idea of a chosen leader undecided.

"And if anyone really needs to be *castigado*," Pedro added, "then we can
vote on whether he should do something else, like confess to his father and let
him do the punishing, rather than try to get away with it like we have before."

"Right," Berto agreed, "so let's vote. Do we do this, or not? I say sí."

Tino and Pedro nodded their response, the three waiting tensely for Horacio's and my response.

I debated for a moment, my grandmother's words echoing in my thoughts
until, with a start, a certain understanding came over me. Though I had broken
no Commandment, I had experienced much to mold my character this
Cuaresma. My encounters with La Muerte and el difunto, as well as my uncle
and father's wise *consejos*, my vision of the night before, and my grandmother's
sage explanation, all had been designed by a higher power to assure my readiness
to become a novicio. What better way to fulfill my destiny than to act in the ex-

ample of los Hermanos? I followed my intuition. "Sí," I nodded, completely relaxed in my decision.

We all turned to Horacio, who squirmed in his seat, seeking mercy in our eyes.

"You don't have to, you know," I told him quietly. "Just remember to keep
quiet for the rest of us if you say no."

"Sure," Berto nodded, "it's okay, Horacio. You can say no."

"No," Horacio shook his head, a faint smile momentarily softening his features, "I mean yes. I just meant no, I don't want to say no."

The blush covered his face as it always did when he rambled on with confusing explanations which only served to confuse us more. It made us laugh, as
though we needed the relief of laughter now that we made our decision. But
we muffled our giggles, remembering that Horacio's mother was just inside,
ready to make us feel like children once again. Then, too, remembering that
we had just made a choice that would come to be the most important one for
our futures, we forced ourselves into a sobriety befitting the conclusion to our
lives as children.

"Bueno," Berto began, "why don't we at least elect a secretario to take down
the rules and minutes of our meetings?"

"Well," Horacio began, hesitantly, "I have a ledger Mamá didn't need, and
I could go get it now and write down everything we decide." He paused. "But,
whoever gets elected can use it anyway." He rose from his knees, and looking
back over his shoulder periodically, stumbled his way to his house.

"Well?" Berto, still acting as spokesman and leader, asked, "¿Está bien if
we elect Horacio secretary? He does have the best handwriting, and he does
take the best notes for tests. Raise a finger if you all agree." All of us lifted a finger, a unanimous decision.

"Okay," Tino agreed, "but he better keep that ledger hidden."

"Right," Pedro nodded, "but where?"

Horacio returned, carrying the long gray book and a pencil, looking at us
warily, and sat down without speaking. We returned his gaze, trying hard not
to smile, our eyes twinkling with unconcealed mirth enough to give us away, I
was sure. He wanted to be our record-keeper, but the desire to ask was killing him.

"Well?" he finally blurted. He looked impatiently from one of us to the other.

Berto regarded us, shaking his head soberly before breaking into a wide
grin. "It was unanimous," he smiled, "you're our secretario, Horacio—unless
you decline, of course."

Horacio blinked and his face broke into a proud smile when we all nodded
our agreement. Opening his ledger importantly, his pencil poised and ready,

he replied, "I accept, thank you, guys—uh, hermanos," he corrected, blushing again as he waited to fill in our rules.

"Where were we?" Pedro asked. "Lemme fill Horacio in about hiding the ledger."

That done, Berto continued, "Look, it's almost time for the Estaciones. I really don't think we can even get to the rules today. But how about we conduct all our meetings at the caves? Papá gave me a couple of big pieces of *tarpolios* I use for a lean-to. I can cut a piece of canvas and wrap the book up, hide it. No one but us goes there anyway."

"I don't know," I added, "sometimes the little kids go out there. What if they find it?"

"Not if we bury it," Pedro suggested. "We can dig a hole by the caves and cover it up. If we mark it with stones like a *descanso*, no one will bother it. Descansos are holy."

He was right. Descansos were holy, and no one dared to bother the piles of stones, some of them with crosses carved into a piece of laja or some with a small wooden cross in their center which marked the resting places and the passage of the processions made by los Hermanos to the campo santo from the capilla. How many of these descansos, which still dotted the countryside, marked the passing of one of my own ancestors, carried in the wooden coffin made by his fellow Penitentes, and the mourners who stopped to rest while singing alabados for their departed brother or a member of his family? I lost count of the number of funeral processions I had attended for those of our little cañon who had passed on, lost count of the *sudarios*, prayers for the dead, and the many descansos I, too, had had a hand in making for someone I had loved while the Hermanos sang.

I wondered if we could effectively conceal our own descanso, which would not really be a descanso, so that los Hermanos and everyone else would think it was a real one and leave it undisturbed. "We'll have to put it sorta close to the path from the church to the cemetery," I spoke, "but like hidden by a bush or trees so the Hermanos don't notice it. I'm sure they know where all their descansos are."

"And we certainly don't want anyone stopping to pray over it like my gramma does," Tino added. "Whenever I go with her to visit grampo in the campo santo, she stops to pray a sudario for the dead ones at every descanso. She even makes me get another stone and place it on the pile every time, so that her prayer will be marked and so that the descanso will never be erased."

"Can you imagine?" Horacio whispered, trying hard not to laugh, "I can just see it now, Tino and his gramita walking to the campo santo and she spots our pile of rocks. She kneels down to pray, and Tino adds another rock to our pile."

"What a thought." I smiled, holding my sides to restrain my giggles. "You would have to say something funny knowing we can't laugh."

Tino was, by far, having the hardest time holding his laughter in, clapping his hands over his mouth as his mind supplied a most vivid picture of his little grandmother praying to a pile of stones which would mark our hiding place. Even Berto pinched himself and Pedro made faces to prevent the emergence of a smile, which made us get the urge to giggle all over again.

"Okay, okay," Pedro finally got hold of himself enough to speak. "Why don't we think about if and who we want to be hermano mayor until tomorrow, and we'll meet at the caves to vote and start working on our rules?"

We agreed, Horacio hiding the ledger in the barn temporarily and Berto reminding us to remind him to take the *tarpolio*. We resumed our whittling in silence as each of us pondered the question of trust between friends or perhaps our own desires to be the leader of our own secret society. Our heads slowly raised in unison only a moment later, our ears discerning the faint tintinnabulation of a pipe, not unlike that of a flute. Our eyes locked for an instant before our heads turned in the direction of the morada. In the quiet of the breezy spring afternoon, the indistinct melody of the Penitentes' alabado floated over us, surrounding us with tranquility. When the door to the morada opened and the Hermanos began to shuffle out, I knew the feeling was mutual. Pedro rose and held his palm out to the center of our group. The rest of us stood together, Tino placing his hand over Pedro's, and Berto, mine, and Horacio's following. The circle of our brotherhood was complete.

"We'll be Hermanos yet, you guys," Pedro vowed, a grin escaping his usual restraint.

"Hermanos," Berto breathed.

Touched by a kindred emotion of togetherness, we felt assured that we had made the right decision to watch out for one another. We indeed felt as close as brothers.

We broke apart, watching as los Hermanos stood as a group, breathing the fresh mountain air deeply. As some stepped into the shade beneath the trees and others stretched their arms and took the kinks out of their knees from many hours of kneeling, I found myself searching for the Hermano of my vision. I looked for the one whose grimace of pain when he leaned his back on a rock or who hobbled in anguish as he walked would alert me to his identity. I didn't find him.

I looked away, perplexed for a moment before realization dawned. I knew who he was. My grandmother had already confirmed that what I had thought a dream was, in truth, a vision: an aviso, or premonition of my destiny that I alone was destined to fulfill. I willed my thoughts to focus on the day and the somber celebration that was to follow.

We knew that this day los Hermanos would wait for their families and vecinos to accompany them, for the Estaciones would be recited while they walked to the campo santo from the morada. The bell of the capilla tolled its first call to the people of Cañoncito, summoning everyone from their homes. Overlooking the road from the mountainside where we stood, we could see all the way up to the Luceros, the large family already trudging up the road. So were Prima Marta, my tía, and my mother, the three then stopping at Filiberto's for his mother and sister. Glancing down the road, we could see all the way to Prima Raquel's, and the two black-shawled women that were she and Comadre Sara making their way to the capilla where they would wait to join up with the procesión. Before long, most everyone congregated outside the gate on the road leading from the morada to the capilla, most of the older girls and women carrying more food inside for the Hermanos, knowing that they had a long night ahead.

"*Ya vienen*," Horacio murmured.

Yes, I thought, here they come. We watched with quiet reflection as los Hermanos took their usual places: my uncle in the lead, raising the bandera high; my father behind, his crucifix in one hand, his black book of alabados open in the other; and the rest in two rows of five men each, now that both Jorge and Pablito were members.

"I wonder if the novicios are full-fledged Hermanos already," Tino whispered.

The boys looked at me for confirmation. I shook my head, disappointing them. "I don't know. Papá doesn't tell me much."

Pocketing our knives and our pieces of wood, we waited as they walked to the gate which opened to the road leading to the capilla. When los Hermanos were in their places in the middle of the road, we moved forward, keeping back about a dozen feet from their group. Horacio's mother and siblings joined us as the *campana* tolled for the second time, and I knew Primo Victoriano had already been there probably for most of the morning, praying alone. No longer able to make the walk from the morada, he was still an Hermano at heart and would be until his death. I resolved to join him the next day, to help him light the candles and ready the wood for the fire, accompanying him at prayer before meeting at Horacio's to follow the procesión once more.

Taking my little black book from my jacket pocket, I opened it to the *Ofrecimiento*, the alabado by which we would appeal to Jesús for the offering of our prayers. The boys drew me into their midst, placing me in the center so they could try to follow the words, which would be rough going due to the ruts in the road to the capilla, the almost non-existent path to the campo santo, and the penmanship of my grandfather's hand blurred with age. It was a good thing we were already familiar with most of the words anyway, yet seeing them in print seemed to bring them that much closer to our hearts, and we strained our eyes to follow along as my father and my uncle's voices mingled together in the first strains of the alabados.

"Amantisimo Jesús, Redentor salud y vida de nuestras almas en unión de aquella divina intención con que en la tierra orasteis a Vuestro Eterno Padre os ofresos y presento por mí y por todos mis prójimos, este espíritual ejercicio en memoria honor reverencia y culto de Vuestra sagrada pasión y muerte y de cuantas pasos distes ...."

The words rose mournfully as my father and uncle offered their hymn to sweet Jesus, their Redeemer of health and life of our love. In his own individual heartfelt voice, each in communing to his Savior confirmed his own faith. In union with that divine intention, which on earth Christ prayed to His own Eternal Father, they asked for His offerings and representation for himself and for all his fellow men. This spiritual exercise was in Christ's honored and revered memory and in the worship of His sacred passion and death and the countless steps He took.

The voices of all los Hermanos rose in their own varied pitches, each one recognizable among his Brothers, while we, in our own little detached procession echoed their voices, feeling the impact of the words like a great weight on our shoulders for all the sins we had ever committed. *"Ohhh, amantisimo Dios, por nuestro remedio y rescate, y pretendo [sic] ganar todas las indulgencias que han concedido vuestras vicarios en la tierra. Y os ofresco todo en remisión de mis pecados y de las penas merecidas por ellos y por las almas de mis mayores obligaciones según el orden de caridad o justicia que debo y puedo hacer ...."*

The inharmonious and hauntingly beautiful unison of los Hermanos' message inspired such pain, for we were reminded that the unselfish love of Christ was forgotten by mankind who, at times, selfishly acted without thought to what our Savior had done for us. The alabado asked us to remember that only through the reparation, redemption, and solicitation that our Savior provided on our behalf would we gain all the indulgences that have been granted judgments on earth. And we were reminded poignantly that His offerings have all been in remission for our sins and punishment for them. Thus, we should live for the love of our major obligations under the rules of charity or justice that are our duty and that we can do.

As we passed over the bridge, the alabado rose in volume, and our own voices found strength not only through our former decision to live more virtuous lives as novicios of our own making, but primarily because the words we sang served to reinforce the reasons for living good Christian lives.

"*Finalmente, os suplico, dueño y señor mío, por el remedio de todos las necesidades comunes y particulares de la santa iglesia … Amén.*"

Our words echoed in a final appeal as we beseeched our Maker and our God for the reparation of all our common needs and the particulars of the holy church. For the exaltation of our sacred Catholic faith, we asked for peace and harmony among Christians, the eradication of heretics, the conversion of infidels and sinners, and for that which is considered appropriate to His divine goodwill and spiritual advantage. We asked for employment in services that would imitate His divine steps so that in eternity we would be in His favor and grace, to be allowed to extol Him in eternal glory.

As the last strains of the alabado drifted away in the breeze, for a moment there was absolute silence. Although we were joined at the church by those who elected to accompany us from there, we delayed greetings in the pregnant pause as the depth of emotion ran through everyone, some shivering outwardly with their reactions. Never unaffected by the dolefulness of alabados, because of our own participation this Lent and because of the secret pact the boys and I held within ourselves, the sorrow the words inspired in our hearts grew in intensity more than it ever had before.

As we reached the church, we stood in silence as Primo Victoriano tolled the campana for the final time, announcing that la *Procesión de los Dolores* was about to begin. Primo Victoriano would wait there for los Hermanos. As his fellow Brothers passed before him, he nodded as if saying, "I am with you, Hermanos, though my physical body remains here, spiritually, I am still with you."

We left the road, making our way up the sloping incline of the hill, which led into the mountains where the campo santo lay, nestled peacefully within a clearing in the midst of towering pines. The alabados began anew, our voices gaining strength and echoing sorrowfully throughout the cañon. We stopped at the crosses which Jorge had told me with pride on Sunday were his and Pablito's responsibility to set up, twelve on the right side of the path before which we kneeled on our way to the campo santo, and two on the left for our return. The fourteen crosses representing the Stations of the Cross, set amidst the backdrop of nature, were both beautiful and terrible, a bittersweet combination that never failed to humble even the most hardened of hearts. We prayed outdoors among the evergreens to remind us of the beauty that is God's creation, our responsibility that we must care for and nurture. Yet in re-enacting the steps that Christ took on His way to *Monte Calvario*, the twelfth Station had been set right outside the campo santo to symbolize His ultimate death.

I shuddered, because the next day, *Jueves Santo* (Holy Thursday), one of los Hermanos—and none of us knew whom it would be—would be chosen to carry the heavy black crucifix all the way to the cemetery, and Friday, *Las Tinieblas*, the most sorrowful and frightening of the ceremonies enacted during La Semana Santa, would occur.

On our return to the capilla, Tino nudged me, pointing with his chin to a thick piñon bush a little removed from the path to our right, the perfect spot for our descanso, he indicated, nudging Pedro who elbowed both Berto and Horacio. I nodded and our voices rose to mingle with the others. At the capilla we entered, seeking the warmth of the pot-bellied stove, for the afternoon had grown cool. The air was abuzz with muted conversations, a restful period before we would kneel for some time again with los Hermanos, to pray a rosario with them before they returned once more to the morada into the late hours of the night.

The boys and I stood in a group, an indisputable nervous tension emanating from Pedro who finally elbowed me and nodded to the Hermano kneeling at the altar alone.

"I noticed him when the procesión started," Berto whispered, the rest nodding that they had observed him as well.

"He did something wrong again," Horacio shuddered, "something that he had to do a penance for." Again, the others nodded their agreement.

"No." Before I could stop myself, the quiet assertion had escaped my lips. I had promised my grandmother I would not speak of the aviso that had come to me in the night, but the conviction I felt instinctively about Jorge made me blurt in protest. I explained, "Don't ask me how I know, I can't tell you, but you have to believe me. He didn't do anything wrong." Dumfounded expressions and gaping mouths greeted my statement, so I added, "He would have been expelled if he had, right?" They nodded, surprised that they hadn't thought of this before. "He did it because he felt it was something he needed." I shrugged. "A reminder, I guess."

The unforeseen certainty of my declaration staggered them. Their eyes told me they believed me, the bewilderment in their faces told me they longed for me to offer more of an explanation. And though I was almost bursting to tell them about the aviso I had received, a sense that my secret premonition would protect them warned me to keep silent.

Before they could rally themselves to rush me outside to question me further, my father beckoned. Foreboding replaced the initial relief that the boys would have no time to cross-examine me. As I made my way to his side, I wondered if he might finally put an end to my doubts, but I also worried whether he had indeed seen me in my vision.

He had only a few minutes before he resumed his responsibility as rezador, the leader of prayers, a duty he shared with my uncle, who was also cantador, leader of hymns. He seemed to be listening intently to the conversation between Primos Donacio and Eufemio, but when I reached his side, his eyes flickered to mine as his primos finished. He waited until I shook both elder men's hands in greeting before pulling me aside.

The question he asked put to rest my fears about the accusation I expected, but the dark maw of a new fear emerged. If he had seen me, and if as I suspected, my time to become a novicio was close at hand, there would be a time and a place for his allegation sooner than I thought.

"Would you like to go to la morada with us?"

My mouth fell open, something that had been happening quite a lot this Cuaresma. Hoping it wouldn't become a habit, I closed it with an audible snap.

Was this it then? Was he saying my time to become a novicio had come? My heart throbbed with anticipation. Was there also a hint of anxiety?

"Just me?" I asked, hopeful and apprehensive.

"No," he answered, "we will invite everyone to pray the rosario with us there, instead of here where we usually pray."

"Oh." Was my disappointment tinged with relief?

He must have read the dismay in my face (mercifully, not the relief) for he added, "And tomorrow, you and the boys catch enough fish at the représ to bring for supper, eh?"

To my chagrin, my mouth repeated its earlier reaction, and my awareness of its betrayal clamped it shut again. "Sí, Papá," I blurted, realizing the importance of the task he asked of us. Though it was no longer guarded by a sentry, the morada admitted no one except the women who would gather in a group when their turns came to take the food up. Yet he asked us to take the fish to them. I wondered, was I reading too much in his innocent request? Hopeful and apprehensive once more, my mind asked what I didn't know: what could it mean?

He smiled, his eyes twinkling in the glow of the lamps before he turned to invite us all to the morada. The puzzled glances of the boys caught my eye, each seeking to snare me for an answer. I shrugged to tell them I was no wiser. If they only knew the half of it! But there would be no opportunity tonight to tell them we had a duty to perform. I knew they would be as honored and perplexed as I was. I resolved I would have to keep my own questions quiet until we met at the caves.

The rosario that evening was especially poignant, for we went to the morada once again in procession, and before the altar of los Hermanos' sacred abode, we knelt right behind them rather than being far removed by the pews which separated us from them in the capilla. Knowing that tomorrow the boys and I would form our own little confraternity, which we would model after that of los Hermanos, a niggling worry chewed at my stomach. As I looked at my father, I knew that none of our gang merited the responsibility of leadership. Knowing I would have much to think about later in the night to keep me awake, perhaps even until my father's return, I willed myself to concentrate on my prayers. I prayed to be released from the fears that tried to override my sincere desire to become an Hermano, holding within my heart the hope that my father would feel I would be worthy soon. I prayed for that as fervently as I could to both the Blessed Virgin and La Muerte to intercede on my behalf and to give me a sign that the gang and I would do the right thing.

Resoluciones

Jueves Santo dawned bright and clear, dispelling the fears that had kept me awake long past midnight. Afraid to fall into yet another pesadilla in my sleep, I had willed my thoughts to turn instead to what the boys and I had planned for the day. The plans I had yet to inform them of had haunted me, finally exhausted me until I fell into a fitful sleep. I awoke tired, but relieved that I had been visited by no apparitions of the past or future.

At breakfast, which consisted of *panocha* and a glass of milk (we were still fasting), I wondered if my father had come home. My mother calmly informed me he would stay until Saturday, my suspicions of what he might be doing, or perhaps readying for, gave me more frightening images.

After doing my chores, I retreated into the mountains behind my house alone, thankful that my mother had seen and let me go without inquiring as to why or where I was going. She must have thought I needed time alone since, after what she had told me about my father, my thoughts left little room for conversation. I finished my breakfast in silence. I felt a twinge of guilt knowing that if she knew I was meeting the gang she would have asked for an explanation. But in my heart I knew that we were meeting for a purpose and not to play around, so I proceeded into the forest beyond our playing field. I caught up to Berto who had the canvas rolled and tied with a piece of string in his back pocket.

The ledges we called the caves were just ahead. Pedro was waiting, and below we could see Horacio huffing and puffing his way toward us. When we gathered to sit atop the largest niche, a scattering of pebbles announced Tino's arrival as he slid down the hill to our left, panting and looking as though he'd been crying.

"What the?" Berto stood, the rest of us crouched, sure Tino was being chased by a rogue bear or hungry coyote. Worse yet, I was thinking, what if he'd seen the serpiente?

He clambered up the ledge until he fell at our feet panting, the rest of us asking, "What?" "¿Qué?" and searching the woods. It seemed to take forever for him to catch his breath. He gasped awhile, laughed hysterically, panted and held his sides until we felt like slapping him—at least, I know I did.

Finally, he spoke. "I got up early this morning, started to make our descanso where we decided yesterday ..."

"So?" Pedro interrupted when Tino stopped to catch his breath.

"When I got home, my gramma was waiting," a giggle escaped before he continued, "and she made me walk with her to the campo santo."

"Don't tell me ..." Berto caught on, slapping his hand over his mouth to prevent a loud guffaw.

"Yeah," Tino panted between bouts of laughter he fought to muffle.

"Oh no," Horacio groaned while I fell to my knees and hunched over to stifle my own giggles.

"Oh yes," Tino gasped, tears were falling from his eyes from his efforts to subdue his laughter. "She ... she stopped at every descanso, and the last one was ... was ours!"

We tumbled onto the ledges, our bodies shaking even though we could hardly make out his words through his gasps and our grunts. "She said something like, '*Madre de Dios, no me acuerdo de este,*' and then she knelt by it and started to pray anyway, even though she didn't remember it being there. Sh ... she cracked me on the back of the knees but good with her bordón when I forgot to kneel and made me fall, then she saw me with my hand over my mouth and knew I was laughing. She ... she clobbered me over the head, calling me *desgraciado malcriado*, until I didn't have to pretend I was crying." He paused to show us the welt on the back of his head, "See," which sent us off again so badly Berto almost rolled off the edge.

What made Tino's story worse was that we knew we weren't supposed to laugh, and it seemed to take even longer for us to quiet down because he kept remembering and adding little details. "Gramma left me on the dirt by the descanso and told me to stay there and pray a Rosario. Look!" He held up the worn beads around his neck. "She practically choked me with it! You shoulda seen her stomping away." He stood and grabbed up a branch, adding "Like this." And he hobbled off, stamping the limb into the dirt, and with every stamp muttering, "*¡Muchacho estupido! ¡Ahora tengo rezar más causa tuya por hacerme decir palabrotas durante de la Cuaresma!*" Angry at Tino for making her curse during Lent, she decried having to say more prayers.

We died a hundred deaths trying to keep our laughter in until our sides ached and Tino made himself sick, vomiting up his breakfast, which made us scatter from the stench and made us all gag trying to hold ours in.

"Brrrr—ugh!" went Horacio in one direction while Pedro went "raaaalph!" in the opposite. Berto just crawled away making "uuugh uuugh" noises, and I covered my nose and mouth with both hands, squeezing my eyes shut as my own retching joined the chorus. We even had to move off some distance from our perch so the smell wouldn't set us off again. I almost asked Tino what he'd eaten, the smell was so pungent, but at the thought of food, I felt the heave rising in my gut once more and tried to think of something else so I wouldn't gag and start the others off again.

After we finally settled down, Horacio took it upon himself to bring up the subject we'd gone up there to discuss in the first place. He opened the ledger, which sobered us immediately, and proudly read aloud what he had written of our decisions the day before for our approval. With a few additions, our records of our own cofradía were complete.

"Did any of you decide if we want an hermano mayor?" he asked, forcing us to focus on the issue none of us wanted to discuss.

Did we? Did we really think any of us could possibly be the one to set the example for the rest to follow? At first we all looked at each other as if by reading one another's faces we could tell who would be the best for the responsible office. But we couldn't see any of the qualities befitting such a powerful position. We looked away, embarrassed by such scrutiny. It was bad enough we couldn't look at one another because not one of us deemed at least one of our peers worthy of discussion (much less nomination). What was worse was knowing that the others had decided each of us had also fallen short of the mark in the process.

"I don't know about you guys," Pedro scratched his chin, "but I thought a lot about it last night, and I really don't think any one of us should be the leader. We should just think of something else."

Looking at him in surprise, I wondered how and when he had come to the same conclusion as I had.

"I don't think so either," Horacio said in that confusing way he had of putting words together, which we all understood.

Berto smiled. "Funny, I was thinking that we should just leave our decision-making the way it's always been, unanimous or nothing. It doesn't seem right to make one of us responsible for everyone else."

"I know," Tino nodded. "None of us is really older and wiser like José's papá."

The breeze, which was drying my tongue, made me realize my mouth had fallen open again. I clamped it shut and swallowed, then I whispered, "When did you guys realize?"

They all thought for a moment, but when they answered, it was in unison: "At the rosario."

I gasped, open-mouthed again.

"¿Qué?" Tino asked, looking around for the difunto he was sure I had seen.

"What is it, José?" Pedro asked, rising to a crouch in case we had to run for it.

Horacio began to shake. Berto only stared, wide-eyed.

Taking a deep breath, I whispered, "I decided the same thing last night, same time, same place."

"So?" Pedro asked. "So it's a coincidence."

"But what's even stranger," I added quietly, "is that I prayed for a sign from the Virgen and La Muerte that we would make the right decision. I guess this is it, eh?"

For a moment everyone was silent, then Filiberto spoke in a quiet contemplative voice.

 "Isn't it strange that three times this Cuaresma we have seen and heard what we have? If I didn't have such a good feeling about what we're doing, I think I'd be scared shi …." He blushed because he had almost cursed as well. "Well, I'd be scared."

You don't know the half of it, my silence replied.

"You ain't kiddin'," Tino breathed. "I feel it, too, like someone out there," he waved his arms, "or up there," he looked to the sky, "approves of us trying to act like los Hermanos."

Horacio added, nodding, "But whoever it is knows that we're still too young to make the really hard decisions, like los Hermanos do."

We nodded in silent acquiescence, a sort of awe lingering in our thoughts that a higher power was pleased by our decision to model our actions more rigidly based on what los Hermanos did.

"Okay." Berto broke the spell. In his back-to-business voice, he asked, "What are the rules of los Hermanos, their duties, besides what we heard that night for ourselves?"

They looked at me again. In the past, I had been the one to supply information that I had gleaned by listening to the conversations of my elders. This time I had more to say than they would want to hear, but looking around at the expectation written on their faces, I could only tell them what I had safely acquired with my father's permission when he allowed me to listen. But then there were times when his mouth would clamp shut and he would tell me to run along, and I knew the discussion was secretive enough that it was not for my ears. And now, of course, there were the words he spoke in my dream, *avisando*, informing me that what I had witnessed awaited my own entrance to their cofradía as a novicio.

"Well," I said, collecting my thoughts, "I don't know all of them, but they follow the rules of the Church and the Commandments. They collect money, you know, for when someone is sick or dies. They call regular meetings and decide when they must go help someone do something. They speak of matters concerning the community, saying it's the responsibility of los Hermanos to take care of their own.

"Then, for now, that's what we'll do. ¿Qué no?" Berto asked.

We nodded, all except Horacio, who busily scribbled in the ledger.

"Okay then, what do we do first?" Tino asked. "Besides attend the Estaciones today."

"I have two things in mind," I said quietly, enjoying keeping them in suspense for a moment, but I understood I would lay a burden on their shoulders with my second disclosure. I weighed my words for some time before Horacio began tapping the pencil on his knee impatiently and Pedro's fist playfully rose and shook before my face. "The first one I decided to do yesterday, and it's something I was going to do alone, so you guys don't have to if you don't want to."

"Well, are you gonna tell us, or do we have to guess?" Tino asked.

"I'm going to the capilla right after we finish and help Primo Victoriano light the candles and chop the wood for the stove," I revealed. "I thought maybe I'd pray with him awhile, maybe talk to him awhile."

Berto groaned, tossing his unruly hair. "It's not like if he needs your help, José. He probably wants to be alone."

"Well, I'm going anyway," I asserted. "If he doesn't want me there, I'll leave. But I'm going to try."

"Okay," he sighed, "count me in."

"Us, too," Tino said quietly after catching the nods of the others.

"Okay then," Pedro echoed. "What else? You said there were two things."

The time had come. I swallowed. "Yeah, and I have a feeling you guys are going to … be surprised." In truth, now that the time had come to reveal my father's proposal. I really didn't know where to begin.

"What?" Tino wailed. "What, what, what!"

Still, I hesitated, wondering if they could put to rest the fears that my father's actions of the night before signaled something more. "Well, last night, you know how we went to the morada later?"

Mutual nods, an exchange of glances greeted my reminder.

"What if that was sort of a trial, too, like the trial period we're making for ourselves? What if it was to get us to see what it's like at night there, to get rid of any childish fears we may still have before we're asked to be novicios?"

"What exactly are you saying?" Pedro's whisper was almost a gasp.

"Besides, everyone was invited," Horacio pointed out, "not just us."

Four pairs of eyes, glued to my face, sought an explanation.

"Yeah," I agreed, looking at each in turn, "but Papá called me over to ask if I liked the idea first."

"Why would he do that?" Berto asked. "Like for your approval?"

"Like your opinion would speak for the rest of us?" Pedro asked. "It makes sense. He knew we wanted to see the morada at night, even though we want to see more than they let us. All those times you asked him and he said no, he knew it was for all of us. ¿Qué no?"

"I don't know." I shook my head, looked at my hands. I looked at all of them. "I'm asking you."

Silence and shrugs told me they had no answer.

"There's more." My inner voice shouted, "And I can't even tell you half!"

"¡Madre mía!" Tino exploded, unable to contain himself any longer. "What else could there be?"

"You're scaring me, José," Horacio put the ledger down and hugged his knees. "I'm not sure I wanna hear this."

Taking a deep breath, I blurted, "Last night Papá also asked us to fish at the représ and take los Hermanos enough for their supper."

"You're kidding, right?" Pedro gasped. "They never let anyone near the morada this week at all."

"And he asked us to actually take the fish there?" Horacio was visibly trembling.

I nodded, wondering if I should voice my suspicions.

"Whew," Berto breathed, "this could be it, alright."

"Wha … what d'you mean, this could be it?" Horacio stumbled to his feet.

Echoing my questions, Berto stood, too. "What if they want us up there for a reason?" He asked quietly, "To ask us if we want to join?"

"Maybe not." A subdued Tino stood slowly. His hands spoke right along with his voice, punctuating his words with quiet gestures. "I know I'm not even old enough. Maybe we're reading too much into this, huh?"

"Maybe," I agreed. "As much as I want to become a novicio, now that it may happen sooner than I thought, for me anyway, is kinda scary. I just have a feeling …"

"Oh no," Tino groaned, slapping a hand to his head, "you and your feelings. You've been having strange feelings and strange things have been happening; don't tell me about your feelings. Leave me in suspense, please."

"Oh, gaaak!" Horacio squeaked. "I'm not ready for this."

No one heard me mutter, "Are any of us?"

The levity we'd experienced over Tino's gramma's error was erased by my revelations. Berto and Horacio wrapped the ledger in canvas, securing it against moisture with the string, and we trooped down to the spot we had chosen for our "descanso." Using sharp rocks and sticks, Tino had dug a shallow hole and placed a few large rocks over it. Now, using our hands, like dogs, we scraped the dirt away before Horacio reverently deposited our secrets in the earth. Replacing the dirt, we gathered stones the size of *calabazitas*, concealing our secret from the eyes of mortals, sensing that immortal sight would watch over it and keep it safe. Little did any of us know we would never see our secret ledger again.

At the church, we sat around the cross, whittling our carvings quietly, immersed in our creations to avoid the fingers of fear that ran across our backs, making us shiver in the sunlight while we awaited the arrival of Primo Victoriano. I recognized the shapes of a figure in Pedro's carving and unique characteristics in each of our crosses by the time the elderly man rounded the corner.

"Eh?" Primo Victoriano's bony head rose, then his hands, then his eyebrows as he suffered a start at finding us there.

We rose quickly, gathering around the elder to shake his hand and offer greetings. Pedro asked if he would like our help in preparing the church for the arrival of those who would come to pay their respects later in the day.

Surprise registered on his face for a moment, but then his eyes narrowed in suspicion. "I know you boys are up to something." He shook a finger at us. "¿Por qué?" he asked, looking suspiciously from one of us to the next.

He knew us as the gang from the past, the gang that had gotten into hot water for practical jokes and pranks that we had pulled on nearly everyone in Cañoncito. Once, on one of the many patron saint's days followed by a fiesta outside of the church, a huge *comida* had been prepared for the community.

We had snuck to the outhouse opposite the road earlier that morning, and Berto and Tino applied black paint to the toilet opening while the rest of us served as lookouts. When one is enclosed in the tiny shed, it is almost pitch black. The following week many of our little Cañon inhabitants, including Primo Victoriano himself, noticed that the underwear they wore that fiesta day had a peculiar ring of black inside. They clucked their tongues and shook their heads observing their backsides in mirrors, as had spouses or mothers, who also found that their efforts to scrub the notorious rings were futile.

Though no one could prove it had been our doing, our reputations being what they were made our guilt a certainty, especially when Berto's father couldn't find the pint of black enamel paint he knew he had in his workshop. What we considered an innocent prank brought huge complaints to our door. The offended parties or their parents shook their fists in our faces and demanded punishment from our fathers. After our own backsides were marked by strappings, everyone who had been "tattooed" by our hand, so to speak, had the cleanest outhouses in the entire cañon.

Primo Victoriano's wife stood by, a chicote in her hand, the entire time we had worked on hers, painting it first brown, which she later made us change to green, all the while giving us a tongue lashing and many sharp strappings to our already sore *nalgas*. Whenever she took the willow rod to the seats of our pants, our howls echoed through the canyon, and to our added shame, we heard much laughter at our expense. The only consolation we had, though our consciences told us we were wrong, was that after our nalgas ceased to bear the mark of our father's whips, those who had sat on our "artwork" bore our tattoos on their rear ends for weeks.

"Why?" Primo Victoriano repeated.

I knew he would need some convincing to know that we had undergone a change of heart from the unthinking youngsters we had been. "*¿Tiene tiempo para platicar?*" I asked.

He looked at us warily for some time, but a slight nod told us that, yes, he had time for a talk. He hobbled over to the edge of the laja which served as a front stoop for the church, slowly seating himself as he leaned upon his cane. He looked from me to the others as he waited for us to speak.

Interrupting one another, we told him of our experiences during this Lenten season with La Muerte and el difunto, of our decision to live like los Hermanos, of our fears and our longing to become one of them in the future.

And though he listened quietly, he squinted like he was still wary, still suspicious of the sudden change we had seemimgly undergone. When we finished, he sat in silence, then finally asked, with a tilt of his chin to the woodcarvings in our hands, "*¿Que hacen?*"

Tino, Horacio, and I told him we were making crucifixes and Pedro revealed that his was a santo. "For ceremonies when we are Hermanos," I explained.

A soft smile replaced the suspicion in his face and wrinkled his withered cheeks. Reaching for the half-finished saint in Pedro's hand, the elderly Hermano turned it in his own, nodding. "It will be a beautiful carving. Make one for me, one that I can take to my grave when my time comes."

Pedro protested. "No, no, Primo. You'll live much longer." The rest of us nodded our agreement.

"We n … n … need your guidance, Primo." Tino stuttered. Primo Victoriano blinked, and tears gathered in his eyes. He was touched by our words, by the gesture that our carvings implied, and by his own belief that we had indeed changed.

Looking at all of us, he offered his consejo from the depths of his wisdom. "*No tengan miedo,*" he told us, shaking his hoary head, "there is nothing to fear in being an Hermano if you live as though it is your last day on earth. Hurt no one, for you will only hurt yourselves. And remember always, *Cristo* waits for us all, mis hijitos, but so does el Diablo."

It was true. I nodded, and the sudden realization unburdened me of the fist of fear that had clenched around my heart each time I thought about surrendering myself to a life of penance. This time the fist opened, freeing the longing I harbored. There really is no reason to be afraid for myself, I rationalized. In following the Commandments thus far, I had proven I could be responsible for myself. The Brothers took vows to assure that each would be the responsible voice of the others' conscience if he strayed, and I had already done that with my friends. I had already decided with the gang that we would take our responsibilities for one another more seriously. Even counting the times Berto's schemes had backfired, we had never really broken the Commandments.

But, I thought, how would it be, really, to have such a serious hold over the heads of one another? To be a witness against one of my dearest friends and a party to his penance? My fear for myself was gone, yes. The aviso had shown me my own face, serene and resolute, in the face of the Hermano who had entered from the darkness into the light of the morada. When I turned, clothed in white, before kneeling to await my penance, a punishment I would willingly request, I witnessed what I would undergo during my initiation as a novicio. I knew why I would kneel before my father and take the lashing of the scourge—

by my own hand. For against the better judgment of my conscience, which I had willingly ignored, I had borne witness, both awake when I had gone with the gang and in the subconscious state of my dream vision when I had gone alone, to the most secret of rituals performed by Penitentes. I knew I couldn't live with myself if I did not fulfill the destiny my premonition had revealed. I resigned myself to the possibility that my time was near, I resolved to meet it with the courage befitting an Hermano.

But the fear for my friends remained.

I looked at them. There was Filiberto, hands in his pockets, head down. What was he thinking? Of the time Padre gave mass and his sermon was about "doing unto others," looking at Berto all the while. The gossip of the cañon always reached Padre's ears, and he always strove to remind us of our actions and the consequences—especially before his entire congregation. That time, Berto had been caught just the Friday before putting dried cow dung in Maestro's bag of punche. The far-sighted man would have never known what he was smoking until he inhaled and the smell of manure alerted him. His yell of outrage preceded Berto's yelps of pain, and his voice punctuated each strapping, "How—would—you—like—it—if—I—put—manure—in—your—frijoles?" By evening everyone had heard, and that morning in mass, many eyes turned accusingly to Berto and many childish snickers were shushed as he tried unsuccessfully to slither down in his seat.

I looked at Tino, who looked, as always, like a tiny angel of innocence, except for his eyes which failed to disguise his impish nature. I wondered if he thought of the time he had almost given Gregoria a heart attack when he snuck up behind her and thrust a bull snake into her face. As it was, the panic caused by her asthma attack was enough to scare even Maestro. The sermon that Sunday had been "We are responsible for our own actions …" Padre, implying with examples how innocent pranks have been known to cause injury and death, never took his eyes off Tino.

Even Horacio and I had been lectured indirectly before the congregation. A glance at my friend's blushing cheeks indicated that he recalled his own thoughtless actions. Padre's eyes that Sunday morning had flicked from me to Horacio and back again, his words rubbing more salt into our wounds during the sermon he began with "Think before you act ..." We had thought only to cure Tino of scaring us at any and every opportunity by giving him a taste of his own medicine. We had waited for him in the monte, where disguised with branches and brush, we had jumped directly into his path and yelled like banshees, little knowing we would scare him enough to run pell-mell down the mountainside, screaming, "¡Serpiente! ¡Serpiente!" before smacking into a tree. Needless to say, with Tino out cold sporting a bloody nose and two blackening eyes (not to mention a slight concussion), the incident ended up scaring Horacio and me more.

And lastly, there was Pedro, a horse of a different color. He stood, blushing a bit, and I wondered if he was pondering his weakness: women. To clarify, the female species overall. He treated the weaker sex (as he saw them), from baby girls to the oldest *viejitas*, with a sense of awe as though he saw in them something precious. And his tenderness with the young, his respect for the old, drew them to him in differing ways. But with Luciana, his desire overpowered his better sense, and it was no wonder that Pedro's overactive hormones where his "wife" was concerned always got him into trouble.

For though Pedro had won her love, she held steadfast to her virginity, frustrating his frequent attempts to get her to consummate their wedding vows. Not that they were married, but Luciana, much to his delight, had been betrothed to him when she was born. Now at the age of sixteen, Pedro could take her as his wife when he could provide for her. It was either that or marry and live with her parents while he tried to find work. And though she could still go to school one more year, she didn't have to. Back then the ambition of most women was to bear children and have a house to care for, and the sooner the better, so I wondered about Luciana.

I was reminded of the time Pedro was caught looking at Luciana bathing in the river. She probably would not have said anything, for where she bathed the water was deep enough for him to see nothing below her shoulders—until Pedro dropped her clothes a few yards away and sat, waiting with a patient grin, like that of the fabled wolf who hungered for his prey. When her threats to scream turned to the real thing—the water was cold, and she was only thirteen—her outraged shrieks brought her father running. Pedro raced for home where the irate father-in-law-to-be appeared at the kitchen door, demanding an apology for his daughter—a formal, written apology recited before the entire family, no less, or he would call off the betrothal.

Before church that Sunday, Pedro had dutifully written and recited his apology before Luciana and her family. He had described her father's glowering face, wordlessly telling him this was his last chance; her mother's eyes, their silent accusation screaming "pervert"; her brother's sly expression, saying he knew what Pedro had tried to do; and the snicker of her younger sister, inwardly laughing at his discomfort. But what affected him most was the unspoken challenge of Luciana's smugness that told him that no matter how he tried, she would not be swayed until their wedding night. Nonetheless, he was determined to try again.

Only hours later he realized the error of his ways, for the Padre's sermon revealed the sins of the flesh and the Church's stand on virginity. Under the eyes of the Padre and his assemblage, cowing like a turtle trying to retreat into his shell, Pedro came to the realization that he couldn't escape the omnipresent eyes of God. And though the eyes of the community, too, would be ever vigilant to assure that his efforts to seduce Luciana in the future would be in vain, he left a changed man. A new determination to control his passion formed. There would be no further attempts.

"*¿Entienden, qué no?*" Primo Victoriano, respectfully having allowed us a few moments to let his words sink in, finally broke the silence. We could hear his hope that we did, indeed, understand.

When the boys smiled and nodded, I knew my thoughts reflected their own. We understood what we had done in our youth; we knew what we had to do now. We had changed.

Rising stiffly, allowing Berto for the first time to clasp his elbow for support, Primo Victoriano beckoned us into the church, where, at his direction, we replaced burnt candles with new ones, chopped wood and readied the stove with kindling, filled lamps with kerosene, and swept out dirt from the floor. Our conversation with the old man was muted while we worked. He explained that he had volunteered to be the one to ready the church because of his desire to continue to serve his fellow Hermanos, attaining an inner peace in his solitary task. But as the years passed, he also found that the stiffness of his joints caused by rheumatism seemed to abate only within its sacred walls, and he was convinced that only in this blessed house of God could he find relief from his pain. With the help of his crooked bordón, handmade by a fellow Hermano, he walked stiffly to and fro as we worked. Indeed, it seemed that after a short while his gait was less awkward.

As he spoke, his trembly voice revealed that his was a soul ready for death, for what came after death. It revealed a man in need of our company to keep him alive by reliving old memories, a need that I would come to know in the future. "I am content," he told us, "to wait for my time, as long as I can still pray with mis Hermanos, still tend to my jardín." But he was tired, and he wondered when the day he would enjoy with such pleasure would be his last. "I know now," he told us, "what my life as a Penitente has prepared me for, and I am not afraid." I knew as I looked at the boys that we would be spending more time with him as he waited. And though I realized, too, that I had spent my own life waiting to become a Penitente, waiting for my time, his was the culmination of an Hermano's preparation throughout his life.

In his quivering voice, Primo Victoriano led us in prayer when we finished, and we sang with him the alabado which he deemed appropriate, leaving him, finally, to commune with God in solitude. We promised to catch a fat trout for his supper.

We hurried quickly in our separate directions, gathering our rods and pails and returning to the représ in the hopes that God would provide. I prayed that we would again experience the blessing of an abundant catch, like the last time we had fished. To my amusement Berto crossed himself, shrugging when he realized I'd seen him, and muttering, "Couldn't hurt to ask for a blessing." Our sport had taken on a new meaning, and we weren't disappointed. Only a little while later, first Tino's and then Berto's rods gave evidence of the tugging that meant a hooked fish. Before long our buckets began to fill with flapping trout.

About noon the faint rising of voices came from the morada in yet another alabado, sung with such strength and conviction. The prayer floated above us like a welcome cloud, blanketing us in its protection. With the last dying notes, the Hermanos began emerging from the building, stretching and conversing quietly, some rolling cigarettes as they stood beneath the trees. Tino propped his rod on a rock and lay on the ground to listen. The rest of us followed suit, Horacio and I crawling up the steep but shallow embankment to lie on our stomachs with our chins propped in our hands, hoping to hear something of their plans for the evening.

We heard nothing but a sudden watery plop and a loud yell of surprise. I turned, amazed to see Tino flailing in the now murky water for his rod, jumping for the trailing stick, which was being pulled just out of his reach by a large trout, its silvery iridescent shadow visible just beneath the surface. Forgetting the need for quiet, we yelled our support in our excitement, and with a lunge, Tino grabbed his rod, straining against the weight of the fish, which fought for its life. Stumbling backward in the waist-deep water, he made his way to the shore, where Pedro yanked him onto the ledge by the collar. Berto and I pulled at the rod, all three of us heaving until we fell as one backward onto the bank. The fish, rising and squirming from the water, flew back, flopping with a resounding smack into Horacio's face.

Amid our groaning struggle against the bubbling laughter threatening to explode from deep in our stomachs, rolling on our backs in the mud-spattered weeds, clutching ourselves and muffling our mouths, Horacio opened his own to howl. He bit back his cry with an attempt at bravery. However, when a clearing of throats and muffled chuckles from behind made us turn, we still trembled with the effort of trying not to laugh out loud.

Los Hermanos stood just above on the ledge of the bank, watching, some smacking their thighs in an effort to control their own laughter, a few hiding their mouths with a hand and turning away quickly before the sight of us made them forget themselves. We looked at one another, sprinkles of mud covering all our faces, our clothes, and Tino soaked to the skin, teeth chattering as he blushed from ear to ear. But he proudly held up the still flapping fish which had to have been the largest any of us had ever caught. We fought another battle against our giggles, but a few fell out of our mouths; and not surprisingly, from the mouths of the men when Horacio's father, gasping for breath, pointed a shaking finger at his son. Forcing ourselves to hunch over, holding our stomachs with one hand while the other pressed against our mouths, we all, old and young alike, fought to hold the peals of laughter that threatened to spill forth and turn to genuine howls when we looked at Horacio wearing the evidence of the fish's wrath on a reddened cheek he proudly refused to rub.

Rough, calloused hands, the hands of our fathers and our primos, reached down firmly, helping us to the top of the riverbank, where our heads were tousled and our arms were punched good-naturedly, wordlessly. When our mirth finally subsided, Pedro and Berto made their way back to the two buckets, now overflowing with trout. Horacio held back, his disdain toward cleaning fish etched in a grim line on his face before he sensed his father's teasing eyes upon him. Don Juan knew of Horacio's aversion to the task, and motivated rather by the playful urge to make his son overcome his revulsion rather than by a spiteful urge to torment, he nodded toward the others, hiding his smile.

Horacio failed in his own effort to smile back before shuffling slowly to the river. Tino, teeth chattering and knees knocking, stood nearby. Dying to go home to change, he ran in place as he whined for them to hurry and clean his large trout first.

"Why?" I asked.

"T ... to ... take ... t ... to Pri ... mo ... Vic ... Victoriano, wh ... why, else?"

Oh, of course.

My father's voice made me turn in his direction. He was walking purposefully toward me, the twinkle of his eyes assuring me that we had done well, even during our unintentional comedic performance. Resting a hand on my shoulder, he smiled, still shaking his head. "¿Como pueden ser tan traviesos y tare grandes?"

The words, meant in jest, implied that though we were maturing, we still acted like mischievous children. Did I hear disappointment in his voice that there was still enough youth in us to make us buffoons at times? Worse, yet, was this a flaw in our characters that would jeopardize our becoming novicios?

His next words, spoken quietly as his face grew serious, dispelled that last thought immediately, leaving in its uncertainty again the unsettling question of why.

"After las Estaciones, run home to your chores, then come back to the morada for supper."

I caught my mouth with a sliver of awareness as it began to open, closing it as I swallowed. "Me? Us?" I asked, sweeping an arm toward the gang. Just like that! We were to accept his invitation as if it were commonplace, as if we were not to make a big issue of it. But I did, and I knew the boys would, too. I could imagine the surprise on their faces when I told them. I could also imagine their happiness that would be overshadowed by their apprehension.

He shook his head. "*Esta vez nomás tú y Pedro.*"

Why? I wanted to ask. Then I knew. We were old enough; the others weren't. Disappointed for Berto, Tino, and Horacio intertwined with joy for Pedro and me. I didn't know how to feel. But I smiled, willing the anxiety that grew in my chest not to show, trying instead to summon the pleasure into my face, for my father could read me so easily. I fought the impulse to throw my arms around him, the actions of the child that lay dormant within me but would express what I was feeling. My heart burst with happiness knowing that the impulse with which he had invited us was meant to put us at ease, yet the very real possibility that tonight would mark our induction into the cofradía overwhelmed both the boy and the man that I was becoming at age fifteen.

Being alike in our natures, we were not physically affectionate, my father and I. And while I could accept the countless hugs and kisses from my mother (and even my brother and uncle), it was somehow different with my father. By keeping his own emotions in check, he tried to make me feel like a man, and not the boy I was still inside. I hoped my eyes would convey to him that though I struggled with my desire to fling myself into his arms, I also searched for words to show him that I was touched by his gesture more than I had ever been by anything he had ever done.

He waited for a moment in our mutual silence, and I heard the words that came from his eyes but didn't touch his lips. "Está bien." His eyes said, "It's alright, I know what you want to say."

He moved toward me and touched my cheek lightly. His tenderness, showing his own affection, touched my heart more than any loving gesture from other members of my family. He turned then, walking slowly toward the morada, and left me to get a hold of myself before my friends could see.

La Última Cena

Subdued by the hopes that surfaced and the fears which overshadowed them, I summoned my friends back to Horacio's after we'd cleaned the fish and trooped proudly to leave them at the morada. Retelling their versions of our fight with the fish, they struggled anew to contain their laughter while I listened half-heartedly and resumed my whittling. I momentarily forgot the thought that I had a reason to gather them together after our chores, until Pedro noticed my lack of attention and asked what was wrong.

"Nothing," I said shortly, but after a pause, I added, "but there is something I have to tell you. I was only waiting for Tino."

They didn't prod "out with it, José," or "spit it out, José." They only turned back to their carvings in silence, and I wondered it if was because they didn't want to hear it or if by waiting for Tino they could postpone something they suspected might be unpleasant.

It wasn't long before Tino came jogging up the hill. Smiling broadly, he announced, "Primo Victoriano nearly cried," he said. "He told me to thank…." Noting the apprehension in our faces, the smile fell from his own as he knelt in the grass at our feet, waiting like the others. For what, like they, he didn't know.

With his arrival, our gang—our circle—was complete, and I could no longer contain myself. Longing for the relief I sought by sharing the burden of my thoughts with my "brothers" I blurted, "My father invited Pedro and me to supper with them after las Estaciones—at the morada."

Silence. They were completely, utterly shocked into silence. I wasn't

132

surprised. What need was there for words when the silent air, heavy with unspoken fears and unrequited longing, spoke volumes?

Las Estaciones were prayed that afternoon just as they had been conducted the day before, the awareness of the words both spoken and sung affecting everyone. As the boys and I sat together in the last pew with Primo Victoriano and his wife, I was aware of the resolute silence in his expression throughout the constant kneeling and rising, knowing that he held within himself the pain such movements caused in his bones. Not once did he sit back to rest his knees when our backs were turned, nor did he take unnecessary steps when he rose occasionally to feed the fire, relieving the stiffness of his joints for short intervals. I counted the shuffling steps he took and the tappings of his cane as he completed his task: ten to the woodbox, five to the stove, and five to return to the pew. My respect for this ancient man grew with each step, and my heart filled with a mixture of sorrow and joy that his life was almost at an end. For though we whom he would leave behind when the Lord called him would be saddened at his departure, I knew he would rejoice to have finally completed his life as an Hermano and that he would be welcomed into the arms of God.

From time to time throughout the ceremony, Pedro and I caught the glances of our mothers, sometimes etched with pride when a soft smile turned our way, yet at other moments carved with concern, which accompanied the hands that rose with linen kerchiefs to their eyes. For by then, they were aware of the invitation. They, too, wondered if this night would signal the end of our childhoods. For Pedro and me, the dolorous ceremony held a double meaning, striking our hearts with a bittersweet mixture of pride and apprehension. We were caught between seasons—being yet children but becoming men. On one hand, our actions bespoke that we were still children. At heart, I didn't think we could ever outgrow our love of practical jokes and horseplay. On the other hand, we were also considered old enough to marry. The complete paradox governing our lives that year was overwhelming.

Thus, when we prayed fervently, it was the man within us who compelled our voices to rise when we found the courage to meet our rapidly approaching adulthood head on. If our time had come to become novicios, we asked to meet our responsibilities with pride and to be rid of the childhood fears that threatened to emerge in the form of cowardice. But it was the child we had not yet completely outgrown that subdued our voices with the anxiety that this night might indeed mark the end to our wait and the beginning of our lives as Hermanos.

When the Estaciones came to an end, a sense of disappointment prevailed, especially when we returned to the capilla and los Hermanos did not stay for a respite as they had before. Pausing only briefly, the last note of their alabado echoed for but moments as we gathered around the door to the church, muted whispers passing between us as we stood watching. Waiting. They remained in formation, not a word passed among them. We quieted, though my heart, and I was sure the hearts of the others, pounded in anticipation, trepidation. I didn't remember the men not ever stopping to visit awhile with us before they had to leave. Mercifully, my suspicions of what they needed time to prepare for or what it could mean were curtailed when the brief, but pregnant, silence was broken by the rising tenor of my uncle's voice, followed almost immediately by that of my father, a moving contrast of bass. Their sorrowful duet echoed on the rising notes of their Brothers, each adding his voice to the emotional lament offered to their Savior. As my uncle moved forward, the procession of devout souls followed, leaving us at the threshold of the church. My inner voice whispered the question our puzzled glances wordlessly exchanged. There was no need. We all suspected the answer.

There was no putting it off. After we walked our mothers home and did our normal chores—taking in firewood for the evening, making sure there was kerosene in the lamps, checking on the chickens, or bringing in water from the well—the time had come for me to meet Pedro at the arbolera. We walked together to the back door of the morada. Primo Eufemio was gathering an armful of wood when we arrived, a burden Pedro relieved him of while I filled my own arms with sweet-smelling pine. Leading the way, Primo Eufemio pushed the door open, "Éntren, Éntren, hijos," he welcomed. Shuffling up the step, he held the heavy wooden door open as we entered. Glancing at my friend, I could tell from the proud lift of his head that I was not the only one who felt privileged to enter the society of men waiting inside. Even if it might only be for supper (after which we might be told to go home and accompany our mothers to the capilla as we always had before) or if it was as we expected, our time to join the cofradía, our faces reflected the inner peace that we had attained from our elderly primo earlier in the day. We convinced ourselves that we were prepared for whatever lay in the hours ahead.

The smell of frying fish tantalized our noses as we exchanged greetings all around, from the men occupied at the stove to the others conversing while they worked at the table, we shook hands with each, capturing the moment of feeling like men. Since we had to endure a bit of good-natured ribbing in the process, the moment fled, leaving in its wake the reminder of our youth, and we were caught again within the capricious period of adolescence.

Addressed by all (except Jorge and Pablito who were almost as young as we) with the personal title of *hijo* or *hito* or the collective *hijos* or *hitos*, all the elder Hermanos were like fathers to us. Coaxing us out of our awe, they welcomed us into their conversations as our opinions were asked and discussed, either with nodding concurrence or quiet disagreement from time to time. Our first self-conscious responses conveyed our nervousness. I wondered whether Pedro thought this was another test, a judgment of our characters that would somehow indicate to them if we were ready to become novicios. But in the atmosphere of camaraderie, enveloped by acceptance in their midst, we soon relaxed enough to enjoy the discourse of the men.

Pedro took out his carving as we talked, handing it over to his father when he asked to see it. Don Esteban expressed his pleasure in the intricate details before passing the half-finished santo among the hands of the rest of los Hermanos. They all admired Pedro's talented workmanship in the folds he had created in the robed figurine. Again, when asked which saint it would be, Pedro only smiled, saying he didn't want to tell just yet.

I proudly took out my almost completed cross, and much to my chagrin, the conversation abated, ceasing completely when the men saw what I had thought would arouse as equal a pleasure as Pedro's instead brought only silence. My father looked at my crucifix in the stillness before resting his gaze on my face.

"I had thought to give you mine when your time came," he said quietly, handing it to my uncle, "but I think it best that you have your own; your time as a novicio is near, and I still need mine."

As my cross passed from one to the other of los Hermanos for their approval, and the men offered suggestions of how or what should be done to finish it, Pedro and I exchanged anticipatory glances. My father's words struck our hearts. Our time was near. How near?

After a while, we helped set the table, sitting among the men we looked up to with the utmost respect. Los Hermanos—our fathers, uncles, cousins— were each dear to us in his own special way. And when my father led the blessing for our supper, I was again touched by the vision before me. Their heads, some bald, others crowned in the thick browns or blacks of youth as well as the sparse or thinning grey or white of age, bowed. Their clasped hands were calloused evidence of the hard work, and their eyes, filled with such earnest love for life in the young and such sincere devoutness and wisdom in the old, closed in prayer. In their work clothes, darned pants, flannel shirts with patched elbows, and worn shoes, they might have looked poor to anyone else, haggard. To me, they looked like a vision of the Apostles come to life, and I was honored to share this moment with them.

We shared the fried fish and the tortillas, and Pedro and I were allowed even to share in a small glass of wine. The combination made for the best meal I had ever tasted—although I was sure it was more because of with whom I ate and where, rather than what. As the light faded from the windows and lamp wicks had to be raised to shed a brighter, buttery glow, a silence fell like a cloak of warmth over us. I was moved by the imagery the humble meal inspired, evoking a bittersweet sensation of impending sorrow. It was as though I were living through the actual Last Supper and I experienced the powerlessness of being in it as it occurred. The thought of the inevitable death of our Savior weighed heavily on my heart throughout the first supper I shared with los Hermanos.

Novicios

When the meal ended, Pedro and I exchanged a glance and rose quickly by mutual agreement, not waiting to be asked or told, to clear the table and do the dishes, allowing the men time to enjoy an after-dinner cigarette or another cup of coffee before resuming their duties. As we finished, they began rising or stretching, going in turn to the outhouse or out for a breath of fresh air before making their way to the prayer room. It dawned on me at about the same time as it did to Pedro that not one had said goodbye or goodnight. We looked at one another in both perplexity and anxiety, wondering if we were expected to leave quietly or to follow in their wake.

As we retrieved our jackets reluctantly, a sense of disappointment overcame us that it was time to leave, yet an overwhelming sense of expectation made our movements slow. And when the kitchen door opened, my uncle and Pedro's father entering at the same moment my father returned from the prayer room, we moved forward. Drawn into the circle of the men who stood before us, we sensed that there would be more to this night than we had envisioned.

"¿*Están listos?*" my father asked, the seriousness of his eyes visible, confirming both the elation and the trepidation in our hearts.

This was it! With no preamble, with no forewarning from any one of los Hermanos, Pedro was stunned. At least I had received an aviso, my only hint of what this night would mean, and I had sworn to keep it secret. Our time had come. "¿Estamos listos? Are we ready?" my thoughts asked for both of us. "Am I ready?" I asked of myself.

Sighing deeply, my father said, "Normally, those who want to become Hermanos must petition el Hermano Mayor, that is me, of course. But since all members are already aware of just how much you both want to enter the Brotherhood, we decided unanimously to forgo that formality and welcome you to our cofradía tonight. What you need to understand is that you will remain novicios for one year, during which time we will all watch over you to assure that you are ready. Your behavior from this night on, for the duration of that year, will be monitored by each one of us," my father explained, looking directly at me, "and if any act, any word, any thought even, does not show that you are trying to live like Christ, you will be ejected, never to return. Do you understand? Never." He looked from me to Pedro and back to me again before he continued somberly, "As novicios, you will witness *La Procesión de la Santa Cruz* tonight. Let me warn you that it will not be like las Estaciones. If you stay, you will be asked to take the vows of Penitencia before you leave." My father paused for a moment, letting the significance of his words seep into our consciousness. "There will be no turning back," he added. "Search your hearts, hijos míos, for if you leave now, you will have yet another year before you may petition me in the traditional fashion."

Looking deeply into the face of my friend, my father's eyes sought his answer. Coming to rest on mine again, his gaze, though serious, reflected a calm assurance that he trusted me to be responsible for myself, trusted my judgment to make myself accountable to my Brothers, both young and old. In that instant, I knew I was ready to live my life according to my religion, in preparation for a good Christian death. I didn't want to wait another year.

I nodded. Out of the corner of my eye, I looked at Pedro. Surely he, too, was honored to finally become a novicio in our first service alone with the men—as men—without the company of women and children. Pedro, his face shining with pride, nodded wordlessly. And after another moment my father nodded, satisfied at what he'd found, not because of our actions, but because of what he'd seen in our souls and in our hearts when he'd looked into our eyes.

Pedro's father beamed. Heaving a loud sigh at the end of our momentary hesitation, he had wondered if his son would decide to wait. My uncle stood proudly as he led us into the middle room. We followed, the child in us a little afraid, the men in us confident in our desire to meet whatever our destinies had finally deemed was rightfully, finally, ours.

Our wait was over; our lives as Hermanos had begun.

I can not, in good conscience, describe the entire ceremony that followed, for being yet, until my death, an Hermano, it is not for me to divulge. I can only say that it began as we fell to our knees in the dark flickering shadows at the back of the room, moving as one toward the light of the candles shining on the faces of the santos before us, beckoning silently to take part in the age-old ritual with our elders. And I can allow for the images inspired by the first verse of the alabado which marked our entrance to the sacred room:

Todos por union,	All in unison,
Entren de Rodillas,	Enter on Knees,
Adorar la Sangre	To Adore the Blood,
De esta Disciplina.	Of this Discipline.

It set the tone for the poignant mood of the next few hours, hinting at the discipline that would be endured by the Hermano chosen to portray Christ, by the men made to revile him, by the men who asked for Penance, and by me fulfilling my premonition. Our first celebration as novicios ended when we took our vows. We left feeling like men. It is the fond memories of times such as this with my friends that I shared with my grandchildren, not the disclosures which I can not reveal.

Brujas

As if we didn't have enough to think about, on our way home we encountered yet another surprise to remind us that we could still be frightened like children. We left the morada with only a candle in a tin holder to illuminate the pitch-black night. We came to the fence by the river where we had seen the difunto only weeks before, both Pedro and I trying to shake the beginnings of a shiver down our spines. Laughing it off, Pedro only added to my fears. I thought we had sensed something and had learned a valuable lesson in not shrugging our intuitions off.

"I keep thinking we're going to see some ..."

Pedro cut me off. "Don't say it, don't even think it." In his voice was the desperation that if we did neither, the feeling would go away.

We hunched between the wires of the fence, stumbling over our feet as we crossed the edge of the field to the river and hurrying over the bridge without mishap. We found both Berto and Tino waiting for us.

"Are you alright?" Tino asked.

"Fine. What are you guys doing here?"

"Waiting for you," Berto confessed, "in case you, er, you know."

I smiled, for the first time wishing we were more affectionate with one another so that I could hug my primos for their concern. Tino, on the other hand, gave way to his emotions and threw his arms around both Pedro and me with what sounded like a sob. Before I knew it, Berto's arms were around all of us and for a moment I was afraid I wouldn't be able to choke back the cry building up in the back of my throat brought on by both by the deep love I felt for these guys and by the pain of my wounded back.

"Let's get you guys home." Filiberto let go, the gruffness in his voice betraying that he, too, had been affected.

Arms thrown over one another's shoulders, the four of us trudged away from the river. Suddenly, Berto sucked in a deep breath. Pointing to the arbolera, our meeting place, he squeaked, "¡*Miren*!"

We looked, almost falling in our tracks when our knees gave way. We clutched at one another, our eyes trying to make our minds digest what we were seeing. It was a ball of fire, like a tumbleweed set to flame, only brighter, the center pulsating in a dark orange glow as if lit from within!

"*Una bruja*." I breathed.

Indeed, we had all heard that the fireballs seen by others were witches. Never having seen one for ourselves, until now, we had always suspected they were myths. I remembered Berto's boast the last time his father had told him of his own encounter with balls of fire. He'd once said he wished he could see one to which my uncle had warned him to be careful he wished for, just as he had told me at the morada. Berto had scoffed, afterward when we were alone, that if he ever saw one, he'd throw a stake through its center and see who it was that died the following day. But now, there it was, and I shuddered hoping he didn't remember his boast.

Tino clutched my arm so tightly it began to grow numb, and I forced myself to loosen my hold on Pedro, just a little. We watched in shocked silence, made mute by our fear. When the ball began to move, it rose about a foot from the ground, slowly revolving round and round in a small circle. Its unhurried up-down revolution was almost beautiful in its execution, as though flitting lightly to a melody only it could hear. Both mesmerized by the waltzing flame and afraid, I felt the hairs on the back of my neck begin to prickle with an unseen vibration that seemed to emanate from the dance in the orchard.

And when its ring widened and it circled with more velocity, I was sure the now audible throbbing made all our hair stand on end. We watched, frozen, as it slowed, breaking away from its circular orbit. Bouncing close to the ground yet not touching it, then rising a few feet above, it moved, coming directly toward us!

"Why do things like this have to happen to us?" The whine that emerged in a whispered squeal from Tino's mouth released the tense muscles of our limbs, and we backed away huddled together. Too late to realize what was behind us, we tumbled over the riverbank. Each clutching the one beside him with one hand and fistfuls of weeds in the other, we prevented, just barely, a midnight dunking in the icy river. The plop of the candle into the water plunged us into darkness.

If the ball of flames coming our way was truly a witch, then it probably laughed at the four pairs of eyes peeking from the ledge of the bank. It seemed to waver for a moment as it floated before us, and Pedro whispered, "It sees us. We can't make a run for it."

"Should we yell?" I proposed. "Maybe we'll scare it off."

"Not unless we have to," Berto whispered, adding under his breath, "Wake everybody up, why don't we, on the night you were supposed to become men. Let's wait, maybe it'll go away."

"If it don't?" Tino couldn't finish; the ball began to move.

"If it doesn't we can always fall backward into the river," Berto reasoned impatiently, "stay in the water till it goes away."

Good idea, I thought, but how long would it remain? Staring at the approaching ball of flame, I muttered, "If it is a witch, it'll probably stay until just before sun up, watching our skin turn blue."

The ball closed the distance slowly, as if sensing our fear, tormenting us with its elusive presence. And when it reached the edge of the river on the other side of the bridge to our left, we breathed a collective sigh of relief. We turned only our heads as we crouched, ready to hit the water if it lunged. We could feel on our faces the heat emanating from the flames only a short distance away, but the chill of fear circulated too deep in our bones to be eliminated.

It hovered only a moment, as if waiting to make the leap over the river. Then it bounced gently inches above the water and crossed to the other side.

Suddenly remembering my gramma and my mother's method of warding off bad storms by making the sign of the cross in the four directions of the compass and faking a courage I didn't quite feel, I stood suddenly and formed the cross in the air in the direction of the ball of flames, saying, "*En el nombre del Padre, del Hijo, y del Espíritu Santo.*" As I began to turn to my left, the east, to finish my rotation, the ball seemed to pick up speed, bobbling up and down as though bidding us an eerie good night and moving more quickly in a wavering path on its midnight journey. Unfortunately, right then Berto remembered his boast. When his fist rose just inches from my head, I saw what he was up to.

"No!" I yelled, hoping to deflect the rock at the moment he let it fly from his grasp.

Through the blanket of darkness, we imagined we saw the rock. But all we really saw was the fluttering of the ball of fire, which paused as though it shivered.

Had Berto's rock met its mark on some inhuman entity and caused injury or was the ball of fire really a witch who got scared at my blessing? We had no clue. Or perhaps it became bored with the fun of scaring us out of our wits and simply decided to reach its destination. We didn't know why, but the flaming ball suddenly took flight, racing over the meadow with such speed that the blink of an eye would have missed its departure into the forest beyond.

"What have I done?" Berto whispered. None of us knew. Instead, we asked questions of our own.

"Did you really hit it?"

"D'you think it—she's—hurt?"

"Will anyone be sick tomorrow? Or worse, hurt maybe, without a good explanation?"

"I can think of something worse … what if someone dies?"

That Berto's action might cause anything in the days to come intensified our terror. We picked up our pace as much as we dared in the dark, our spines tingling and our legs shaking so that we huddled together in case one of us fell. When we left Tino at his home first in the welcome beam of light from the open door, we collected ourselves as best we could, supplying courage to one another with words we'd been too frightened to speak in the darkness. But when the door closed behind him, the black arms of night closed once more around the three of us shaking on his stoop. After Berto and I left Pedro standing safely in his doorway with the light pouring out behind him, there were only two of us to walk the remainder of the way alone. I took my turn waiting at my door to watch Berto run down the road to be the last of us to reach home safely. His impulsive act haunted me and probably the other three, all except Horacio, who for some reason had been spared our midnight encounters twice.

Going into the kitchen quietly, hoping I wouldn't wake my mother, I removed my shoes and jumped into bed fully clothed.

"¿Estas bien?" I heard my mother ask quietly from the bedroom.

"Sí, Mamá," I replied, "Buenas noches." I wasn't sure I was supposed to disclose what I had undergone only an hour before, so my telling her good night was my way of assuring that she would go back to sleep and leave me to my own thoughts. Huddled in the cocoon of my own blankets at last, I shivered so badly I wondered if my bones would come apart.

I feared for my grandmother. The unwelcome suspicion that gnawed at my mind, biting into my subconscious dread and filling me with the morsels of doubt, was that she could indeed be a witch. My mind filled with images of the tiny woman in the meadows, her long silver hair braided in a bun on the nape of her neck, the hem of her long dress wet with early morning dew, her apron folded over with one hand while the other gently picked plants that her keen eyes discerned were remedios, ignoring those that were poisonous. With her wonderful innate ability as a médica, she knew which herbs and plants were for what ailment and whether they should be applied to the skin or taken internally as a tea. She could tell just by laying her hands on your body whether it was your stomach that ailed you and you could be cured with *manzanilla* or *yerba del manzo* or if it was your appendix and she could do nothing but offer to ride with you in Maestro's automobile to the doctor in town.

I remembered the time I had snuck away with a handful of still hot bizcochitos, their centers soft instead of crunchy. I relished the savory cookies as I gobbled them down, only to suffer terrible stomach cramps a little later. My grandmother had clucked her tongue, telling me that now I knew why I had to wait for the masa of the cookies to harden and cool. And she had cured me by making me swallow an awful-tasting combination of baking soda in tepid water before rolling me on my protesting stomach and gently pulling at the skin from my lower back kind of the way a cat likes to knead fabric with its claws. I remember feeling relaxed under her skilled hands until, clutching fingers-full of skin, she yanked me up quickly and painfully so that my skin cracked loudly. Before I could cry out, she released me and playfully spanked my bottom instead. Being *empachado* had been agony. I was cured, though, and I never ate another pastry hot from the oven again. Although I personally never attempted this "cure" on anyone myself, my wife and later on my daughter mastered the act, which by the way, works on animals, too.

I remember another incident of my youth when my abuela was accused of being a witch. The misunderstanding developed from my gramma's mischievous nature—for she loved to play a good joke on others from time to time, a love inherited by both my uncle and me—but what followed planted the first seed of doubt in the few who believed in *embrujeria* and supplied the fruit of evidence in those who were convinced she was a witch. Of the latter, there were only two, an old woman who lived far up the road (thankfully) and had been the cause of the entire fiasco in which she accused my grandmother of bewitching her and Horacio's little brother, Julio (who, if the truth be told, was afraid of everybody and everything and didn't count).

Now, this old woman was a new addition to our valley. Having only moved here a few years before, she kept to herself. She may have become well liked in the community had we gotten a chance to get to know her, but she never tried to strike up a friendship with anyone. We all thought she was either a recluse or a nose-in-the-air who wanted nothing to do with us.

The evening of the accusation was the first time she had ever tried to mingle with the people of Cañon, and the disastrous episode marked only the beginning of her vengeance. During a dance thrown in the schoolhouse (the only building big enough for community affairs), much to our surprise, the recluse walked in. Arriving in a long, dark velvety dress, the tall woman had come late enough to make a noticeable entrance, yet early enough to saunter about with a haughty air, as though she had decided to hobnob with the rabble.

Before long, she made her way to the refreshment table where my grandmother was filling a cup with liquor. The woman, who towered over my gramma, rudely shoved her to one side. Ever the patient, well-behaved lady, my grandmother waited quietly for an apology. When it didn't come, my tiny gramma smiled, offering the woman her cup.

The woman looked with disdain down her long nose at the tiny lady with such twinkling eyes. If she had only looked deeper into the depths of my gramma's eyes, she would have seen the impish mischief that lay just below the surface. But after only a slight hesitation, she took the drink, suspecting nothing.

What the woman didn't know was that the cup had been for my uncle, and it was filled to the brim with moonshine. Unlike those who have drunk mula full knowing the effect of such powerful home-made liquor, she gulped a good portion down before choking She didn't know that the queer burning in her stomach and the dizziness were caused by the seemingly innocuous drink, not from the spell of a witch.

Her drunken screams echoed through the room when she could finally wheeze out a breath. When the shrieks began, so did the denunciation: "¡Bruja!" Though there was already quite a bit of distance between them, she had staggered away from my grandmother. Already swaying on her feet, her accusing finger pointing shakily before her at the tiny woman who smiled smugly as her eyes twinkled with glee, the newcomer screeched loud enough for all to hear. By this time a trio of primos who played guitar, violin, and an accordion had ceased to play, and everyone's eyes were glued to the scene enacted before their disbelieving eyes: "She gave me poison and now I'm dying!"

Now, being a tight little community, we were all aware of how the woman had purposely stumbled into my gramma. And we were all too aware of the power of moonshine on an unsuspecting soul not used to such an infamous brew. Thus, when the woman wavered on her unsteady feet and screamed that my grandmother had bewitched her, we understood that my grammita had only taken the woman's conceit down a notch, put her in her place for her rudeness.

We didn't mean to be mean, but we couldn't muffle our laughter. The crowd went wild practically rolling on the floor in spasms of uncontrollable mirth. Everyone who had ever drunk moonshine knew that she had been bewitched alright. Though my abuelita's hand had offered the drink, it hadn't been she who had cast the spell. It had been good old-fashioned mula.

Screaming that she was in the midst of witches and lunatics, the inebriated woman took on a look of wild-eyed disbelief. Panic-stricken, she fled, staggering and stumbling dizzily out the door. To top it off, the full moon illuminated the comic scene as we collectively stumbled outside, our now hysterical laughter following the woman's delirious flight, and as she weaved away into the night in her car, her shrieks echoed in her wake. "¡Brujas!!"

There was no forgetting the incident in the years that followed either, for each time the haunted woman drove up or down the road passing our house—or anyone near the road—screaming those infamous two words that we are a community of witches and lunatics, our laughter echoed behind her. Our community gave the woman who had accused my abuela of bewitching her the name *Lunática*. And though my grandmother says that she is sorry for the part she played in teaching the woman a well-deserved lesson in manners, she always smiled when the woman passed.

Though I know what happened was an innocent prank on my grandmother's part (with a little help from the spell of intoxication from the mula), and not the spell of a witch, the first seeds of doubt had been planted, growing in the thriving soil of my subconscious, budding into a full flower of suspicion when she did something that could not be explained.

That my grandmother had an unnatural ability was something I knew with a certainty, for there were many times when she could read my innermost thoughts like a book, just by looking into my eyes as if she could indeed see into my soul. And though from time to time my mother could sense that something was wrong with me, I knew it came from a mother's intuition. Even though that, too, is inexplicable, it is expected from women. But what explanation was there for the premonition I received that my grandmother had shared in her own restless sleep? The question was staggering, and I worried at the unspoken implication.

Unfortunately, the inquiry raised yet another worry, and this one rose like a dragon from the depths of snaking questions in the bottomless pit of my mind, threatening to devour me with the razor-sharp teeth embedded in the open jaws of my doubts. My father had it, too, the uncanny power to know my thoughts and respond with his own. Quaking uncontrollably, I panicked. If I suspected my grandmother of being a witch, then my father would come under suspicion as well. Were there male witches? I didn't know.

You're being ridiculous, my conscience chided. You might as well suspect yourself, why don't you, you carry the same genes. That bit of information to chew, I really didn't need. It snaked through my mind, now leaving images of myself in its trail—the evening I fled from the voice of La Muerte alone—in the night as I encountered what she had warned—the night I witnessed myself clothed in white as the Hermano who received his penance in the morada.

The image of me as a novicio brought a welcome warmth to my quivering body, but then it changed. The ball of fire hovered over me for an instant before the dragon, which had grown as it gorged on the multitude of my questions, opened its gaping maw. As the jaws closed over the flaming ball, plunging me into merciful darkness, I agonized that the morning would reveal my grandmother had been hurt.

Sangre de Cristo

The next morning, Good Friday, found me in bed with a high fever. The chill that permeated my body had increased during the night, but anxious to join the Hermanos at the morada, I struggled to rise, only to fall back weakly against my pillow. My grandmother, who was drinking coffee with my mother in the kitchen, came to the doorway. Silhouetted in the rays of the sun in the window behind her, she seemed enveloped in a cloak of white. My fears of the night were dispelled, there was no bandage, no limp to her walk; and in the light of day I chided myself for my foolishness, convinced that my fever had caused such disturbing thoughts.

That my abuela was here was no accident, no inexplicable coincidence to agitate my imaginings. For she knew that I had become a novicio the night before, and as médica, she had come to see how I fared. She moved to my side with a jar of her remedio, turned me to my side to rub the *romerillo*, or silver sage, on my back, and then tucked the quilts around me once again without a word.

My mother placed a mug of warm broth in my hands, brushing a gentle hand over my cheek and pulling a chair by my bed for my gramma before she left for the church with my aunt. A few of the women would give the capilla a light cleaning before covering the saints with cloaks of black this morning to symbolize the dark day of Christ's death. They would remain concealed until Easter morning, the day of His resurrection.

Settling herself comfortably, gramma took from her apron pocket a small kerchief with a trailing thread and proceeded to continue her embroidery on its edge, the needle whipping in and out of the intricate design with a delicate, almost birdlike fluttering of her hands. I sipped the warm soup watching her, waiting for her to speak. I knew I had inherited my physical appearance from her, the small, thin stature, the nose, and her humor. Had I also inherited a mental power I didn't understand, or want, from my beloved grandmother? Before I could ponder the question further, before I could think of a way to phrase my question without hurting the feelings of the tiny woman seated beside me, she spoke.

"You have a gift."

Her words revived my concerns that the warm broth had begun to dispel. She looked up from her embroidery. Although this was one time I wished I could turn away, I forced myself to look into her eyes. Bright with tears, hers held a mixture of sadness and regret. When she blinked the drops away and smiled softly at me, there was also pleasure and expectation in their depths. "The gift of sight," she began, "is strong in our family though inherited by some, not all, through the generations. And," she added, "while some seemed only to possess a strong sense of intuition, there were others who had the power to know other's thoughts, especially of people with whom they were close.

"I will tell you a story, hijo, a cuento of a young girl you know well." Putting her embroidery aside, she settled back into the pillow at her back and continued. "When this girl was very young, she began to have disturbing dreams, dreams which frightened her because in the days that followed, they would almost always come true. More and more often as she grew, the dreams plagued her. And her abuelito, the only one who believed her, died before he could explain the gift she had inherited from him. She learned to keep the dreams secret because whenever she told anyone, they looked at her as if she were loca. And people, ignorant and afraid, had started to think she was either crazy or a witch. Years passed, until one night she saw her father in her dream and knew what real fear was. In her vision her father was being dragged by horses in the field he was plowing, his leg entangled in the reins behind the arado."

She paused, taking her sack of punche from her pocket to roll a cigarette. I squirmed restlessly on the bed. From past experience, I knew that it was an effort in futility to urge her on, for if prodded to finish a cuento before she decided she wanted to, she was known to teach me a longer lesson in patience, sometimes making me wait for days, or until I had even forgotten the beginnings of a story and her teasing reminder would set me off, begging for the end. I had to hand it to my abuelita; she knew how to build up the suspense in her stories like no one else. I was forced to wait as she took a laboriously long time rolling her smoke, her eyes twinkling with mirth at my discomfort.

"Where was I?" she asked, striking a wooden match on the sole of her shoe.

"Oh, yes, the dream." Puffing a small stream of smoke, she continued, "The next morning, much to her dismay, the girl's father had already begun to plow the fields when she awoke. Without breakfast, the girl ran out of the house, straight to the field."

When she paused to puff her cigarette again, I could have screamed from the suspense; it was killing me. "Now, the neighbors had honey bees," she reminisced, "and the hives were just across the river. For some reason, I never knew why, they swarmed—and the girl's father with his horses were right in their path. It was a good thing the girl got there when she did, for her father, strong though he was, was already struggling to keep the horses from running away with the plow. When she looked down, the girl saw that the end of one of the reins had tangled around her father's leg, just like in her dream. And just as the panicked horses took off, shaking the bees from their heads, she jumped forward, unwrapping the rein just in the nick of time to save her father from a very bad injury—perhaps even death."

Gramma puffed at her cigarette a moment before she added, "That was the day the girl finally realized that her dreams were not the curse she had thought they were all along, for years having been afraid that perhaps she was a witch and that she had dark powers from the devil. They were forewarnings, a gift from God, and she had learned to read their meaning to help others."

Putting her cigarette out, she looked at me closely, searching my eyes for understanding. "Sí," she said quietly, "I have been called bruja many times, hijo, but only by the ignorant or the envious, God help them. They do not know that what I have is a gift from God and that I have learned to use my gift to avisar or to give consejo to those I see in my dreams."

I breathed a sigh of relief, knowing that no matter what happened in the future, I would never suspect my abuelita of being a witch again. And I understood that my father possessed a different gift, a power to read my thoughts and to respond in the voice of my conscience to guide me in the journey of life. But at the same time, I was troubled. Hadn't I also inherited such a gift, a power to see or hear things others didn't?

I knew she picked up the apprehension in my eyes, for my gramma said softly, "*No te preocupes*. Do not be worried, hijo mío. Instead, thank the Lord that you have something not many people do and learn to use your gift to help yourself and to help others if you're able. And if your friends question your intuition, you do what your conciencia tells you. If they are real amigos, they will look to you for consejo. Advise them well. If they are not, then you will have to live with their suspicions and their accusations just as I have. And though it will be hard, you will have to learn to leave them to their own consciences."

I nodded, and we sat in companionable silence for a while. My gramma took up her embroidery again as my mind digested the importance of her story, her counsel. I knew that I would have to find within myself the strength to overcome my disquiet, to listen and watch for any avisos in the future, to use my gift of intuition wisely.

Suddenly remembering what I had seen the night before, I asked, "Do you believe there really are witches?"

"¿Por qué?" she asked, looking at me quizzically.

I described our encounter with the ball of fire and what Berto had done as it had fled.

She nodded, "There are many, including myself, who have seen them. And since there is no explanation for the balls of fire, there are many who believe that they are witches. No one knows for sure. But it has been a long time that any have been seen around here."

"What do you believe?" I asked, a little uneasy about her answer.

"I believe that there is a power of good, which is God. But the Bible tells us that there is also a power of evil. Just as Dios gives His children gifts which help them to live as good *Cristianos*, then so could el Diablo guide those he chooses with the powers of darkness."

She crossed herself before she looked at me for a moment. "That you saw one during la Cuaresma disturbs me. This is one of the most sacred seasons of the year. If it was a bruja or some other work of el Diablo, then they seem to have no fear that this is Lent, and today is Viernes Santo, the day our Savior died."

"What could it mean?" I whispered.

The heavy silence of our thoughts spoke volumes, for we both knew that this afternoon *La Procesión de Sangre de Cristo*, the procession of the Blood of Christ, in which a chosen Hermano would carry the crucifix from the morada on his back, would be enacted. And even though the Penitente would not be crucified, the re-enactment of the most sorrowful day in the life of our Savior would take its toll on the Brother who played the crucial role. I wondered if it would be the Hermano who had portrayed Christ the night before in la Procesión de la Santa Cruz.

Before either of us could speak, my mother rushed into the house, bringing with her a bit of news that brought an unwelcome confirmation and a bit of relief to our uneasy thoughts. A neighbor found the Lunática sprawled unconscious and bleeding from her head outside her house. He had summoned her hired hand to transport her to the doctor in Las Vegas.

"What do you think happened to her?" my mother asked, looking from my grandmother to me and back at her again.

My abuela's face mirrored my thoughts: a bruja! Could the one who had protested the most loudly that she was surrounded by witches and lunatics in fact be a witch herself? Could Berto's rock have met its mark on the floating ball of fire, leaving in its stead a wound in a witch that would cause her death? I knew that neither my abuela nor I wished the woman harm, yet I saw in her eyes the question I felt in my heart. If the woman died, then would the significance of the ball of fire we suspected be dispelled by her own death?

Unable to rest and unable to sleep, I rose when Berto appeared at my door about noon, sent to see if I was well enough to go to the morada before the procession began. At first my mother protested, having heard of my induction from my father earlier that morning. But rising unsteadily, I assured her that I felt better and that if los Hermanos had sent for me, surely I was needed at the morada. Physically, it was the truth, for my chills had subsided and I was no longer dizzy, but my mind whirled with questions and an impending sense of doom.

Concerned about how Berto would react if he heard of what had happened to the Lunática from someone else, I broke the news to him gently. Though I tried to convince him that we didn't know whether the woman was only an innocent recluse who had fallen, perhaps even attacked by a thief (which was unheard of in our community), I heard the doubt in my own voice and saw the disbelief in his eyes. Berto remained convinced that the woman was a witch and that she had been injured by his hand, the hand which had cast the stone. He ran his fingers through his shock of hair again and again, upset about her probable revenge. I, too, worried for Filiberto, remembering my grandmother's words.

When we arrived at the morada, the Hermanos were resting beneath the shady cottonwoods outside. I went from one to the other exchanging greetings, touched by their concern. My father beckoned to me, moving a little away from the others so we could speak in private. He asked if I was up to the long hours ahead. After I assured him I felt fine, he told me what had been decided during the morning in my absence.

When he told me who would be the Cristo in the procession of the afternoon, I frowned. My Tío Daniel who had been chosen for the honored role the night before had asked for and received permission to again portray Christ in the reenactment of His walk to Monte Calvario. I needed to tell my father about the premonition of impending death I sensed, but there was no way to explain without beginning with the ball of fire the boys and I had encountered the night before. So I took a deep breath, plunged in, watching his eyes widen when I told him what Abuela and I had discussed, and finished with the account of the neighbor woman's mysterious injury. I breathlessly waited for his reaction.

He took it all in, quiet with thought before he spoke. "I am glad that your abuela explained about what it is to be a gifted member of this familia," he said, "for from now on you will listen more closely to your intuition to guide you on the right path in life."

"But that's just it," I blurted, "I have a queer feeling about what gramma said about someone dying. As much as I don't like that lady for how she treated gramma, I don't wish her dead, but if she does die, at least that might mean Tío Daniel won't."

"Perhaps Mamá is right," he said. "I trust her judgment," he added, laying a hand on my shoulder, "as I also trust yours."

He stood, and I felt a surge of pride that he spoke to me as one man to another. I waited for him to say that the procession to follow would be canceled or that he would put it to a vote of all the Hermanos, but when he spoke I knew that it wasn't something he had the power to do. The rites and rituals of the Penitente Brotherhood were clear, and the reenactment I dreaded would proceed as usual.

"We will do what we must," he said with determination, "and we will pray that Daniel will not be the one who has to die with Cristo tonight."

We walked together back into the morada where the rest of los Hermanos were in prayer. The window, covered with a dark cloth, let no welcome warmth or light into the room. In the chill of the thick adobe walls there were only the flickering flames of candles to shed a wavering glow on the altar and the men kneeling before it. As we joined them, I took the crucifix I had finished carving, painted black the day before, and placed it among those of my Brothers and the small covered santo Pedro had carved. Kneeling, I waited for the peace I always felt when I prayed there. I longed for the solace I would have received if I were able to look into the face of the Savior. But every retablo, every santo, was covered in shrouds of black. I felt a sense of loss, of foreboding—until I closed my eyes. From the dark recesses of my mind the face of Christ emerged, filling me with strength to face whatever might occur.

It was a little before two o'clock when we emerged from the morada, blinking our eyes in the welcome light of the sun, warming our stiff bodies in its rays as we were surrounded by the friends and relatives who had come to join our procession. Women bustled into the cocina with pots of food while others entered the prayer room for a moment of contemplation before we began.

I greeted my mother and grandmother with a hug, reluctant to let either of them go, for in their arms I felt the comforting reassurance of my youth. I found myself close to tears, realizing that the innocence of my childhood was lost to me, only to be remembered in their embrace with the bittersweet knowledge that I had willingly forsaken the child within me and let the man in me emerge when I took the vows of a novicio.

Collecting myself as best I could with the tumultuous emotions and frightening premonition looming over my thoughts, I made my way over to the boys who were resting beneath the trees, knowing if anyone could take my mind off my worries, it would be the gang. Horacio was speaking as I joined them.

"My gramma told me a cuento once," he said quietly. "She thinks it's only a legend though, 'cause she never really heard of it happening in her lifetime. Her own abuela told it to her when she was a girl. Do you wanna hear?"

Berto nodded. "Anything, if it'll stop me from thinking about the bruja."

We all looked at Berto sympathetically, wishing we could relieve him of the burden of his fears and knowing there was nothing we could do except keep his mind off them.

Horacio began, "Well, you know how Tío Daniel is going to play the Cristo and carry the cross on his shoulders in a while?"

"Don't remind me." I waved a hand at Horacio to continue when the boys' confused looks turned on me. I was thinking of my uncle's nightmares about the war and wondering if this was his penance for some unimaginable act.

"Anyway," Horacio continued after looking at me askance, "my gramma told me that one of the descansos up there," he pointed his chin to the mountains beyond the church, "is supposed to be a real grave, the grave of an Hermano who died while he was acting the part of Christ."

We gasped. Pedro added, much to my discomfort, "It could be true, you know. I heard my papá and my grampo talking once, and they said that in the old days the one who played Cristo was really crucified on Viernes Santo, only instead of nails, they used ropes to tie him to the cross."

I was unable to shake off the chills that rose up my spine. Though I noticed the others squirming as well, I knew my distress for my uncle was greater than theirs because they had no knowledge of my conversation with my grandmother.

"All I know is what gramma told me," Horacio finished, leaning toward us. "She said that if it was true, then the Hermano who died would go straight to heaven. In those days, no one was allowed to witness the procession, but what was stranger was that the dead man's shoes were left on his doorstep so that the family would know how he had died, and for a whole year no one but the Penitentes knew where they had buried him."

We all took this bit of news in silence. I pictured the scene Horacio described and thanked the Lord silently that we didn't do things the old way anymore, and then Pedro spoke up as if reading my mind.

"I'm glad we don't do it that way anymore."

We all agreed. However, as we rose to join the men already getting into formation, I saw the black crucifix carried on the shoulders of two Hermanos who emerged from the morada. The moment for which I had longed for so many years—and only today had come to dread—arrived. For the first time, I would take part in the procession of Penitentes, but the pride I felt was overshadowed by the knowledge that my uncle, whom I loved like an older brother, would be in the lead carrying the heavy cross. I knew my eyes would be upon him all the way. Coupled with my foreboding that someone would be dead before morning, my first procession became a penitence indeed.

I sighed heavily, lining up with Pedro at the rear of the group. As everyone who gathered to join the procesión took their places behind us, I was surprised to see Primo Victoriano, leaning heavily on his bordón, directly behind me with his wife, Prima Juanita. I noticed Berto and the others positioned behind him, ready in case he needed assistance.

I turned and offered the elderly man my hand. "If you get tired, everyone will understand if you have to stop," I told him in a whisper.

"I will," he promised. "I just had to come one last time, you understand?"

The longing in his withered face was enough to tell me that this might be the last Lent he would see in his lifetime, that this might be the last chance he had to join his Brothers before age or ill health took its toll.

I nodded in understanding, but I saw the weariness of his eyes, in the way he leaned on his cane, in the way his breath emerged from his mouth in short, tired gasps. "Don't overtire yourself, primo," I warned, but he only waved my concern away with a hand.

The procession began when my father's voice rose to announce that this was the reenactment of the Passion of Christ. My Tío Daniel, the massive black cross on his shoulders, moved forward, setting the pace for us to follow.

"Oh—ohhh, *imagen de Jesús doloroso para ejercitarse en el santo sacrificio de la misa como memoria que es de tan sacrosanta pasión*," my father intoned, telling us to imagine our dolorous Savior fulfilling His destiny in such a sacred sacrifice in our reenactment of the memory of such a sacrosanct passion.

I read along as the rest of the Hermanos joined in, my voice blending with the varied pitches of the men, rising and falling with each line. The music emerged as if from our very souls to waver and float around us as we spoke to our Savior in a somber hymn rather than with mere words. The very tone of our combined voices and the reverence with which we sang spoke volumes as our words conveyed how much we believed in the passion of our Savior.

My father's words conveyed that Jesus had revealed many times to his faithful servants what was to follow. And though no one actually did the things to my uncle that my father told us, he paused with each recitation, and the weight of the words he spoke with such tremulous emotion made us feel that just by describing the terrible things done to Christ he felt them in his heart as he carried the symbolic cross.

Then the first time he stopped, Tío Daniel spoke loud enough for all to hear the words that indeed seemed to be the words of our Savior: "*Primeramente me levantaron del suelo por la cuerda y por los cabellos viente y tres veses.*" My uncle revealed, "First they lifted me from the floor by rope and from my hair twenty-three times."

As he resumed the pace for the procession to follow, my uncle paused twenty-one more times. His pace slowing with each pause, Daniel fought the trembling of his legs. I saw his shoulders bend under the cumbersome cross, symbolically weighing heavily in our hearts each time he staggered under its massive bulk. Even from where I stood, with twelve men before me, I heard his breath come more heavily, his voice emerged more tremulously, the words quaver as he described the countless terrors suffered by Christ in His passion.

"They gave me six thousand, six hundred, sixty-six lashings of the whip when they tied me to the column …. I fell on the earth seven times … before I fell five times on the road to Mount Calvary …. I lost one thousand twenty-five drops of blood."

By the time we were halfway to the church, many of the women were sniffling, wiping their eyes with their kerchiefs. But the worst was yet to come as my uncle continued, weakened but undeterred in fulfilling his role.

"They gave me twenty punches to my face …. I had nineteen mortal injuries … they hit me in the chest and the head twenty-eight times …. I had seventy-two major wounds over the rest."

By this time some of the women were weeping openly, and the smaller children, frightened beyond belief—I knew because I was at their age—began to sob quietly at their mothers' distress. Primo Victoriano stumbled behind me, and I stepped back to grasp one elbow as Berto took the other. The determination in his face to reach the capilla, to finish the procesión as an Hermano one last time, was heart-wrenching. And as I took some of the weight off his feet with my support, I felt tears gather in my eyes.

"I had a thousand pricks from the crown of thorns on my head because I fell, and they replaced the crown many times," my uncle's weakened voice continued. "I sighed one hundred nine times … they spat on me seventy-three times."

The tears flowed down my face. I heard Primo Victoriano's labored breaths at my side. I thanked God the procession had come to an end, for the words were too painful to bear, humbling our Christian souls to the core of our being.

"Those who followed me from the pueblo were two hundred thirty," my uncle finished, "only three helped me …. I was thrown and dragged through barbs seventy-eight times."

As we reached the capilla, my uncle was barely moving, his feet shuffling wearily in the dirt, his breathing labored. When he leaned precariously forward, the cross threatening to smash him into the earth, several women cried out in alarm. Leaping quickly to his aid, my father and Primo Esteban each grabbed an end of the beam lying on his shoulders, relieving him of his burden just as his knees buckled beneath him and my uncle fell to the ground on hands and knees.

When I saw him fall, his face grimaced in pain, my heart throbbed in fear that he could be gravely hurt, that my premonition of an impending death would come true. I would have rushed to his side but for Primo Victoriano, whose arm clutched mine tightly, his shoulder leaning heavily against me. If I left him, he too would fall.

All the women were now sobbing as they looked at my uncle, trying in vain to stifle their uncontrollable cries because of the children, who, too young to understand what we did, cried with distress and sympathy for their mothers' tears. A few of los Hermanos rushed to help my uncle to his feet, supporting him as they took him into the church. Though he was exhausted, my tío appeared to be unhurt, and a collective sigh of relief shivered over us. The women calmed themselves and mothers or older sisters hushed children's cries into soft whimpers.

Primo Victoriano continued to shake against me, his legs quaking with his effort to remain standing, his breathing heavy. Beginning to falter under his weight, Berto motioned for Pedro to help us, knowing that my scrawny frame wouldn't be enough help to get the elderly man into the church. Relieving me quickly, they placed our primo's arms over their shoulders, supporting his weight between them as they moved slowly into the capilla with his wife at their side. Following with Horacio and Tino, I heard Primo Victoriano mumble disappointedly at himself that he had no strength left to light the fire or the candles inside. Exchanging glances and nods, we hurried inside, so that when our Primo reached the door, I was busily feeding the flames of the kindling I had lit in the stove and Horacio and Tino were moving from candle to candle quickly. Turning as he entered, I smiled, glad that we were able to relieve him in his duty now that he needed us. Primo Victoriano only nodded, but the gratitude in his eyes said it all before he allowed the boys to settle him comfortably in the pew nearest the stove.

When the Estaciones ended that evening, there was a silence unsurpassed by any service we had yet attended. I knew that for those who prayed with los Hermanos it was in part because of the anguish of witnessing la Procesión de Sangre de Cristo and the terrible sorrow of las Tinieblas that was to come back at the morada afterward. For Pedro and me, it was something more. We knelt with los Hermanos as novicios in the center aisle of the capilla as we made our slow and somber revolution of prayers and alabados around the retablos of the Stations of the Cross. I found my place in my faith, and it affected me as nothing before had done. It was awesome to contemplate.

When my father signaled that it was time for our return to the morada, I retrieved my black crucifix from the altar. I blew out a candle with a fervent prayer for my uncle's health and took another taper with me to the door of the now darkened church. Spotting Primo Victoriano, supported between his wife and Berto's mother, I went to say good night. Someone had gone for a wagon to take the elderly man home, Prima Cleofes explained, for he felt tired. Prima Juanita clucked her tongue at her stubborn husband, but he didn't need to say a word. The soft smile that lit his face told me that he had done what he had set out to do. He was content that he had accompanied his Brothers one last time, and he would toll the bell also for the last time that night before he would allow himself to be taken home.

When I saw los Hermanos taking their places in the center of the road, I bade him good night, telling him to rest and not to worry, I would be there to help him on Easter Sunday as well.

In the soft glow of the lanterns and candles, his eyes grew moist. Blinking back his tears, Primo Victoriano looked at me gravely. He said, "I will be here on Sunday, hermanito, and you will light the candles for me, but I will not see their light. I will not feel the warmth of the fire you will make."

Confused by his cryptic message, I searched his eyes. From the quiet contentment and resoluteness of his gaze, a silent tear that rolled down his withered cheek and touched my heart. My respect and admiration for the elderly Hermano who had fulfilled his desire engulfed me. On impulse, I hugged him close for the first, and for what would also be the last, time in my life.

Las Tinieblas

———

"*Ven*," my father said when I reached the group in the center of the road. Holding his lantern out for me to take, for a moment I forgot my qualms, forgot my worry over Primo Victoriano's weakened condition, and forgot his enigmatic words as well. I was overwhelmed again by such a powerful surge of pride, knowing my father intended to let me walk beside him, lighting his way to the morada. Pedro's father did the same for him, and I knew without looking at my cousin that he, too, felt as I did. We began our walk, my father on one side of me, my Tío Daniel with an arm draped over my shoulder from the other side, their voices rising through the black of night to signal our approach. The campana of the capilla began to toll, slowly, solemnly, the elderly Hermano we had left behind announcing to the valley that los Penitentes were on their way.

The soft golden orbs of lanterns cast very little light in the darkness that enveloped us on our way to the morada for what we thought would be the last time of the Lenten season that year. The alabados echoed hauntingly in the night, evoking a more terrible feeling of dread than at any other time during the Cuaresma. As we passed the meadows on either side of the road, the chirping of crickets quieted and even the screams of the bullfrogs ceased, as though God's creatures sensed something somber in the air.

Only los Hermanos' voices—our voices—rose and fell in the sorrowful notes of the hymn we sent spiraling upward into the starry sky. Our Lenten processions and ceremonies had always been open to the public. Even though families and friends were welcome, there were not many who had elected to attend the most painful of Penitente ceremonies. Emotions ran high during la Procesión de Sangre de Cristo. Witnessing my uncle's reenactment of Christ's faltering steps beneath the heavy crucifix had left some, especially the women and small children, exhausted with grief. The few people who accompanied us—and, of course, Berto, Tino, and Horacio—followed in subdued silence. The anxiety we felt worming through our thoughts as we walked can only be compared to the way one feels when one knows a loved one is about to die and is helpless to prevent the inevitable. Our dread permeated our hearts and was heightened by the night, symbolic of the dark ceremony that was to come: Las Tinieblas.

We reached the shadowy morada, blowing out our lanterns one by one as we entered the inky shadows of its shell. One of los Hermanos closed the door and locked it securely. The door would remain closed throughout the ceremony, but whether to lock us in or to keep someone or something out, I wasn't sure. The sound of the bolt falling into place imprisoned my heart. I had embarked on a journey from which there was no return.

One by one, an Hermano lit thirteen tapers upon the *candelero*, a large triangular candle holder, also known as a *talandario*. It was about four feet high on a pedestal and stood to one side of the altar holding the shrouded saints. Six candles ascended on each side of the triangle toward the one on the top. Tonight, for only a short while, those thirteen candles, representing Christ and the twelve Apostles, would be the only illumination in the room, and after would be utter darkness.

We knelt in a group before the altar. Las Tinieblas began. My father's voice rose in prayer: "*El Miercoles de Ceniza, fue día tan senalado, se comenzó la cuaresma de Jesús Sacraméntado,*" announcing that Ash Wednesday marked the beginning of the Sacramental Lenten season of Christ, that most sorrowful of periods in the lives of Christian souls.

The alabado which followed, los Hermanos' voices raised as one echoing my father's, bespoke of our Savior during the time of His death: "*Ver una corporación que es cosa muy iminente en un encumbrado serro, Nazarino Penitente.*" "See the gathering," he announced, "that is a thing of such imminence on that lofty mountain, a Nazarene Penitent."

The first candle was extinguished.

The second prayer began: "*Pues el Señor escojio, por su voluntad y amor, algunas cuarentas días la culpa del pecador …*"

The words pierced my heart with guilt, eating at me to the core because as one of God's children, a sinner, I must share the blame for all that occurred during the forty days chosen by His son because of His love for us. As the second alabado followed, "*su majestad que es cosa muy eminente, aquí cay, aquí levanta,*

Nazarino Penitente," images of Christ, in His majesty and imminence, falling, rising, intertwined with that of my uncle that afternoon in reenacting the steps beneath the weight of the cross on his shoulders. When I cast a glance from time to time at my tío, he appeared none the worse for having endured such a poignant ordeal of both body and mind. He looked exhausted, yes, but kneeling with resolute inner strength, he raised his voice in prayer, in song, determined to complete his duty with his Brothers one last time this Cuaresma. I prayed that this would not be the last time ever.

My trepidation about what this night might bring increased with each prayer, with each verse of the alabados intoned with rising sorrow. The second candle was extinguished. Words and phrases stuck to my awareness, heightening the fear that my premonition would in fact come true. "Mother Mary, look at Your Son … see the cross on His shoulders …. His body bathed in blood …. His head crowned with thorns …. His final day has come …."

Flickering candles cast many images in the shadows of the ceiling. I saw Christ, bound and led by the soldiers with flowing red capes that reminded me of the devil. I saw their whips fluttering through the air above me. The guilt for all that He had endured, for which I was partly to blame, increased with each prayer, each word adding to castigation of my soul. The alabados, because of the sorrowful way in which they were chanted, became so much more poignant with each verse, I succumbed to the visions floating in the meager light of the dark room.

"*Te pido de corazón, por la llaga de costado, que de alcanzar el perdón … por los golpes que sufriste de los Judíos armados, pido perdón a mi Dios … por la corona de espinas con que fuiste coronado … yo soy un gran pecador, pues si vivo descuidado no dejes de perdonarme, oh Jesús Sacramentado.*"

I spoke the words, asking with all my heart, because of the wound in His side, to be granted forgiveness … because of the blows inflicted by the armed soldiers, I asked forgiveness from my Savior …. because of the crown of thorns with which they crowned Him …. I am a great sinner, and if I live unguardedly, do not forgive me, oh Sacred Jesus.

When I thought of how my Savior had suffered because of my sins, I prayed fervently to be forgiven this night, to be relieved of the weight of guilt that settled so heavily in my heart.

"*Viernes, Viernes de la luz cuando Cristo caminaba por la calle ….*" Friday, Friday of light when Christ walked through the street….

"Friday of light" echoed in my thoughts. I wondered at the paradox—Holy Friday, that darkest of days when our Savior died, we called Friday of light. And then I remembered something Primo Victoriano had said, something about waiting for the time being an Hermano prepared him for, that time of light when he would be called to his Maker. I recalled my uncle's words, "Do not fear death, it is life that should be feared," and I knew that as an Hermano, I would have to accept the fact that I should strive to accept death as my goal in life, the good death of a Christian so that I would be granted eternal life. The paradox was bittersweet with double meaning.

I felt a renewed surge of guilt, for I loved life and I still feared death. I had to learn to love death as well, for if I lived as a good Hermano, I had to have faith that I would be resurrected in a new eternal life that would be better than the one on earth. Somehow, I had to overcome my lack of faith in my fear of dying. I would confess to my father that I was not a good Hermano and take his advice as Hermano Mayor to heart. The last verse added to my despair. I, one of God's imperfect children, had caused Christ's death by my very faithlessness.

"*La Madre con que dolor cuando lo vió clavado, el corazón se le habrió …. El Viernes Santo espiró a los cielos fue llamado, de su Madre recibido … hoy de los duros lamentos, alerta, alerta, suspiro, lagrimas y sentimentos.*"

Sung with only one remaining candle to shed a meager light on us all, the words evoked such pain in the images that assailed me. "His Mother's heart, with such pain when She saw Him nailed, Her heart opened … on Holy Friday He died and was called to Heaven from His Mother who had received Him … today, a day of hard lamentations, alert, alert, sighs, tears, and sentiments."

When I thought of how Christ died for me, because of me, I found myself swallowing the lump in my throat, threatening to bring tears to my eyes again. As the last candle was extinguished (or so I thought), the echoing notes of the last alabado surrounded us in the heavy darkness. One by one as each of the candles was snuffed out, symbolic of the Disciples' abandonment of Christ, the guilt mounted, left me feeling utter despair that I could not escape blame nor could I change what had occurred in centuries past to the one man who could have saved the world.

Our journey into the netherworld began. The palpable weight of blackness engulfed us. I could see nothing, not even shadows or silhouettes of those around me. Utterly blind, my eyes were useless, yet my sense of hearing was heightened. I jumped when the first ominous clattering of the matracas came from across the room. Fingers of fear came from the darkness and ran lightly over my skin. A second, then a third, then more matracas clacked loudly from the outer edges of the tightly knit circle of Hermanos and vecinos around me. The flutelike notes of the pito rose in a melancholic discord, and those around me began to clap, to stomp their feet, to cry out.

The voices rose, the cries of distress turned to screams of agony as las Tinieblas reached toward its climax.

The words of the Apostles' Creed came unbidden into my consciousness: "He died, descended into hell …" Chills raced through my body, again evoking such utter hopelessness that I shared the blame for the death of my Savior. I became aware that tears ran unchecked down my face in grief.

A sense of doom came down out of the darkness, surrounding me, permeating my inner perception with such renewed strength that I knew Death walked among us. Though I couldn't see her, I knew La Muerte sat in her corner to my immediate right with her grimace of death, her sightless but all-seeing eyes focusing on her victim. I sensed with utter conviction that her bow and arrow were poised to strike, and I knew with a certainty I could not explain that she had come for one of us this night.

Amid the sobs, the sound of the agonizing cries of those in the middle room and the shrieks of horror from those around me, I heard one scream rising for a moment above the rest. I realized when it stopped that it had come from the depths of my own soul; and my throat felt raw as I fell to my knees before La Muerte, sobbing my plea for her to spare the soul of the one for whom she came. Reaching out through the darkness, I touched the shroud she wore, shivering when I felt through the silky cloth the skeleton fingers. They seemed to quiver on the bow she held tight in her bony hands. I didn't fear her for myself, but I feared for the soul of the one she had chosen to take with her. I prayed from the depths of my heart for her to leave this night empty-handed. But when I heard her voice come from the shadows around me, I knew my pleas would go unheeded—for she had been called.

"*Vengo,*" the grave voice intoned. "*Llevo a un Penitente que me ha llamado.*"

At her words the pito blew loudly, the matracas clacked more rapidly, the agony of the screams rose to a crescendo around me, rising from the hoarse throats of los Hermanos. For a moment, I wondered if they had heard the voice, too or sensed that Death had come for one of their own.

After about a half an hour as if by some unspoken and pre-ordained plan, the cacophony of horror ceased. The pito fell silent, the matracas stopped their awful whirring, the voices turned from screams to whimpers and hushed sobbing as names of our deceased ancestors were called out and teary sudarios were prayed for the eternal peace of their souls. From behind me an Hermano made his way to the front of the room with the last remaining candle, the white one that symbolized Christ, which he used to relight the rest. Las Tinieblas had come to an end.

In the utter silence, the words of La Muerte echoed in my troubled thoughts: "I come. I take with me a Penitent who has called for me."

As the first candle was lit, I wiped the tears from my face. Rising, I turned to look for my uncle with a terrible feeling of dread at what I might find. I didn't see him, and the sorrow that rose from my heart threatened to make me cry out in anguish.

More candles were lit. As my eyes adjusted to the light, I moved among the people, searching through the weary, tear-streaked faces around me with a heightened sense of despair. I sighed with relief when I saw my father across the room; I saw my friends and the rest of los Hermanos and vecinos around me, and I rejoiced silently that they were all safe. As I rushed through the crowded room, my feet seemed to barely shuffle across the floor, taking me everywhere and nowhere. Under the weight of my terrible apprehension, I moved in slow motion as in a dream.

By the time I saw Tío Daniel in the doorway, desperation had taken its toll on my emotions. I flung myself into his arms, breathing a silent prayer to La Muerte for sparing him from the mortal wound of her arrow of Death. My uncle's arms closed around me tightly, reassuringly strong in his embrace. Pulling me into the small room away from the others, he held me until I composed myself, until the silent sobs rushing through my body ebbed in his arms.

He stepped back, brushing the hair from my eyes and searching my face for explanation. I saw confusion in his eyes; I felt his thoughts. Las Tinieblas were the most frightening of Penitente rituals because of the depth of meaning they symbolized: our Savior's own descent into hell. And though they had frightened me badly when I was younger, surely now that I was a novicio I should have been able to handle them better.

"I was afraid you would die tonight, tío," I confessed, blushing from the desperation of my actions.

He smiled gently. "Because of what I did this afternoon?"

I nodded. "I've heard stories of Hermanos dying from what you did, and I was afraid for you."

"But I'm alright … a little tired, that's all." He explained, "I did what I wanted to do, hijo, and for that I hope I will be blessed with a long life." He waited for my nod of understanding. "Tomorrow I'll be sore, I'm sure, but there's nothing for you to worry about. In a few days, it will pass."

Though I felt great relief at his words and knew he was alright, the terrible feeling that Death had struck close was still there. It didn't leave me as I thought it would in finding my uncle safe; the words that came to me in darkness haunted me.

When we returned to the prayer room for our last alabado, the welcome hue of the candles bathed the room in light. "Brothers of light," the flickering candles reminded me; that is what los Hermanos represent. I shook the gloom from my thoughts, thinking instead of what it was to be an Hermano: the light of illumination in living a life exemplified by our Savior, the purpose being the light of salvation when our lives came to an end and we were welcomed home. The weary voices of los Hermanos rose in unison, gaining strength now that the netherworld was behind us and resurrection awaited. As before, the hairs on my head stood on end as the alabado rose in volume and the chills the music wrought from my body raced up my spine. Kneeling there in the midst of my Brothers, I knew then that the chills the words inspired in me came no longer from fear, but from awe. I realized how much these pious men of my valley, and I among them, longed for the embrace of our Savior's love; and I knew somehow that His heart was surely touched by the intense faith which emanated from our humble souls. A sacred communion with our Lord formed through our words, and He, as though hearing our voices raised in such a devoted endeavor to reach Him, came among us, to bless us with His presence. I knew then that it was this that made the room itself glow with such a golden radiance, that made the air electrified, and that touched our souls with pride. We were honored by His presence.

As the last notes died out, I came to as if out of a dream, not unlike the vision I had experienced before. I became aware of Horacio shuffling on his knees beside me. And glancing at him out of the corner of my eye, I felt that he had experienced something akin to what I had. Hearing yet more shuffling, I looked to our right where Tino was kneeling beside his father, seeing in his face a radiance which made me wonder whether mine looked the same. With our backs to both Berto and Pedro, I wondered momentarily if they, too, had been affected. And when I heard Pedro's gruff voice and Filiberto's murmur raised in prayer moments later, I was sure that they had. We all recited the final prayer as I was sure none of us had ever prayed before.

When the service ended, I sought to hang on to the moment, to keep it with me for the rest of my life. It has been with pride that I have treasured the memory of my first Cuaresma as a novicio. I have never forgotten that season of my adolescence when los Hermanos prayed so fervently and sang their doleful alabados with such heartfelt emotion. And what makes the memory so strong is that my friends and I had joined in, our young voices blending with those of our elders, my Brothers, for the first time in my life.

When it was over and the men began to rise stiffly to their feet, my friends and I made our separate ways to the elder Hermanos, hoisting an elbow here and there, acting as supports for them to rise. We retrieved all the jackets and hats from the kitchen, passing them to their owners, assisting those whose rheumatism or arthritis made it difficult to don their coats alone. They clapped us on the backs tiredly and commented proudly that we had become good novicios, or as in the cases of Berto, Horacio, and Tino, would be soon, for the elders had indeed heard our voices raised with their own in our earnest endeavor to be devout Hermanos. We waited our turn as the men stepped up to the altar, to kneel and rise in a final parting to our Savior, some snuffing out candles while others retrieved lanterns from the middle room before moving to the door.

We didn't say a word, only looked at one another in a kind of stunned shock over the darkest experience we had ever been through, before we, too, bade good night to the symbols of our faith which we thought we wouldn't see again until Easter morning.

Walking home after midnight with only a few lights to keep us from stumbling too much on the rutted road, we were all bone-weary, barely shuffling along, yet longing for the warmth of our beds. We trod the path for home, like exhausted horses after a day of work making their way to their stables by instinct rather than by sight. I felt a renewed sense of trepidation as we neared home, shaking the inner peace from my heart with which I had left the morada for what I thought would be the last time for prayers this Cuaresma. Eating at my soul with ever-increasing certainty was the dreaded fear that Death had indeed come for one of us.

"La Muerte," I found myself whispering, cutting into the thoughts of los Hermanos around me. The silent procession halted, and my father turned, putting the lantern near my face. I looked into the confused eyes on their barely discernible faces. They waited for an explanation. Urgently needing them to understand, I looked at my father, who of them all, understood the powers of my intuition.

"I know she came for one of us tonight."

In the silent faces of those around me, I saw perplexity in the flickering glow of the candlelight. Did they believe me? Perhaps they thought I had gone mad with the terror inspired by las Tinieblas. It didn't matter—what did matter was that I saw resigned acceptance in the eyes of my father. He believed me. As we passed lanterns to those who would walk farther up the road to their warm abodes and the night reigned once more over our final steps to our home, the words from the ceremony of las Tinieblas came to my mind. I was sure I would hear them on the morrow and be alert to our sighs, tears, and sentiments.

"¡Alerta, alerta!" the voices in the dark chapel cried out in the depths of my memory. I felt certain that within the next few hours the others, too, would hear and believe.

Resurrección

The anguished wail that permeated my dream with the first rays of the dawn made me wonder for a moment whether I was still at the morada in the darkness.

"¡Alerta!" my mind screamed in response.

Startled out of an exhausted sleep, I ran outside, watching my aunt and mother race across the road to Prima Juanita, who stood holding a kerchief to her eyes, her frail body shaking with sobs. They reached her just as her knees gave way beneath her, and supporting her between them, they led her back into her house with my grandmother trailing behind, a glass jar of yellowish-brown herbal tea in her hand. When they reached the corner of Prima's house, my gramma turned, and her eyes told me what I already knew: This day would indeed be filled with sighs, tears, and sentiments.

Primo Victoriano had died during the night—the deadly accurate arrow that La Muerte had let fly into the darkness had met its mark, piercing the heart of the elderly Hermano who had awaited his time.

I remember dressing mechanically, shuddering with the sobs that emerged in my solitude. I struggled against the sadness that accompanies death, trying instead to feel the joy that Primo would have wanted me to feel for him. His time finally came. He was ready, and he would find himself at the gates of Heaven, welcomed into the arms of his Father in finally going home—the home he had longed to reach. But then I remembered my vow to spend more time with the old man, and I cried with loss. I would never see him in this life again.

As Hermanos, we all had our work cut out for us this day that we had thought would be a restful interim before Easter. Two of the men had gone to Prima Juanita's the minute her cries alerted us to our Hermano's passing and stood guard over his body until they were joined by the rest. Then we went back to the morada, staying in shifts to keep our departed Brother company until he was laid to rest. My father and uncle had gone to Las Cañadas to check on the cattle and would return around noon, little knowing what sadness awaited them upon their return.

As Hermanos, Pedro and I went with the rest to Prima Juanita's, all of us, young and old, trying to stifle the tears of sorrow at the elder Brother's passing and trying instead, as one, to be filled with the joy that he would have wanted from his fellow Brothers. As the people of our valley lined the road weeping in grief, we all took turns carrying between us the body of the elderly Hermano in a white sheet. He had been tall, lean, frail with age; however, as it is with the dead, he was extremely heavy. Only the shell of the man remained; and I wondered if the weight came from his soul, waiting for something to happen or someone to bid him forward through the gates of heaven.

As we slowly trod the quarter-mile path from our Hermano's home to the morada, the heaviness in our hearts made the distance longer. My mind turned inward, trusting my faith to answer my questions. I sighed despondently, accepting yet more inquiries and the self-doubt they raised. I had few answers for this time of leaving childhood and opening my arms to manhood as a novicio. Yet, my Conscience spoke to me in its confident inner voice, reassuring me that when my thoughts turned inward, some of the puzzle could be solved. As I grew, as I learned to trust in my faith, my Conciencia told me, more and more pieces would fall into place—perhaps only to reach completion when I, too, was welcomed into the arms of my celestial Father.

With that welcome realization, I concentrated on my inner voice, asking to understand my primo's death and for the solution to the inquiries that confused me about death. If his soul still held him bound to the earth, was it because he held it? Was he waiting of his own volition? Or did the higher power I knew as God call my primo, only to have him wait for something or some specific time before welcoming him into His eternal home? And where was his soul then, since it was caught between the living and the dead? Was he enduring some kind of penance that being an Hermano had prepared him for on earth?

The answer came to me in the words he had spoken with such faith when we had met him at the capilla. He was ready, he'd said, in his old age of constant physical pain, to welcome the final moment of what being a Penitente had been all about. He had been ready to go with Death, the sorrowful woman in black who had to break the news that his time had come before taking deadly aim with her arrow and letting it fly, piercing him with a mortal wound that would take him quickly. But after so many years of painful penance, so many years of trusting in his faith, I sensed that she had spoken to him in that moment before her arrow met its mark, reassuring the humble Penitent that he would be going to the final home which awaited him. Her words at the morada the night before reminded me that she had come for the only one of the Brothers who had called her. And though her skeletal countenance and bony, black-shrouded body were ominous because of what she represented, leaving the life we knew and reveled in on earth, the darkness of her coming signaled to a Penitente strong in his faith that he would be going to a place filled with eternal light. I was sad with grief at Primo's death, but he had known his wait was at an end because he had called La Muerte to come for him. Something told me that it was he who awaited Easter Sunday, just as his Savior had so long ago, of his own free will, for it would be his own day of resurrection.

I caught many eyes watching me from time to time. They were the people I had known all my life. Friends and relatives looked at me as though they had never really seen me, as though they didn't know me at all. I had deceived them all by the silence my unwanted inheritance required, for word had spread that I had the gift of my ancestors and that I had known one of us would be taken by La Muerte during the night. I bowed my head from those eyes, for I felt somehow accused.

I had gone to see Prima Juanita just before the Hermanos arrived at her home, though two Brothers stayed outside while we talked. She rose quietly and told me in tears that she was somewhat surprised to see Primo Victoriano still asleep because he normally woke with the sun. A twinge of apprehension overrode her first thought that he was simply overtired. Something, or someone, had told her to check on him. There was no breath to warm her fingers when she placed them beneath his nose, no pulse at his wrist, already cold in her hand. And though she had dreaded this moment, she gave thanks that he had gone peacefully to his home. She said her goodbyes, knowing the moment for which he had lived and awaited had come.

"He was so tired," she cried, moving into the circle of my arms. "Tired of the pain and so tired of the waiting."

"Yo se," I told her. I knew.

"But I should have known it would be last night," I protested, remembering his last words to me at the capilla the night before, falling like yet another adobe to add to the wall of guilt that was rapidly building within me. I looked down at her tired, tearful face. "Remember," I told her, "remember he told me I would light the candles he would not see, and I would light the fire he would not feel?"

She looked into my eyes deeply before she nodded. "Sí, I remember." She added with a shake of her head, "He knew."

My grief was tenfold, and I felt anger at myself. Why hadn't I remembered his cryptic words until now when they had so confused me the night before? I should have looked more deeply into myself for the answer. If I was given the gift of sight, then I was cursed because I had been unable to see whom La Muerte had marked as her target. With the anger came yet another inexplicable question: if I had known, could I have done anything to prevent it? The guilt was overwhelming, eating at me. As certain as I had been that one of los Hermanos would go with Death the night before, why hadn't I insisted upon going to Primo Victoriano, whom I had last seen in such weak condition, on our way home? I blamed myself, the inescapable wishes of hindsight plaguing me, if only, if only … as I left with my primo and los Hermanos.

Just as I thought I would never be able to face the people in my community with the weight of the wall of guilt I had erected around myself, we reached the morada. And I was filled with a sudden realization. There were limitations to my intuition and limitations to my understanding of God's plan for us. I realized that though I had known that one of us would die on Good Friday and though I knew later that Primo Victoriano had in fact chosen the day of Christ's death to call La Muerte to his side, there was nothing I could have done to prevent either. The omnipotent power which reigns over us all had pre-ordained our Brother's demise, perhaps had even told him somehow that his time had come. The reconciliation that came over me in knowing that my Brother found peace shook the bricks of remorse from my heavy heart, and the barricade of self-blame tumbled down.

We carried Primo Victoriano into the kitchen where we would prepare his body for burial. I went back outside for a moment and stood in the fresh early morning to be alone with my thoughts. The trees stood like sentinels around the sacred building. Looking up the road, I saw my father and my uncle approaching. My father and uncle's steps indicated the heaviness in their hearts, too.

When they saw me, the young man inside of me fought to restrain the child who wanted to run into their embrace. My father came to stand before me, holding out his arms as he sensed my inner conflict. I returned his hug, fighting tears, and felt my uncle's hands on my shoulders from behind. After a little while, holding me at arm's length, my father searched my face. "You know there was nothing any of us could do, hijo," he said, his tone one of statement rather than inquiry.

There was no accusation in the eyes of either my father or my uncle, only silent sympathy for my own conflicting emotions. My uncle added quietly, "Don't blame yourself, José. When one of us calls for Death, it is because he is ready. We must be happy for our primo now that he has found his own happiness; we must be strong."

I nodded, sighing deeply before I squared my shoulders and wiped at the tears that had filled my eyes. Though I had come to the same conclusion only moments before, I had feared I would see in their eyes the condemnation I thought I had seen in the tearful eyes on me along the road earlier. My uncle hugged me briefly as both turned to enter the morada where their Brothers waited, leaving me to compose myself alone. After a few moments, I joined them, watching as los Hermanos exchanged sympathies for the Brother each had lost.

As I worked with los Hermanos to prepare the prayer room, tranquility grew within my heart because of the peace I had attained within my conscience at the passing of our elder Hermano, reaffirmed by my father and uncle. From time to time an arm fell across my shoulders with reassuring pressure or eyes spoke understanding, I knew that los Hermanos didn't blame me for my gift of sight. In fact, in the quiet words they offered, my faith was strengthened in knowing they, too, had resigned themselves to their Hermano's death. However, I felt an uneasy quiet emanating from Pedro who worked silently and kept his distance. I sensed his confusion, looking quickly away when I glanced up and saw him. And when I wondered if I saw fear in the eyes that looked away, I was saddened that he had become alienated from me because of my unwanted ability.

I tried not to think of the gang chopping wood outside as Pedro and I took the shrouds from the santos and the black cloths from the windows to let in the light of day, leaving the doors open to air out the sense of death that remained within. We would stay the night with our departed Brother. We would celebrate his death, celebrate his emergence into a place of light.

We bathed his body with warm water, clothed him in the only suit he possessed, and enveloped him in the sheet, his death shroud. We measured and cut and nailed the pine boards, each of us taking a turn at making the old man's coffin, our last gift to him. Horacio ran home, returning with a satiny white tablecloth, which he reverently placed and tacked inside as a liner. We gently lifted our primo and just as softly laid him within the pine box that we had laid across two burros, sawhorses, in front of the altar. When we finished, Tino entwined his own rosario between the man's folded fingers, running from the room, stifling his sobs.

Pedro motioned me outside, took the saint he had carved from his pocket, and covered it with his hands. Tino, standing under a tree near where we stood, blew his nose into his kerchief loudly before shuffling over to us, his face still red and blotchy. Berto and Horacio joined us beneath the cottonwoods in subdued silence.

Pedro's voice broke into our thoughts. "I was keeping it secret because I was making it for you," he said, looking at me and then at the others in sudden shyness.

He removed the hand hiding the santo, revealing a most beautifully carved Saint Joseph, the baby Jesus in his arms. The folds and creases in their robes were vividly detailed; the tiny fingers of Jesus' hand grasped a finger of His Earthly Father's hand. Pedro had done an exquisite job of making the features of the faces appear so perfectly at peace, from the intricate lids of their eyes to the delicately soft smiles that graced their lips. It was the most beautiful carving I had ever seen. My patron saint, I thought, swallowing the lump in my throat.

I blinked back the tears that would mark me still a child, wondering how many more emotional moments would distinguish this day to keep it so vividly embedded in my memory. But I saw that each of my friends was affected, and I felt that their memories of this day would be ingrained as deeply as mine. None of us could find the words to express our admiration of its intricate loveliness. I was touched beyond belief that Pedro had thought to make a carving of my own patron saint for me, and a tear ran silently down my cheek at the thoughtfulness of my friend, my cousin.

He cleared his own throat, blushing at my evident emotion, "It was to say thank you for all the times when we weren't novicios but you kept me out of trouble, or tried to anyway."

I didn't know what to say to express the depth of emotion caused by my friend, especially on this already poignant day. A simple thank you was not enough. As I admired the beauty of Pedro's best carving, which lay lightly in my palm, it dawned on me that after Easter Sunday I would never see it again because it was with a twinge of sadness that I remembered his promise to make Primo Victoriano a saint. Pedro's gift to me would be the one our primo would take with him, a gift from all of us which no mortal eyes would ever see again after tomorrow.

Before I could voice what I felt or what I wanted to do with it, Pedro said softly, "I can make you another one, that is, if you want to give this to …"

I nodded, giving him a quick hug, which he briefly returned before pushing me gently away, blushing to the tips of his ears.

When I passed the santo to Berto, who passed it reverently to the others, the boys finally found their voices to tell Pedro how they were affected by the beauty of his creation. Tino returned the saint into his hands, saying we would have to get it blessed before Primo Victoriano's cajón was nailed shut. We nodded, standing awkwardly quiet for some time, making no move to re-enter the morada. I sensed that my friends had something else on their minds, something they wanted to say but didn't know how. When their eyes shifted to me and looked quickly away, I knew that they wanted to speak to me, and all of a sudden I didn't think it was something I wanted to hear.

When I stepped away from the circle, Filiberto's hand reached out, clasping my arm with gentle firmness. "We just wanted to say we're sorry," he blurted.

I nodded. I knew what they had to be sorry about. They never knew there was something about me that none of them understood, something strange in the way I could read their minds sometimes and the way I saw and heard things none of the rest of them could?

Tino admitted shamefaced, "You used to scare me with your funny feelings because something always happened when you got them."

"Especially last night, on the way home when you said La Muerte had come for one of the Hermanos," Pedro explained. "I couldn't sleep all night, worrying about who it was. I kept checking on Papá because your feelings always come before something happens."

"For a while," Horacio added, "I was afraid you were a brujo, like the way some people think your abuelita is." Blushing with shame at his confession, he looked away.

Berto interrupted, "But your gramma called us all over this morning when you were at Prima Juanita's, and she explained as good as she could … well, you know." Raising his eyes to mine, he added with a soft smile, "I'm not afraid anymore; I'm just sorry about how awful it is for you to know things and not be able to do anything about them sometimes."

Shuffling his feet in the dirt, Tino admitted, "I'm still kinda scared of the way you can see things, but I'm not scared of you."

"He's right," Horacio pointed his finger at me, "and when you get another one of your funny feelings, you have to tell us …"

"Only if you can, that is," Filiberto interrupted again. "Your gramma said sometimes you might be warned not to say anything."

"But maybe like your gramma said, there are some things we can do something about sometimes," Horacio finished, with a self-conscious shrug, "and besides, telling us maybe can make you feel better than keeping it in."

They looked at me then, expectantly, hopefully. I looked at each of my friends who were also my primos, I knew that this gang of my youth would stand beside me through thick and thin as Brothers for the rest of my life. For the second time this day, I let my emotions govern my actions. This was the first of what would be many times in our future that I let myself express my feelings freely for my Brothers, for even though only two of us were novicios this year, I knew the next would make Hermanos of us all. Moving within their circle, I held out my arms to them. When the five of us embraced each other for those few moments, heartfelt kinship raced through my arms, passed through us all like a current of electricity, binding us for life before we broke apart, self-consciously succumbing to embarrassment.

We moved to enter the morada as a group with Pedro in the lead. My Tío Daniel stood in the doorway, inquiry in his eyes mingling with pleasure, probably witnessing the bond of our friendship.

I shrugged. "Pedro made a gift for me, but we decided to give it to our primo." I pointed to the saint in Pedro's hand, "What do you think?"

Tío's eyes widened as he noticed the santo Pedro held out. He turned it in his hands, expressing his admiration of our cousin's talent before returning it and standing aside to let us in.

We went directly to the coffin, quietly whispering our goodbyes one by one to the elderly Hermano, whose memory we would keep in our hearts. I hoped Primo Victoriano would somehow know that we wanted him to hold a memory of us as well. When Pedro placed his santo reverently beneath our primo's folded hands, for the first time, we noticed the silence in the room. We turned to leave, blushing, self-conscious before the teary eyes of some of the elder Hermanos, their gazes expressing pride and pleasure at our gesture. Many arms embraced us as we left to rest for a few hours before we had to return.

Needless to say, the santo became the object of much wonder throughout the rest of the day, Prima Juanita crying her gratitude in Pedro's arms, and everyone quietly exclaiming over its intricacy, saying surely Primo Victoriano must see it and appreciate its beauty, and it would provide company on his lone journey to his eternal rest.

For the rest of the day, we Hermanos took turns velando or guarding our Brother in twos while some of us went home to do chores andor to rest before our turn came again. My father joined me for a while after a short rest, bringing by my grandmother who added more food to what had already been brought by others. Constant was the flow of vecinos and primos that came to accompany us in our vigil. Though at first I was reluctant to meet their eyes, I came to see that the silent censure I thought I had seen in their faces before was really a sympathetic understanding. For though they didn't understand any more than I the gift of sight I possessed, they were sensitive to my confusion and the helplessness that it brought me. They sat in turns, quietly recollecting with tears or subdued smiles this or that about the devoted Brother whom we would lay to rest on Easter Sunday.

We all had thought the night before marked the last time we would pray there since Lent was officially over, yet that evening we crowded into the three rooms of the morada to pray a rosario. The altar, with its revered retablos and santos, was no longer hidden beneath shrouds of black. It seemed to glow with the wavering candlelight, but it was the black crucifixes that caught my eye. The one belonging to Primo Victoriano beckoned silently to take part in this age-old ritual with our elders in his memory.

As always, my father knelt in the center of the first row and my Tío Daniel made his way to his side, moving quietly around those who knelt behind. Pedro and I took our places behind the rest, with Horacio, Filiberto, and Celestino just behind us, crossing ourselves as we waited in silence for the prayers to begin.

"En el nombre del Padre, del Hijo, y del Espíritu Santo," my father began, the rest of us echoing his words solemnly.

"*Ofrecimiento del Rosario*," my father continued, praying to the Virgin Mary to listen to our offering of the rosary.

To this day, as old as I am, I will never forget the first time I prayed as one with the men I respected—los Hermanos Penitentes, the society of which I was finally a part—for the loss of a Brother. It was a moment suspended in time, a moment which I had thought I would wait for years to experience. Yet there I was, only fifteen years old, invited to kneel in prayer for an Hermano who had reached the end of the path where I had yet to tread. And so I prayed, determined to seek within myself a purity of spirit, a purity of thought that would make me into a humble soul who would be ready when my own time came.

My father began the alabado offering our rosary to the Blessed Mother. Our voices rose as one in entreaty, and our hearts filled with desire to be heard on this night. "*Oh María, con tierno y devoto pecho, de nuestra fe sacrosanta, la conservación y aumento. Torna sus divinos ojos hacia tu Cristiano pueblo*," we prayed in song.

My friends and I sang the words with such sorrow, offering our rosary to the Blessed Virgin, who was of tender and devoted heart. We asked from our own hearts to be maintained in Her sacred faith, to have our restitution increased. Our voices rose in harmony as we pleaded for Her to turn Her divine eyes to Her Christian pueblo. Our voices, reaching as high a crescendo as was possible, seemed to make the very rooms tremble with their powerful attempt to reach our Holy Mother's ears.

I let myself become enveloped in the strength of our conviction, looking to the altar and focusing as if in a trance upon the jaspe statue of the Virgin Mary. She held her dead Son in Her arms, Her face a vision of sorrow as She, too, longed for the reunion She would earn at His side in eternity upon Her own resurrection. As though it had no will of its own, my voice joined with theirs, softly at first, then rising among those of my Brothers, to mingle in the air above. I, too, wanted to reach the pinnacle that would make the Holy Mother hear my own pleas to accept our Hermano into Her heart so that he would indeed reach the eternal rest made possible by Her Son.

Although we knew Primo Victoriano had an impeccable and admirable character, we also knew when one dies, one must be accountable for the discrepancies which make us mortal and imperfect. We prayed for the power of our prayers and hymns to reach Her ears. We had faith that She would intercede on our Brother's behalf for the sins he may have committed. It was this faith that we knew would make our prayers heard by omnipresent ears, and we were confident that our primo would be welcomed to his eternal home with the open arms of his Savior whether we prayed or not. Our faith in the omnipotent, all-knowing eyes of our Holy Mother was so strong.

When the rosario ended, we rose to extend our sympathies to the diminutive woman who sat quietly weeping into her handkerchief in the pew at the front of the altar beside us. We who had been his Brothers (even if for only a few days, in the case of Pedro and me) rose first, followed by the rest of the people of our Cañoncito. Everyone had seen Prima Juanita off and on all day, the women bringing food and staying in turn to serve those who came by to extend their sympathies, and we with the men sitting beside her to share remembered moments in the life of the man she had called her husband.

Sleeping at the morada in blankets we spread on the hard wood floor for the velorio, the customary wake for the dead, we took turns resting and waking to pray quietly throughout the night, keeping vigil over the soul of our departed Hermano. Rising with the first light of day on Easter Sunday, I felt a sense of elation mingled with a sense of loss. The day would be of two-fold significance and bittersweet emotion. There would be two ceremonies: the regular Easter Mass, in which the children would make their First Holy Communion and we would celebrate our Savior's resurrection from the dead, and then the Mass for the Dead, marking the resurrection of our Brother.

The mood of the first mass was poignant, to say the least, because we rejoiced with the children and their families that they had reached such an important stage in their religion, but we exulted the words which proclaimed that Christ had risen on this day so long ago to eternal glory so that we might do the same at our moment of death. We were given hope, reaffirmed in our faith of our own salvation and in the salvation of the Hermano we would bury today. But the happiness we should have felt was overshadowed by the sadness of the service we knew would immediately follow.

We listened during the mass for Primo Victoriano to the padre's plea, asking that we try to dispel our sorrow and replace it with joy for our Brother who had indeed chosen the most special day of our Christian faith to meet his Maker. His words reassured us that this day should indeed be marked with celebration, for surely our primo had been blessed with resurrection and eternal life. And though the mass began in tears and grief, we left reminded of the hope our Brother inspired by reaching his eternal home.

Near the end, the boys and I feared our absent-minded little padre would forget to bless Pedro's santo before closing the coffin for the last time. But for once his memory served him well and he raised the beautiful carving high, sprinkling it with holy water as he blessed it before replacing it. Closing the lid over our Hermano with Pedro's gift cradled in his arms, the padre hid both from our sight for the last time.

We took turns carrying our Brother between us up the quarter mile of the barely perceptible path to the campo santo, resting only twice to sing alabados as the people who walked with us to his resting place gathered stones in a neat pile to mark our descansos. The first rest, to the dismay of Berto, Tino, Horacio, Pedro, and me, was at the "descanso" we had erected to guard the ledger of our secret brotherhood and the pact we no longer needed. As more rocks were piled upon the stones we had erected, we exchanged nervous glances. We knew that in good conscience, we would never be able to disturb the rocks of Primo Victoriano's descanso to retrieve our book. Our ledger would remain undisturbed, forever hidden. And when we looked at one another in the silence of our realization, there was also bittersweet acceptance. With quiet resignation, we each placed a stone on top of the pile. No one would ever know our youth was buried forever beneath the rocks and guarded by our Brother's memory.

As the last alabado began, intoned with echoes of sorrow and joy, I took my turn with seven of los Hermanos, raising the coffin between us to carry our Brother to his final resting place. When I found it a much lighter burden than the day before, the sorrow that had haunted me at our Brother's passing rose from my body. At last, his soul was gone from the shell of the body we placed above the hole in the earth. With los Hermanos, I threw the first clumps of dirt that fell with such finality upon the coffin. I heard Primo Victoriano. His voice was a melancholic note rising for the last time into the heavens before his body was lowered into the ground. "Estoy en mi casa," he whispered through the breeze amongst the towering pines. "I am home."

The teardrops that flowed from deep inside of me, coursing down my cheeks, were tears of happiness, releasing me from the last vestiges of guilt that burdened my heart. I knew with certainty that our primo had indeed marked this day—Easter Sunday—as his own day of ascension and resurrection to the place for which he had so longed and awaited. But for the weeping of the women around me and especially that of his grief-stricken wife, I would have shouted my happiness into the heavens. I knew that he was no longer here.

Amor

That Lenten season of 1928, the year I said goodbye to the child I had been and welcomed the young man I was to become, indeed marked the turning point in my life in which I learned to embrace adulthood and all that came with it.

My father and uncle went to Las Vegas early one morning to pick up my brother Miguel, who had completed his basic training and was coming by bus. I hadn't seen my brother since he'd taken his own vows. Though we wrote a couple of letters in the months that had passed, I wondered if he had changed. After about an hour of doing my chores, I heard the rumble of Maestro's vehicle as it rounded the curve in the road between the capilla and our casa. I ran up the slope from the barn to the road to watch as the car stopped in front of our house.

Of course, my mother, grandmother, and aunt had their arms around Miguel before I even reached the car. When everyone finally got their fill of welcoming him home, he turned and said simply, "I missed you, hermanito."

The young man, standing erect in the uniform of a Marine, was a stranger. Miguel had left home not so long ago with my same tall, scrawny stature, the lean frame of a boy barely out of adolescence. Yet, here he was, at a few inches under six feet tall, his broad shoulders straining the cloth of his shirt, which held two ribbons over his heart. His arms bulged and his legs were now long and muscular. Physically, this was not the brother I remembered.

But, head held high beneath the military cap on his short hair, he had the same face; here was a face in my memory. Though it had filled and looked more mature, the mouth was Miguel's, upturned, as always, in the soft shadow of a smile. When his hand rose to take the cap from his head, the gently teasing eyes were revealed, dark brown like ebony, their depths always hinting at mischief. It was his eyes that told me this proud young Marine was my brother; and I forgot the young man who fought to grow inside of me, letting the child emerge as I ran into my brother's arms.

Miguel had always been emotional, sensitive to affection, before he'd left home. He never failed to let us know that he loved us. On countless occasions, whenever the mood struck him, he would sweep my mother or grandmother into his arms and dance with them. Whenever they happened to pass close to him, he planted countless kisses on their cheeks. And how many times did he come up behind my father or uncle with a bear hug that lifted them off their feet and left them sputtering with the surprise? Miguel laughed every time at their reaction, as if they hadn't said the same thing hundreds of times before. How many times had Miguel tossed me high in the air before lowering me for a brotherly kiss that left me swiping at my cheek in embarrassment at his display of emotion?

In his embrace, I remembered the many ways he showed his love for us, his family, without the usual reservations exhibited by men, and I realized how much I had missed his affection and his fun-loving character. We held one another tightly for a long time, and when our weeping ebbed, we wiped our eyes, and a bit of self-conscious embarrassment made us smile sheepishly at our emotional outburst at his homecoming. But we hugged again briefly, chuckling.

"You've grown, hermanito," he said, holding me at arm's length.

It was true. For the first time my head had rested on his shoulder as I wept. What I noticed more was that twice he'd called me "hermanito," one word with double significance, a word, he had never used for me before. He knew I was now his Penitente Brother, and his role as an elder brother both at home and in our religion changed without our awareness. But with the tears came the shared joy of welcoming the men we would become together, sharing that time in our lives of treating one another with mutual respect, of lending support and of giving advice. I was content to know that the teasing, a remnant of our childhoods to which we would cling, would always remain.

"You've grown, too." I smiled, slugging his tough shoulder. My brother had indeed lost the wiry slenderness of his boyhood, returning with the physique of an athlete, exhibiting the muscular hardness that came from rigorous military training.

He shrugged, his face sobering with his statement, "You're a novicio now." The concern in his eyes asked for truth. "Are you happy?"

I nodded with excitement. "So much has happened, Miguel. I have so much to tell you."

He looked at me deeply before a quiet smile replaced his worry, and laying an arm across my shoulders, he propelled me forward as we walked to the house. "We'll have to talk later, hermanito." Nodding his head toward the women, he laughed, "We have to let Mamá, Tía, and Gramita feed me … you know that's why they're standing there waiting."

They'd been at it all morning, cooking all his favorite dishes at once because they only sought to please him and didn't know what he'd prefer. So the wood stove held pots of pinto beans and menudo for side dishes, and sweet rice and *natillas* for dessert. The oven held two platters of enchiladas, one made with green chile and the other with red. Sopapillas and tortillas were already on the table waiting to be used as *cucharitas*, or little spoons, the way we New Mexicans like to eat. The meal that day was celebratory, and those in the next nine days Miguel spent with us were the tastiest of that summer, primarily because all of us were together, even if it was only for a short while.

Before Miguel left again, he found time to tease my grandmother with kisses and sweep my mother and aunt off their feet while they kept his appetite whetted with as much of his favorite foods as they could make. He helped my Tío Daniel and father work, laughing and joking with my uncle so much they made my father impatient (which was what they always set out to do with their merciless humor). But he also found the time for me, sharing what we had learned about ourselves and about life. We went up to the caves where the gang and I met in secret, recalling with laughter the fun we shared in our past, and at times our retrospection was full of sadness. I told him everything about the past Lent, which was so etched in my mind. I left no detail undisclosed. As I spoke, I watched his eyes for the disbelief I hoped I wouldn't see. Though his brow unconsciously rose as it did when he was shocked into speechlessness and his eyes widened several times with surprise, there was only acceptance and understanding in his gaze. And the words of his youthful wisdom offered solace as only a brother's can.

"When we became Hermanos, we pledged to live Christian lives and to help one another," he told me. "I took a longer time to take my vows; you were ready way before I was. I'll bet you'll be Hermano Mayor one day; will you be ready for that?"

I thought about the responsibility the position entailed for only a moment before I nodded. "*Con Cristo todo es posible. Sin El soy nada.*" Miguel just looked at me and I wondered what he thought.

"Yes, with Christ all is possible and without him we are nothing," he repeated. "I think you'll be more help to me, hermanito, than I will ever be to you." That little discussion became the basis for our lives from then on.

Miguel made time for us all during that visit, but he also found the time to fall in love. Before he had left for the first time to join the military, young love had already begun to bloom between himself and Gregoria's older sister, Carolina. And when their eyes met on the day of his return, the bud of their former attraction began to unfold once again. Only the year before, the young pair had been allowed to wander off together pretty much alone, for theirs had been the innocent friendship that exists between a boy and a girl who have grown up together and have barely begun to see hints of the young man and woman they were becoming.

This visit, however, in the smoldering look of Miguel's eyes when he looked at Carolina, we all knew that he saw the young woman who in his absence replaced the girl she had been. And in her blushing face when she caught his gaze, we all knew that she was more than pleased at the young man who had come in the stead of the boy who had left. They spent many hours getting to know one another in this new awareness—under the watchful eyes of an adult who would ensure that they kept their passions in check. It was evident to all that theirs was a love that grew with each passing day, blooming like summer flowers in the fields.

Sure enough, not even two days after his arrival, Miguel asked my mother to write the formal request to her parents. The whole family trooped proudly to Carolina's home the next day, before Mass on Sunday, and my father presented the letter to her parents. Tradition called for them to read it after our departure and, if the answer was affirmative, to respond within a reasonable period of time with a letter of their own. If the response was negative, the father of the prospective bride would gift the suitor with a *calabaza*, a pumpkin. To this day, I don't know why this was the traditional symbol of rejection. However, Miguel decided to begin a tradition of his own and explained to Carolina's parents that he was pressed for time due to his imminent departure and formally requested her hand from Don Juan. On bended knee, he asked Carolina to be his wife.

Miguel and Carolina married the following Wednesday before he left, not seven days after he had seen her with the eyes of a man who saw in her the woman who returned his love. Though her parents protested that perhaps they should wait until his return, it was evident that they approved whole-heartedly of my brother as their future son-in-law. They were assured that his intentions were sincere and that he had the means to provide for their child. Their real fears lay in having to release their eldest daughter from their protective nest and in their reluctance to let their first child fly on her own wings with the man she had chosen to protect her. They reasoned further, along with our own parents, that they had no time to prepare, that Primo Victoriano had recently been interred. What would people think? But when it became clear to our elders that Miguel and Carolina would not be dissuaded from their desire to become man and wife, all four parents had the young pair kneel before them, extending their hands over their heads as they formed the sign of the cross, blessing their union.

The next two days were chaotic, to say the least. My mother and the mother of the bride, along with most of the women and girls in our little valley ran around like chickens that had indeed lost their heads in the confusion of having to prepare a wedding feast. Since Miguel was to leave the following Sunday, there was also the problem of posting the banns in the church bulletin for three consecutive weeks; but our little padre came through with flying colors, his happiness at performing a wedding spurring him on. He reminded his congregation that, in the wake of our celebration of death not so long before, there was also the continuing celebration of new life. And so in a quiet ceremony, Miguel in his military uniform and Carolina in her grandmother's ivory lace dress met at the altar before our bespectacled and over-excited padre to exchange their vows to love one another for the rest of their lives. The mass—though sad with the memory it brought of having said good bye to the elderly man whom we missed sitting quietly in the last pew—instilled in us the meaning of life, of marriage, and of procreation. Our hearts rose with the joyful promise that only a wedding can provide, much to our padre's delight.

An equally quiet reception followed at the schoolhouse with only a single violin to provide a quiet melody for the celebration. The women, knowing that the nuptials had been arranged post-haste, outdid themselves in helping their comadres to provide a feast for their children's wedding. I lost count of the varieties of chiles, green and red, chunks of savory beef in some, fresh tomatillos and onions in others. Pots of beans, some with chicharones (pork cracklings), some with chicos (smoked corn kernels), graced the table alongside menudos, posoles (another cooked corn soup dish), and platters of chicken or beef enchiladas and burritos stuffed with refried beans or carne adovada (pork marinaded in red chile). There were enough tortillas to go around as well, stacked high, some thick, some thin, depending upon who had made them. And the desserts? Empanaditas (mincemeat stuffed pastries), bizcochitos, varieties of pies, and a most beautiful wedding cake rounded out the plentiful menu that left all of us stuffed with both food and happiness on the day of my brother's wedding.

Though the day was the happiest of my brother's life, there were two incidents to brand his wedding in my memory as well. Halfway into the reception, the Lunática arrived. The woman who had accused my grandmother of bewitching her strolled in as though nothing had ever happened. Since our account of the ball of fire and the rumors of the woman's injury had made their rounds throughout the valley in the week after Primo Victoriano's death, her entrance into the makeshift sala was greeted by hushed whispers, and some of the younger children ran to hide behind their mothers' skirts.

She took a seat in an unobtrusive spot of the room where she sat for most of the next hour observing the gaiety of the wedding feast, which, I might add, was somewhat muted by her presence. Though we tried our best to ignore her, most of us were affected by her eyes roaming over us. The fear that she would break out in screams of "¡Lunáticos! ¡Brujas!" cast a somber pall to our mood, made worse by the fear that she would rise and recite some kind of incantation that would cast a spell over any one of us. My concern for my grandmother was great as the boys and I eyed the woman warily. I watched her every move, wondering if anything she did might signal the casting of a spell. Would she avenge herself on my abuelita by doing something to overshadow Miguel and Carolina's future? Berto trembled and whispered, "If she's really a bruja, I hit her with a rock when she was a ball of flames! Is she here for her revenge?" We sat quietly next to Berto, as if our nearness could protect him from the witch's wrath. Yet really we were convinced if the woman possessed powers of darkness, there was nothing we could do.

It was my diminutive grandmother who saved the day. Making her way over to the woman, she sat next to her where they conversed quietly for some time. For the rest of the reception, my grandmother took the lady in tow, making the rounds from one cluster of vecinos or compadres to the next. My gramma introduced her to everyone. When they were close enough, I heard the woman offer her humble apologies for her previous actions and treatment of the people of our small valley. My abuelita's offer of friendship changed her.

The boys and I sat nervously observing their slow revolution around the room. When they came by us, we stood and shook her hand—with wariness, you can be sure. Tino braved an inquiry that dumbfounded the rest of us. He asked about her health, to which the woman replied, "Fine, just fine." She only smiled, offering no explanation for her accident, which would remain a mystery. But she seemed to look at us closely. Was it my imagination, or did she narrow her eyes at Berto before they moved on to the next group?

We tried to convince ourselves that afternoon that the woman was harmless, that there were no witches, that there had to be a reasonable explanation for her accident. We chastised ourselves for our fears. In the end, finally remembering that as Hermanos or soon-to-be novicios, we mustn't judge people by our suspicions.

Horacio nudged me. "What do you think, José? Is she a bruja?"

I shrugged. I had no intuitive feelings of badness about the woman. Having seen her up close, I saw her for what she was: a lonely old woman who had finally come to realize that her neighbors were not a bad lot. Granted, many of us were superstitious and suspicious of strangers, but as a whole, we were ready and willing to give friendship with the woman a chance if that was what she wanted. Though my grandmother was not to live much longer, the woman became a constant visitor to her home, offering her companionship until my abuelita's last day and thereafter coming by regularly to remain a friend to my mother as well.

That night the second incident that marked Miguel's wedding left questions that would haunt me through the months that followed. I had trouble getting to sleep, like the way I toss and turn after a day of hard work when I'm so tired I ache for the sleep but it evades me. Perhaps it was all the excitement of having been a best man for the first time, perhaps it was the woman who had finally ceased to be an enigma, or perhaps it was all the food I consumed which left me bloated. When sleep finally came, it was again the troubled slumber of a pesadilla. My dreams were haunted by a young girl wearing blue, with hair so black it seemed almost midnight blue in the light which came from behind her, enveloping her in an aura of gold. In my mind's eye, I strained to see her face. I caught glimpses of her dark brown eyes, which beckoned to me in the silence of my dreams. I shuddered when I woke, for though I never saw her face clearly, her eyes continued to haunt me through the days and nights which followed, as though she wanted something from me, as though she promised me something of herself.

Miguel left four days later a married man and was joined by his new wife after he acquired housing for them on the base, and though it would be over a year before we would see them again, my brother kept our brotherly relationship intact, made even stronger by his wisdom.

In the few weeks that followed, Carolina and I became close, bound together by the love we shared for the young man who had made us brother and sister. Though our relationships with Miguel were definitely different, the many hours we spent sharing our memories of him helped to ease the emptiness in our hearts felt by his absence. In the months after Carolina left, she wrote constantly, sending gifts and post cards from time to time, making me see what it was like clear across the country. But it was her long letters which gave me solace, for in their words I saw that she and Miguel were happy. And though I missed them terribly, I felt comfort in knowing they missed me, too.

School came to a close for another year for some; for Pedro and me, it was over for good. We completed the eighth grade and had the diplomas to prove it. I threw myself into the workings of the farm with my father and uncle with happiness. Miguel wrote that when his time with the Marines came to an end, he would come home to stay. His letters provided me with purpose, and keeping it secret from my brother, in my spare time I began to lay the foundation for an additional room to his home. I couldn't wait to see the surprise on his face to find it at least partially completed upon his return. My father and uncle helped from time to time when they weren't too tired, so did the gang, and my mother and grandmother kept my secret from Miguel. Though when he returned it would be with a surprise of his own, and I would have yet another incident that even then I little suspected.

Esperanza

Our days in Cañoncito were filled with countless chores, our nights with quiet conversation. I was content; we were happy. But within the year, my grandmother suddenly grew older, her strength dissolving day by day into weariness, even her eyes taking on a visible haze as we watched her month after month get progressively worse. Her refusal to see a doctor was adamant, and her acceptance of spending the last of her life waiting reminded me of Primo Victoriano, who had also waited patiently for the end. I awoke each day expecting the worst, dreading the day when my uncle would come to say that she was worse—or gone. My abuelita, always attuned to my feelings, finally called me to her bedside one evening in late September, chastising me terribly for the sorrow that had begun to shadow my eyes. Reminding me that she was happy she would be joining my grandfather, she exacted my promise that I would try to be happy for her, telling me that she would wait if she could until Miguel's return. She felt in her heart that he would bring with him a wondrous surprise that she had to see before she left this world for the next. And though I prayed for the strength to go through the days watching her grow ever more frail, the anxious waiting for my brother's return was overshadowed by the knowledge that my grandmother would leave us shortly thereafter.

By October, Pedro had done so well in his welding apprenticeship that his uncle gave him a plot of land in Las Vegas with a three-room house in dire need of repair. The boys and I went down every chance we got, helping him reinforce the walls, making adobes by the dozens, eager to help him finish before the heavy snows. We knew that Pedro desired, beyond anything, to marry Luciana before the end of the year, and for that we worked until we fell. The house was finally decent enough to inhabit by early December, and to Pedro's profound happiness, he became a husband the day before Christmas. To Luciana's delight, she became a mother the following September—almost to the day of their wedding night. But I remember with hindsight that the night of his wedding the young girl with black hair came again into my dreams.

Filiberto had left school a year before he had to, finding his niche in Mora, working at the butcher shop and dairy farm, commuting each day with three other men who had jobs in the small community twenty miles to the north. Finding his own true love in the young beauty who was his employer's daughter, Berto married the month before Luciana gave birth to Pedro's first son. He brought Esmeralda home to live with his parents until he could build a house for her, and the young woman found herself enveloped in the love of Berto's family. She brought with her a wide knowledge of culinary and homemaking skills, much to the delight of Berto's mother, who was getting old and needed a helping hand, and much to the gratitude of Berto's father, who loved nothing better than a skilled cook.

Horacio remained at home, and under the tutelage of Maestro Rubel; by the following year he obtained his teaching certificate. He found a position in nearby Terromote where he was bitten by the love bug almost immediately. She was a young woman from Rociada whose younger siblings were enrolled in a school ony a few miles northeast from were we lived. She took a bit of him from us to our dismay and to the obvious displeasure of his mother because he spent all his spare time courting her, both having decided to extend the period of their betrothal until he could save enough money to build her a house.

Between our friends' weddings in 1928 and '29 and Horacio's betrothal, only Tino and I remained, reluctant to be bitten by the virus known as love. Yet many times, now that I look back, I searched for the young girl who had haunted me since the day of my brother's wedding. I had learned to trust my intuitions, and I felt that the girl in my visions would someday come into my life to capture my heart in the depths of her eyes. I found myself going to dances or other events around our community at my abuelita's bidding, looking for a raven-haired girl with ebony eyes, but I never found her.

I spent time most evenings at the bedside of my beloved abuelita, listening to the cuentos of the past, memories of her youth she wanted to leave with me when she left, always reminding me to keep her memory alive when I had my own children to entertain and to inform with her stories. The fact that I had no apparent desire for marriage became the brunt of a battle she began to wage against me. Her constant reminders that time was short became her ammunition, and the final sword thrust into my heart was that she would like to know whom I would take as my wife before she passed. When I told her finally that my dreams both in the darkness of the night and in the light of day were haunted by a black-haired girl, her eyes brightened with hope. "Esperanza," she told me, "you have given me hope, but you have to search with your heart, hijo mío, search quickly." She left me exhausted after each visit, though her combat came in the form of teasing banter to lighten our mood, telling me she wasn't angry, only impatient, because she felt that her time was quickly running out. My gramma shared my conviction that when I found her, I would find the woman I would marry. In truth, I wanted to find the girl quickly myself, but not for the hurried wedding my abuelita desired, rather because I was eaten by curiosity to see the face my dreams withheld. But when I crawled beneath my blankets each night, I felt my gramma's disappointment in my unfulfilled quest. I began to wonder if, at the ripe old age of sixteen, maybe I should give the idea of marriage more serious thought and intensify my efforts in my search.

Between the countless chores of the ranch, with Tino's help I continued to add to the walls we had already raised for Miguel's bedroom. We were occasionally joined by the rest of the gang, either singly or together, when they weren't too busy with their own lives. By that time we'd all become Hermanos, so we met at regular intervals within the walls of the morada to discuss our affairs and to decide who needed assistance in times of sickness or financial hardship. These were lean years, and five or ten cents from each Hermano added to a few dollars when one of their own needed medicine or other goods which required money. Although the Depression was starting to affect many Americans from coast to coast, we really didn't feel it much because we were already poor, struggling to make ends meet, and relying on ourselves for assistance and support. So we cleaned the irrigation ditches and the dam, we herded cattle and sheep, we replaced the log bridge to the morada when the crecientes took it away in the spring run offs. And we prayed, strengthening the ties of our Brotherhood that bound us together.

I remember vividly going with Tino to a wedding dance November of 1929, at Filiberto's invitation, no less. We went somewhat reluctantly since we had hit every dance possible the past few months, and both of us were tired of Berto's attempts at playing cupid. I had danced my feet off with each black-haired girl I encountered, from Mora all the way to Las Vegas, and my fruitless search for the deep dark brown eyes that haunted me had left me disillusioned, not to mention exhausted with my efforts. But we went, more to satisfy our friend than because we really wanted to go, especially when Berto, his eyes twinkling, teased that there would be many young *bonitas* there that we didn't know.

He ignored our pleas to stop trying to get us married. Little did I know that up at La Cueva, a small village between ours and Mora, I would find the bride of my dreams.

I remember entering the small sala and I remember Berto rushing over to us to introduce us to the newly wedded couple, and I remember following him back to the table where his wife waited, talking to two other girls seated demurely beside her. Just as we had feared, Filiberto and Esmeralda were playing matchmakers. I frowned, rolling my eyes at Tino, who shrugged, whispering that we could leave soon if I wanted. I nodded as we reached the table where Berto's wife sat.

I kissed Esmeralda's cheek, teasing her about the roundness of her stomach. "I pray your child won't look like Berto, with that wild hair!"

Berto waved off my insult. "Esmeralda will deliver a girl who will look just like her beautiful mother." He kissed his wife on the cheek and then moved aside, motioning to the young women seated before us. The first I recognized as his sister-in-law, Dora, whom I had met at his wedding. Small and a tiny bit plump, she reminded me of a wren from her gray eyes to the constant fluttering of her hands when she talked, her bubbling voice animated with her perpetual joviality. I hoped for a moment when we exchanged hellos that Tino would like her because, with their fun-loving characters, they made a perfect match. And they were both small.

The second was a girl I had never seen before. Berto whispered, "She's my wife's cousin from Las Cañadas. She was too ill to attend our wedding where you would have met her months ago." He poked me as if we were ten years old. "Besides," he explained behind his hand so she wouldn't hear, "her father is so strict that it's a miracle she could come to this dance at all."

In a daze, I heard Berto tell me her name was Esperanza: Hope. But then his voice faded, and I heard only the strains of the waltz surround me as if in a dream. My legs shook, my palms began to sweat for I heard the girl's name repeated in my head in my grandmother's voice. "Esperanza," she had said, "you have given me hope." I looked down at the raven-haired beauty, and when her dark eyes looked into mine, she smiled hello before her gaze lowered shyly to her lap. My pounding heart told me at last I had seen the face that so eluded me in my dreams, and I realized my soul had been caught in the depths of her eyes.

Never having been in love before, I remember sitting next to her in the awkward silence, my mouth suddenly gone dry, my knees shaking with some malady I didn't understand. In the flashes of heat that made my face blush like a schoolboy when Berto got up to dance and motioned us to follow, I feared if I stood I would faint for the first time in my life. But my legs didn't fail me, and the dizziness ebbed when I put an arm lightly around Esperanza's slender waist. I remained self-conscious at the sweat I was sure she would feel in my palm when she laid her small hand over mine. I blushed anew when I stumbled for a moment, but she only smiled at my mumbled apology, letting me find my balance to lead her through the steps. She never took her eyes from mine as we danced, not once did she look down, not once did she look away. Under her observation, I felt myself grow warm, and I longed to ask her what her thoughts were, longing, as well, to tell her that I knew her from my dreams. As whiffs of her gardenia fragrance surrounded me and the soft tendrils of her blue-black hair brushed my cheek, the pounding of my heart increased. When that first dance with her ended, I released Esperanza from my arms with reluctance. I felt as I had never felt before, as though I was the only one who could protect her, and I longed to keep her in my embrace forever.

To my delight, we danced almost every piece after that from the polkas and the *valses* to the intricate *varsouviana*. When we sat quietly getting to know one another, I also felt, for the first time in my life, the gnawing teeth of the green monster—jealousy—when many a young man sought a dance with her. With a polite thank you, Esperanza smiled and told them all her dances were taken, and the monster returned to the pits of my inner being quietly, replaced by a pleasure that made me want to shout with happiness. Sharing a cup of punch, we looked deeply into one another's eyes, finding confirmation of our innermost thoughts.

When I left her that evening, it was with a most terrible reluctance. But when my promise to call upon her soon met with her obvious pleasure, I left with hope dwelling in my heart and Esperanza's face in all her quiet, demure beauty etched in my mind. My joy reached the heavens that night. I had indeed found the girl of my dreams, the woman I vowed to myself then and there to marry someday.

My sleep took a long time coming that night, but for once I didn't mind. At last I had a face upon which to focus, and Esperanza's dark beauty swam before my eyes. I had much to think about, for the next day I knew I would have to ask her father for her hand. The youth of today might think me rash, that I moved too quickly, for I had only met my future bride a few hours before. But that was the way of my past. If a young couple had not been betrothed at birth or in childhood, instead guided to one another by their hearts, they were protected by a betrothal or a fast marriage. Enmeshed in their attraction and desire—for even then passion was hard to curb—they would be allowed to meet only under the watchful eyes of an elder no matter how long the betrothal period, ensuring that both remained chaste until the day of their nuptials.

My thoughts turned to myself in the role of husband: at sixteen, suffering under the heat of desire, I knew I wanted more than anything to experience the dizzy queasiness I felt when I held Esperanza in my arms. I knew I wasn't ready for the responsibilities of a wife. I had no money with which to build a house, and my parents' two rooms were certainly not big enough for all of us to share. Besides, the way I was affected even by my thoughts of Esperanza, I was certain I would want the privacy of our own house when we married.

It obviously would be some time before I could even think of taking a wife. I would need time to start a house, and I would need to find part time employment to begin saving money. I would have to strike up an agreement with my father in which I could sell cattle or wood, maybe both, for the amount of money I would need. And if he refused because the Depression had driven prices down? Then I would have to wait until Miguel returned for good before I could leave home to find a job. I began to wonder how long Esperanza and I would have to wait for the day we'd be joined as man and wife, and I prayed until the sun began to rise that she would wait.

The next morning after mass, my family gathered together for Sunday lunch at my grandmother's. I ate distractedly, suffering the teasing my quietude inspired in my uncle. As dessert was served, I offered to take a slice of pie to my grandmother, who lay bedridden in the next room, listening to our quiet conversation. Sitting beside her as she ate, I sat still while she looked deeply into my eyes for only a minute before her face lit with amusement and she nodded with assurance. She knew what I had come to say. I only smiled, brushing a strand of hair from her forehead before returning to the kitchen. There was no need for words between us.

When the dishes were done and we sat around the table, I knew I could no longer postpone the inevitable. I longed more than anything to rush to Esperanza's house, but I knew that would be impossible unless I told my parents where I was going because by horse it would take a few hours. When there was a lull in the conversation, I gathered my courage and quietly announced that I had finally met the young woman of my dreams. My disclosure was greeted at first with a silence so great I feared my family would protest. But when my uncle realized that I had finally been bitten by that flighty little bug called love, he howled his joy loud enough to wake the dead, catching me up and dancing me around the kitchen in a jig as my aunt clucked at his noise, rushing to check on my grandmother who waved her concern away, her voice coming through the door. "¡*Ya era pa' tiempo!*" My uncle's laughter resounded through the adobe walls as he agreed that it was about time before clapping me on the back so hard I choked. My father, ever the staid far-sighted man, shook my hand soberly, asked how I planned to support a wife and family. My mother, teary-eyed with that bittersweet mingling of joy and loss at the marriage of a son, scolded my father for his questions, saying there would be time enough later to discuss any plans I had. Her questions would have to be answered first, and they came one after the other with hardly a pause between: "Who is she? Where is she from? Where did you meet her? Do we know her family?"

I answered as best as I could, longing for her approval of my choice for a bride, yet knowing that I had only met Esperanza the night before and really knew nothing about her or her family—other than that her father was strict (which gave me a stomach ache every time I thought of having to speak to him). But with my few responses, my mother's eyes brightened with recognition. Indeed, she knew who Esperanza was; she had grown up a neighbor of her family. In fact, she filled in so many blanks I had about the girl of my dreams that by the time we left for home a half hour later, I knew more about her family than I could have learned in a year.

We decided then that my parents would submit my proposal formally to Esperanza's parents the following Sunday. Like Miguel, I, too, wanted to take part in the formal request for Esperanza's hand and collaborated with my mother to come up with a well-thought-out letter, one which would impress Esperanza's parents with my literacy skills while simultaneously impressing the love of my life with my heartfelt desire to be her husband. Although the request must be written in my parents' point of view, I finally came up with this:

Cañoncito de las Manuelitas, Nuevo Mexico
Noviembre 27, de este año 1929
Señor y Señora Nazario Montoya
Las Cañadas, Nuevo Mexico
Respetables Señores:

Queremos decirles que nuestro hijo, José Valdez, nos ha anunciado su deseo de entrar de matrimonio con su amable y bellosa hija, Esperanza Montoya. El esta listo para hacerla una vida comfortable y alegre. Tiene un gran amor para su hija, y tiene propiedad, vacas y dinero para darle una vida buena. Por estas rasones, José desea extender su mano para jurarla amor para siempre en el sagrado sacramento de matrimonio. Como padres que aman a su hijo mucho, decidimos cumplir con este acto sagrado para que nuestro

hijo y su hija puedan comienzar su vida juntos si ustedes son agradable con
*   este proposito.*
Esperamos recibir contesta faborable.

> *Con alto respecto,*
> *Señor y Señora Aniceto Valdez*

In short, the letter says that my parents want to tell hers that I, José Valdez, have announced my desire to enter marriage with the congenial and beautiful Esperanza Montoya. I am ready to give her a comfortable and happy life. I have a great love for their daughter, and I have property, cattle, and money to give her a good life. For these reasons, I desire to extend my hand in marriage to their daughter whom I will love forever. Like parents who very much love their son, my parents decided to complete this sacred act so that their son and the Montoya's daughter can begin their lives together if her parents are agreeable to this proposal. We await their favorable reply with much respect.

If that didn't convince them, especially her strict father, nothing would. Now, Las Cañadas, where Esperanza lived, was approximately nine miles to the north of us. Las Cañadas where we took the cattle for summer grazing was in essence the same place. However, it was located way west, behind where she lived and so mountainous it could only be reached by horse or by foot. Even on the county road, by wagon it would take us at least a few hours to get there and back, so I took it upon myself to ask Maestro Rubel if I could do any work around his house or at the school as payment for him providing us with taxi service.

So for an hour each afternoon that week I met him at the school and he set me to do all the little chores he couldn't stand to do until each was done. And that Sunday morning after mass, we all piled into his car and set out on our errand. Along the way, I confessed that though I knew in my heart that I truly desired Esperanza as my wife, I had decided to wait until I could provide for her. My father, thinking guiltily about his initial reaction to my news, I supposed, looked at my mother and consulted silently with her before he looked back at me. When he spoke, it was to tell me that, as a betrothal gift, he and my mother were giving me five of the cows that were mature enough to sell. If I wanted to marry in the immediate future, he added, he was sure los Hermanos would help me build a house.

Though I was touched by his gesture and nothing could ever change my mind about Esperanza, I had to confess that at my age I didn't think I was ready to be a husband, even given the means to provide for her. My father only nodded, saying he understood; he'd been twenty-six when he married my mother.

My mother sighed wistfully, admitting that though she was only fifteen when my father swept her off her feet, she didn't want me to marry yet anyway while in the same breath telling me she wanted to see me settled, wanted me to give her grandchildren. Laughingly, I told her not to worry, Miguel would probably provide her with her last wish soon enough. So when we pulled into the road to Esperanza's house, we had decided I would sell the cows anyway when the prices were higher (hopefully in the not too distant future), putting the money away until I felt ready.

My heart began to pound when Esperanza emerged from the house to stand on the wide veranda. Though her father stood on one side and her mother on the other, I don't remember seeing them at first, for I only had eyes for the girl who had come to me in a dream. For a moment seeing her there in a cornflower blue dress that blew with her black tresses in the light breeze, the cold November weather tingeing her cheeks pink, I forgot my decision to wait in my longing to kiss the lips that turned up in a soft smile of welcome when she saw me.

But when I finally laid eyes on her father, the large, burly man on the porch, the feeling fled in the wake of the sudden fear that I would be refused. He seemed to scowl at me and introductions were exchanged before Esperanza's nervous mother beckoned us inside. I remember how anxious I was when we entered the large parlor and the women promptly moved to the kitchen to gather refreshments. Tradition dictated that this particular ritual be conducted by the men of the family. So my father handed her father the letter, which her father promptly tucked away into his shirt pocket. The two men began conversing, getting a feel for one another as they discussed mutual acquaintances and shared interests. I sat on a stiff-backed chair and looked around. The parlor was large, almost larger than our two rooms put together and I wondered about the rest of the house. My eyes moved slowly around the room with its large windows and shiny wood floor, until my gaze reached the staircase and I saw one—no—two, then three children perched on the ascending steps. My eyes wandered higher and I found four more toward the top of the stairs—seven children with fourteen wide eyes stared back at me. I slowly turned my attention back to the men just as the women returned with trays of coffee and bizcochitos.

That visit was only preliminary, a feeling out of one another's families for the father of the bride to take measure of the prospective groom and his family and to determine suitability. I don't think I spoke more than a dozen words to Esperanza's mother, even less to her father, and only hello and good bye to her. So the visit was fairly short, maybe a half hour. We all breathed a sigh of relief as we exited the main gate to the Montoya house. The entire visit had been an ordeal because of the formality of the situation, because we were all strangers, and because we had all been so nervous to begin with. But the deed was done and now all I could do was await the response from Esperanza's parents, which traditionally would take about a week.

Throughout the next seven days, between working on Miguel's addition when the gang was available, I found many other chores to do. I tried not to give myself time to think. I tried to make myself so tired that when I fell into my cot at night, I would fall directly into sleep. Alas, quite the opposite occurred. I worked myself into exhaustion and took forever to finally nod off. That was when the gate I put up against my negative thoughts opened and those dreaded thoughts leaped out: what if Esperanza's father didn't think I was suitable for his daughter? What if he kept their reply from me longer than a week? I wasn't sure I could keep up working the way I was without killing myself in the process—round and round the questions swirled in my head until I turned to prayer and eventually fell asleep.

Thankfully, Saturday brought a welcome surprise. Around one o'clock we heard the sound of an automobile coming around the bend in the road and watched through the kitchen window as an unfamiliar vehicle came to a stop in our driveway. Of course, all the adults proceeded to go outside to greet whoever it was while I strained my eyes at the glass, hoping yet dreading that it was who I wanted it to be. Esperanza's father emerged from the car, followed by her mother and lastly the black-haired girl I was in love with. My heart beat so fast in my chest I looked down, sure she would be able to see the thumping through my shirt—even through the window. I quickly joined my family who was already greeting hers and joined in the "*buenas tardes, gusto de verles, como estan todos,*" followed by an awkward silence. We settled in my grandmother's parlor since we didn't have one and because my grandmother was mostly bedridden and one of us stayed with her at all times. My mother made sure each had cups of coffee and that the plate of fresh empanaditas held center court on the coffee table. Señor Montoya pulled a folded sheet of paper from his breast pocket and handed it to my father, who opened and read it silently while I stood as still as a statue and held my breath. My abuelita, who had been helped into the only armchair in the room, caught my eye and winked at me with a slight nod of her head. Finally turning to my mother and me, my father handed her the letter and I forced my eyes to look at the words.

En repuesta a su carta de fecha de Noviembre 27, 1929, en la cual nos demuestradon que su honorable hijo, José Valdez, desea entrar al estado de

matrimonio con nuestra hija, Esperanza Montoya, permitanos decirle que
después de haber consultado con ella, ella nos ha dicho que es favorable con
el idea de matrimonio con su hijo y que acepta su propósito de matrimonio ...

This was the only sentence that interested me, the gist of which says that after having consulted with their daughter, Esperanza's parents discovered that the idea of marriage to me is favorable and that she accepts my proposal!

I moved to stand before Esperanza and her parents. I remember looking directly at her father and then her mother as I stumblingly told them they made me the happiest man on earth. I looked at Esperanza and told her that I would provide for her for the rest of her life, and when I finished, her mother dabbed at the tears in her eyes while her father's scowl deepened and he brushed a finger over his eye. That's when I realized that to a father, his daughter's marriage is bittersweet—full of promise for her but full of uncertainty for the parents who were losing their little girl from their home. The only way I could assure them that their daughter had made the right decision would be to prove myself the best husband I could be for her. Only then would their fears be alleviated.

Her mother asked if Esperanza was pleased while I held my breath in hopeful anticipation, and I felt my heart soar when she said yes without hesitation. But her father scrutinized me closely for what seemed like an eternity, and when he gave me a curt nod, six heavy sighs of relief met his silent reply. He only added that our betrothal should last a year, for Esperanza was only fifteen and it was his wish that she finish school before she became a wife.

I nodded quickly, for I feared that if I disagreed, he would change his mind. Just then, my grandmother caught my eye with a raised finger. "*Llevan me pa' mi camalta,*" she asked tiredly. Esperanza and I assisted her back to bed, and gramma began putting her own plan into play.

Once settled under her quilts, she motioned me to one side of her bed and Esperanza to the other. Holding our hands in her own, she blessed our union and proceeded to inform my future wife about just what kind of a man she was getting. Mostly, gramma tried to convey my positive qualities in her anecdotes. However, here and there, she managed to include a few memories of my less than stellar moments. But with that almost omniscient tenacity she possessed, gramma took it upon herself to explain our "gift" to Esperanza without scaring her. Esperanza's innocent inquiry of how I had known that she was the one for me sent a sliver of foreboding through my mind, and I told my grandmother I didn't know how to explain. My silence worried her, I knew, and now I knew my gramma had also known it had been bothering Esperanza.

Looking deeply into her eyes, my abuelita told Esperanza I had seen her in my dreams. When her brow raised in perplexity, my grandmother did her best to explain and to reassure Esperanza that what I had was a gift, her legacy. She needed the time our betrothal would afford in which to attain understanding. I knew that not to tell her now would be an omission of something so inherent to my character. Though this admission could alienate her from me, it would be better for both of us if she were told now because, if her fear of me was too great to be conquered by our love, then it was best to know now, rather than to see the fear in her eyes after our love had blossomed.

I told her I had been afraid that I would scare her away, and to my surprise, before I could continue, her gaze softened and she covered my mouth with her fingers. "José, I knew there was something about you that drew me to you at our first meeting. I saw something special in your eyes." She smiled. "I could never be afraid of you." The understanding the three of us achieved that afternoon was truly special. My abuelita had seen through both of our confusions and our questions and made everything clear from the beginning of our betrothal. It made our relationship stronger, even before we ever took our wedding vows, which was her intention all along, of that I have no doubt. Saying she was getting sleepy, my gramma bade us both a good afternoon and closed her eyes as we tiptoed from the room.

We spent the rest of the day together, our parents establishing a comfortable friendship that would have to last throughout the years because of their children who would bind them together. Esperanza and I were allowed to sit on the porch in view of the kitchen. Nervous as cats to be left alone, at first we barely spoke.

In the end, we decided to agree with her father and wait so I could build a house for her. Neither of us wanted to live with her parents who had a large house that housed a large family. And of course, we couldn't live with my parents who had a small family housed in a small house.

Our waiting decided, we turned our thoughts to all the questions we wanted answered from one another. We distracted ourselves with topics which afforded countless other discoveries of one another. Before long, we found the comfortable friendship we had attained the night we met. We became animated with our colorful anecdotes of what our lives were like, laughing quietly at the frivolous characters of our youth. Though when our fingers intertwined sending prickles through our touch that ignited the fires of our growing love, we knew we would be hard-pressed to content ourselves with the long betrothal period ahead. When it became clear that her parents were about ready to leave, we quieted, knowing that this would be the farewell of our betrothal, the first of many throughout the coming year. And we realized how hard it was to say goodbye even for a day and wondered how we could endure a year of such bittersweet parting.

Knowing how long it took for adults to leave anyone's house after the first "Bueno, pues," which signaled their imminent departure, I knew we had some time. When we were the visitors, sometimes we stood at the door, coats wrapped around us, the car started or the horses pulling at their bits, only to sit back down for another fifteen minutes, then another and another, until my father ushered my mother out, saying we would surely run out of gas or frustrate the animals. I told Esperanza that I would see her in my dreams as I had seen her elusively throughout the past months. She replied with a soft laugh that she would be there, just as I would be in hers.

Before our parents finally came outside, we snuck a glance to see whether their eyes were averted before our lips met in a soft kiss, the first real kiss of love either of us had ever received or given. And though it was only a small kiss that lasted only seconds, the innocent touch of our lips kindled a not-so-innocent flame in our hearts that left each of us weak-kneed. We looked deeply into one another's eyes as if to brand our images into each other's minds. And we quietly exchanged our vows of love before letting our hands go, leaving our hearts with one another.

During the month that followed, we wrote one another once a week, our letters like small novellas with all that we wanted the other to know, and so our love continued to grow with each passing day. Toward the end of December 1929, Esperanza's father finally allowed her to visit our house for the weekend Miguel and Carolina were due home, primarily because my mother assured him she and Esperanza would sleep together.

When they returned amidst our first heavy snowstorm, my aunt chose to stay behind with my grandmother while my parents and uncle, Esperanza, and I awaited at Miguel's formerly two room house. In those days, practically every room, unconnected by modern hallways, had a door that opened outside on one side of the structure, so we were ensconced in what appeared a cozy long one-roomed house. In reality, before Miguel left, the house was much like ours: kitchen and bedroom. Now, however, with the boys' help, I had added a door to the back wall of the kitchen which opened into a short hallway with two additional doors leading to what could be used as a parlor and a small bedroom. Although the rooms were not finished, now that Miguel was home he and Carolina could decide how they wanted them completed.

Stoking the fire while my mother and Esperanza set food to warm on the stove, I saw my uncle run out of the house, flagging Miguel and Carolina down as Maestro, who gladly consented to serve as taxi again, drove by. For so anxious had they been to reach our house that none had even noticed the welcoming smoke from the chimney concealed by the swirling snowstorm. We ran outside shivering without our coats to tell them of our surprises, a remodeled house for them and a bride for me, only to fall silent with shock at the quilted bundle in Carolina's arms. Their own surprise to us broke the silence. From the folds of the quilt came gleeful gurgling at the snowflakes that fell upon the tiny face.

We found our voices, running into the house and laughing with joy. We chastised Miguel for not telling, only to be reprimanded playfully in return for our having kept secrets, too. He and Carolina looked at the large kitchen, the exposed vigas gleaming from the ceiling, the table and benches that Pedro and the boys had made as a house-warming gift, the wooden floors scrubbed to a shine by my mother. She laid out two handmade rugs, another gift to them. Most of their wedding gifts were displayed on counter tops or shelves I had built, Esperanza having decorated them after we white-washed the walls the day before. If I hadn't been able to give him a completed house, at least we were determined to make their home as comfortable as possible.

It was a house warm with both loving care and love radiating from those who had made it possible. My brother and sister's eyes spoke their gratitude as they went from one set of arms to another, so touched by their homecoming that they let their actions speak to us, finding no words adequate.

Welcoming Esperanza into the family, Miguel's brow rose in impish deviltry and I knew that my uncle was joined once again by the master of merciless mischief. From then until I married, I knew I would suffer in interminable teasing about being in love.

I shook my head, grinning at the blush I couldn't prevent from rising to redden my cheeks. Looking away from the laughing eyes of my brother, I saw that my niece, born the month before, was passing gently, reverently, from one pair of arms to the next as everyone cried tears of happiness. They blessed her with silent prayers and visible signs of the cross over her cherubic face for fear of giving her *el ojo*, or what others called *el mal ojo*, meaning the evil eye. Even today we Hispanics are a superstitious bunch. To prevent this curse from happening at all, babies wear coral, typically on a bracelet, which stops the evil eye from taking hold of the victim. If for some reason the baby isn't wearing coral, however, there is a cure which seems incredible but which can be attested to even to this day by New Mexican Hispanics.

I had personally witnessed both the curse and the cure the year before when one of Pedro's older sisters had her second child, and one of their primas actually gave the little girl ojo. Let me explain: when a person admires the infant too much, whether the admiration arises from a positive emotion like love or whether the act comes through envy or any other negative sentiment, the child becomes the victim of el ojo. This malady causes almost immediate discomfort in the infant, who cries as though in pain and who will not stop unless "cured" in one of two ways. Either the offender or a male named Juan or a female named Juana must give the infant water directly from his or her mouth. I don't know the reason for the "curer" having that particular name, nor do I know why coral and not, say, topaz protects the child. And although this cure sounds ridiculous, I can say firsthand that it works, as can hundreds, if not thousands of other Hispanos from the southwest and Mexico. When Pedro's prima gave the infant, named Rosa, a kiss on the cheek prior to departing and after a few minutes she began to cry, no one thought much about it—but when about fifteen minutes had passed and Rosa just wouldn't stop—no wet diaper, no hunger, no cause for her discomfort found—the only conclusion was that she had been given ojo. Pedro was dispatched to bring Prima Juanita to the house forthwith. Almost immediately after Prima Juanita opened her mouth and dribbled a small amount of water into the infant's mouth, Rosa stopped crying and her fussy motions ceased. She was cured, and Pedro's mother immediately began to search for her own children's coral bracelet, stored at the bottom of her hope chest. Adjusting the talisman on her granddaughter's wrist, she chastised herself for forgetting to have done so before guests arrived to see the new addition to the family.

When Miguel took his daughter from my mother's arms, placing the tiny bundle into mine, quietly introducing me as her uncle and her padrino, I was speechless for a moment. I looked from the cherubic face of my niece up into my brother's eyes in surprise.

"Well," he began, "I can think of no one better equipped to be godfather to my daughter than my own hermanito and godmother, my soon-to-be-sister."

"Sí," Carolina echoed. "And as her padrinos, you and Esperanza get to choose her name."

Since Esperanza was motioning for me to relinquish the baby to her, I placed a gentle kiss on my niece's forehead, made the sign of the cross over the spot my lips had touched, and handed her gently over. As a tiny wrist waved in the air, we both smiled as we noticed the coral bracelet. I, personally, breathed a sigh of relief that she would be protected from ojo.

Making arrangements for the baby's baptism post haste the following day with the Padre, it was decided she would be baptized at Sunday mass the day before Miguel and Carolina had to return to California. It was my mother who made sure the parents handing over the child to her godparents was done with the traditional decorum of our ancestors, just as she had when I requested Esperanza's hand in marriage through the formal letter writing ritual. For the next three days, all the women busily sewed and crocheted the baby's christening outfit until it was done to their satisfaction; then they began the cooking. The wood stoves at my aunt's, at Miguel's, and at our house were stoked twenty-four-seven as all the cooks prepared the meal for Sunday's celebration. Finally, on the evening before the mass, my mother and Miguel sat at the kitchen table and wrote the letter the parents would present to the godparents as they turned their baby over to what would essentially be her second set of parents. In the event of something tragic happening to the parents, the godparents would raise the child in the Catholic Church. The padrinos' responsibility was great indeed.

Sunday dawned with a golden sunrise in a cloudless sky, and after a light breakfast, Miguel and Carolina arrived with the baby dressed in her beautiful ivory dress, edged in lacy embroidery. They stood formally just inside the kitchen door as Miguel read aloud their request to Esperanza and me:

Muy Señores míos,

Como que mi esposa ha dado a Luz un infante el día tantos del corriente por la gran voluntad de Dios.

Saliendo de su parte con felicidad gracias, y felicidad infinita a la divina providencia: En primer lugar ofrecemos a ustedes esta niña como un servidor de ustedes. En segundo lugar como que esta criatura ha nacido en los tinieblas por el pecado original con el qual somos heredados de nuestros primeros padres y para que esta criatura sea lavada de esta mancha es necesario llevarla a la dulce fuente del Bautismo y de esta manera colocarla al gremio de nuestra religión. Yo y mi esposa mirando que ustedes posen un corazón humano y omas reunen en nuestro concepto todos aquellos cualidades honoríficas de honor y virtud, nos podemos a sus plantos suplicándoles, se dignen socar a esta criatura de los tinieblas en que se halla. Si así lo hicieron despues viviremos reconosidos de tener tan honorados compadres y de entrar con ustedes en este parentesco spiritual.

Sin otro asunto quedamos de ustedes con mucho respecto a sus plantas y ordenes."

Translated as best as I could, this is what he said:

"Because my wife has given Light to an infant on the day forecast through the great power of God, we come with felicity and infinite thanks to divine providence: firstly, we offer to you this child as your servant. Secondly, because this creature was born out of the darkness of the original sin we inherited from our first parents and so that this creature will be cleansed of this stain, it is necessary to take her to the sweet fountain of Baptism and in this manner place her in accord with our religion. Because I and my wife see that you possess a human heart and moreover represent our concepts of all those honorable qualities of honor and virtue, we place her in your hands asking for succor for this creature of darkness where she finds herself. If you agree we will live hereafter knowing that we have such honorable godparents and we enter with you in this spiritual relationship.

Without further issue we remain yours, with much respect at your feet and at your orders."

Though the language was lofty and the subject heavy, the overall message was indeed touching. To know that my brother and sister thought my fiancé and I were worthy enough, honorable and virtuous enough, to oversee the upbringing of their daughter was almost more than I could take that morning, especially knowing I wouldn't see any of them for a whole year after the morrow. I was blinking back tears again as Carolina placed the baby in Esperanza's arms and Miguel handed me his letter.

During the ceremony when we got to the part of the mass when the baptism was to occur, the padre asked the parents what name they'd chosen for their daughter. Both Miguel and Carolina's eyes widened in panic and with jaws agape, both pairs of eyes swung my way. Esperanza and I had communed at prayer the evening before and come up with two which we then combined, hoping the name we chose would please everyone. But we didn't know we were supposed to tell the parents before the mass! As the confused little priest turned his gaze to me and Esperanza, I elbowed her, giving her the opportunity to speak the name aloud before the entire congregation. But she just elbowed me back. I would've elbowed her again except for the look she gave me which warned that the duty was mine and mine alone.

"María del Carmel," I said loudly and clearly. "*María, por la Madre de Jesús, y Carmel, por la primera parte del nombre de Carolina combinada con el fin del nombre de Miguel.*" I felt compelled to explain. María because of the Mother of Christ and Carmel, a combination of the first part of Carolina's name with the last part of Miguel's. When I looked into the eyes of my niece's parents, I saw they both wore a glimmer of tears, and I was relieved and pleased that they approved. Needless to say, the rest of the mass and the feast which followed passed all too quickly, and by dawn of the following day, Miguel and his small family were gone.

Miguel's arrival, even though he would leave for yet another year with his small family before returning to our valley for good, signaled the beginning of new life with the birth of his daughter. It also brought the end of the life of our grandmother. She had waited to meet and approve of the woman I would marry, telling Esperanza that she had indeed given her hope. My betrothed spent many hours at my abuelita's bedside where they established a strong friendship, even if only for a short time. And true to her word, my grandmother had seen for herself the surprise that my brother brought home with him. Her time had come. She died on Esperanza's birthday, December twenty-ninth, after quietly reassuring us as we sat beside her that she was ready to join her husband.

The year of 1930 began slowly, as if stopped in time by my grandmother's leaving. My Tío Daniel and my Tía Estrella moved to town in February. He was tired, he told us, tired of the endless farm work, and he had taken a job as a custodian. When they left, my grandmother's house stood empty, and my uncle deeded it to me, saying that it would be far better to remodel it than to build another. Esperanza and I quickly agreed. I continued to work on Miguel's house with the help of los Hermanos, then we started our remodeling by early March, the month Berto's daughter was born.

Lent was especially poignant that year, for with my grandmother gone, Miguel away, and my uncle coming only for the Penitente meetings and services and to help my father when he could, there was an atmosphere of change that we couldn't dismiss. Our prayers were filled with earnest pleas for understanding, for acceptance of all that was to change in our lives. We were soon welcomed into yet another change that would take the melancholy sadness from our hearts and leave eternal rest in its place.

The summer finally passed, and with the fall, Miguel came home. We finished his house and took over the majority of the farm work, unburdening our elders. Carolina became pregnant once again, as did Lucía. Maestro Rubel finally decided to retire. Horacio had spent so much time in Terromote with his betrothed that we wondered where exactly he lived, but he came home to teach in the rock-walled, one-room schoolhouse where we all had gotten our educations. The year we turned eighteen, Horacio married, much to the disapproval of his mother, who had taken an immediate dislike to the young woman of her son's desires. It was a good thing for Horacio that he had become somewhat of a miser, for he had saved enough to build a small house. And so our gang re-united once again, to assist our Brother each Saturday for the last few months of 1930 in the building of his home a mile away from that of his mother's.

Esperanza had indeed given me hope that in my journey through life I would not be alone. She had waited as she had promised, and on November twenty-seventh (exactly a year after my proposal letter), in the midst of a three-foot blizzard, my little valley shared in my happiness as we took our vows as husband and wife with my brother and sister at our side in the small Capilla del Santo Niño.

During Lent of 1931, I called our gang together for the last time to the caves where we had had our first meeting as Brothers. Arriving first on the morning of Ash Wednesday before we were to meet with los Hermanos at the morada, I watched as each of my friends trod up their separate paths toward me.

Pedro came first, as usual, the sullen-faced concentration of the boy I had known still visible beneath the countenance of a man with a purpose. He had already begun to establish his fame as the youngest *santero* in our county, his intricately beautiful saints selling in Santa Fe for enough to provide a comfortable little income aside from his work as a welder. Becoming a master santero when he reached the ripe age of nineteen, his reputation and the demand for a santo created by his hand grew, promising the wealth of an artist worthy of his talent in the years to come.

Next came Filiberto, the most devious of us all, the impish smile that etched his face reminding me of the boy whose countless schemes caused us such trouble. What would his father-in-law, who held him in such high esteem, think if I chewed his ear with stories of all the hot water Berto had gotten us into in our past? I wondered. His father-in-law was already in the process of making his son and Berto equal partners in his combination butcher shop and dairy farm, and in his face, I saw the responsibility that marked him a changed man.

I saw Tino jogging up the hill, teasing Horacio who trailed behind, huffing with the added weight he carried from the contentment of his wife's cooking and his new-found happiness as a husband. Horacio had become one of the most respected members of our community as the teacher of the new generations. And Tino, no longer the tiny boy of our youth, had grown into a hard-working farmer, appointed mayordomo of our irrigation canal by the men of the community who respected his fairness. It was Tino's duty to grant permission for irrigating with equal justice, assigning equal time for those of us who had gardens or orchards to use the water, in turn leaving plenty for everyone.

Tino, too, had finally succumbed to the yearning of his heart, had seen a kindred soul in Esmeralda's cousin Dora. Though it would be another year before he married, the betrothal was announced at Horacio's wedding, on the first day of January 1931.

That year, that day we met at the caves, we relived our memories in the laughter we shared and in the tears we fought for the boys we had been. True to his word, Pedro gifted me and the gang with santos created by his hand. In the poignant moment suspended in time we accepted with pride the intricate carvings, which would hold places of honor on each of our altars in our homes. And as we walked down the path from the cemetery to the morada, we stopped at the stones where we had said goodbye to our secret pact, bidding a last farewell to the boys who had made a descanso forever holding our secret ledger within the embrace of our old primo who guarded it. And as we shared a prayer for our Brother, Primo Victoriano, we also shared a prayer to bind us for the life we now embraced as the men who were bound by our shared youth. Our circle was complete. We were Brothers of Light.

Aceptación

———

Throughout the years that followed, we raised our families in decades that brought even more changes to our little valley. Electricity came to brigten the darkness of the nights and to make our lives easier with the countless gadgets that came with it. And though I was happy to see Esperanza's face light up when I bought her such appliances as a washing machine or a radio, and even later, a stove or a television, I missed the quiet of our home, the warm glow that ony a kerosene lamp can shed, the taste of food cooked on a wood stove, among so many other of life's little pleasures before the invention of electrical energy.

When farm equipment was made available, she was happy when I no longer had to walk the fields behind the plow pulled by our horses, so exhausted each day that I fell into bed sometimes before I could even taste her suppers. I couldn't admit, even to her, that the noisy tractor took away from the quiet communion with the land that had inspired such peace in my heart when the horses and I had done the job alone.

When bigger and better schools were established in Sapello and Las Vegas, our little school closed and Horacio taught at Sapello where we delivered our children into his hands. In the 1960s when they reached ninth grade, they were bussed into town to the high school. However, since our little valley had only a small amount of children, no bus would come down the road to our houses. Yes, the few who lived here walked up to three miles one way to catch the bus to town, even in four feet of snow, until the 1970s when the school authorities finally decided to allow a bus to come our way. Oh, and did I mention that the girls weren't allowed to wear dresses to school until the '70s?

But I get ahead of myself.

With the approach of the 1940s came World War II, and Esperanza and I decided to leave Cañoncito to see how we could help in the war effort. Having failed the physical for the armed forces due to my flat feet, I joined the Civilian Conservation Corps and was sent to San Fransicso to work on the shipyards. Meanwhile, Esperanza found employment on the assembly line of a munitions factory making bombs. After a year I was transferred and we both worked at the Denver Munitions Factory for another period before deciding to return to New Mexico.

In our absence a few of los Hermanos had moved to nearby Las Vegas, returning to Cañoncito regularly to tend to the remaining vecinos and to conduct their Lenten ceremonies as in the past. When Esperanza and I returned, we opted to move to the city as well where I found employment on the maintenance crew of a school and she worked at a parachute making factory with her mother and her sisters.

Esperanza and I were as content as we could be throughout this period of our lives with our work and our hobbies, returning to Cañoncito every weekend, every Lent, and every summer to plant jardínes and to care for the arboleras and the livestock we kept. But we were also childless, having experienced three miscarriages. Losing three daughters one after the other, we'd resigned ourselves to our fate and relied on one another for support and for solace.

Almost fourteen years later, when the miracle of life began to grow within Esperanza once more, we spent nine months of living on pins and needles, nine months of praying and wondering if it would all be for naught. But our fourth daughter survived. I wondered many times why my so-called gift didn't alert me to the troubles we would undergo in trying to have a family; sometimes I wondered if it hadn't just been something I outgrew. It took much praying in solitude on my part to restore my faith in God's plan for us.

During these decades of the '50s through the '80s, our gang made a name for ourselves as humble, hard-working men and devout Hermanos, taking over the cofradía as, one by one, the elder members died. I was elected Hermano Mayor, a most heavy responsibility, which I took to heart, learning that I had the capacity for justice in the faith of my Brothers who followed my guidance. However, with the inevitable change that came over the years, our Penitente practices were shunned by the younger generations who wanted nothing to do with what they looked upon as a horrifying practice, rather than the beautifully poignant exercise of our Penitente faith that served to mold us into good men. And so our cofradía died out.

Now that I have reached the wise age of seventy-four, I remember Primo Victoriano's words. Like him, it is my own memories of my youth that keep me content in this life, for my heart has already gone to the life which awaits. And as my faded vision rests upon the santo Pedro made for me so long ago, a replica of the San José which rested with Primo Victoriano on his eternal journey, I vow it will accompany me as well when I make my final good bye to my earthly home.

My dearest friends have all departed. As each one left to his own eternal rest taking with him the santo Pedro had made with such loving care, each took with him a piece of my heart—as did my Esperanza. Having lost three of our four babies, one of her brothers to electrocution, and her mother in a horrific fire, Esperanza was my inspiration throughout my life and my hope for eternal happiness. She never lost her faith in God, and she continued to devote her free time to serving our local church as a Catholic Daughter and caring for our grandsons.

I never regret my passionate faith to live the life of a Penitente and what it entailed, even though I know it is too late for most of the men of the new generations to renew the fervor which led my cousins and me to become Hermanos. Most have grown up without experiencing the awe-inspiring procesiónes, the desire to keep our ancestors' acts of faith alive, those very acts which influenced those of us of the nineteen twenties to continue our tradition.

When Esperanza left me in her sixty-fifth year, the last of my heart went with her. She calls to me each day, her dark eyes look down upon me each night, and the hope she still provides enters my soul. I know that soon she will come to me in my sleep for the last time.

I am the last of los Hermanos del Cañoncito de las Manuelitas. As I await the passage for which being a Penitente has prepared me, I am ready to join those who went before. I will go with Esperanza, and the circle of Hermanos will again be complete.

Afterword

—————

As José and María del Carmel's only child, I chose to write this story to honor their memories, to enlighten those who want to know more about los Hermanos, and to provide a little insight into what life was like in rural New Mexico in the early nineteen hundreds. Most of my story regarding los Penitentes comes from my own memories of praying with them and of being cared for by some of them or their wives when I was young. I have intertwined real people from my past into my narrative and taken liberties with timelines to insert fact with fiction. Although the majority of the people are (were) real, there are very few who I've identified by their real names.

Some of the cuentos I included were told to me by my father and my tío, such as the serpiente, el Diablo, and el difunto (which my father asserted they really saw). La Llorona I learned from practically everyone in my youth, but the story of the ball of fire was my mother's, and the woman at the campo santo was told to me by a vecina, a neighbor. Both women swore they saw what they did; and since I never knew either of them to lie, I believe them to this day. It was my mother who told me the story of the bee attack, revealing that it really did happen to a neighbor and that the man was actually pulled to his death by the scared horses. Although I now live on the very spot where my father built his wife their first home (the two room house I depict where José actually grew up), I've never seen the serpiente for myself. Recently, on some educational channel, however, the bones of such a snake were discovered; so who's to say our primo didn't actually see one for himself back in the day?

The traditions of the past were also real: the letter-writing ritual of asking for the bride was performed by some of my relatives (not my parents). In fact,

My parents, José and Esperanza (her real name was
María del Carmen) in either Berkley or Denver when
they worked for the war effort

my father and mother only met once before they married—he at 26 and she at
only 15. The formal giving of the child to the godparents I did at my mother's
bidding, and the letter in this story is the real letter she wrote for me to read to
my sons' godparents as I turned my babies over to them for baptism. In some
places here in New Mexico some communities still have active Penitentes and
church functions for certain saints with community fiestas and comidas for all.
And of course we still believe in and fear la Llorona and some of us are still
scared of la Muerte.

　My memories are rich with scenes of those real cattle drives (I was the one
who playfully pushed my mother, not intending her to fall face-first in the mud
and lose that fateful loaf of bread). Both my mother and I had scares sinking
into the quicksand of the arroyo, but it was my husband who did the really
"bad" things I attributed to Filiberto: painting the outhouse seats black and
steering his blind uncle through the ditch. Oh, and the man who was robbed
by Vicente Silva was actually my own grandfather, my mother's father. (Appar-
ently my grampo had quite the skill and the audacity to make mula during
those Prohibition years). So you see, this story is based on quite a bit of reality,
just swirled around with different characters and mixed into the time frame
concocted in my imagination.

GOOD-BY TO THIS WORLD

Good-by, all this company,	*Adiós a companimiento*
Who have been here at my wake,	*De los que me están velando*
The hour and time have come	*Se llevarla la hora y tiempo*
When you must take me out.	*De que me vayan sacando*
Good-by, my loving parents,	*Adiós mis amados padres*
Who conserved my life,	*Que conservaron mi vida*
The hour and time have come	*Se llegó la hora y tiempo*
For me to take my parting.	*Ya se llegó mi partida*

Two stanzas from an alabado sung by the Hermanos.

But the gist of the story—what I wanted to convey most—was how praying with los Hermanos affected me profoundly. I remember even as far back in my memory to when I was about five, accompanying them in the black of night to and from the morada to the capilla, while clutching my mother's hand with a fear of something I couldn't quite understand. I was the one who was deeply afraid of La Muerte back then, I was the one who could never stand before her; and to my regret, when the Hermanos disbanded, I refused to take her into my own home because I was so afraid of her even then (and I was in my mid-twenties by that time). A relative in town cares for her, and to this day no one is allowed to see her.

I was the one who begged year after year to be allowed to join los Hermanos in their prayers at la morada; and time after time, I was the one who was always turned down. I was the one who asked why no girls were allowed, especially by the '70s when I was old enough to protest on behalf of equality for women and had discovered through my bilingual studies that women and even babies were active participants of la Hermanidad in Spain. Why not here? But I was denied entry every time I asked. So after my father's passing in 1986 when we began going through the morada, we brought everything home with us: the trestle table and the benches, the cabinet with all their dishes and utensils, the wooden coat rack, the candelario and the stools with sharp metal barbs on which to sit (I still have no idea how those were used), the cross borne by the Penitente who played Christ, the santos, my grandfather, uncle, and father's prayerbooks, the candle holders—everything came home with me.

Including the wooden box.

Procesión de la Semana Santa. José on the left, carrying la *bandera*; Miguel's house in the background.

I can still capture that moment of anticipation when we unlocked the padlock and opened it for the first time. The yellowish smocks and loose-fitting trousers of los Penitentes were there, most bearing rust-colored blood stains (I still have them all in my closet, unable to bear throwing them out because, to me, they aren't trash; they're treasures of my ancestors). I remember how at the sight of the blood I burst into tears, realizing that some of what my imagination had always supplied and what I'd studied in college about los Hermanos was really true—they did practice penance actively.

Beneath the garments we found the pito, the matracas, the horsehair scourges, the tin holding sharp pieces of glass, the homemade container of gravel—evidence of the mysteries I'd always suspected finally coming to light.

Cross from la morada, recrafted with extra crosses on top, rounded edges on the arms, and cut at the bottom after los Hermanos stopped the practice of recreating the crucifixion in their own ceremonies.

Oh, how I cried. A memory suddenly came to me—my father in his seventies, having to visit a specialist periodically for his breathing difficulties, and I, sitting in the waiting room, startled to hear the doctor gasp, "What happened to your back?" Not once in all my childhood had I ever seen my father's naked back—never. Only his knees, which bore angry scars and indentations, gave any clue to what he did to himself in those late hours of the nights at la morada.

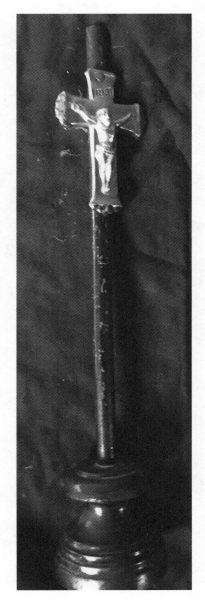

So although some of my suspicions proved true upon our discovery of the contents of the box, I still have no clue how or when the self-penance occurred—nor do I want to; it's not my place to speculate and it's not up to me to reveal what los Hermanos who are still active today don't want known—even if I knew. I can only tell you that all the rules los Penitentes follow reveal their desire to live humbly and reverently, caring for their own and for their communities while emulating Christ in their daily lives. And that's all any of us who aren't Hermanos need to know about them.

Los Hermanos de la Cofradía del Sagrado Corazón made or bought the wooden crosses, painted them black, and attached the tin crucifix with small nails so each had their own unique symbol of their faith.

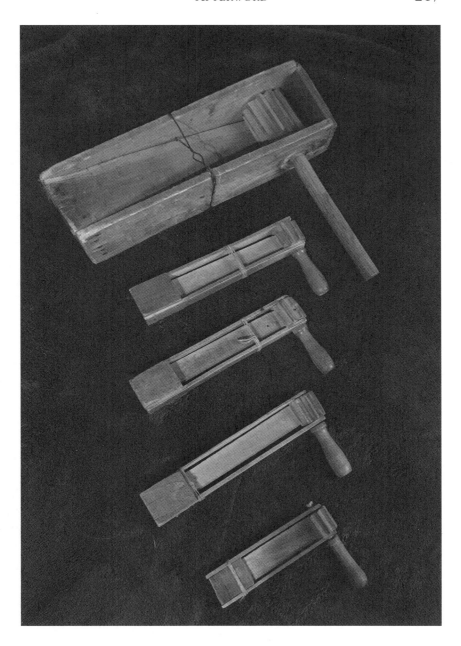

Matracas

This is the ledger where el secretario wrote every record of los Hermanos' rules, charitable acts, and lists of Hermanos Mayores over the decades, established in 1850.

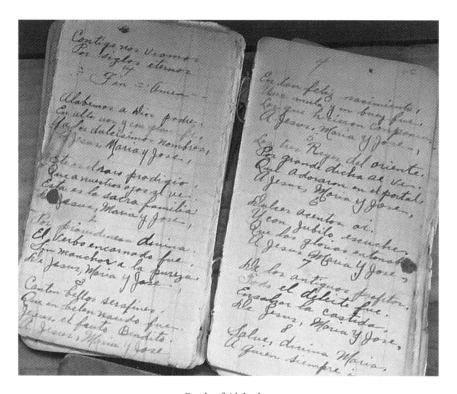

Book of Alabados